Guardian

of the

Crown

Melissa McShane

Night Harbor Publishing
Salt Lake City, UT

Night Harbor Publishing
www.nightharborpublishing.com

Cover design by Yocla Designs www.yocladesigns.com
North sign and shield designed by Erin Dinnell Bjorn

First Printing
10 9 8 7 6 5 4 3 2 1

For Jana,
because Willow is your favorite

Cast of Characters

THE TREMONTANANS

Willow North—a thief

Felix Valant—eight-year-old King of Tremontane

Serjian Kerish—former dowser to Terence Valant and Willow's ex-
fiancé

Terence Valant—Felix's uncle, usurper of the Crown of Tremontane

Giles Rafferty—a rebel lord

Rickard, Ellie, Fern, Kev, and Samuel—Rafferty's fellow rebels

THE HAREMS OF ESKANDEL
(Eskandelics put family names first)

The Serjian Principality:

Janida—*vojenta* (harem leader)

    Kerish and Imara—her children

Maitea

Catrela

    Amberesh, Gessala, Posea—her children

Giara

    Jauman—her son

Alondra

    Caderina—her daughter

Salveri—the Serjian Prince

The Serjian Allies:

Dekerian Mireya

Torossian Kharalin (Caroline)

Khasjabi Donia

Ajemi Sovea

The Serjian Enemies:
Abakian Raena
Gharibi Ciera
Hovanesian Melirra (allied with Gharibi)
Mahnouki Adorinda
      Mahnouki Ghanetan — the Mahnouki Prince
Sahaki Beppinda (puppet of Mahnouki)
      Sahaki Karalhi — the Sahaki Prince

Neutral:
Jamighian Issobela
      Jamighian Vijenci — the Jamighian Prince
Hajimhi Fariola
Sarhafian Jennea
Takjashi Lucea
Najarhian Yesemia

OTHER ESKANDELICS:
Caira — Willow's servant (*zetesha*)
Fedrani — Felix's servant
Khurkjian Gianesh — keeper of the zoological collection
Abakian Terjalesh — Raena's *zuareto*
Gharibi Cammean — Ciera's *zuareto*
Hajimhi Jherjesh — Fariola's son
Khazanjian Ojman — friend of Serjian Amberesh

A glossary of Eskandelic words appears at the end of this book.

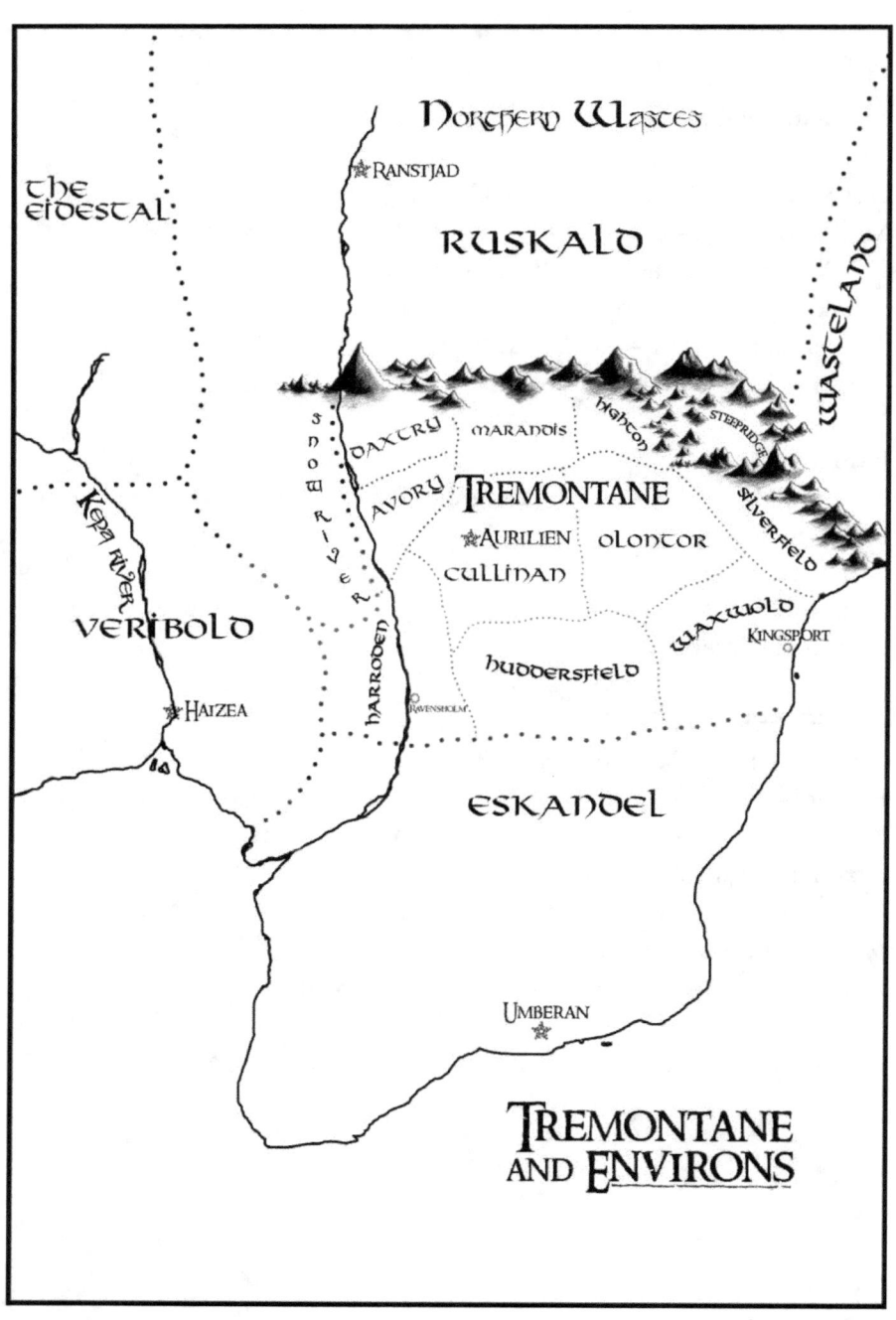

NORTHERN WASTES

★ RANSTJAD

THE EIDESTAL

RUSKALD

WASTELAND

SNOW RIVER

DAXTRY

MARANDIS

HIGHTOP

STEEPRIDGE

TREMONTANE

AVORY

★ AURILIEN

OLONTOR

SILVERFIELD

CULLINAN

KEPA RIVER

VERIBOLD

HARRODEN

RAVENSHOLM

WAXWOLD

KINGSPORT

HUDDERSFIELD

★ HAIZEA

ESKANDEL

UMBERAN

TREMONTANE
AND ENVIRONS

Part Four

Chapter One

Willow's golden gown whispered to her, *swish-swish*, as she passed through the corridors. It would be terrible for hiding in, what with its bright color and the sound of silken skirts rubbing against each other, but tonight she wasn't going to hide. Tonight was for standing out, for keeping the attention and, she hoped, the good will of more than a score of women who needed to be convinced that their best interests matched those of Felix Valant. If they chose to reject Janida's proposal...no, it wasn't time to consider ways to make Felix disappear, because they hadn't failed yet. And as far as Willow was concerned, they wouldn't.

The hemispherical room in which the Serjian harem handled business was not just full, but overcrowded, with women dressed in variations on the clothes Willow and Caira had packed into Willow's closet that afternoon. They were all engaged in low-voiced conversations that Willow could hear the murmurs of down the hall, but every one of them turned toward the door when she entered, and every voice fell silent.

Willow reflexively took hold of the door frame with her right hand, realized she'd left her left hand free to defend herself, and made herself let go of the smoothly painted wood. *Focus, Willow,* she told herself, *orient,* and let her inherent magic feel out the shapes of the women before her.

They all wore jewelry, necklaces and earrings and many, many bracelets, including the wide golden bracelets like Janida's that Willow assumed were the mark of a *vojenta*. There were four other women wearing those bracelets, and Willow marked them by eye as well as magic.

Janida, of course, stood at the center of the room next to an elderly *vojenta* who wore a silky black headwrap that made her tan skin look lighter by comparison. Another *vojenta* stood well off to one side. She held a silver goblet (*They're not serving drinks like that, are they? How can I get out of that?*) and wore a broad silver necklace like a collar studded with amethysts. Her short black hair fell loose around her face, which was narrow like Catrela's and blue-eyed like Janida's; she might have been about Janida's age.

A third *vojenta* was at the center of a ring of women. She looked as if she'd been telling a story, and frequently pushed her long brown hair back behind her ears. The last was right next to Willow, close enough to touch, and Willow was startled to see that she was not Eskandelic. Her hair was as bright blonde as Felix's despite her evident age—she was probably near fifty—and she was much taller than the women surrounding her.

She perceived Willow's surprise and smiled at her, a friendly expression with none of the calculation even Alondra frequently displayed. Willow was accustomed to it, knew that attitude was just a reflection of the political realities of Eskandel, but the idea that the leader of a harem might be so unabashedly friendly was a surprise.

"Welcome, Willow North," Janida said. "Sit and make welcome, all."

The women settled onto sofas and cushions on the floor with a great rustling of skirts and trousers. Willow found a seat on a maroon sofa that made her skirt look orange and clasped her hands in her lap, and looked to Janida for some signal. The rest of the women seemed to feel the same way, because their attention turned to Janida, who'd remained standing. Janida settled her golden bracelets straighter on her wrists.

"Welcome," she repeated. "It is good once again among friends to be. I have said to you all that Eskandel faces its greatest challenge in a century. Our northern neighbor Tremontane on the verge of civil war is. Terence Valant has laid claim to the Crown, which by Tremontane's laws illegal is. He says the heir Felix Valant by an assassin killed was, but Felix Valant alive is and here under the protection of the Serjian Principality is. This principality asserts that Felix the rightful heir is and that Eskandel should recognize him as such, and return the Crown of Tremontane to him."

The room was silent. Willow had expected at least some audible expression of surprise, but no one said a word. "Willow North the guest of the Serjian Principality is. She *eskarna* for the young King is."

That got a response, women muttering to their neighbors and all of them staring at Willow. She stiffened her spine and gave them the look she gave Rufus Black when he tried to cheat her. Of course, Rufus's cheating was always a joke between them, and she knew him well, unlike all these powerful women who were accustomed to political infighting and didn't know anything about Willow except what Janida claimed. *This is for Felix, he can't do this for himself,* she reminded herself.

"You claim *eskarna* in public?" said one of the women. Willow examined her, noted how her clothes were plain and dark by comparison to the others, how she wore no jewelry, and concluded she was probably *eskarna* herself. Willow stood, made her hands relax by her sides, and fell into the comfortable stance she used when she was observing a place she meant to rob—knees slightly bent, shoulders straight, head and neck loose so she could quickly look in any direction.

"I know those who are *eskarna* work in secret, here in Eskandel," she said. "It's like that in Tremontane, too. If I were openly a thief there, I'd be punished or maybe even killed. But I'm told Felix can't speak for himself here, and I think everyone should know why I'm qualified to speak on his behalf. A thief is what I am, and I'm not ashamed of that. And my skills are what got him out of Aurilien alive. So yes, I'm claiming *eskarna* in public, and I hope that demonstrates my desire to be open in my actions on the King's behalf."

"And you would have us support this King," said the black-haired *vojenta*. "You would have us put Eskandelic lives in jeopardy."

"I'm not going to dictate to Eskandel what kind of support to give Felix, though I have some suggestions," Willow lied. She definitely hadn't thought that far ahead. "I hope to convince you to support his claim, to refuse to recognize Terence Valant, and the rest will come later."

"Felix Valant was killed by an assassin. An Eskandelic assassin," the woman said. "You should prove otherwise to us before we consider your claim."

3

"If you've heard that rumor, you probably also heard the assassin was the Eminence's dowser. His name, in case you're interested, is Serjian Kerish." Another muttered reaction. "Kerish helped rescue Felix from the palace and was almost killed in the process. Terence thought he looked like a good candidate to pin his murder of his brother on, so he lied about Kerish's involvement in the coup. He wants everyone to believe Felix is dead because he's ruling illegally and Felix's reappearance would set the provincial rulers of Tremontane against him even more than they are right now. I'm sure we can arrange for all of you to meet with Felix later, if that would help, but I give you my word that he's who he claims to be."

"Your word as *eskarna*."

"My word as his guardian. As *eskarna* too, if that means more to you. I wouldn't have done all of this if I didn't believe he's who I say he is."

"What is 'all of this'?" the blonde *vojenta* said. She spoke Tremontanese with a northwestern accent, something Willow hadn't heard often in Aurilien but which was unmistakable.

Willow let out a deep breath. "I left my life behind," she said. "My friends were endangered. I can't return to my home unless Felix is restored to the throne. I was nearly killed by bandits and I'm in a country where I don't even speak the language. Because of him—no, for his sake."

"Dramatic," said one of the women, a redhead who looked as if scowling were her permanent state. "Suppose we believe you for argument's sake. The question most important is, why do we care?"

"You don't, really," Willow said, startling the woman. "It's not your country and he's not your King. You don't have to do a damn thing except watch Tremontane go up in flames, taking your economy with it."

She straightened a little. "I can't say I understand much about the way countries trade with each other, but I've seen wars between the dukes—the criminal bosses—of Aurilien, and I know that when two dukes are fighting over territory, the wars hurt anyone who depends on the stability of those territories for trade.

"Usually such wars mean those people go elsewhere for what they need, which is complicated and almost always more expensive. So I'm pretty sure you'll be increasing trade with Veribold for a while, maybe a long while. Which means, first, that you'll be paying more for the same thing, Veriboldans being who they are, and second, you'll lose out on the things that only Tremontane produces while that country resolves its problems. Or you'll pay more for *Tremontanan* goods, funneled through the black market. But that's really up to you."

The room fell silent. Finally, the brown-haired *vojenta* said, "You speak with force. Janida, you support this woman?"

"Serjian Principality stands behind her," Janida said, emphasizing the first two words slightly.

The *vojenta* stood up, prompting five women nearby to stand as well. "Ajemi Sovea swears that Ajemi Principality will stand with Serjian in this thing," she said.

"Willow North," said the black-haired *vojenta*, "can you guarantee Tremontane will follow your King?"

"I can't," Willow said, then wished she'd lied, because the woman's eyes flashed with amusement. *Mistake!*

"Honesty in *eskarna* is of the most importance," the woman said, rising from the floor and bringing three other women with her. "Khasjabi Donia speaks for the Khasjabi Principality, which stands with Serjian in this."

"As does Dekerian," said the woman in the black headwrap, "by oath of Dekerian Mireya."

Willow looked down at the blonde woman, who hadn't moved. "You're from Aurilien?" the *vojenta* said.

"Born and raised. This is the first time I've been out of the capital," Willow said.

"I was born in Barony Daxtry," the woman said. "I've lived in Eskandel since I was twelve, and it's my adopted home, but I respect the place of my birth and I don't want to see it ruled by an Ascendant any more, I think, than you do." She stood and offered her hand to Willow. "Torossian Kharalin, or Caroline Anders as was, and Torossian Principality stands with Serjian in this."

"Thanks," Willow said, clasping Kharalin's hand.

"We'll have to speak later. You have the look of someone bursting with questions," Kharalin said with a smile. "But for now I think we have strategy to plan."

"We will need the question on the roster to be written," Mireya said. "I think we will have the better of Mahnouki if we can keep this secret. Surprise, and curiosity, friends to us are."

"Mahnouki has spies," the dark-clad *eskarna* said, with some scorn. Willow guessed spies weren't the same thing as *eskarna*. "But I think Catrela and I can misdirect them."

"I have conceived ideas," Catrela said with a nod. "But we must not too soon put our question to paper. It too easy to find will be."

"Understood," Janida said. "In three days the Princes vote. Salveri prepared on this matter to speak is, Serjian Principality its sponsor to make. This we do first, Willow North. All principalities wish things enacted to be, decisions made to be, but too many to vote in Conclave there are. Thus does each principality with a thing they desire add this question to the roster, which brought to the harems is the morning before the Princes vote on which of those questions will be deliberated and voted on in Conclave and which will not.

"The harems decide and tell their Princes. It is meant that no principality has time to instruct another on how its Prince should vote, which things to vote against, but many times the roster...is found by some harems in advance. We must give Mahnouki no time to control the vote, because Mahnouki Adorinda will not wish this question to be part of the *adjeni*, the final list of questions to vote. Better for her that it rejected at the start is."

"What can I do?" Willow asked.

"We will prepare our strategy as if this on the *adjeni* is. Otherwise...no point in acting at all. You must learn those we will try to sway and those we must...neutralize, the word is. Then you will know which words to which principality to speak."

"There much to learn is," Mireya said, "and three days in which to learn it. Are you prepared, *eskarna*?"

"Not really," Willow said, sending a laugh rippling through the room, "but I guess I have to be."

"Indeed," Janida said. "Then tomorrow we will begin."

This seemed to be the sign for everyone to rise and begin chatting in Eskandelic, which told Willow she was free to leave. She nodded at Catrela and left the room. Once outside, she walked down the hall until she was out of sight of the door, then leaned against the wall and let out a deep breath. And that had been a gathering of…not friends, but at least allies, and people friendly to her cause. How much worse would it be facing her enemies?

She leaned down to unfasten her soft shoes, which pinched at the toes. She wished she'd come up with a reason to wear her own shoes, specially made by her to be perfect for midnighting, but Caira had made a face Willow interpreted as "stop being a heathen foreigner" and Willow had given in. Would she be able to wear them again here in Umberan, ever? If she got caught midnighting, it would look very bad for Felix…on the other hand, suppose she had to learn something, or take something, that would aid his cause?

She rolled out her shoulders. She was certain she wouldn't start making up reasons to climb the walls of Umberan. Mostly certain. Certain enough that she wouldn't ask Caira to hide her shoes as a precautionary measure.

The lights were off in the stairwell leading to her and Felix's room, which seemed odd. She looked around for a switch like the ones that operated the lights in her room before remembering there were no switches in the halls; the lights burned all day and all night. Well, it wasn't as if she weren't used to working in the dark. She began ascending the stairs. There were no lights coming from—

She cursed and ran up the stairs. No lights in the stairs, no lights in the hall. As if in tandem with her horrified thoughts, a scream echoed down the stairwell, then another, and a high, frantic yapping filled the air. She yanked her stupid skirt out of the way and tore down the hallway, shouting, *"Felix!"*

"Willow!" Felix screamed. *"Help!"*

Willow yanked at her sleeve, which was too tight thanks to her knife—she'd insisted on wearing it and overridden every one of Caira's protests. She tore it free from its sheath, heedless of ripping fabric, and flung open the door to her room. The only light came from the half-moon just visible through the windows, but Willow's eyes had adjusted to the darkness on her flight and she could see the hulking forms of two men tussling. Ernest's silvery-gray form darted around them, yipping wildly. Felix wasn't visible anywhere.

"Felix!" Willow shouted, and threw herself at the men just as one shoved the other hard, making him fall in a heap. The one still standing turned on Willow, and she ducked under the shining silver of his knife and slashed at him, making him stumble backward. "Stay down!" she said, hoping Felix would understand.

She crouched, knife at the ready, caught the man's blade on hers when he struck and swept it out of the way. She thrust at his midsection and forced him back again. The man snarled something in Eskandelic and made a grab for her with his free hand.

She stepped to the side, ducked under his hand, and made another thrust at his belly. This time she connected solidly. He made a pained grunt and moved back out of the reach of her next slash, toward the doorway. "Don't even think about it," Willow said, moving to intercept him.

She realized she'd put herself within his reach when he grabbed her arm, drew her close and brought his knife around to slash at her throat. She went limp, sagging in his arms, and his strike missed. When he fumbled with her unexpected weight, she ducked away from his knife and aimed another blow at his stomach.

He turned at the last minute and her knife caught in his dark, loose clothes, pulling it out of her hand. She swore and punched him in the stomach. It was like punching a wall, sending a sharp pain shooting up her arm and making her assailant cry out. He shoved her away, sending her sprawling to the floor, and took off running down the hall.

"Stay down!" she shouted again. She jumped up and tore after the man in time to see him hoist himself awkwardly over the nearest windowsill and drop. Willow ran and took a brief look down before climbing out herself, gathering her skirts out of the way. They were near the top of the house, and he'd made a wild leap to the next window down and was dangling by his hands, reaching for a foothold.

Willow felt around the wall for something to hold onto. The walls of the Serjian Residence were smooth, too smooth for free climbing, and there was no way she could replicate that leap of his in this dress. She cursed again and made for the stairs. If she could get down and outside before he did —

She dashed out of the front door and around to the side of the Residence. The assassin was gone.

She stood, slightly bent over with her hand pressed to the stitch in her side, and looked around. One of her fists was bloody. She'd definitely wounded him with the knife, and maybe he'd left a blood trail she could follow.

There were a few drops by the base of the wall, and more about ten feet on. She tracked him to the wall surrounding the Residence, lined with hedges on this side. A smear of blood marred the top half of the wall where the assassin had dragged himself up and over.

Willow climbed to the top and dropped lightly down on the other side. The skirt snagged and tore, but she barely noticed. There was a matching smear on the street side of the wall, but no more blood spatters, and Willow ran a few dozen yards before concluding she'd lost him. She cursed. Someone had attacked Felix, and she needed to know who.

Felix.

She ran back, scrambled up and over the wall, then raced as fast as she could back to their room, her heart pounding faster than exertion would warrant. She shouldn't have left him. What if he was dead? Who had been fighting the assassin when she entered? She skidded around a corner in her bare feet. She'd heard him scream. That meant he was alive. Everything was fine. She clung to that thought.

The lights were back on in the stairwell and the hallway when she pelted up them, hearing the noise of a dozen people all talking at once coming from her room. She came to a stop in the doorway, breathing heavily. Felix was sitting on his bed with Rafferty next to him. He was hugging Ernest so tightly the puppy was whimpering and struggling. Willow crossed the room and went to her knees in front of him, holding him close.

"He's all right, Willow," Rafferty said. "Just scared."

"That's more than bad enough," Willow said. "Felix, take a deep breath. Try to calm down. You're safe."

"He killed Fedrani, Willow," Felix sobbed. "Fedrani fought him, but he had a big knife and, and Willow, he was going to kill me, where were you?"

"I'm sorry," she whispered, "I'm sorry. I tried to catch him, but he got away."

"He's going to come back!"

"That is not a thing that will happen," Janida said grimly. "We will place a better guard on this house, and you will have bodyguards, young King. I blame myself for not imagining this would happen."

"How should we know?" Giara said. "No one knows of the King's presence yet except our allies."

"There many were who saw him at the Conclave," said Catrela. She was kneeling over Fedrani's body and examining it, though Willow couldn't tell for what. "We do not know how many know the truth behind Terence Valant's lies. Anyone might have drawn the right conclusion." But she didn't look convinced. Willow was certain she was thinking what Willow, fellow sneak, was thinking: *which of our allies is a traitor?* The *vojentas* had come with escorts, and with so many extra men milling around, anyone could have slipped away, sneaked through the Residence, silently climbed the stairs...

A heavy tread in the hallway became Serjian Salveri, imposing in an embroidered dressing gown, followed by Kerish. "We have learned how he entered, and have taken steps to see it cannot happen again," the Prince said. "I apologize, young King. We have failed to protect you."

"Two more retainers are dead," Kerish said. "Felix, I'm so sorry. It won't happen again." He came to kneel by Felix's side and put his hand on the boy's shoulder.

"So what you're all saying," Willow said, freeing Ernest from Felix's grip, "is that someone knows who Felix is and wants him dead. But why? Don't they just have to make sure his question doesn't get approved by the Conclave?"

"There are likely those who do not wish that risk to take, that the Conclave votes to return the Crown of Tremontane to King Felix," Janida said. "And some of those would not blink at killing a child that to prevent."

"We will find the truth, Willow," Catrela said.

"With my help." Willow smoothed Felix's hair. "He's my

responsibility."

"You will have much to do. Better to let the *eskarnas* take this burden."

"I'm *eskarna* too, right? And you and the others will have enough to do making sure the vote goes our way. I've done this sort of thing for years, finding things that don't want to be found. You tell me which of the principalities might be behind this, and I'll figure out who it is. And you'd better not say I don't have the right."

Catrela shook her head. "I will not say that." She stood back as a couple of Serjian servants, big and well-muscled, brought a sheet to wrap Fedrani's body in and carry him away. Felix burst into noisy sobs and Willow drew him closer and rocked him in her arms. "We will move you to another room now. Tomorrow is soon enough to begin your lessons. All of your lessons."

"I'll show them the new room, Mother," Kerish said. "Why don't you let me carry you, Felix?"

The new room was also on the highest floor of the Residence, but the stairs led directly to the door instead of to a hallway and rose from the floor where Janida and Catrela's suites were. "There will be a guard inside and out," Kerish said. "Tomorrow there will be guards for you, Felix."

"All right," Felix said in a small voice.

"Are you hurt at all, Willow?" Kerish said. "Your dress—"

"It's the wrong kind of clothing for climbing walls, that's all," Willow said. "I'm fine."

"Good. I don't—if that man had hurt either of you—"

"I know. Everything's all right now." His dark eyes were fixed on Felix, but she knew his attention was on her, and suddenly she wanted to put her arms around him and let him hold her. She chased the impulse away. That couldn't lead anywhere good. "We'll see you in the morning."

Finally, he looked at her, and she regretted her words, how dismissive they'd sounded, because he looked hurt. But he said, "Good night," and disappeared down the stairs.

Felix let Willow lead him to his bed and tuck him in, then welcomed Ernest into the crook of his arm. "Willow?" he said when she would have moved away.

"Yes?"

"Is it all right if I don't want to be King?"

Willow came back to sit on the floor near his head. "I think only crazy people *want* to be King, because it's very hard work. I wish..." She decided not to say *I wish I could take that burden away from you*, because there was no sense encouraging him in thinking that way. He was the King, and nothing could change that. "Right now, you're scared, and I don't blame you. What was Fedrani doing there?"

"He brought me something to eat before bed. It was just a little thing. He wouldn't have been killed if—"

"Stop that right now," Willow commanded, and Felix wiped the beginnings of tears from his eyes. "I wish Fedrani was alive, too, but he cared about you and he didn't want you to die. Sometimes people have to choose what's more important, their own lives or someone else's. I'm pretty sure Fedrani would have hated himself if he'd run away and let you be killed. So don't blame yourself. Blame the bastard who killed him."

"Hilarion says profanity shows a lack of imagination and is the last resort of the half-wit."

"Hilarion never heard Rufus Black in full flower of obscenity. It's a thing of beauty, unless he's directing it at you." She patted Felix's cheek. "Try to sleep. Don't worry, no one's getting in here tonight."

"I know. Good night, Willow."

Willow turned off the light and awkwardly stripped out of the golden gown, wishing she hadn't sent Caira to bed. She'd forgotten how she was dressed. She'd destroyed it anyway, what with climbing the Residence wall twice and going through the hedge both times. She threw it into a corner and got into bed in just her underwear, since they hadn't had time to bring her wardrobe to the new suite.

Felix was already asleep, breathing through his nose with a quiet whistling sound. If she hadn't come back when she had, he'd be dead. Willow shivered, not from cold. She'd gotten so complacent, surrounded by the Serjian Principality. She'd forgotten that Terence still needed Felix dead, that he had all sorts of resources available to him to make that happen. She had to be lucky all the time. He only had to be lucky once. Well, starting tomorrow, she was going to track that assassin down. *And pray there's only one principality behind it*, she thought, and ruthlessly chased the thought away.

Chapter Two

"Let me go over this again," Willow said. She rubbed her temples, vainly trying to make her headache disappear. "Most of the principalities are allied with more powerful ones. But those more powerful ones may give their votes to an even more powerful principality. So the goal is to identify those...I don't remember what to call them."

"Our word is *parjeni*," Alondra said. "It means, to rule by proxy. The *parjeni* are all those who command the votes of others. *Parjenisur* is the ones who themselves control the votes of others, but give that control to someone above them in power."

"The *parjeni* are the ones we want to sway, but we also want to encourage the ones who haven't given allegiance to choose one of our allies. Or us."

"That is so. Best still if a strong *parjeni* attracts more principalities and then brings those votes to our cause."

"And we do this by promising our support for their interests and convincing them that our enemies—sorry, our opponents—can't help them." She still called them enemies in the privacy of her own mind. This was Felix's future, the future of Tremontane, at stake, and anyone who stood in the way of that couldn't be considered a friend. Not to mention that at least one of them was an actual, potentially deadly enemy. "Which means knowing what those interests, those questions, are."

"It is much to remember. But you understand much already."

"Only because I took notes." Willow tapped her pen against the sheet of paper, which was whiter and thicker than what she was used to in Aurilien. She'd never had more than the most basic education in reading and writing, so her handwriting looked like that of a child, but at least she was literate, which was more than most of her acquaintances could say.

"This list is our primary allies, the ones who will vote with us when they see Serjian is sponsoring the question no matter what it is.

Then there's the enemy *parjeni*—I mean, the opponents, and their *parjenisur*. And the long list is the ones who don't know about our question and who won't automatically be for either side. That's the confusing one. All those principalities, even after we eliminate the ones whose side we know already."

"It is complex even to us. We must court the *parjeni* and *parjenisur*, but we cannot neglect those who give their allegiance to them, who might give allegiance instead to us. There it is we must understand the most."

"Treat them as if they matter as much as the most powerful *parjeni*."

"You understand it." Alondra stretched and shifted Caderina to her other breast. "I think this child draining me is."

"I'm surprised you don't have someone else nurse her. The nobles in Aurilien all have wet nurses for that."

Alondra cuddled her baby more closely. "That is not a thing we do, except when the mother cannot. It is…complicated, to bring an outsider into the harem even for such a thing. Giara could not feed Jauman, so we took Berena among us for a time. She much loved was and we still her friends are."

"I guess it doesn't seem to slow you down at all."

"It is another way the harem cares for its own."

Willow decided not to follow that conversational trail. She wanted to know how the wives managed not to feel jealousy over Salveri, or maybe they did and just hid it really well, but it felt like an awkward subject, as if she were judging them for being so well-adjusted. Instead, she said, "Are you all sure you want me to concentrate on wooing these four? Wouldn't it be better if I talked to some of these, um, less powerful principalities?"

"You may also do so," Alondra said, "but these four are not only *parjeni*, they are among those who will control the decision of the *vojenta mahaut*. They must be convinced that Serjian Principality the best for Eskandel is. If you speak well for Felix, and if Serjian Principality recognizes his claim, then logic it is that Serjian Principality best knows how to resolve the Tremontane question."

Willow drew a box around a set of four names:

Jamighian Issobela
Hajimhi Fariola
Sarhafian Jennea
Takjashi Lucea

"Jamighian Issobela is logical and cautious, maybe overly so," she recited. "She will want facts and information. Be honest with her, because if she thinks I'm lying, she'll turn on us completely. Hajimhi Fariola wants Gessala to join her harem — Alondra, I don't think I should make that promise. Isn't it up to Gessala?"

"You will not promise, and she would not believe you if you did," Alondra said. "She will try information to gain from you and will not respect you if you give it. Her respect is of the most importance. Hajimhi prides itself on its honor."

"I can understand that." The dukes of Lower Town had a system of dealing with each other that depended heavily on their complicated sense of honor, hundreds of rules and nuances of behavior that could literally mean the difference between life or death. Probably it wasn't that dire in the Conclave — though it might be a bad idea to assume that. At any rate, honor was something Willow understood.

"Tell me about Sarhafian Jennea."

"She'll want an exchange of favors and will want more from us than she gives. Pushing too hard will make her withdraw and look for another alliance." Willow drew a line under the last name on her list. "And Catrela doesn't know anything about Takjashi Lucea."

"She was a scholar, not one of much consequence but not the least of her scholia. It was a surprise when she became *vojenta*. She and Abakian Raena *suorenas* are, and Lucea may follow where Raena leads, but we have no certainty in that. Catrela will continue her responsibility to pursue, and you must observe her closely."

"I will." Willow dropped the pen on the table, making a little ink splatter, and stretched. "I think I understand how this works. Now, what about the assassination attempt?"

"That a thing Catrela should tell you is. I *eskarna* am not."

"But you know who's powerful enough to try assassination, and who would want to."

"There obvious choices are, yes." Alondra sighed. "Mahnouki.

Abakian. Gharibi. Sahaki. Hovanesian might do it at Gharibi's urging, and might believe it their idea to be, but it unlikely is that Gharibi Ciera would risk discovery by revealing such a plan to another principality. But none of them know of Felix's existence."

"That we know of. Terence Valant was in communication with Sahaki when they were still *vojenta mahaut*. He might have told them about Felix if he thought they were true allies. Who knows what he might have promised in exchange for them killing his nephew? And you said Sahaki was a puppet of Mahnouki, so Sahaki might have told *them*. Once that sort of secret gets spread...you know the saying, two can keep a secret if one of them is dead?"

"That is an Eskandelic saying, too. But I think we would have heard rumors...though perhaps Catrela has learned more. I think—" Her voice became quieter, making Willow lean in to hear her clearly. "I think she worried is that one of our allies is not as honorable as they seem."

"I don't blame her. I'd suspect them over your enemies, since they for sure know about Felix."

"But these are women we have trusted for many years. Some of those principalities have been Serjian allies for over two centuries. I am unhappy at the thought."

"Well, I intend to find out the truth. And speaking of finding things out, I'm going into the city now."

"Alone? You cannot speak our language, and outside the harems you will find few who speak yours."

"I know. But if I don't get out of this place for a few hours, I'll start climbing the walls, and I mean that literally. Don't worry about me."

"I worry more for the city," Alondra said with a wry smile. "Very well. We will continue this later."

Willow ran back to her room and rummaged through the closet looking for something simple to wear. Silk, fine linen, more silk, something trimmed in velvet...why wasn't there anything sensible? Then she stopped with her hand wound into a gauzy scarf and laughed at herself. She wasn't here as a thief, looking for a safe place to stay in whatever the Umberan equivalent of Lower Town was. She didn't have to worry about hiding. *Even so*, she thought, selecting linen trousers, a long-sleeved shirt in pale rose, and a white headwrap, *I'm not going out there in a robe it will be hard to run in.*

She managed to put on the headwrap in only a few tries, strapped her knife to her forearm, then examined herself in the mirror. She *almost* looked Eskandelic. Blue eyes were uncommon but not unheard of, but her fair skin wasn't yet tanned enough by the sun and her cheekbones and eyebrow ridges weren't prominent enough. At least her nose had stopped peeling. Well, it wasn't as if she were trying to conceal her identity.

She still found it easy to get lost in the many passages leading between the buildings of the Residence. The walls were all unadorned pink stone with few windows, cool and comfortable no matter how hot the day. Finally she reached a familiar walkway that led from her own rooms to the main house and strolled along, enjoying the smell of the sea breezes. The walkway turned into an open colonnade that overlooked the courtyard, and to the smell of the sea was added the faint whiff of horses from the adjacent stables.

She began to hear strange noises, the *thock* of wood striking wood and the scuff of feet, and hurried along the colonnade until she could see down into the courtyard. Half a dozen men and two women dressed in sleeveless tunics and loosely-fitted trousers lunged and darted at each other, their wooden practice swords clashing and disengaging with incredible ferocity. One man grunted loudly enough to hear over the noise as his partner thwacked him in the stomach with the flat of her "blade." Small clouds of reddish dust kicked up from the hard-packed earth of the courtyard obscured Willow's vision slightly, but not enough that her eye wasn't immediately drawn to Kerish, fighting another man in the far corner.

Willow watched, breathless. She'd never seen him fight before, though she knew the kind of training he'd received as a child and a young man. Seeing him now…he moved gracefully, as if this were some dance, his weapon flicking here and there, never letting his opponent land a stroke. Gradually, he forced the other man back, a step at a time, until the man was nearly to the wall. He blocked the next swing, struck faster than Willow could follow, and then his opponent's weapon was on the ground and Kerish had the blade of his sword pressed against the man's throat. They stood like that for a moment, both breathing heavily, until the other man laughed and clapped Kerish on the shoulder. Kerish stepped back, shaking his head. He bent to pick up his opponent's weapon and handed it to him.

The man caught sight of Willow and nudged Kerish, who turned, sword still in hand. Willow felt an intense desire to hide, as if she'd witnessed something intimate and private. From that distance, Kerish's expression was difficult to see, but he didn't seem to be smiling, or frowning, just regarding her with that steady, familiar gaze. She put her hand on one of the columns to steady herself against an unexpected rush of desire.

Kerish raised his sword to her in salute, still unsmiling, and her heart beat even faster. It was the gesture of a champion to his lady, a courtier's salute. It threw her into such confusion that she turned and ran from the colonnade to the stairs without responding. She stood at the top of the stairs, out of sight of the courtyard, cursing herself. How rude, to spurn his gesture—but how could he behave as if nothing were wrong between them? She felt dizzy enough to sit on the top step and put her head between her knees. Was he mocking her? She wasn't his lady, not anymore, wasn't anyone's idea of a lady. But at that moment she wished she were.

She retreated all the way around the main building to the front and left by that route. The Residence's front door was some distance back from the street, opening on the garden Willow had caught a few glimpses of from the upper floor galleries. A long covered walkway lined with bulbous white pillars extended from the front door to the gatehouse, but Willow took the opportunity to go into the garden and get a closer look at the frond-trees, trying to calm herself. Their trunks looked as if they'd been woven out of short, fat lengths of bark, and most of them bowed under the weight of their fronds. Barefoot, it wouldn't be difficult at all to climb these trees.

Willow walked around the Residence until she could see the windows of her new room, then estimated the distance between the walls and the nearest tree. Too close. Would the glass of the window, not made to open, be enough to deter an assassin? She'd have to come back later and test the theory.

She took one last look at her window, then turned to look at the trees again. Her attention was caught by someone hurrying along the walkway, someone who moved furtively from pillar to pillar and therefore stood out as obviously as if she'd run its length, shouting and waving her arms. Her head and face were draped in a veil, a fashion Willow hadn't seen outside the Conclave, and without thinking Willow set out to follow her. The woman was leaving the Residence, not entering it, and it was probably none of Willow's business, but after the assassination attempt she was inclined to suspiciousness.

Despite the woman's obvious desire for secrecy, she was terrible at watching her surroundings for anyone following her, and Willow barely had to make an effort to stay concealed. The woman passed the Serjian gatehouse without being hailed—of course, she wasn't trying to get in, but even so Willow expected at least to see the guards acknowledge her—and turned left. Willow wasn't hailed either, though in her case she was sure it was because no one saw her. She ought to speak to Janida about the alertness of the guards. That explained a lot about how the assassin had been able to get inside so easily.

The house—Residence?—next to the Serjian Residence was as elegant and huge as its neighbor, though built from creamy white stones instead of the pinkish-tan blocks she was now so familiar with. It, too, had a gatehouse flanking its driveway, which was paved with smaller cobbles than those of the road. The road itself was odd. The paving stones were too clean, the road completely empty of people except for her and the woman, and it unnerved Willow so much she began touching her left arm every few minutes, assuring herself that her knife was still there though she couldn't perceive anyone she might need to use it against.

She observed the houses more closely, the narrowness of the road, and realized it was a private road like the one leading to the palace in Aurilien rather than a public street. There were neighborhoods like this in Aurilien, little cities within cities, gated off from the rest of the capital. This made her less unsettled, since it made sense the people who lived here would control the traffic and keep undesirables out of their enclave, but knowing that by some definitions *she* was undesirable kept her from relaxing entirely.

She followed the woman down the private road to a black stone arch, pointed at the top and wide enough for only one carriage to pass through at a time. Now Willow heard the noise of people, and carriages. She hadn't realized how much she missed being in a city until that moment. She saw no guards at the black arch, which she found odd. Was the power of the principalities who lived beyond the gate enough to dissuade thieves? It certainly wouldn't stop *her*. But then, she wasn't likely to go in via the gate.

Once past the black arch, the woman moved more freely, and Willow had to speed up to keep within sight of her. The street beyond the arch was paved with gray bricks the width of her two hands whose edges were rounded from centuries of traffic. The current traffic was doing its best to round off those edges further. Willow didn't quite have to push her way through the crowds of pedestrians, but she was pressed closely enough that she was glad she'd left her belt pouch in the Residence. All she had in the pouch between her breasts was Tremontanan money, but this was a thriving center of trade, wasn't it? Even if there weren't moneychangers, which seemed unlikely, there was the Tremontanan settlement Rafferty had gone to. She could probably find a way to spend her money if she really wanted to. At the moment, she had more pressing concerns.

The air was filled with the delicious smell of roasted meat and hot, rich Eskandelic coffee, *khaveh,* sweetened with burnt sugar, beneath which she could barely perceive the odor of animal waste. Umberan was as clean as Kerish had always said. The sound of hundreds of people all talking at once in Eskandelic really was like rainfall. In Aurilien, she'd have paid attention to the conversations with half her attention, listening for indications that someone was coming after her. Here, none of it made sense, and the chances of her picking out the few Eskandelic words she knew were vanishingly small, so she followed her quarry feeling as if she were caught in a hot, dry rainstorm. The woman continued to be oblivious to her presence.

Willow kept one eye on the Jauderish, which dominated the skyline and provided a perfect landmark to keep her from getting lost, and tried not to think too hard about how easy it would be to scale the sides of some of these buildings. It was all the arches, and the balconies, and the jutting window ledges which bore colorful pots filled with trailing greenery, that made the idea so tempting. At street level, the doors were set into pointed or keyhole arches, every one of which was outlined in bright colored painted patterns, none of which matched each other. Willow examined a few, hoping to work out an underlying system, but it seemed they were all just expressions of the householders' whims.

The woman turned onto a smaller street, one which led to what Willow thought was a residential area. There were fewer people, and the narrow streets were empty of merchants and wagons. There were no windows at ground level, at least not facing the street, and the stone houses all butted up against each other the way they did in Aurilien, though these were much taller and narrower and brightly painted. Pots full of red flowers like tiny trumpets hung next to the upper windows, which were open to the breezes that came off the ocean. Gauzy fabric fluttered at many of them.

The woman knocked at a blue door and finally looked around for someone observing her. Willow had been expecting this and turned toward another door, pretending to knock but covertly observing the woman. The blue door opened, and a man appeared. He was handsome, with dark blond hair and dark skin that contrasted nicely with it, and he put his hand on the woman's shoulder as if in protection. He looked up and down the street before welcoming her in and closing the door.

Willow immediately moved toward the door. Too bad there were no convenient windows. Now, how curious was she? She moved on down the street, looking for a back entrance, and found an even narrower street about five houses down that cut across the one she was on; it was practically an alley. It led to an actual alley that ran behind the houses where refuse was thrown, stinking of human waste and rotting food. So much for Umberan's legendary sanitation. She picked her way through the muck, counting houses, and found no ground-level windows on this side either. Of course. Who would want to look out on this mess?

She reached the rear of the house the woman had entered and looked around. It rose four stories into the air and had one window at each of them, all of them either open or without glass to block the breeze. Now she had to make a decision.

She eyed the window immediately above. It would be hard to reach, and this wasn't her city. If someone saw her apparently trying to break into this house, she could be in serious trouble. She didn't know how Eskandelics punished thieves, but they couldn't be more lenient than Tremontanans were. On the other hand, if this woman, whoever she was, had had some part in arranging the assassination, Felix's safety could depend on Willow finding out the truth.

She came to a decision and stripped off her shoes. The fronts of the houses had smoothly plastered finishes, but the backs were rough, unfinished red brick that had crumbled with time. Willow rubbed her hands on her trousers, then rubbed her palms together and began feeling around for a gap big enough for her to fit her fingers into. She only had to climb far enough to get her hands on the jutting windowsill, and if she didn't see anything, well, she'd make that decision when she came to it.

The stillness of the air, broken only by her heavy breathing as she climbed one painful inch at a time, made her feel as if she were moving through treacly water, as if the ground were trying to assert its hold on her. She kept moving, knowing from experience that stopping to indulge that feeling would only leave her trapped midway between her goal and the so-hard earth. She reached up and got a grip on the windowsill, shifted so she could put both hands on it, and found a couple of toeholds to help support her weight. Then she raised her head and peered over the sill into the room beyond.

A couple of gauzy curtains blocked her view somewhat, but she could see a narrow bed covered with a multicolored woven blanket and a couple of floor pillows like the ones in the Serjian dining room. The door was just closing behind the man and the woman. The man had his back to Willow, blocking her view of the woman, who had her arms around him. They were kissing, feverishly, their hands working at disrobing each other as fast as possible. Just as Willow was about to turn away in embarrassment, the man swept the woman up in his arms and deposited her half-naked on the bed.

Sweet heaven. Imara.

Imara pulled the man down to lie atop her. He kissed her throat, began moving down her body, and Willow ducked away, her face hot. Imara. She hadn't expected *that*. She made her way back down the wall and put her shoes on. Imara probably wasn't plotting against Felix, but what *was* she doing? Aside from the obvious. Janida certainly didn't know about this, and Willow doubted any of Imara's *majdrani* knew either. A daughter of a principality, meeting with…it was tempting to imagine a forbidden love with a poor man of the streets, but for all Willow knew, he was of high rank and this was just where they met.

She retraced her steps and headed back toward the Residence, not allowing her preoccupation to distract her attention from her surroundings. Telling the harem the truth…it went against every principle she had. And it was really none of her business what Imara did.

On the other hand—she remembered something Rafferty had said once, about being nervous about other people's secrets. If Imara was doing something she didn't want her family to know about, who knew what she might be willing to do to keep that secret—including endanger Felix? Willow would have to find out more, possibly by talking to Imara herself. As if she didn't have enough worries already.

There were still no guards visible at the black arch or at the entrance to the Residence, and Willow considered sneaking into the guard tower just to prove a point, but decided against it. She would climb that tree near her window, decide whether something needed to be done about it, then join the family for supper. Maybe ungoverned heaven would give her inspiration. She could certainly use it.

She crossed the grounds to stand at the base of the tree, then unfastened her shoes and rubbed one foot against her shin. The linen of her trousers had a slightly slick finish, and the sole of her foot slid before catching on the weave. Soft grass grew throughout the garden, but the ground beneath the frond trees was bare and gritty, with coarse grains that stuck to her feet. She wiped her other foot, then reached up as high as she could and grabbed hold of the trunk.

Climbing was as easy as she'd anticipated. Willow shinned up the trunk until she reached the spot where the fronds emerged. The tree dipped and swayed, bending slightly under her weight, and she gripped the base of one of the fronds to steady herself. She was a foot or so beneath her window. The fronds brushed the side of the Residence, but when she tried to move further, they bent alarmingly. They wouldn't support anyone bigger than a child, and a child would have trouble reaching the window.

"What are you doing?"

Willow grabbed the fronds to steady herself and looked down at Kerish, who was dressed as casually as she was and sounded just as casual. He stood with one hand on the trunk and had his head tilted back, squinting against the sunlight. "I didn't even think of the trees," he said.

"Is it ungrateful to say I don't think much of the Serjian Principality's security measures?" Willow said. If he was going to pretend the moment in the courtyard hadn't happened, she was happy to do the same.

"If it is, we're both ungrateful. I just came back from the scholia and the guards at the gate didn't challenge me." He took a few steps back as she descended. "They're not sufficiently paranoid."

"Neither were you, once."

Kerish shrugged. "I did listen to you, you know."

Willow brushed off her feet and bent to put her sandals on. The urge to say *Not about the important things* was compelling. Instead, she managed, "I never thought you'd need my midnighting skills."

Kerish was silent. She glanced up from her feet to see him looking away from her, into the distance, his jaw tight. "I guess," he said, "there are a lot of things neither of us expected."

Willow rose and wiped her hands on her trousers, leaving pale streaks of dirt. "That's true."

"Willow—" Kerish bowed his head. "I'm sorry."

"Sorry? For what?" *For pretending you still care about me?*

"For not being with Felix last night. He would have died if you hadn't returned just in time."

"Kerish, his safety isn't your responsibility."

"Isn't it? I saved his life once; I feel it's my duty to keep him safe. And you—"

"I can take care of myself. You know that."

"I'm a better fighter than you are. *You* know *that*. And Fedrani would still be alive."

His hand was slowly opening and closing with that regularity that told her he didn't know he was doing it. She went to him and took his hand in hers. "Kerish, we both felt safe here. If you're at fault, so am I. So how about you let me bear a little of that burden?"

"You don't understand."

"Don't I?"

Kerish looked at her finally. "No."

"Then explain it to me."

His dark eyes were intent on her the way they'd been so many times before. Then he sighed. "I don't know. It's nothing. Look, will you go over the Residence with me? I've been searching for places where someone could get in, and you'll see things I've missed."

"Kerish—"

"It's really nothing. I just didn't sleep well last night." He removed his hand from hers. "Come on."

He turned and walked away, not looking to see if she was following. She stared after him. "Kerish," she began, but he didn't stop. It wasn't as if she knew what to say, and throwing her arms around him, kissing him, was the wrong thing to do. She hurried to catch up to him. At the very least, the two of them could do what they could to protect Felix. Even if they'd totally failed at protecting themselves.

Chapter Three

"No," Willow said. "Absolutely not."

Caira threw the multicolored skirt on the bed and brandished the short jacket with its full sleeves at Willow. "Is to wear," she insisted.

"I realize you don't speak Tremontanese well, but do you understand *no way in hell?*" Willow kept one arm crossed over her bare breasts and reached for her shirt with the other. The healing scab itched, and she wished she had a third hand free to scratch.

Caira snatched the shirt out of Willow's reach and rolled her eyes. They'd passed the point where Caira's fumbling grasp of Tremontanese vocabulary could break their impasse about five minutes earlier. "Is *all*," she said irritably.

"Is all but Willow," Willow said. "Give me my shirt."

Caira tossed the jacket on the bed and, to Willow's surprise, took off her own shirt. Naked, she shrugged into the jacket, which ended a few inches above her waistline and was open at the front. It didn't have buttons and was clearly intended to reveal the skin beneath. Caira tugged both sides forward to cover her breasts. "Is to naked not," she insisted, pointing at herself. "Is to all wear. Janida, Alondra, all."

"All right, so you're mostly covered," Willow said, "but there's nothing keeping that thing from flipping open whenever it wants and revealing everything I've got."

Caira glared at her. "Wear not, go not," she said. "Janida say, Willow is, and I say, is…*sulk.*"

"I am *not* sulking!"

"To say, not have…" Caira held her hands in front of her breasts and made cupping motions, indicating much larger breasts than her own, which were still bigger than Willow's.

"That's got nothing to do with it! Tremontanans don't go around half-naked!"

Caira took off the jacket and stood in front of her, not bothering to cover her breasts. "You Tremontane, you not Eskandel. You Esk — to say, *in* Eskandel, be Eskandel. I in Tremontane, be Tremontane. You

27

not, then..." She made an irritated noise and began chewing on a fingernail while she groped for words. "Proud. Disrespect. Look wrong."

"You mean if I don't follow Eskandelic customs, it will look like I don't respect you all." Willow scowled at Caira's nod. Of course, she was right, but the thought of going out in public like that, even if it wasn't actually very public according to Janida, made Willow cringe. It was just unnatural, that was all. She scowled more fiercely and held out her hand. "Give me the damn jacket."

Properly clothed in the multicolored skirt, which was fuller than it looked thanks to two deep pleats in the front, and the skimpy jacket, she stood in front of the mirror to brush her short hair, which really needed to be trimmed. The jacket didn't reveal as much as she'd feared, though the pale skin of her chest and waist did make an odd contrast to her tanned face and arms. She laid the brush aside and picked up her mother's ivory bracelet, slid it over her wrist, then spun it around a few times, enjoying the cool smoothness against her skin.

"You look different," Felix said, and she squeaked and pulled the front edges of the jacket close together.

"I thought you were with Kerish," she said.

"We came back to have dinner. Why are you dressed like that?"

"This is traditional Eskandelic clothing. Men and women wear it to special events, like this thing I'm going to with the harem and Imara and Gessala. And it's extremely uncomfortable. So please stop staring."

"Hilarion says women should cover themselves because women's bodies are a snare and a temptation. I don't understand what that means."

"It means Hilarion wanted to blame his urges on someone else. Look, Felix, this isn't something you'll understand until you're older, but Eskandelics don't think there's anything wrong with this kind of clothing, and we're going to respect their customs unless those customs want us to do something bad. But I don't have to like it, so I'd rather you didn't stare." The jacket was too loose and was already starting to chafe her nipples despite the soft satin lining. The only thing that could possibly make it worse was for it to be covered in solid gold sequins. Chafing *and* burning, that was what she needed today.

"I think you look nice." Felix sat on his bed and began taking off his shoes. "I want to go barefoot all the time. Will you have dinner with us before you go?"

"We ate already. Did you have fun at the scholia?"

"Yes!" Felix stood on his bed and started jumping. "They have a man there who teaches about animals, and he said I knew more than a lot of his students, and I can go to where he keeps a lot of animals to teach with and learn more about them!"

"That's nice. Stop jumping, you're going to ruin that bed."

"Felix, it's time for—oh," Kerish said from the doorway, and Willow turned to face him, still clutching the jacket together over her breasts. He looked stunned, and Willow blushed hotly even though all he could see of her skin was the three-inch space between the jacket's hem and the waist of the skirt. A vivid memory of his hands stroking that same skin flashed across her mind, and she gripped the jacket harder.

"You look wonderful," Kerish said. "And you don't have to—it's not immodest, here—"

She took refuge in belligerence. "If it's not immodest, why are you staring like it is?"

"You have bad manners, brother," Imara said from behind him, and slapped him lightly on the back of the head. "Willow, it is time to leave."

Willow nodded, then had to push past Kerish, who stood in the doorway as if he'd forgotten why he was there. She followed Imara, who wore the same clothing as Willow, but strode confidently through the Residence as if she didn't care if anyone saw her. Which was probably true. Imara hadn't left the Residence alone since she'd gone to meet her lover, at least not as far as Willow could tell, and Willow hadn't figured out how to get her alone to ask what she was doing. Some of that was reluctance to interfere, but mostly she'd just been busy. The *adjeni* had been decided the day before, and Serjian Principality's question was on it. From here, the real work began.

She let go of the jacket and tried not to feel conspicuous and foreign and naked. *He still thinks you're beautiful, he still wishes*—she tried not to remember Kerish's look of stunned appreciation, how for half a breath she'd wished they were alone together to explore the possibilities of the jacket. Now was not the time to daydream about impossibilities. She was about to step back into the world of Eskandelic harem politics and she didn't need distractions, however pleasant they might be.

They entered one of the Serjian carriages and settled in for a ride. It was another scorcher of a day, tempered only by the breezes that blew in off the ocean, which Willow still hadn't seen except through her window. Unlike Lower Town, whose walls seemed to trap the hot air at ground level to suffocate its inhabitants, Umberan's stone arches felt as if they were designed to collect the heat and store it away for release in the cool of evening. If not for the sun beating down on her head and the black embroidered satin of the jacket, she would have felt almost comfortable.

She envied the people thronging the streets in their white headwraps and loose robes. There were fewer people about than before. Probably they were all sensibly indoors, eating their dinners, possibly in some cool garden enjoying the spray of a fountain. If she were home, she'd be doing the same, but in far less comfort, and she felt a little guilty that she didn't feel any homesickness at the idea.

The carriages brought them through the sprawling marketplaces that sprang up wherever the narrow streets widened to a street lined by a ten-foot-tall hedge. It was dense enough that Willow could have climbed it easily, if she weren't here as a guest. A gate of delicate iron filigree stood open to admit the carriages. No one stood guard there, the way they would have if this were an estate in Aurilien. But no one would ever mistake this place for an Aurilien estate.

Shorter hedges defined sweeping sections of lawn, connected to each other by stone-paved paths that gleamed white in the noonday sun. Ahead, a lake gave off sharp reflections of sunlight that burned Willow's eyes when she tried to estimate how large it was. Easily two hundred feet across at its widest, she guessed, and the road they were on became a bridge that crossed the lake's narrower end.

Brightly colored fish swam just beneath the surface of the lake, as if they were enjoying the warmth of the sun. Definitely not an Aurilien estate. There were plenty of poor people there who'd see those fish as a source of food.

Ahead, a number of other carriages were depositing women at the doors of a palace built of yellow limestone, arched and pillared and delicately latticed with contrasting white marble that glittered as if someone had dusted it with diamonds. Willow cast an experienced eye over the façade of the palace. It was probably best accessed at the far end, where a shaded porch extended in a grand curve out of sight. The porch roof led to a small door in the side of the main building, but there were also trellises meant to conceal that little door that could probably be easily climbed to the roofs. That had all sorts of potential. Not that she would break into this place, but it was nice to know she could if she had to.

They waited a few minutes in line to reach the front door, whose iron-banded doors stood open to admit streams of women both entering and leaving. Though all wore the same open jacket and pleated skirt Willow did, there was such a variety of color and pattern that the overall effect was of a rose garden overgrown for ten years with no one to prune back its excesses. Exotic garb aside, these could have been Tremontanan noblewomen attending a ball at the palace. None of them looked at all as if they ruled a nation.

She suppressed a tiny shiver of nervousness as they passed through the doors and into a wide hallway floored with tiles two feet square, cobalt blue and as shiny as if they'd been waxed. Conversations in Eskandelic echoed off the ceiling, which was painted a deeper blue than the floor and supported by more of those white marble arches.

The tingling, itching, burning, fizzing sensations of too much jewelry in too small a place made Willow dizzy, as if she'd had a little too much wine, and she breathed deeply and wished Janida would walk faster. This might not turn out to be the best idea she'd ever had, but it wasn't as if she'd had much choice. The Review, as Kerish had helpfully and concisely translated it for her, was the most important event of Conclave, where the opening moves in the political dance were made, and as Felix's *eskarna* she had to be there.

Her palms were sweating the way they did about an hour before she tackled a complicated theft. This was nothing to be nervous about. Her palms didn't believe her.

"Stay close," Janida murmured to her. The red-haired *vojenta's* lavender and gold skirt and deep purple jacket somehow complemented her hair perfectly, and she settled her bracelets on her wrists in a way that told Willow she wasn't the only one whose nerves were troubling her. "You are Serjian Principality's guest and therefore we obligated to guide you are."

"Catrela said we would meet people here."

"Our question on the *adjeni* is and received much attention. There will be many interested in discussing it with us."

"This is a lot of people. How does that happen?"

"The Review lasts two days and all harems do not come at the same time. We have let it be known when we attending are, and those who wish to us to speak will come at the same time."

"So we just…wait for them to find us?"

"We will visit the exhibits and congratulate those *harimi* who have completed their negotiations and will soon married be. Gessala as *harima* will be observed by those harems who wish her to join with them. And as we proceed, we will encounter those who have an interest in our question, and we will converse."

"And one of those is probably the one who planned the attack."

"Yes. Now is the time for you to observe them and see what conclusions you can make."

"That sounds subtle. I'm good at observing, but I'm not sure I can manage subtle."

"Most will understand that you are a foreigner and will forgive your missteps. The ones who do not, undesirable allies are. You need not worry."

They reached the end of the hallway, and Willow gaped at the enormous room beyond. "I won't worry," she said, "but this is a little intimidating."

The chamber wasn't quite the size of the Conclave bowl in the Jauderish, but it was still larger than any other single room Willow had ever seen. Rows of arches made of striped stone filled it from one end to another, some of them supporting lengths of white silk that divided the chamber into smaller…could you call them rooms, when their walls were only fabric?

She could only see into three of them before the silken drapes blocked her view, but Catrela had, with some pride, explained everything to her before they left: members of the harems, as well as women desiring to join a harem, displayed some work of art or music or literature that demonstrated their skills and achievements. From where she stood, Willow could see a bronze sculpture, a painting, and a wall hanging with something written on it in Eskandelic. The last two spaces were occupied by young women wearing the red headwraps that marked them as *harimi*. They both looked at Willow with some curiosity.

Janida slowed to examine the sculpture, then ran her finger along a small plaque beside it. "Gharibi Esyana," she said. "Middling work, but Hovanesian Principality will not be interested in her artistic talent."

Willow gave the sculpture a wide berth—bronze filled her vision with the kind of sparkles you see when you're about to faint—and went to look at the painting. Two children fought over a toy that on closer inspection proved to be a doll with a very detailed face. "Markhosi Jeneta," Catrela said in her ear, and Willow startled at the unexpectedness of it. "The doll, that is. This is her *zuareta* Tammena's work. Striking, and probably true, but it will win Tammena no invitations, that she has aired her principality's secrets here."

"I can imagine. That painting…I don't even know the woman and I can feel her pain."

Catrela took Willow by the arm. "Let us continue. I wish to see how Gessala's work received is."

The silken dividers turned out to be spaced widely enough apart that it was easy to move between displays. Willow stood for a time in front of a young woman who sat on a cushion with her head bowed and plucked the strings of a long-necked, full-bellied fiddle, or at least that was the only instrument Willow knew to compare it to. It made a low, throbbing sound, the sort of noise stones might make if they wept, and she had to be nudged more than once by Catrela to walk away. The written displays, of course, meant nothing to her, though she could admire the beautiful calligraphy and the creative ways the women had found to make their works visually appealing.

She was on the outskirts of a small crowd, listening to a *harima* speak, not that she could understand the words, when an unfamiliar voice said, "What do you think it means?"

Willow turned to see three women grouped close together, all of them intent on her rather than the speaker. The woman at the front of the group was tall and angular, taller even than Willow, and her black hair was cut short to brush her collarbones and partially obscure her face. She seemed curious rather than antagonistic, and Willow said, "I don't know. I wish I understood your language. It sounds lovely."

"It is a lecture on how ancient Eskandelics worshipped the lost gods," the woman said. "Their actions were not lovely. But this young woman is exceptionally intelligent, an excellent writer, and her research is impeccable. She has no fewer than ten principalities courting her."

"Is that a lot? I'm sorry if that seems ignorant."

"It is unusual. Only one woman has surpassed that in recent years, and that was Bejdrossi Alondra. Serjian Alondra, now." The woman eyed Willow as if waiting for a reaction. Willow made a guess and went with awed surprise. "It was a great political coup for Serjian Principality. They already had great power, and Alondra made them *vojenta mahaut* that year."

Willow glanced quickly around. None of the Serjian harem seemed aware of this interaction—or was Catrela perhaps a little too intent on the lecture? "They all seem very astute." No wonder Janida was willing to put up with Salveri's infatuation, if the result was power for Serjian Principality. Not that Willow thought Janida calculating enough to take advantage of either Alondra or Salveri, but she was certainly capable of sacrificing her own desires for the sake of the principality.

The woman made an abbreviated bow Willow had never seen before. "I am Hajimhi Fariola," she said.

That was a name Willow knew. Hajimhi wanted Gessala to join their harem. Her mind went blank briefly. Should she return that bow, or use the one Fedrani had taught her? She made a quick decision and returned Fariola's bow. "Willow North," she said.

"You want Eskandel your boy to support," Fariola said.

"I want Eskandel to acknowledge Felix as King of Tremontane,"

Willow said, "and then we can talk about what kind of support you might give."

"Terence Valant is King. We have acknowledged him."

"It's illegal for Terence to rule because he's an Ascendant. My country is rising up against him already. Eskandel should support the true King, not someone who murdered his way to the throne."

"You think to tell us what to do?"

"No, I'm just pointing out the facts."

"And the facts say Eskandel should wish a boy of eight years to rule? Better the stability of an adult King."

"It's hardly stability if there's no agreement. That's what they're fighting about."

"Then go to one of your lords. Ask him to take the Crown for this child."

"They want the Crown for themselves. If they were willing to follow Felix, it would be to install themselves as the power behind him. He'd never be able to become King in his own right. We want Eskandelic support because your country has no interest in Tremontane except as a stable, peaceful neighbor."

Fariola nodded slowly. "How fares Gessala?"

The abrupt transition left Willow groping for a response. "Um…she's well? I haven't seen her display yet."

"Those harems interested in gaining a new sister do not speak to their *harimi* here. But we wish to assure her of the sincerity of our offer. Perhaps you will tell her this." One of the other women standing behind Fariola, a plump young woman with thick, curly brown hair, looked as if she wanted to say something, but glanced at Fariola and subsided.

Willow glanced again at Catrela, who was practically rigid. "I think it's not for me to convey that kind of message," she said. "But I imagine she knows you are sincere."

"Knowing and hearing are not the same," Fariola said. "Gessala receives many invitations and needs some way between them to distinguish. It is a small thing, but one that may have…large results."

"I can imagine," Willow said. "But I can't interfere." *Please let Catrela be right about this, please don't let me ruin Felix's chances with this woman...*

The curly-haired woman looked as if she were almost bursting with what she couldn't say. Fariola nodded at Willow. "I see," she said. "Hajimhi Principality honors you. We will speak again, Willow North." She bowed again, smiled, and turned away. Her sisters followed her, though the curly-haired woman gave Willow what was almost a pleading look as she left.

Willow let out a deep breath. So, Hajimhi believed Terence was the rightful king. Or at least felt he'd bring more stability than Felix would. But could that translate into a desire to get Felix out of the way permanently? Willow moved Hajimhi Principality onto her list of possibles. They bore closer attention.

"Excellent," Catrela said, and Willow jumped again. And she thought *she* was sneaky. "She will respect that you understand our customs enough not to break them. Though I wish I knew why they so intent on courting Gessala are. I love my daughter, but she an indifferent artist is, with skills other than those on display, and Hajimhi...they are not so powerful as we, but they weak are not. I dislike not knowing others' motives."

"Maybe they just like Gessala. She's very sweet." *Or maybe they're playing a very deep game.*

"'Sweet' is not a thing harems put first, when it a marriage is." Catrela took Willow's hand and squeezed it. "I will learn their secret soon. Let us now see who else has arrived."

They were a few steps behind Janida and Imara, who were having a low-voiced conversation in Eskandelic that was gradually becoming loud enough for Willow to overhear, not that she could understand. It was easy enough to read their reactions, though. Imara held her shoulders stiffly, as if she were under attack, and Janida gestured frequently in the direction of the speaker.

Imara shook her head, then shook her head again when Janida's next words were more forceful. Then she said something that sounded angry and walked away. Janida watched her daughter go, but didn't follow her. One fist slowly clenched, then relaxed. She said something to Catrela, who glanced at Willow before replying. Janida nodded, and walked away in the direction Imara had gone.

"You polite are, not the question I can see in your face to ask," Catrela said, motioning to Willow to join her as she moved toward another display. "It a secret is not. Janida wants Imara herself *harima* to make, and Imara refuses."

"Why doesn't Imara want to be *harima*?"

"She says only that it the life for her is not. But she will not say what life she does want. Janida wants great things for her because of her talents. She would be more courted even than Alondra was, if she chose."

"Is she that good an artist?"

"She is that good a writer. Better than that young woman. It is part of the Conclave that the princes speak to one another on behalf of their question—a speech, you understand—but it is the harems who write the speeches, and one as gifted as Imara in the art of rhetoric and persuasion would be...she would mean great power to a principality."

"But if she doesn't want to join a harem...." Was Imara's secret affair the reason she couldn't, or wouldn't, tell Janida the truth?

Catrela shrugged. "Janida believes she simply does not understand the joy we take in our sisterhood. That she fears choosing poorly. But I think Imara fond of politics is not, and has other desires for her future. If she would tell Janida...but it is not my place to interfere."

Willow stopped to admire a woven wire sculpture made of fizzing silver whose parts shifted to change its appearance: a sun, a tree, a bird taking flight. More moving parts, these of copper and brass, were hidden in the base. A Device. It wasn't drawing nearly the attention of its neighbors, but Willow couldn't stop looking at it.

"I guess it's hard when you want things for your children they don't want," she said. "And when you don't want to disappoint your parents." It felt like her blood was fizzing along with the silver, an enjoyable feeling Willow knew would turn uncomfortable before long. She turned away and saw Catrela had moved on to the next display. Had she even heard Willow's words? Not that it mattered.

"Dua! Comeiti duesh almeti terojman khes adenuti!"

The strident sounds rose above the general murmur of the crowd, silencing those nearest Willow. A large, elderly woman pushed past a few women who weren't quick enough to get out of her way and stopped just inches from Willow, leaning forward to loom over her. Willow took a single step backward, toward the sculpture, before regaining control. "Excuse me?" she said.

The woman's slightly protuberant eyes bulged more. "You do not belong here," she said. "You foreign are and you defile this gathering with your presence. How dare you dress as if you one of us are?"

Willow took a deep breath. The fizzing was getting harder to ignore. "My name is Willow North," she said, "and I represent King Felix of Tremontane. Who are you?"

The woman's eyes narrowed. "I Abakian Raena am," she said, "and you represent an impostor."

Chapter Four

"I beg your pardon," Willow said, "but that is a serious accusation you don't have any proof of." She remembered that name. Abakian, definitely on the enemy list, possibly controlling the Takjashi Principality. "Are you suggesting that King Felix isn't who he says he is?"

"Felix Valant murdered by an assassin was," Raena said. "Terence Valant King of Tremontane is."

"Terence killed his brother and tried to kill Felix. Serjian Kerish and I smuggled Felix out of Aurilien. Are you calling us liars?"

That got a rise out of the women around them, though Willow was afraid to look away from her opponent to see exactly what they all thought of this. The silver was making her irritable, and she knew her patience was slipping away. In a few minutes, she'd say something undiplomatic, and who knew what that would do to Felix's cause?

"I say you saw an opportunity to take power," Raena said, raising her voice. "You have deceived Serjian Principality with this boy who is not Felix Valant. You think our country to mock by dragging us into war?"

"I think you—" *are delusional? Want to destroy us?*—"are mistaken. I'm *eskarna*, no one who could benefit from pretending to have the heir to the Crown in her care or from getting Eskandel involved in Tremontanan politics. Before Kerish came to me for help, I had a good career as a thief and I was happy with my life. This whole thing is nothing I would have chosen."

"Then you admit you have no loyalty to this child? Your words prove what I have said. He an impostor is."

"You're twisting my words. He's my King." Raena was trying to make a point, but what?

Raena smiled, a thin twist of her lips. She resembled Maitea when she did that, but where Maitea's eyes were dark and piercing and looked as if they could read someone's thoughts, Raena's bulging eyes made her look like a fish. A dangerous one. "Eskandel has an opportunity like no other," she said. "The discovery of a southern continent means great economic expansion. You, on the other hand, would sap our resources to benefit another country, on behalf of a child whose identity unproven is."

"I wasn't aware it was appropriate to make such bold statements about the questions on the *adjeni* here," Willow shot back, no longer caring about diplomacy. "You must not be very certain of yourself, to take advantage of this gathering like that. But that's all right, I don't mind if you want to make a fool of yourself."

"You—" Raena began, her face reddening. She drew in a great breath, said loudly, "Abakian will never support the Serjian question," and left, forcing the crowd to part or be run over. Willow immediately took several steps away from the sculpture and took in a deep, calming breath. She'd been so stupid. True, Abakian was never going to be an ally, and they were high up on Willow's list of possible assassins, but how many people had she alienated by insulting Raena so publicly?

"I will not tell you how foolish that was, because I certain am that you already know," Janida said in her ear. "Come with me."

Willow followed in her wake, passing several displays and dozens of women who were definitely staring at her. "I'm sorry," she said under her breath.

"It will pass," Janida said. Safely headed toward one corner of the vast chamber, to Willow's relief some distance from the metal, she added, "You correct were that Abakian displayed poor behavior. Many will judge them harshly for it."

"And many will judge *us* because I lost my temper," Willow said.

"True, but not something that fatal is. However, you should more cautious in the future be."

"I will be."

Janida's steps slowed. "Now is the time to prove it," she said. Willow was about to ask what she meant when Janida said, "Mahnouki Adorinda," in a sort of rushed, breathless voice, as if she were hurrying to push the words out.

"Serjian Janida," said Adorinda, half a breath behind Janida.

"A pleasant day, yes?" Janida said with a polite smile.

Adorinda flicked a glance at Willow, the tiniest movement of her dark eyes. "For those who can appreciate it," she said, smiling just as politely. "Serjian Gessala's art lovely is."

"Thank you for taking the time to observe it."

"I am certain Serjian Imara will as successful be."

Janida's hand twitched. "We wish only for her happiness. As you know."

"Of course. As you did for Bejdrossi Alondra. She seems very content."

"Your interest in her well-being, touching is. And what of you? Mahnouki Ghanetan pleases you?"

Now Adorinda's smile was smug. "In every way."

"A pity Mahnouki Ihtzian could not...please you," Janida said, and Adorinda's smile disappeared for a moment. "But of course one cannot endure weakness in a Prince."

"Of course," Adorinda repeated, less pleasantly. "But Ghanetan clever and well-spoken is. He did present our question in Conclave most successfully."

"A daring question. One that places much demand on the hearts of Eskandelics."

"As does yours. But we both know how much our people care about Tremontane."

"As much as they do for the possibility of your success."

Adorinda's smile widened, and then she said, "Willow North. How do you find our hospitality?"

"The Serjian Principality has been very kind," Willow said. "Eskandel is a lovely country."

"A fair refuge for your young King. Do you intend to stay long?"

"Long enough to secure Eskandel's support of Felix." She was certain that superficially pleasant conversation had concealed something vicious, but she had no idea how to follow Janida's example. Straightforward politeness would have to do. "I hope the Conclave sees the benefit of doing so."

"The Conclave has many concerns and will consider yours as carefully as any other." Adorinda tilted her head, the barest inclination. "We always act for the benefit of Eskandel."

"Well, supporting Felix benefits your country, and I hope others will see it that way."

"I think they will see the truth." Adorinda smiled again, then walked away without a nod, without a bow.

Janida stood watching her for a few moments, then said, "Let us find Gessala and then leave."

"But we haven't spoken to hardly anyone."

"My sisters have been meeting with others. They are competent and will garner support for our cause. This has been productive."

"I'm certainly convinced Mahnouki could be behind the attack. What was all that with Adorinda?"

"Old battles. She thought to rattle me, but I think she unsettled instead was. Though I will make her regret bringing Imara into it."

"I don't know where the insult was in all that, but I could tell there was one."

Janida snorted, the least delicate sound Willow had ever heard her make. "Gessala has not a fraction of the talent Imara does. To suggest her success will only be as great as my *zuareta's*...she has always been jealous because she childless is. But this is a conversation for another place. There is Gessala now."

Gessala was near the back of the room, standing next to an easel displaying a landscape in oils that Willow thought was very good, but then she didn't have an Eskandelic eye for beauty and form. Janida stopped to talk to someone—it sounded like a genuinely friendly discourse, not the veiled viciousness of the exchange with Adorinda— so Willow proceeded alone.

Gessala was speaking to someone rather intently, their heads close together, and as she approached Willow identified the second woman as the curly-haired companion of Hajimhi Fariola. Willow slowed down, not sure of the etiquette involved. The interested harems weren't supposed to talk to the *harimi*, and Gessala looked furtive enough that Willow was sure she was doing something that was at least frowned on.

The curly-haired woman glanced around as if ensuring they weren't observed, saw Willow looking at them, and after a few quick words to Gessala and a brief squeeze of her hand, nearly ran away from her. Gessala deliberately didn't look at Willow, but she had a mulish look on her blushing face. So, definitely frowned on, but—

Willow thought about how close the two had been, the way they'd looked at each other, and suddenly she had a very good idea of why Hajimhi Principality wanted Gessala so badly—or at least why one of their sisters did. It had never occurred to her to wonder what women who were attracted to other women did if they wanted political power, but surely it couldn't be that uncommon an occurrence? And if Catrela didn't know…no, meddling would probably make things worse. How many of Serjian Principality's secrets would Willow have to bear? Well, Catrela would figure it out eventually. And it wasn't enough to take Hajimhi off her list.

"I like your painting," she said when she neared Gessala.

"Thank you. It is a place I love," Gessala said. She didn't meet Willow's eyes.

"I understand about love. You never know where you'll find it," Willow said.

"That is true," Gessala said. "I painted this because I cannot go there again. I think it is the most terrible thing, loving someone— something you cannot have."

"I completely agree," Willow said. "But you never know whether things might change."

"Do you love my *fuoreno*?" Gessala asked.

It was so abrupt Willow couldn't think of a glib, deflecting response. "Do I…why do you say that?"

"I watch, and make conclusions," Gessala said, "because one day I will *eskarna* be, and Kerish and I were close once. I think something there is that drives you apart. But it causes you pain, and I will say nothing more."

Willow once again couldn't think of a response. She turned her attention back to the painting. Even looking more closely, she had no idea how good Gessala was, but she now saw more than just the artistry. Gessala had included tiny details, the color of the fish in the pool, a squirrel hidden in the depths of a shadow, that only the most observant eye would see. Willow was certain she'd painted the scene as she remembered it, that the squirrel and the fish had been there and weren't just features she'd added to the scene to make it interesting.

Assuming the viewer even saw them. Catrela might be right that Gessala's skill as an artist was indifferent, but her skill as potential *eskarna* was exceptional.

"You see what in the painting is?" Catrela said.

"Do you always have to sneak up on me like that?"

"If I can conceal myself from one like you, that a challenge is. Do you see the squirrel?"

"I do. So you meant you thought people wouldn't appreciate Gessala's real talent."

Catrela sighed. "It is difficult an *eskarna* to find, because she cannot be known as such to other harems. *Eskarnas* must their talent display in secret, may not reveal it even to the harems who court them, and until the marriage it known may not be. But there are ways to know what a harem seeks, and I see none of that in the harems courting Gessala. I do not want my daughter her abilities to waste."

Willow struggled briefly with herself, and discretion won the day. "I'm sure whichever harem Gessala chooses will appreciate her," she said.

Footsteps sounded behind them. "We will leave now," Janida said. She straightened the front of her jacket, revealing a little more skin, and added, "I had hoped to see Takjashi here. That unfortunate for us is."

"Because it shows they aren't willing to listen to our request?" Willow said.

"Indeed. They may choose to avoid us as a sign that they will follow Abakian's lead. We must approach them more directly."

They took the long way around the edge of the hall, examining displays they hadn't yet seen. Willow saw a few more Devices, none of which did anything practical. Not that she could come up with any ideas for practical Devices herself, but then she didn't understand enough about them to know the possibilities. Kerish probably did. How worried should she be that Gessala had seen the remnants of what they'd had between them? That others might see it too? The last thing she wanted was for Janida to know Willow had been in love with her son.

The carriages were waiting for them when they emerged from the palace. The sun was setting behind it, throwing cool shadows over the

44

courtyard. No one spoke much on the journey back to the Residence aside from a brief comparison of notes on whom the harem sisters had spoken to, so Willow leaned back and closed her eyes and let her mind wander, soothed by the flowing sound of Eskandelic words.

Back in the Residence, she changed into more comfortable clothes and put away the formal wear with a shudder. All right, it hadn't been that bad except for some chafing, but it was still a reminder that she didn't belong here.

She crossed to the window and looked out at the ocean, which was golden in the light of the setting sun. Now that she knew where to look, she could see ships sailing away to the west, from the docks that lay beyond her sight. It seemed the Eskandelic love of beauty extended to putting their important but utilitarian activities where they wouldn't intrude on anyone's sensibilities. The ships were all too far away for her to see whether or not they were beautiful. They probably were.

"Suppertime," Kerish said, and she half-turned to see him standing in the doorway with his hand on the frame. "How was the Review?"

"Fascinating. I didn't really realize how much your culture cares about art until today. Do harems really choose their members based on how well they draw?"

"Sometimes. Artistic skill reveals much about someone's character. But there's more to it than that—there's personality, and compatibility, and the kind of man the Prince is…it can take months for a harem to know enough to make a decision. Or for the woman to make her choice."

"So who has the final say? The harems, or the women?"

"Before the end of Conclave, the harems will make offers to the woman they believe is best suited to them. Then the woman decides whether she wants to marry that principality. It's more complicated than it sounds. My *majdran* Alondra had many offers, I'm told."

"I heard that today." Was Salveri the reason she'd picked Serjian Principality? Willow still couldn't imagine sleeping with a man old enough to be her father.

"Anyway," Kerish said, "I wondered if you'd like to see the scholia tomorrow. Felix wants to show you the animals, and I thought you'd be interested in the Devices."

"I thought I was busy all day tomorrow."

"Tomorrow the harem will sort the invitations they receive and plan their schedule for the next few weeks. They won't need you."

"Then I'd like that."

"We might have time to see the ocean." He sounded slightly too casual, and it made Willow uncomfortable, as if he were offering something intimate. Which he sort of was.

"All right," she said, just as casually. "If there's time."

Felix wasn't there when they arrived at the dining room. "He asked to eat with Posea," Catrela explained. "I thought he might enjoy being just a child for once."

"And this meal is for talking," Salveri said, as he and Janida took their seats on the fat cushions, leaving Willow and the rest to follow their example. "I have learned much today, and not all of it good is."

"The show trials," Jauman said. He was a tall, thin boy of about fourteen who cared for only two things: dogs, and his *fuoreno* Kerish's approval. He held a bowl of steamed vegetables above his plate, forgotten, and his eyes gleamed excitement. "Did Nanitan do well?"

"Very well," Salveri said, "and next year you will an adult be and see for yourself. But it is not the dogs that disturb me. All the talk was of Mahnouki's proposed voyage. It has captured the imaginations of the princes. Promised riches, new lands...they think little of the dangers and uncertainties of such an endeavor. For the most, they see our question as unimportant next to that."

"It is not the princes we must sway," Giara said, and reached across the table to take the bowl from her son.

"No, but it may be the princes will sway their harems," said Janida. "Who were those not allured by Mahnouki?"

"Jamighian," Salveri said, "which is not surprising, because Vijenci as logical as Issobela is. Though this does not mean they intend us to support. Still, they are worth courting. Haroutjian, Bokaji, Tangheli—they all will not follow Mahnouki. Also, surprisingly, Abakian. Benjedan is set in his ways and dislikes novelty. Unfortunately, Raena will not allow him to vote for us. Still, it means one vote fewer for Mahnouki, unless Adorinda can convince her."

"They are still names to add to my list," Janida said, "and I think we will host a gathering for them."

"What of Takjashi?" said Alondra.

"I am increasingly convinced Lucea is following where Abakian leads," Catrela said. "They have rejected every attempt I have made at contact, and I have yet to find a way into their residence."

"Could I try?" Willow said, trying not to sound too eager.

"You would not know what information to look for, and you cannot read Eskandelic," Catrela said, "though likely you would more capable than I of entering be. No, for now I think we should act as if Takjashi an enemy is."

"The kind of enemy that would send assassins into another principality's Residence?" Willow said.

Catrela exchanged glances with Janida, who nodded. "Takjashi has strong trading ties with Tremontane," Catrela said, "and they almost certainly knew of the pretender's coup before anyone else did. They also a strong contender for *vojenta mahaut* are. Terence Valant might have reached out to them as potential new rulers of Eskandel. We must find some way of learning what they know."

"Then tonight is for sending invitations," Janida said, pushing her empty plate away, "and tomorrow for accepting them. Be ready, Willow North."

"I will," Willow said, and tried to feel as certain as she sounded.

Chapter Five

They took a carriage to the Domian scholia the next day, though it wasn't very far from the Residence. "No sense exhausting ourselves and getting sweaty," Kerish said, "and this is easier on Felix's guard."

The guards Janida had assigned Felix were a pair of very large men armed with swords and knives who looked as though they had no sense of humor whatsoever. They wore Serjian livery, which matched what was on the pennant they'd carried with them on their entrance to Umberan: crimson and white, with a red eagle on the chest of the slim robes they wore over their leather armor. They were sweating despite not having to walk, which made Willow feel sorry for them, but she was pretty sure expressing sympathy would get her nothing except a disdainful look. Their eyes were constantly moving, watching for threats against Felix, and she had a feeling they'd only protect her if her injury or even death endangered their actual charge.

"I can't wait to see the animals, can you, Willow?" Felix said, and Willow once again had to tug on his shirt to get him to sit down. "He said there are jungle cats, and wild boar, and snakes—"

"That's exciting, Felix," Willow said, shuddering. "Are they poisonous?"

Felix gave her the same disdainful look she'd imagined on the guard. "They're *venomous*," he said. "Poisonous means something you eat that is poison, and venomous means an animal that has poison in it."

"I beg your pardon for not knowing that extremely vital and obvious difference," Willow said. "Now can we talk about something other than snakes? What about Devices? Can you build them yet, Kerish?"

"I'm still learning how they work," Kerish said. "I can imbue motive forces with source—that's easy, it's just like dowsing—and I've designed one or two. But I learn more every day. Oh, here we are."

The carriage passed beneath a low arch of twining green branches, inside which Willow could sense the chill of iron bars bent into hoops to give them a framework. It opened on a long avenue lined by tall, thick hedges that smelled fresh and wet in the muggy morning air, so different from the dry heat of an Aurilien summer. Later in the day it would feel like being swathed in wet cotton wool, but for now it was comfortable, if alien.

Beyond the hedges Willow glimpsed the tops of white domes. From her position at the base of the hedges, they looked like they were pushing their way up through the dark greenery. At the far end of the avenue, the grounds opened up on the same kind of grass she'd seen at the place where the Review was held. It all looked beautiful, and wealthy, and Willow once again felt uncomfortable, like an imposter welcomed into Eskandelic royalty by accident. It reminded her that she was completely out of place here.

They emerged from the avenue into a wide, grassy lawn crisscrossed by paths made of gray stone that looked as ancient as the paved streets of the city. Men and women dressed casually in multicolored robes over white or tan linen trousers and shirts and white headwraps strolled along the paths, some of them leading slim dogs, others carrying books or scrolls. They paid no attention to the carriage, which came to a stop in front of a domed building with a pillared portico that curved around its front.

One of the guards stepped down from the carriage and passed through the opening beyond the portico that looked very dark to Willow's light-adjusted eyes. The other put a hand on Felix's shoulder when he would have followed. "Not yet, your Majesty," he said in thickly accented Tremontanese.

"Is it really likely there's danger here?" Kerish asked.

"We have to assume there's danger everywhere," Willow replied. The guard looked at her with something approaching approval. Felix sat back down.

The first guard returned. "You can enter, your Majesty," he said in the same thick accent, and Felix hopped down and followed the man inside. Willow and Kerish came behind them at a slower pace.

"This is the Devisers' hall," Kerish told her. "Dowsers from all over Eskandel, and a few from Veribold, come here to learn Devisery."

"And Devisery is…creating Devices?"

49

"That, and imbuing motive forces, and repairing Devices. It's fascinating. I hope you'll like it."

He was more animated than she'd seen him since the night he'd set all this in motion, and her uncomfortable feeling increased. She'd seen him dowse, and he clearly loved it, but this…this was something else entirely. She smiled, but said nothing. Anything that excited Kerish this much had to be interesting.

The dark doorway, once Willow's eyes adjusted, proved to open on a hall lined with doors labeled in Eskandelic script. Kerish opened the third door on the left without knocking and gestured for the rest of them to enter, then had to step back as the burly guard went through first, nearly shoving him out of the way. "Your Majesty," he called out, and Felix and Kerish entered, followed by Willow and the other guard. Willow tried not to be annoyed. This was to keep Felix safe, and that was more important than politeness.

The walls of the room were tiled in beautiful abstract mosaics and lined with black lacquered tables ornamented with burning gilt. All of them held small filigree boxes made of aromatic woods, some of which glowed with pale blue or white or green light. The smells from the boxes blended with each other to make a soft, subtle scent that permeated the room without being overwhelming. It seemed a perfect metaphor for Eskandelic culture in general.

Two women in bright robes, one embroidered with purple butterflies and the other unadorned red and orange patterned silk, stood at the tables sorting through the metal objects the boxes contained, while a man stood with his fist outstretched over a circle painted on the marble floor. It was lopsided and coarse by comparison to its surroundings.

The woman in the butterfly robe looked up at their entrance. Her eyes widened as she glanced from one bodyguard to the other. She asked a question in Eskandelic that Kerish answered briefly, then he said, "This is Willow North, King Felix's guardian. She's interested in what we do here."

"Of course," the woman said. "Excuse that I do not speak your language good." She beckoned to Willow, who gave the man at the circle a wide berth. He ignored her. "See, is *ezdalha*, gives power to *surabhi.*"

The box she was sorting contained disks of all sizes, some thin as paper and others almost fat enough to be spherical, in a variety of metals, mostly copper and iron, but a few silver and gold. None of them were glowing, but the box next to that one contained the same objects and all of those glowed with a pale green light.

"Motive force," Kerish said, "and you remember *surabhi* translates as Device."

"And the…motive force…is what makes the Device run," Willow said.

"Watch this," Kerish said. He picked up an inch-wide button made of solid gold and took it to the circle. He held out his hand, palm-up, with the button at the center. "It's just like dowsing, only instead of the source going into a person, it goes into the motive force."

Nothing happened. Willow waited. She was used to this. Nobody could see source unless it was being used by an Ascendant, and only a dowser—well, or a Deviser—could sense it. Kerish said to him it was like a melody of chimes.

"Oh, sorry," Kerish said. "This is Gomelia, and that's Pelara, and this is Lorjezi." He indicated, in turn, the butterfly-gowned woman, the other woman, and the man. "Pelara and Lorjezi don't speak Tremontanese." He said something in Eskandelic that included Willow's name, and Lorjezi briefly focused on Willow, nodded, then returned to staring at his fist, which glowed dark blue. Willow smiled at him out of politeness, but her attention was on the button in Kerish's hand, which had started glowing a deep gold that was almost a visual representation of the burning Willow sensed from the metal.

"We don't know what causes the different colors," Kerish said. He sounded distant, the way he always did when he was working with source, as if his attention were divided. "It's not like with Ascendants, where the color of the source is a reflection of the kind of magic they have. It's one of the things they investigate here."

"That seems, well, practical," Willow said, and Kerish smiled.

"Aesthetics is important, but so is logic and reason," he said. The button's hue was becoming lighter, still yellow-gold, but bright. Lorjezi's fist radiated a pale blue now, and he opened his hand and revealed a button smaller than Kerish's that glowed with pale blue light. He said something to Kerish, who replied in that same distant voice, then asked a question. Lorjezi nodded and walked away. "We only have three sources, and those came from far away," Kerish continued. "What they do here, in this room, is study motive forces, not just to figure out the colors thing, but to see which materials work best to contain source. And then the motive forces go to other...you'd say 'study groups,' for using in Devices. Mostly lights, because the scholia wants to light all of Umberan by Device, but there are other artistic and scientific uses."

"Can we see the animals yet?" Felix asked.

"I want to see the Devices first, and then we can look at as many animals as their keeper will let you," Willow said. "So be patient."

"I'm good at being patient. I just don't like to wait."

"Don't forget we have something special to show Willow," Kerish said.

"Oh! I did almost forget. You're going to love it, Willow!"

"What is it?"

"A surprise. A big one." Felix grabbed her hand. "Let's go see it now!"

Kerish spoke to his colleagues briefly, then started to offer the brightly glowing button to Willow before remembering himself and tucking it away in a pocket in his robe. "It's just across the hall."

They repeated the dance with the bodyguards before Willow and Felix were allowed to enter. This room was far bigger than the other, with a domed ceiling supported by arches and a floor tiled in a random pattern of browns and reds. Pedestals topped by slabs of carved mahogany made a pattern of their own across the floor, their plinths spaced six or seven feet apart. Most were empty, but a few held gold or brass or silver Devices, not enough to leave her feeling drunk, but enough that she could feel them even from the doorway.

"These are the prototype Devices," Kerish said, taking Willow's elbow and gently urging her into the room. "Devices that were approved by the Magister for their beauty and artistic value. He has the final say on which Devices are allowed to be reproduced, or put on public display, or purchased for private use. It's important that Devices meet a high standard, since in a sense they represent our country. Go ahead, look around."

Willow moved to the nearest pedestal, trying to ignore the itchy feeling its copper-sheathed neighbor gave her. It was a framed picture on an easel, but made of hundreds of tiny pieces of wood, all shades from pale blond to black ebony, with an intricate weave of fizzing silver and tingling brass concealed beneath it. The mosaic of wood depicted a jungle scene, trees with drooping branches and exotic flowers and vines looping through the trees, all of it so realistic that if it hadn't been obviously made of wood, she could almost imagine it was moving. Then she caught her breath. It *was* moving, the pieces shifting slowly so the trees moved in an imperceptible wind. A bird swept across the scene, disappearing into the foliage. One of the vines turned out to be—Willow shuddered—a snake. She watched in fascination until the thing completed its cycle, then said, "It's amazing. Is this what all the Devices are like?"

"They all demonstrate artistic unity," Kerish said, and made a face. "I have to say I'm getting tired of hearing that. I don't have the artistic training the rest of the Devisers have, so I'm always proposing new Devices, or putting them together, and being told they lack artistic unity."

"We have to show Willow the Device now," Felix said, tugging on Kerish's robe.

"Let her look at what she wants first, Felix."

"If he's so excited, maybe we should see that one first," Willow said.

Kerish grimaced. "Now I'm afraid you'll be expecting something magnificent. It's just a little thing."

"It's *wonderful*," Felix insisted. "Come on, Willow."

"All right." She let Felix take her hand and drag her through the room, passing the few occupied pedestals and seeing only glimpses of what they bore: a book, a lantern like the ones in the Residence, a lady's fan, more framed pictures, a sculpture similar to the one she'd seen at the review. Then Felix stopped in front of one near the back of the room and said, "See? Kerish made it."

Willow blinked. She was looking at Felix's old doll Rebecca. "Um,

Felix," she began.

"No, you have to talk to her," Felix said. He picked up the doll and handed it to Willow. She sensed a fizzing knot of silver nestled into the stuffing of the doll's head. "Just say hello."

"Um," Willow said again, and held Rebecca up to her face. "Hello, Rebecca," she said.

"Hello, Willow," Felix's voice said back to her. She nearly dropped the doll in surprise.

"See!" Felix was jumping with excitement. "Kerish made her do that! I had to do the voice because Posea doesn't speak Tremontanese. Say something else!"

"Uh…do you like to play, Rebecca?"

"I like games!"

Willow looked at Kerish, who managed to look smug and embarrassed at the same time. "You did this?"

"My first Device," he said. "The final version has to go into a porcelain doll so it can have *artistic unity*," he made another face, "but I thought you'd appreciate it better this way."

"I do. This is incredible. Imagine how popular it will be. Rebecca, can you say 'thank you' to Kerish?"

"Thank you, Kerish," Rebecca/Felix said.

"Now can we see the animals?" Felix said. He looked as if he wanted to start jumping again. Clearly he'd learned bad habits from Posea.

Willow set Rebecca back on the pedestal, but Kerish picked her up and held her out to Willow. "She's for you," he said. "I know it's silly, but I didn't think she ought to be abandoned."

Willow smiled. "I agree," she said, "and thank you." His first Device. It felt so personal, but she couldn't reject the gift and, she realized, she didn't want to reject the gift, no matter what message that sent. Kerish turned away, but she saw him smile too.

The bodyguards flanked them as they left the Devisers' hall and followed one of the stone paths across the lawns and between other domed, pillared buildings that gleamed in the noon sun. "This is the largest scholia in Umberan—in Eskandel, really," Kerish said. "Most scholias specialize in one field of study, but the Domian scholia allows men and women to work together on cross-disciplinary projects. It's also one of the few that emphasizes natural philosophy and logic equally with the arts and history. That's why Khurkjian Gianesh's zoological collection is sited here."

"What's that?"

"It's *animals*, Willow, lots of them," Felix said, taking her hand to urge her along faster. "Mister Khurkjian talked to me the last time we were here, and he said he really wanted me to see his collection. Hurry, Willow, he might have gone to have his dinner and I don't want to wait!"

"I'm sure he'll wait for you, Felix," Willow said, refraining from adding *because you're a King*. No sense letting Felix start thinking that he could get special treatment because of his rank. He'd learn that soon enough. She hoped the man wasn't just humoring Felix and his enthusiasm.

They'd left the lawns behind for an overgrown thicket that shielded them from the heat of the sun, something Willow was grateful for. She was also starting to feel hungry and half-hoped Khurkjian had, in fact, gone to dinner so they'd have an excuse to eat something too. Though she had no idea where they'd find food in this maze of buildings. The scholars had to eat, yes?

Felix shouted and pulled free of Willow's hand, only to be brought up short by one of the bodyguards. "Wait here, your Majesty," he said, and Willow once again took Felix's hand while the bodyguard forged ahead, out of the thicket and into an open space Willow couldn't see much of. When he returned, Felix dragged Willow forward and into the open clearing beyond, where Willow stopped and stared in amazement. "I can't believe this," she said.

Giant cages of elegantly worked iron dotted the open space through which the path meandered, all of them occupied by creatures Willow could never have imagined. She'd seen some of them in the one picture book she'd owned as a child, before Nan had destroyed it as punishment for some chore Willow hadn't done right, but others were completely unfamiliar.

A giant black cat lay sprawled under a tree that grew up within its cage and emerged from the bars over the top. A boar rooted around in the soft ground, moving its head restlessly from side to side to let each of its tusks have a turn at digging. A pair of monkeys climbed the bars of their cage and swung from the top, chittering at each other and their neighbors. Something that looked like the monkeys' older, fatter brother sat with its back against a boulder, surveying the landscape and settling its gaze unnervingly on Willow.

The musky smell of animal bodies filled the clearing, making the air feel even warmer than the sun's rays could account for. She could see more cages beyond the first, lining the path, and moved forward in a daze interrupted by the monkeys shrieking at her. "This is..." she began, and her voice trailed off. It was nothing she'd ever imagined. "Don't they feel confined, living in those cages?"

"They do not stay long," an unfamiliar voice said. "We study, and then return them to the wild before they can grow too familiar with captivity." An older man approached them along the path, his dark beard streaked with gray at the chin. He was bare-headed and wore a very plain robe, and he was trailed by a Kazhari sighthound wearing neither collar nor leash. The pure black animal paced him as exactly as if it were on a lead.

"Good morning, Mister Khurkjian," Felix said. "May I pet Maresh?"

"Of course," Khurkjian Gianesh said, and Felix ran to the dog and began scratching behind its ears. "She likes you."

"I like her almost as well as Ernest," Felix said. "This is Willow. She's my guardian."

Willow had never heard him call her that before, and to her embarrassment she felt her eyes grow moist. "Mister Khurkjian, it's good to meet you," she said, bowing respectfully to cover her embarrassment. "Felix is very impressed by your animals. Thank you for letting him visit."

"It is I should thank you," the man said. His voice was deep, his Tremontanese barely accented. "Felix knows much about many creatures. His interest exceeds that of most of my students."

"He certainly talks about them enough," Willow said, and Khurkjian laughed.

"Come, let me introduce you," he said, "and please call me

Gianesh. My mother was Tremontanese and I cannot be formal with anyone who reminds me so much of her."

It took only five minutes for Willow to realize that, first, Gianesh cared very much about every animal in the place, and second, that he was in no way humoring Felix in his interest in those animals. The two fell into a conversation in which Gianesh asked nearly as many questions as Felix did, though Willow judged he was assessing Felix's understanding rather than asking for information. Willow admired the creatures and tried not to sound too ignorant in her questions. She lingered by the great black cat, who eyed her with mild interest and yawned as if she knew Willow was no threat. "What kind of cat is she?" she asked Gianesh.

"*Najabedhi*," Gianesh said. "In Tremontanese...the word is not exact, because you have none in your country, but it is cousin to the wild cats that live in your hills."

"Panther," Willow recalled from that long-lost book.

"Yes. But bigger. As you see. You know she is female?"

"It was just a guess." The cat's relaxed presence, that languid pose, suggested she could go from lying down to a full leaping attack in half a breath, but why that had made Willow think "female," she had no idea. Alondra had said something about *najabedhi* once, but she couldn't remember what.

"The indoor cages now, I think, and then you will join me for a meal?" Gianesh said, indicating a low-roofed building surfaced in gleaming white plaster that reminded Willow of the Serjian Principality's outbuildings. The bodyguard had to duck to enter the doorway, and Willow was about to follow him when she heard the man say something in Eskandelic that had to be profanity and rush back out, making his partner stand protectively behind Felix. The guard spoke rapidly and with great feeling, and his eyes were wide.

Kerish drew in a breath and stepped closer to Willow, but Gianesh laughed and prodded Felix, who was grinning. To Willow's surprise, Felix came out with a few halting words in Eskandelic that made the guard relax, though only fractionally. He shook his head again, and Gianesh said something that sounded like he was teasing the big man.

"What's going on?" Willow murmured to Kerish.

"He says—" Kerish pointed at the distressed guard—"there's a giant snake in there."

Willow sucked in a breath and grabbed Kerish's arm with both hands. "What?"

"He's in a cage, Willow," Felix said. "His name is...it means Thunder. He's a python!"

"Kerish—" Willow said, not letting go of his arm.

"It is quite safe," Gianesh said. "He is not venomous. He kills by squeezing his prey. But the cage is strong."

"Is it," Willow said.

"Come on, Willow, he's what I wanted you to see," Felix said, prying her fingers loose from Kerish and urging her along. "There are lots of snakes. It's what Mister Khurkjian studies most."

Willow directed a pleading look at Kerish, who glanced at Felix and then shrugged. Willow closed her eyes and tried to still the hammering of her heart. Then she let Felix drag her into the building.

It was dark and cool inside and smelled distantly pungent, like burning sage. She let her eyes adjust to the dark, then had to bite back a scream, because dangling from a branch right next to her head was the biggest snake she'd ever seen. She guessed it was about eight feet long, judging by how much of it was hanging off the branch. Its body was thick enough that she was sure she wouldn't be able to fit her hands around it, assuming she wanted to touch the thing, which she absolutely did not. The bars were closer together than in the cages outside, which comforted her only a little. She took a step back, hoping her fear didn't show—Felix would be so disappointed in her—and said, "It's certainly big, isn't it?"

"It's the biggest," Felix said. "They eat rabbits *live*. They squeeze—"

"Thanks, Felix, I can imagine," Willow said with a shudder. "How about we look at some of the other snakes?"

She let Felix's chatter wash over her, appreciating only that he never seemed to run out of things to say, trying not to think about just how many millions of snakes Eskandel seemed to be home to. Finally, Felix said, "Isn't that interesting?" and Willow nodded, not sure what she was agreeing to, but it sounded like the sort of thing someone would say at the end of an event—or in her case, an ordeal. "Let's eat now," he added, and Willow nodded more fervently.

She sat and ate without saying much, mostly listening to Felix's questions and responding to Gianesh when he spoke to her. He was good at drawing people out and at gently reminding Felix that there were other things to talk about than animals. "For example, Kerish is beginning to make a name for himself in the scholia," he said with a wink.

"Yes, and the name is 'you there with no romance in your soul,'" Kerish said wryly. "I blame Tremontane for teaching me pragmatism. I just think there are so many things Devices could do that aren't restricted to the arts."

"I liked the idea of a Device-powered fan for the reptile house," Gianesh said. "My friends are sun-lovers, but they are still so uncomfortable in such heat."

Willow realized the "friends" he was talking about were the snakes. "Why can't Kerish just build one?" she said, suppressing a shudder.

"I can, but I'd have to justify it to the Magister," Kerish said. "Though I did bring this." He fished out the glowing golden button. "I was thinking I'd build the Device and test it, and then have something to show the Magister. He's proud of the zoological collection, and he might make an exception if he can see the Device benefits it."

"I am happy to provide you with space for your experiment," Gianesh said with a smile. "And a cool drink to finish this meal."

Having said goodbye to Gianesh, they returned to the carriage, where they waited while one of the bodyguards erected a canopy to shield them from the sun. The other stood watch, his eyes restlessly scanning their surroundings. "I have to admit I feel safer with them around," Kerish murmured to Willow.

"So do I," Willow said, but remembered her earlier thought about who they were really intended to protect and wasn't sure if that was true.

Felix fell asleep on Willow before they'd left the scholia grounds. Willow pushed his damp hair back from his forehead, noting again that the mariseed oil was fading quickly. Should they let it go, or dye it again? "I think I want to take a nap, too," she said quietly.

"It's the heat. A lot of people do nap in the early afternoon," Kerish said. "But I meant it about seeing the ocean. If you still want to."

He wasn't looking at her, he was watching another carriage approaching theirs, but Willow heard tension in his voice, as if his words didn't match his meaning. He couldn't possibly believe they could go back to what they'd been, could he? What did *she* want, really? She took advantage of his attention being directed elsewhere to look at him, at his so-familiar profile and the sweep of his hair that needed to be trimmed as much as hers did. She wanted —

Someone stood up in front of the approaching carriage and raised something to shoulder height. Willow had just enough time to recognize it was a crossbow, and shriek a warning, before he fired directly at Felix.

Chapter Six

One of the guards lurched across to throw himself in front of Felix. The other cursed and leaped from the carriage. The assassin threw down the crossbow and fled into the crowd. The guard took off after him, shouting something over his shoulder, and the carriage sped up until it was pushing people out of the way, fast enough that the jolting made Felix stir and then sit up. Kerish grabbed the guard and pulled him upright slightly, but he was already sitting up, swaying and clutching his shoulder. "Willow?" Felix said sleepily.

"Lie still," Willow said. Blood was seeping up around a hole in the guard's leather armor, from which extended the butt end of a crossbow bolt. "Everything's fine."

Kerish and the guard had a quick conversation, Kerish's words clipped, the guard's pained, then Kerish spoke to the driver and the carriage sped up again. "Assassin," Kerish said, unnecessarily as far as Willow was concerned. "We're going back to the Residence and praying to ungoverned heaven there was only one."

"What about the other guard?"

"He'll catch the man." Kerish didn't sound convinced. "We need to get Haroush back to have his wound treated and get Felix to safety."

Felix's face was white, and he didn't seem to realize he was clutching Rebecca. "He'll be all right, won't he, Willow?" he said, his eyes fixed on the wound.

Kerish stripped off his robe and tore a large chunk out of it. He offered it to the guard, who pressed it against his shoulder. "He will," he said.

"Stay down, Felix, just in case." Willow put her arm around his shoulders and hoped it gave him comfort. "We were careless," she said. "We shouldn't have taken the same route both ways."

"I didn't even think of it."

"Well, I should have." Willow scanned their surroundings. They were approaching the black arch of the entrance to the Residence complex, which made her more nervous. This was a natural ambush spot, the one place anyone leaving or entering the Serjian Residence's neighborhood would have to pass. She squeezed Felix a little tighter and flexed her wrist, feeling the pressure of the knife that would be useless against another projectile attack.

No one waited to attack them at the arch, but Willow kept having to remind herself to breathe, in and out, to relax some of the tension that made her useless rather than alert. When they reached the gate to the Residence, the guard, despite his condition, made Felix walk in the shadow of his great bulk, his halting steps making Willow want to scream with frustration and snatch Felix up and run inside with him. Finally, *finally* they reached the front door, and Willow took Felix's hand and hustled him up the stairs to the safety of their room. "It's all right, Felix," she said, hugging him tightly and feeling his heart beat as rapidly as her own.

"Will the guard be all right?"

"Yes." Willow felt safe assuring him of that. "They'll catch the man who did it."

Felix knelt to hug Ernest, who'd woken from a nap to come bounding over to meet them. "And he'll tell them who sent him?"

"He will." Willow realized she had her knife in her hand and sheathed it. *And then I'll go after his employer.* "We'll be more careful next time."

"I don't want to go outside anymore." He laid his cheek against Ernest's face and didn't smile when the dog licked him.

"I know. But we'll be more careful. It was my fault for not remembering to be sneaky, and that's my job. I'm sorry."

Kerish pushed open the door. "The bodyguard came back," he said. "The assassin—" He looked at Felix. "Can I talk to you privately, Willow?"

"Did he escape?" Felix said, his eyes wide with fear.

"No, he…" Kerish gave up. "The guard killed him in self-defense. I *know*, Willow, and he's as angry about it as anyone. They brought the body back and I thought you might want to have a look, in case there's anything that might identify who sent him."

"I'll come. Maybe you could stay with Felix?"

"All right. Let's go have a bath, all right? You don't want to smell like those monkeys, do you?"

Felix gave him a weak smile. "I guess not."

With Ernest trailing them and yipping occasionally with happiness at being allowed to roam the Residence, they went down the stairs, where Willow left them to go to the courtyard. The afternoon sun beat down on the hard-packed earth, and Willow felt even sweatier just looking at the glare. Men and women gathered around a supine form Willow recognized as the assassin. She pushed through the crowd and knelt beside the body. His face was already sunken in death, his lips and eyelids bluish. Blood soaked the front of his shirt, which was torn above his heart. He was Tremontanan.

Willow saw the second bodyguard standing nearby, his own clothes bloody. He saw her in the same moment and began speaking rapidly in Eskandelic, gesturing at the dead assassin and then at himself. "Why didn't he capture the bastard?" Willow said to Catrela, who was kneeling beside the body.

"It an unfortunate accident was," Catrela said. "He apologizes to you and asks you the young King's forgiveness to ask."

Willow scowled at the man, whose words became more urgent. "It's all right," she said. "Better you didn't let him kill you." She crouched beside Catrela. "I don't suppose he's wearing easily identifiable clothing or carrying a note that says who sent him?"

"Unfortunately he has no such things," Catrela said. "His clothing gives no sign of who he is." She sat back, squatting near the body, and added, "A Tremontanan assassin the work of Terence Valant will be."

"Or one of the principalities wants to disguise its involvement by hiring a Tremontanan," Willow said. "But either way, what matters is someone really wants Felix dead, if they're willing to send an assassin to strike in the middle of the city."

"Someone with resources," Catrela agreed.

"This is my fault," Willow said. "I was careless."

"So were we all," Janida said. She gestured at a couple of the men standing nearby. "Dispose of the body, and see that your patrols are extended past the main gate."

"Inside, now," Catrela said to Willow, "and we will discuss."

Once inside the hemispherical room, Janida removed her

headwrap and tossed it on a nearby chair. "This should not have happened," she said to Willow. "The young King will not be able to endure these attacks for long before it makes him too fearful."

"Then we need to be more aggressive," Willow said. "Somebody is behind these attacks, and I want to know who."

"A Tremontanan assassin tells us much," Catrela pointed out. "Terence Valant may independently acting be."

"True. But we can't ignore the possibility that a principality did this, and there are only a few with the means and desire to carry it out." Willow paced from one side of the room to the other. "Mahnouki has the most to lose if Eskandel supports Felix's claim. Sahaki has close ties with Tremontane and contact with Terence, and so does Takjashi. Abakian is staunchly opposed to our question and supports Terence completely. Hajimhi—"

"You cannot suspect them. They are neutral in this," Janida said.

"Except Hajimhi Fariola was clear she wants Terence to rule because he'll provide stability. Or at least she thinks he will. I don't want to disregard that."

"I think you are wrong, but your logic makes sense. Very well. Hajimhi."

Catrela ticked the five names off on her fingers. "I am reluctant to say it," she said, "but we must add Khasjabi Donia to the list."

"You had better have evidence for that," Janida said. "Khasjabi has been a loyal friend to Serjian for over one hundred years."

"Didn't she swear to stand with us?" Willow said, remembering a dark-haired woman with a narrow face and blue eyes.

"Donia has been treating with Mahnouki Adorinda for something I have not been able to learn," Catrela said. "They have had little in common for many years, so I am suspicious, the more so because she has kept it a secret from us. Not the action of someone whose motives pure are."

Janida looked sour. "That does not mean she would kill a child," she said.

"Donia is ruthless, as ruthless as you are, sister," Catrela said. "She will do what is best for her principality and she might consider that action best for Eskandel as well. And she knew of Felix's presence here before it was public knowledge."

"Then we must prove her loyalties soon, because we cannot have allies we do not trust." Janida sat on the chair, picked up her headwrap and twisted it into a short rope.

"I'm going down to the harbor, see if I can find Giles," Willow said. "I'm better equipped to find out who hired our assassin than you are."

"Very true," Catrela said. "I think it unlikely is that a principality would risk being found out by involving others, but it not a possibility to ignore is."

"Then I'll be back for supper. Tell Felix not to worry." She left the room at a near-run, propelled by a new sense of urgency.

She saw guards at the entrance to the Residence now, all of whom paid her close attention but didn't try to stop her. She made a rude gesture in their direction that, judging by their lack of reaction, didn't mean anything in Eskandel. What was the point of their being alert now if they'd let an assassin past before? She still didn't see guards at the black arch. Several Residences lay beyond it, not just Serjian. Who was responsible for security there? The whole situation made her furious. Felix might be smart not to want to go outside anymore, if no one could guarantee his safety.

The crowds were thinner now, probably because of the noonday heat. She ought to be indoors as well, napping, but she was too keyed up to sleep. With luck, she'd find Rafferty easily, and he or his fellow expatriates would know where to look for the kind of men and women who would take money to murder a child.

Rafferty had bid them all farewell four days ago, saying, "I've appreciated the hospitality, but I find I'm impatient to be among my own people. A few months, and I can probably go home again."

"Good luck, Giles," Willow had said, and had been startled when he caught her up in his giant embrace and thumped her hard on the back in a comradely fashion. Then he'd knelt in front of Felix and said, "Good fortune to you, your Majesty."

"I still don't like you," Felix had said, "but you were honorable, and Hilarion says honor is prince among the virtues. I don't know which virtue is king, though."

"When you find out, let me know," Rafferty had said, and then he was gone. Now, as she made her way through the jostling, noisy crowds that smelled of hot sun and roasted lamb, she wondered if he'd found what he was looking for. She would find the enclave today... it never hurt to have a backup plan, and hers was to make herself and Felix disappear if Eskandel wouldn't back him and Terence Valant's minions came calling.

Willow dodged around a donkey who looked like it might have been Rosamund's ill-tempered cousin and nearly tripped over some running children. She half-turned to watch them go and caught sight, briefly, of someone ducking quickly around a corner with a furtive movement that drew her eye as surely as if the person had just stood and waved at her. She pretended she hadn't seen anything and kept walking. If someone had picked her as an easy mark, they were about to get a painful lesson in underestimating foreigner women.

The street she was on was full of shops, though Willow only called them that because there were wares on display and people were giving other people money for them. Instead of store fronts, the sellers laid out their goods on bright rugs in front of open doors and sat cross-legged on thick mats next to them, not calling out to passersby the way an Aurilien merchant would do, but silently waiting for people to stop, admire, and buy. A lot of business was being transacted this way.

Willow passed a woman sitting next to a display of brass pots that made her skin vibrate, then doubled back quickly as if to examine the pots more closely. Her eyes watering, she quickly scanned the crowd behind her and identified her shadow just before he ducked back behind a tall stand of paper parasols. *Amberesh.* What was he doing in Umberan?

She moved on, keeping one eye on the Jauderish and the other on the road ahead of her, and sought the young man out by his metal. He was armed with a long, straight sword, not one of the curved Eskandelic swords she was now familiar with, and wore a chain mesh shirt under his long, colorful robe. *He must be sweltering,* she thought, and doubled back again just to see how he'd react. He was actually quite good at concealing himself. He was out of sight so quickly the second time that if she hadn't been able to perceive him by her inherent magic, she'd have missed him entirely.

Amberesh in Umberan. Well, Janida hadn't said he had to wander the desert wastes, just that he couldn't take advantage of the Serjian name or wealth. And a big city like Umberan had plenty of opportunities for someone who needed to support himself any way he could. But why was he following *her*? Unless he really did mean to take revenge on her for getting him banished, which didn't seem at all unlikely.

Willow looked around for a place to arrange an ambush, then changed her mind. She was a stranger here, and incapable of explaining why she'd decided to attack an Eskandelic citizen unprovoked, as far as anyone knew. And it wasn't as if Amberesh could do anything to her in the middle of the street, let alone catch her unawares. Even so, feeling him at her back left her unsettled.

She explored the city at random, just to make Amberesh think she was lost, but made sure to stay within the public areas and retreat from the residential streets when she stumbled on them. Umberan was less well organized than Aurilien, but in a pleasant way. The center of the city had houses next to businesses and little parks at random intervals, most of them with cool fountains unlike anything Aurilien had outside private estates. It made her wonder who was charged with keeping it all clean and free from refuse. The principalities? They made and enforced laws, but what about municipal requirements? Something to ask Catrela later.

After about half an hour, she found someone to change money for her and then bought a skewer of lamb chunks with roasted peppers to eat as she walked. Time to find Rafferty and the other Tremontanans. *"Do you speak Tremontanese?"* she asked the first vendor she passed in Eskandelic. The woman shook her head, but pointed in the direction of someone selling cones of sugared nuts. Willow bought one, then repeated her question.

"Yes, though well no," the vendor said. "What is?"

"I am looking for more Tremontanans," Willow said, trying not to speak so slowly he'd take it as an insult. "I hear they live in a group here."

The man nodded. "Toward the harbor," he said, pointing. "Ten and five streets south, ten streets west. You see them. They make neighbors good."

"Thank you," Willow said, and headed off in the direction he'd indicated. Near the harbor, huh? Maybe she would finally see the ocean.

The route didn't take her far enough south to reach the shore, though she caught glimpses of the waves rolling in and the harbor where dozens of ships stood at anchor out in the deep water. Felix would want to see it, too. They should find time to visit, though Willow still felt anxious when she thought of going anywhere public with the young King, despite his formidable bodyguards. It made her angry that someone was making it all necessary, either Terence Valant or one of the Eskandelic principalities or both working together. Felix was still just a child, and he deserved not to have to live in fear.

She realized she'd lost count of the streets almost at the same moment she realized she was passing familiar faces — or, rather, not familiar so much as similar to her own. This street was out of the way, and quieter than the others, but the bright colors and arched doorways were the same. Men and women sitting in a trellised courtyard drinking *khaveh* from tiny brass cups watched her closely. She smiled and veered over to greet them.

"I'm looking for Giles Rafferty," she said. "He came here a few days ago?"

"Never heard of him," said one of the women, who had a livid scar running from her forehead to her cheek across her left eyelid, which sagged as if empty.

"He's a friend of mine. We traveled to Umberan together."

"Still never heard of him." The woman leaned forward, smiling. It wasn't a friendly smile. "You don't look like someone just traveled here from the old country. Look like someone wants to be native." She was dressed in the rough trousers and cotton shirt of a Tremontanan laborer. In fact, none of them were dressed in Eskandelic clothing and none of them looked very friendly.

"Neither did Giles, when he arrived," Willow said. "We're still Tremontanans like you."

That drew a laugh from everyone. "You don't look like anyone who ever slept hard in an attic in the freezing winter," said a man sitting near the scarred woman. "Nor went hungry in summer."

"She's done that, and more," Rafferty said, emerging from the building attached to the courtyard. "Willow. I didn't expect to see you here so soon."

"You said such nice things about the people here, I couldn't stay away," Willow said, straight-faced. Rafferty chuckled.

"Sit and have a drink," he said, taking a seat at an unoccupied table. "Rickard, bring our guest something." The man who'd spoken to Willow stood and disappeared into the building.

Rafferty sipped from his small cup. It looked smaller in his large hands. "Don't be offended by their behavior. If someone comes looking for one of us by name, she's generally the law."

"I see," Willow said. "You could have mentioned that."

"I didn't know you'd be looking for me any time soon. Is something wrong with…our young friend?"

Rickard returned with another of the tiny cups full of hot, sweet *khaveh* with thick foam on the top. Willow took an incautiously large swallow and winced as it burned her tongue. "He's well, but…" She glanced around at the men and women, who weren't concealing their interest in the conversation. "I take it these are some of your fellow rebels?"

"We prefer to be called 'insurgents,'" the scarred woman said. "Giles, who is this woman?"

"This is Willow North, and she agreed to take me south after my little misunderstanding with the law," Rafferty said. "Willow, this is Rickard, Ellie, Fern, Kev, and Samuel. Friends of mine who've had to make a living far from their homeland."

Willow nodded at them. They still didn't look very friendly. Rafferty finished his *khaveh* and set the little cup down with a *tock* on the wooden table top. "Let's take a walk. I'll show you the boundaries of this place so you can find your way back later."

Willow gulped down her *khaveh*, once again singeing her tongue, and followed him into the street. "You didn't come here just for the sake of my charm," he said when they were well away from the others. "What do you need?"

"Felix was attacked again, this time on the street."

"I assume the attack failed, or this would be a different kind of conversation."

"Yes. But the assassin was Tremontanan. I was wondering if you knew of anyone who might take that kind of job."

"Not one of my people, that's sure," Rafferty said. "But there are any number of men and women who are here because of worse crimes than wanting to protect their families from Ascendants. Do you think the pretender arranged it?"

"I don't know. Right now I'm just hoping to find who hired the man and see where that leads. What about Eskandelics? We don't know the nationality of the first assassin."

"The poorer part of Umberan is full of people who'll do pretty much anything for money. I don't know much about it, but my friends do, and some of them speak Eskandelic. I'll investigate, let you know what I find."

"Thanks. I'll stop by occasionally. How do your friends feel about Terence's coup?"

"Most of them don't really give a damn about the home country anymore. If you're asking if they'd support Felix over the pretender, well, most of them will follow where I lead."

"I didn't realize you were so well respected by your fellow, um, insurgents."

"I haven't shared all my secrets with you," Rafferty said with a grin. "Let's just say I command the loyalty of more than a few of my, um, insurgents, here and in Tremontane."

"I'll remember that. I might need a favor someday."

"Don't forget you're the one who owes *me* a favor. I intend to collect eventually."

"I still say you should have asked for the money. I'm unlikely to ever have anything you want."

"You never know." He waved goodbye as Willow headed back the way she'd come.

Halfway back to the city center, she saw Amberesh again, lurking about twenty feet behind her. She thought about confronting him, decided she was too tired, and once again amused herself by wandering the streets seemingly at random, memorizing their pattern while confusing the young man. He might be waiting for his moment to attack her, or he might just want to make her nervous—but if that was so, he'd have made himself more visible. Well, he wasn't very bright, so who knew what he might be up to?

Amberesh disappeared well before she approached the black archway that led to the private street and ultimately the Serjian Residence. Well, she wasn't afraid of him, but that didn't mean she wasn't going to be cautious when she went outdoors alone.

Her route to her chambers took her past the harem's chamber. Something was going on there, something that included a lot of loud arguing in Eskandelic. Curious, she turned down the hallway and walked to the door. To her shock, Janida and Maitea were shouting at each other. Maitea had a sheet of somewhat crushed paper in her hand and was using it to punctuate her sentences. Alondra sat nearby, watching the two wide-eyed. Giara stood with her arms folded across her chest, glaring at the room in general. And Catrela sat at a writing desk, scribbling rapidly.

As Willow entered, Catrela shouted something that carried over the argument and brought it to an abrupt halt. In the silence, Catrela spoke at length, something Willow could tell was chastisement delivered in tones of barely contained anger. Willow took a few steps backward; intruding seemed like a bad idea. But her movement drew Maitea's attention. "Stay, Willow North," she said. "This for you is as well."

Willow approached her. "It sounds bad."

"It *is* bad," Janida said. "Terence Valant has demanded Eskandel return Felix to him."

Chapter Seven

"*What?*" Willow found herself breathless for the second time that night. "He can't possibly—but he's told everyone Felix is dead. How can he go back on that?"

Maitea waved the paper in the air again. "He claims to have wrongly believed Felix to have died in a fire. He pretends great joy at Felix's survival and protests that he would never have declared himself King had he known the truth. Felix is to return to his guardianship as regent. Immediately."

"Is that—will Eskandel agree?"

"Eskandel has no *vojenta mahaut*," Janida said. "No one to speak for the country in this matter. All depends now on who succeeds to that position when the Conclave ended is."

"Except Mahnouki will certainly force this to a vote in Conclave," Maitea said, turning her fierce gaze on Janida. "And a vote may not go our way."

"Then we must ensure it does not happen," Janida said. Her voice once again rose in anger.

"And I say again it a fool's endeavor is," Maitea said, matching Janida in tone.

"You have another plan? Let us hear it!"

"Build support among the harems. Ensure the vote is ours."

"That too much work is. We have no time."

"Forget it," Willow said, cutting them both off. "If Eskandel tries to return Felix to the uncle who will almost certainly arrange a fatal accident for him, I'll take Felix and disappear."

"Leaving Tremontane in turmoil," Maitea said. "You have no loyalty to your country?"

"I care about my country," Willow said, surprising herself, "but I care more about Felix. He's still just a little boy and he deserves to have a life. If Eskandel is going to betray him, I see no point in staying here."

"Eskandel will not betray him," Janida said. "I swear it."

"You swear something you cannot guarantee," Maitea said.

"Either we prevent this decision from being made until the *vojenta mahaut* is sworn—and that might not be Serjian Principality—or we sway the vote to our side. Either is a perilous task."

Janida's expression was calculating, as if she were a cat creeping up on a mouse. "I wonder," she said to Willow. "You will not fear speaking to the *vojentas*."

"No, I—what?"

Janida cast a glance at Maitea. "You think we can arrange such a thing?"

"Mahnouki Adorinda will insist on it," Catrela said. She finished with one sheet of paper and moved on to another. "She believes she will win if she can force it to a vote. But first the *vojentas* must decide whether to allow such a vote to happen."

"Many will already believe the question should be deferred to the *vojenta mahaut*," Alondra said. "We must convince the others of this."

"Giara?" Janida said. "You have done the most to gather support for our question. What do you say?"

Giara shook her head. "We in a good position are not. But we have not lost. And I think *she*—" she pointed at Willow— "should speak."

"The *vojentas* may see it as an intrusion," Maitea said.

"Then she will have to convince them otherwise." Giara approached Willow and walked around her as if weighing her possibilities. "This Tremontane's affair is as much as anyone. She—"

"Could you not talk about me as if I'm not here?" Willow said.

"You the King's *eskarna* are," Giara said. "You have a right to speak on his behalf. Adorinda will wish to unsettle you, to make you believe you an illegitimate participant are. Will you allow her to convince you so?"

"No," Willow said. "I'm just not sure what to say."

"We will decide that together," Janida said. "Go. Eat. Tomorrow we will see what Adorinda does, and match her step for step."

The dining room was empty when Willow arrived, the table cleared of dishes. She passed through the little door the servants always used and found herself in a narrow hallway from which good smells still emanated. She followed her nose to the kitchen, where with gestures and a few words she convinced one of the cooks to give her a *nouhut,* creamy and delicious. She folded it on itself and strolled out of the kitchen, chewing happily. Eskandel had all sorts of compensations for being away from home, much as she missed eggs and bacon in the morning.

She was almost to the stairway leading to her and Felix's room when she heard someone coming down it. She tensed, but it was only Kerish. He seemed surprised to find her there, which she found odd — it was her room too, wasn't it?

"I've just put Felix to bed," he said. "He wasn't happy that you were gone."

"I had to speak to Giles about the assassin. I'm sorry."

"It's all right. I explained to him what you were doing. He just feels safer with you around." Kerish's lips compressed into a tight line, and he looked away.

"Kerish, he trusts you, too."

"It's not the same." He shrugged. "I've spoken with the carriage driver and the bodyguards. Haroush is going to be fine, but Mother assigned a different guard while he's recuperating. And we're going to be more careful of the route we take."

"That black gateway is dangerous. It's the only place you always have to go."

"Then what, Willow?" Kerish exclaimed. "Do we tell Felix he can't do the one thing that makes him happy? Make him stay in the Residence until heaven knows when?"

"We just have to be careful —"

"I thought we were."

"More careful, then."

Kerish swore and turned away from her. "I thought Terence loved Felix," he said in a low voice. "I don't understand how he could want to kill him. Why didn't he just adopt the boy? It's not as if he has children of his own. I'm just a stupid foreigner, but even I can see that solution."

"I don't know. Probably because so long as Felix is alive, he's a better claimant to the Crown, and Terence *is* ruling illegally. Besides, I'm not convinced Terence is behind the assassination attempts. It's just as likely to be a Principality."

"I want to believe you, but I know Terence too well."

Willow laid her hand on Kerish's arm and squeezed gently. "Will you stop blaming yourself? Felix is alive, and he's going to stay that way."

Kerish laughed, a short, bitter sound. "If I blame myself," he said, "I at least have the illusion that I could have acted. I've been so caught up in what I'm learning I haven't really thought about Felix at all."

"Well, I bet Hilarion would have something to say about that."

This time Kerish's laugh actually sounded amused. "Hilarion would say blaming yourself makes as much sense as trying to lift yourself by your bootlaces and is just as productive."

"And everyone knows how wise he was. Kerish, if you're worried about Felix's safety, you're not going to make him safer by thinking about whatever failings you believe you have. You've kept him safe even when you had a three-inch hole in your side, or have you forgotten fighting off those bandits who attacked us?"

"Actually, I had forgotten that. I was sure we were both going to die."

"And you killed that man for Felix's sake. I don't think anyone can ask more than that."

Kerish turned back toward her and put his hand over hers where it rested on his arm. "You're the most sensible woman I know."

"I'm not that sensible. Most people would call me crazy for half the things I've done since I left Aurilien."

"And all of them were in Felix's service. It's no wonder he loves you."

His eyes were fixed on her, his lips quirked in a smile, and five-year-old memories crowded her mind, memories of kissing those lips and being held in those strong arms. She felt a sudden terrible urge to put her arms around him, draw him close and kiss him, and realized she was holding her breath. She let it out slowly and released him. His hand lingered on hers for a moment, then fell away. The smile vanished, and it made her heart ache.

"Did you talk to Rafferty, then?" he said, as offhandedly as if they meant nothing to each other. Which was more or less true.

"I did. He's going to ask around, see if anyone has been

75

approached by someone looking to hire a killer." Did Kerish look disappointed? Or was that just wishful thinking? "Or if he can find out the identity of our assassin."

"Good." Kerish looked past Willow down the hall. "I don't want to keep you up. I'll see you in the morning, all right?"

"Kerish—"

"Yes?"

He was still so close, and she wanted him so badly—not with physical desire, but a longing to once again feel cherished, part of something greater than the two of them. And that was impossible. "I'll...let you know what I learn," she said.

"Thanks." He smiled at her, but without feeling, and strode off down the hall. She watched him go until he turned the corner, then slowly ascended the stairs to her room. Felix was asleep, sprawled out on his bed as usual, but Ernest lifted his head to look at her as she entered.

"We probably shouldn't let you sleep on the bed," she whispered, but she couldn't find it in her to evict him. "Felix ought to be training you."

Ernest sat up straighter and let out a small yip that didn't disturb Felix at all, then snuggled down next to the boy and rested his head on his front paws. Willow shrugged. She had only so much energy to go around, and she didn't feel like expending it on Ernest.

She undressed and put on her nightgown, then dragged a chair to where she could look out the window at the Residence gardens. The black sky, studded with white stars like shattered glass, extended past the limits of her vision, but she could imagine it meeting the ocean; this new room didn't have the ocean view of the first. The fronds of the tree bobbed in front of her, silvery in the light of the nearly full moon. If she hadn't tested their strength earlier, she might have imagined herself reclining in their embrace, rocking to sleep under the stars and the moon with the smell of the sea caressing her cheeks. Knowing they would crack and break under her weight destroyed the romance.

The thought made her curl up on herself more tightly. She'd come so close to kissing Kerish just then, and that could lead nowhere good. It was true, she still cared about him, but love wasn't enough, and she wasn't sure how he felt about her, anyway. Not that it mattered if he still loved her. She rested her head on the padded side of the chair and closed her eyes.

It wouldn't make a difference if he did, she told herself, and let the sound of the fronds moving in the wind carry her off to sleep.

***

Someone, possibly Caira, had sewn the new gold satin dress so it fit better in the bodice than the first had, but Willow still felt uncomfortable—itchy, as if the dress were lined with copper, and over-warm. Kerish's suggestion of a Device that might remove the heat from a room seemed like an excellent idea at that moment. Janida had called the room a reception hall, but it looked more like a funnel lined with uncomfortable wooden seats that were almost all occupied by women dressed in satin in every color imaginable.

Willow tried to shut out her awareness of the jewelry they wore, which was making her a little drunk. She needed to stay focused if she wanted to address these women with clarity and reason. All the golden bracelets the *vojentas* wore burned her senses like sheets of fire and made her warmer. She surreptitiously scratched under her arm and hoped she wasn't sweaty.

Janida sat next to her, also gowned in the gold satin of a speaker. "It good is that you will speak last," she murmured. "But Adorinda gave in too quickly. She has a deeper plan, and that worries me."

"We can but do our best," Catrela said from Willow's other side. "You have nothing to fear."

"I'm not afraid," Willow said. *Apprehensive, maybe. Possibly anxious. But not afraid.*

Janida nodded at her, then rose and stepped to the raised platform at the base of the funnel. It was circular, made of honey-blond wood and only about three feet in diameter. It didn't raise a speaker very high and seemed more symbolic than utilitarian. Janida stood, waiting for the quiet voices to still, then said, "We have an unusual request to consider. The usurper Terence Valant has requested we return his nephew Felix, King of Tremontane, to his—"

"You use inflammatory language," a woman about midway up the funnel said. "Terence King of Tremontane is."

"That discussion for another time is, Sahaki Beppinda," Janida said calmly. "The facts are that Terence has taken the throne and has claimed his nephew dead is. He now says he wrongly believed the boy to have died and wishes his regent to be. Serjian's question on the *adjeni* states that Felix King is. We say Terence's...request...should be deferred until there a *vojenta mahaut* is."

"This request needs no discussion. Terence Valant the boy's rightful guardian is," said another woman whose peach satin clashed with her dark skin. "We should return him."

"Again, that decision must be deferred," Janida said.

Mahnouki Adorinda, seated on the front row and also garbed in gold satin, spoke in Eskandelic. Catrela gripped Willow's hand. "She says we should not accommodate you, as a foreigner, and this discussion is for Eskandelics only."

"It a Tremontane matter is as well," Janida said, "and we must show hospitality." She turned to address the gathering at large. "Serjian says this decision should wait for the *vojenta mahaut* to decide. But you the ones who must choose are. Choose well." She stepped off the platform and returned to her seat.

Mahnouki Adorinda rose and walked at a slow pace toward the platform, raising her skirts daintily as she stepped on to it. She once again spoke in Eskandelic, and Catrela's grip became tighter. "She says nothing but what we knew she would. That Eskandel should not interfere in other countries' politics. That Felix does not need our protection when he has his uncle's. But speaking in Eskandelic is a slight to you. It means...she suggests you are not deserving of hospitality and should not be heeded."

Willow watched the crowd instead of Adorinda and had to make herself breathe slowly, calmly, because many of those heads were nodding and all of them were intent on Adorinda in a way that said they liked what they were hearing. When Adorinda finished speaking, and took her seat, there was complete silence. Janida nudged Willow. "You," she said.

Willow stumbled a little over her unfamiliar skirts and heard a whisper go round the room. Wonderful. She'd lost them even before she began. She stepped onto the platform and took a deep breath.

"I know I'm—" Her voice was lost in the funnel. She was sure it didn't reach the upper tiers. She cleared her throat and tried again. "I know I'm not one of you. I can't tell you how to run your government. What I can tell you is that Terence Valant is lying. He told the world Felix was dead because that gave him a sliver of a claim to the Crown, but he knew the rightful King was alive.

"What is it he said—that he believed Felix had died in that fire? Are we supposed to believe this was some magical fire that consumes even bone and every trace of a body? Terence wants you to believe he means well. He's *manipulating* you. And I don't think you—all of you—have become as powerful as you are by letting others manipulate you." She pushed aside thoughts of Mahnouki Adorinda.

"Here's what I think," she continued. "I think Terence is trying to convince you that you need to act on his demand immediately. But Terence knows damn well he should be dealing with Eskandel's *vojenta mahaut*. And he also knows this is the middle of Conclave. So basically he's showing a total lack of respect for your government by suggesting his demand override your traditions. Not to mention that he has the balls to make any kind of demand of a sovereign state. I don't think Eskandel is subordinate to Tremontane. I'm not any kind of ruler, but I know something of how we trade with you, and I know it's a relationship of equals. Terence wants to change that."

"You speak for him?" Adorinda said. "You know his thoughts?"

"And you don't?" Willow shot back. "I don't think we need to know his thoughts to judge him by his actions. Look. I said I can't tell you how to run your government. But I don't think a nation ought to allow another country to dictate its behavior. Don't give in to his manipulations. Let this wait until you have a *vojenta mahaut* who can deal with Terence as an equal. Maybe they'll decide to return Felix. Maybe they'll ratify Terence as King of Tremontane. I'd hate for either of those things to happen. But at least you'd make those choices as a nation. And I think you'd keep your self-respect."

Muttering sprang up all through the funnel. Willow instantly regretted that last sentence. What if she'd undone whatever good work she'd managed? She could barely remember what she'd said. She made her way back to her seat and dropped into it gracelessly. Catrela again took her hand. "Well spoken," she said in a low voice.

"You mean the part where I implied you're all cowards who bend to prevailing opinion?"

"A chastisement well needed," Janida said. "Leave now. You are not entitled to be present for the decision. But…you have our thanks."

It was a dismissal. Willow nodded and left the chamber, retracing the path they'd taken to climb a very long staircase until she was outside. The reception hall was in one of the buildings attached to the Jauderish, with a low roof that said, along with the stairs, that most of it was underground. It should have been cooler than it was; maybe that was all the women crammed into it. The sun was working its way toward becoming a brassy disk in the sky that broiled everything beneath it. *Now* Willow was sweating.

She stood beneath one of the trees lining the street like a living wall, its fronds drooping as if they too were sweating in the heat. She wished she had her headwrap, but Janida had assured her it would only disorder her hair and make her look unkempt when she addressed the *vojentas*. The carriage had disappeared, and it probably wouldn't take her back to the Residence without the rest of the harem. She should go back inside, but she felt drained, both by the heat and by the confrontation, so she leaned against the curved, ridged bark of the tree and closed her eyes.

With her eyes shut, the sounds of the city were louder: men and women speaking waterfalls, donkeys braying like deep-voiced geese, thousands of feet treading the stony streets. Their metal was at enough of a distance that it didn't disturb her, sparking brass and shining steel and fizzing silver, the faint itch of copper and the occasional burning speck of gold coin. She wished she'd brought coin of her own; she was hungry. Lines of curved steel of varying lengths—and one straight sword, headed her way.

She opened her eyes and stood up straight. There was Amberesh, about twenty feet away. He shoved a few people out of his way, apparently cursing at them. Willow made a lightning-fast decision and went to meet him. She had no interest in speaking to him, but he clearly had something on his mind, and if he were going to attack her either verbally or physically, she was better off meeting him in public, especially since she was unarmed.

"Amberesh," she said when he was close enough to hear her over the street noise. "How are you?"

"You," Amberesh snarled, "you I leave home. You lie."

"Only a little. And you deserved it for what you did to Alondra."

"Not I do this thing. She I want. You…*interfere*."

"That's a big word for you, Amberesh." Willow took a step closer. "You know damn well Alondra hated you. I can't help it if your delusions put you in a position to be exiled. You should be grateful Salveri didn't kill you."

"He not I kill." Amberesh put his hand on his sword. "You I make hurt for lose I name."

"Right here? In the street? Who do you think will be punished for that?"

Amberesh snarled at her again and drew his sword. "I say you lie. You thief. Thief you steal from I."

Willow shook her skirts at him, eyeing the traffic beyond. No one was paying any attention to them. Maybe this hadn't been a very good idea. "With me dressed like this? No one's going to believe it. Now, get out of here. And don't come after me again. You've only yourself to blame for the position you're in, and if I see you following me, I'm going to tell Janida and let her handle it." She stared him down, winding her hands in her skirts so their trembling wouldn't betray her.

Amberesh returned her glare, breathing heavily, then thrust his sword back into its sheath and turned away, pushing his way through the crowd and shoving anyone who raised a voice in complaint. Willow breathed deeply and waited for her heart to slow down. She knew Amberesh was stupid, but she hadn't counted on him being so stupid as to attack her in public. Maybe he was more dangerous than she'd thought. She took another deep breath. She'd have to be more careful.

A carriage drove up to the door, then another, and suddenly women were streaming out of the reception hall, talking over one another so the yard sounded awash in the waves Willow always heard distantly beating the shore. She saw the Serjian carriage in the distance and walked toward it, holding her skirts up out of the dust. Janida and the others met her there. "We succeeded," Janida said. "They will wait to respond until there a *vojenta mahaut* is."

"But it a decisive victory was not," Maitea said. "We should not become complacent."

"I don't feel complacent at all," Willow said. "What happens next?"

"As always. We meet, we talk, we convince others of the rightness of our cause," Catrela said. "You spoke well. There will many be who wish to speak again with you."

The carriage began moving with a jolt that made Willow grab its sides to steady herself. "I still have to discover who wants Felix dead. I have to have time for that."

"It Sahaki is not," Catrela said. "Sahaki Beppinda wishes from Tremontanan politics herself to distance. She has broken with Mahnouki and attempts to become *vojenta mahaut* on her own terms. She cannot risk an assassination to be linked to Sahaki, even though Felix's death would increase Terence Valant's power and therefore maintain stability in Eskandel. But we will not allow her *vojenta mahaut* to become."

"So that's one down. There are still far too many possibilities."

"Including the one that says Terence Valant the assassin is," Janida said. "Better the guard on the King to increase, if we cannot prove the assassin's identity."

"The best way to protect him is to eliminate whoever's trying to kill him. He shouldn't have to live in fear."

"I have not yet given up hope," Catrela said. "You search the docks, I search the principalities. We will find our enemy."

Willow felt the long streak of silvery steel just at the limit of her perceptions. Speaking of enemies... Should she tell Janida about Amberesh? She turned her head casually to look in his direction, but saw nothing but crowds. If Janida knew Amberesh had threatened her, she'd likely assign bodyguards to Willow, and that would mean the end of investigating Felix's would-be assassin. She'd just have to be alert when she left the Residence. And never be unarmed. "We'll find them," she agreed, "but it had better be soon."

Chapter Eight

Caira helped Willow change out of the golden gown and into the plainest clothes she owned: tan linen trousers and a matching tunic-shirt with a deep V-neck, a white headwrap and the complicated sandals. She still didn't look Eskandelic, but she hardly looked Tremontanan, either. Willow settled her pouch around her neck. She was dressed all wrong for the slums of Umberan, but it had been three days since she'd seen Rafferty, and the meeting with the *vojentas* had left her antsy and disinclined to wait for word from him.

She sensed Amberesh on her tail about halfway to the enclave and touched the sheath of her wrist blade. Whatever Amberesh had in mind for her, she doubted it was friendly, and it wasn't impossible she'd have to defend herself.

Time to make his life harder, she thought, and turned the corner into a residential area she'd scouted out the last time she'd been down that way. It had several cross-streets, most of which connected to each other, and she took the second of these and doubled back, paying close attention to where Amberesh and his distinctive sword went. He took the wrong street, then corrected himself and cut across an intersection, heading directly for her. She turned and ran, crossing one of the little parks that smelled fresh and cool even at midday. Amberesh followed. Damn. He probably knew she knew he was there now.

Quickly she worked her way back to the main street and out to a meat market that smelled of blood and warm flesh, then down a side street and around a corner into an alley wide enough almost to be a street. The buildings on either side were old, but well-kept, without the crumbling stucco Willow had seen in other, poorer parts of the city. Strings of hanging wash stretched between the balconies, shirts and undershorts drifting lazily in the ocean breeze. Willow eyed the nearest balcony. Its cold iron railings burned in her senses. How desperate was she?

She took a running leap and grabbed the railing, bit back a scream at how cold it was, and hauled herself up. Without a pause, she climbed onto the rail and reached for the next balcony. She rolled over the rail of that one and lay flat on its floor, grateful it was wood and not a slab of iron. Breathing heavily, she closed her eyes and searched for Amberesh. There he came, moving steadily but not slowly, past the street, past the alley. She flattened herself as low as she could get, praying that he was like everyone else and didn't look up.

The straight sword went motionless at the head of the alley. *He can't follow me even if he sees me*, she thought, but that didn't leave her inclined to stand and wave at the man. The flapping of the laundry sounded like birds flying past, and she heard real birds crying to each other somewhere nearby. Amberesh was silent, unmoving. Willow breathed in the smell of the hot wood against her cheek and licked her dry lips. They tasted of salt. How long would she have to wait?

Finally, Amberesh's sword began moving—down the alley. Willow resisted the urge to peek over the edge of her balcony and prayed no one would come out to collect their laundry. Amberesh passed beneath her without pausing. He was barely within range of her magic, and at some point she'd have to take a chance. Carefully, she rolled onto her back and considered her options. There was one more balcony above her, and then the roof—if she could get that high, she could avoid Amberesh indefinitely. If she could get that high.

She rolled back over and scooted on her stomach to take a peek over the edge of the balcony. Amberesh's steps slowed the farther he walked, and as she watched, he turned around. She ducked out of sight. He didn't shout or do anything to indicate he'd seen her, just walked back down the alley and turned left to follow the street. Oh, he'd lost her, all right.

Willow got to her feet and brushed herself off—and the door opened. A small child, younger than Felix, stood gaping at Willow. She carried a wicker basket bigger across than she was in both hands. Willow realized she had a hand on the railing and snatched it away. "Hello," she said.

The little girl dropped the basket and began speaking in Eskandelic, rapidly and with feeling. "I'll just be going now," Willow said, clambered up on the railing, and reached up for the next balcony. She just had time to see a woman follow the child outside before she was up and over the railing and reaching for the edge of the roof.

She landed in a crouch on rough stucco that had been worn by time to feel like a pebbly streambed, her face inches from a rosebush blooming pale peach. The bush grew not from a garden bed, but from a pot a few feet across that bore the remnants of paint, red and gold and green. More pots stood nearby, all bearing roses of dark red or white or yellow or even a blue-black Willow had never seen before. She walked among the flowering bushes, marveling at the delicate scents filling the air, touching one of the unopened buds that felt like living velvet. Chairs and a wirework table stood at the center of the garden. An arched trellis bore twining vines that put the seats in shade, and Willow almost sat before remembering she was an intruder.

A hatch with a loop of rope for a handle lay at the edge of the rosebushes. Willow left it alone. She didn't want to intrude any more than she already had on the residents, and that woman had probably told all her neighbors about the Tremontanan "thief" who'd gone to the roof. Which meant Willow had to get off the roof as quickly as possible.

She ran to the end of the building. It shared a common wall with its neighbor, so going from one to the other was as simple as stepping over a three-foot wall that was more a marker of territory than a structural support. She kept going, running lightly along the row of buildings until she came to the end. There, a gap of about five feet separated one row building from the next. Willow backed up and took a running leap. It was almost too easy, certainly easier than leaping roofs in Aurilien, where everything was steeply pointed and not nice and flat and covered in flowers.

She stopped on the other side of the gap and peered over the edge. No Amberesh. She was too far up to perceive his metal, but she didn't see him with her natural eyes either, just a crowd of people going about their business with no idea there was a woman leaping walls and climbing balconies above their heads.

She left the wall and looked out across Umberan, which was blistering white and cream in the noon sun. From this vantage, she could see more gardens, some of them growing low to the ground, others with trellises whose flowering vines trembled in the salt breeze. Why didn't Aurilien have anything like that? *Well, the roofs are sloped, and who'd take care of the gardens?* She felt a lingering sense of disloyalty to her city, as if she was blaming it for not being drenched in the southern sun.

With a sigh, she moved on along the new row of buildings until she came to another that had those lovely, if cold, balconies as good as stair-steps all down its back side. She worked her way down to the ground, then stood shivering despite the noonday heat, rubbing her arms and casting about for Amberesh. Nothing.

Someone shouted, and Willow turned to see a man in a dark robe and a white headwrap pointing at her. Willow turned and ran. She didn't need to speak Eskandelic to know she'd been pegged as a thief.

She threaded her way through the thinning crowds, all those people going home for dinner and a nap, doubled back a few times, then finally came to a panting halt near one of the public fountains. No one had followed her, but then she'd found over the years that if you could outdistance your pursuit in the first fifteen seconds, you were usually home free.

She splashed her face with cool water and waited for her heart rate to slow. Amberesh wasn't going to find her again in a hurry. He'd probably search all afternoon, and he'd be sweltering in all that armor. Served him right for trying to frighten her. Running was a short-term solution, but short-term was all she cared about this afternoon.

The streets of the Tremontanan enclave were mostly empty, though the men and women on the streets eyed her suspiciously. Willow strode past, pretending to ignore them. She really needed the right kind of clothes if she was going to come down here frequently. Maybe Rafferty could direct her to an appropriate shop.

The trellised courtyard of the *khaveh*-house was empty, the door to the adjacent building shut. Willow sat at one of the little tables and closed her eyes, feeling out her surroundings. She'd learned that many businesses shut down after dinnertime, when the heat of the day was worst. Not that Umberan, with its cool sea breezes, felt nearly so hot as Aurilien. She sensed short silver streaks, the ubiquitous belt knives of a handful of men or women, in the nearby buildings, but no one in the *khaveh*-house next door. Now what?

She leaned farther back in the little chair and let the sunlight filtering through the trellis relax her muscles. A thick, unfamiliar vine twined through the wooden slats, smelling hot and green and peppery, and it cast interesting shadows over the table and her hands. She could go looking for Rafferty, or failing that, one of his friends. They might be friendlier now that their boss had vouched for her. Or she could sit here and breathe in the peppery air, mingled with salt and brine, and lay down her responsibilities for a few minutes. When was the last time she'd truly been able to relax? Before Kerish and Felix had disrupted her life. Not that she resented it.

And she didn't resent it. She couldn't even summon up irritation at either of them. Leaving Felix was unthinkable, and Kerish was…still the same, and yet so different. Suppose he hadn't come to her that night? He and Felix might be dead now, probably would be dead, and she'd still be midnighting and cursing Terence Valant for an Ascendant King. The thought chilled her.

"We're not open yet," a voice said. Rickard, Rafferty's compatriot, stood just inside the door to the *khaveh*-house, of which only the upper half was open.

"I came to see Giles Rafferty," Willow said. "Is it all right if I wait here? I don't expect service if you're not open."

"I can tell you where he lives." Rickard opened the rest of the door and came toward her, pointing. "Down the street, take the third left, then it's the house with the green door. You'll recognize it when you see it."

"Thanks." Willow stood and nodded to the man, then set off in the indicated direction.

The houses along Rafferty's street were typical of lower-class Umberan, only a few arm-spans wide, three or four stories tall with shared walls, like sheer cliffs faced with brown plaster. Only one had a green door, and it was a vibrant, eye-watering green with a rusty iron knob. Willow knocked at the door and waited.

Eventually, she heard a heavy tread from deeper within the narrow house, and shortly the door opened, revealing Rafferty in his undershorts and a thin cotton shirt, scratching his thick blond hair. "Willow," he said. "Something wrong?"

"Just wondering if you'd learned anything more about our

assassin." Rafferty seemed unembarrassed by his state of undress, so Willow decided not to draw attention to it.

"I have. Come in, let me get you some water or something."

In contrast to the plain exterior, the inside of Rafferty's house was as vividly colored as the door, the walls painted a deep, glowing blue, the floor strewn with fat cushions in multicolored striped upholstery. A mosaic lamp of red and purple glass in irregular shapes hung low over the center of the room. Rafferty disappeared through a doorway to the right and came back with a metal pitcher and a couple of wooden cups.

"I hope you don't mind Eskandelic furnishings. I've gone completely native," he said, gesturing with the pitcher at the cushions, which made some water slop over its sides and speckle the hard-packed earth of the floor. "I'd almost want to move here if I didn't love my own country so much."

"I know what you mean." Willow took a seat on one of the fat pillows and accepted a cup of warm but delicious water. "Eskandel certainly has compensations for being away from home."

"The next time I come here—you know, when I'm not fleeing the law—I'll bring my wife. I think she'd appreciate it." Rafferty sat across from Willow and set the pitcher beside himself. He saluted Willow. "Here's to the comforts of exile."

"I'll drink to that." Willow took another swallow of water.

"But you came on business. You have good timing. I was going to send word to you this afternoon." Rafferty drained his cup and set it next to the pitcher. "I think my people have identified your assassin. His name is James Martin—Hardnose to his friends, not that he has any."

"What makes you think it's him?"

"Well, for one, he's the sort of man who'd kill his own mother if the money was right. He's a thief, but the kind that gives honest women like you—" Rafferty grinned—"a bad name. And it's no secret he's done that kind of work before. So if someone in high places was looking for an assassin, Martin's name would definitely come up."

"That's still not proof."

"No. But there were some high and mighty types poking around here a week ago—some of my people noticed them on account of how they wore fancy livery the way an Ascendant or Tremontanan noble might. Purple and silver, with some kind of snake on the chest, they said. And when I inquired further, it turned out Clara—very observant old woman, I must say—saw them meeting with Martin in secret." He grinned again. "Clara may or may not have gone out of her way to observe this. What's more, Martin hasn't been seen around here in the last three days—specifically, since you came here looking for an assassin. Since he's not exactly the shy and retiring type, I call that strange."

Willow finished her water and set her cup down. "That's good evidence, but I need proof."

"That's the best I can do for you. However…Martin has lodgings not far from here."

"Does he?"

"He does. Lodgings that haven't been rented out yet, given as how nobody's too worried about his absence yet. Lodgings that might have important evidence."

"That's interesting. Too bad his landlord probably won't let just anyone go in, on account of respecting his privacy."

Rafferty nodded and scratched his chin, the very image of a man deep in thought. "Too bad we don't know anyone who might not need the landlord's permission."

Willow stood. "Can you take me there?"

The lodging house wasn't far, but it might as well have been in another city for all it resembled the tidy Tremontanan enclave. The streets were narrower, and filthy, and the smooth plaster surfaces of the walls were streaked with dirt. The windows were empty, dark holes, giving Willow the unsettling feeling that she was being watched. Well, it wasn't just a feeling. The men and women loitering on the corners eyed her and Rafferty as they passed. They were a mix of Eskandelic and Tremontanan, and wore dirty laborers' clothing even though they seemed unemployed. Willow sensed a couple of them falling into step behind them and instinctively drew closer to Rafferty, who was now dressed much as everyone around them was, though his clothes were clean.

"How safe is this place?" she said.

Rafferty glanced down at her. "Safe enough. They just want us to know we're here on their sufferance. I've never been molested in all the times I've come here."

"How many times is that?"

"Two."

"You're not filling me with confidence."

"Keep walking."

They were approaching a larger building, its dirty white façade marked with rust-orange stains trickling down from the window holes and the corners where the roof met the walls. "That's it," Rafferty said, nodding once. "Rents rooms to anyone who can pay. You want to go around back?"

"Not if we're being followed. Come with me." Willow walked straight up to the doorway, which was a dark, empty hole like the windows, and went inside. Behind her, Rafferty cursed, then hurried to catch up.

The little room smelled of old garlic and onions, the remains of a hundred Eskandelic dinners, barely covering the whiff of urine that rose from the hard dirt floor. Another dark opening led deeper into the building, which was cool by comparison to the street, if not entirely comfortable. A white-haired Eskandelic man, his face a mask of wrinkles, looked up at their entry. He was seated hunched over on a tall stool and held a frame strung with beads in his hands. "Two *ryad* a night. Each." His tiny eyes glittered at them.

"We're here to pick up a friend's things," Willow said. "James Martin. Can you show us his room?"

"Very clever," the man said, then coughed long and hard into the crook of his elbow. He wiped his lips and continued, "You think me a fool?"

Willow held two large silver five-*ryad* pieces toward the man. "He also sent us to pay his back rent."

The man eyed the coins, but made no move to take the money. Willow held her breath and tried to ignore the fizzing against her fingers. Behind her, Giles shifted his weight but said nothing. Finally, the old man said, "Back rent is fifteen *ryad*, not ten."

Willow held out another coin. The man set the beaded frame on

90

the floor and took the coins, tucking them away in a purse dangling at his side. Then he stood, slowly, as if it hurt to move. "Follow," he said, and limped away through the dark doorway.

They went down a short hallway off which opened several doors—except they weren't doors, they were heavy curtains, blocking out any light that might come from within. Mallets with heads the size of Rafferty's fist hung at eye level next to each door. The place was so still, Willow found herself slowing to make her steps even more silent. Even the noise of the street was muted to a low hum.

At the end of the hall, slender wooden steps ascended toward a faint glow above that turned out to be a window on the first landing. Another hallway led off this landing, but their elderly guide kept climbing until they reached the fourth floor, where he took them to a curtained doorway like all the others. He held the curtain for Willow, smirking. Willow ignored him and ducked past—and gasped.

Someone had slashed open the bed, which wasn't more than a rectangular cushion against one wall, and straw lay scattered across the floor. A large chest with a flat top was knocked over, its lid flung wide open, and cheap clothes and a much-used razor lay nearby. The light that came through the single window illuminated the rest of the broken furniture, a low table whose legs had been wrenched off and a handful of cushions, also slashed. Down fluff mingled with straw.

Willow took a few more steps into the room, followed by Rafferty and the old innkeeper, who sucked in a shocked breath and then began speaking rapidly in Eskandelic. "We're too late," Rafferty said.

"Maybe," Willow said. Aside from her own knives and the coin she carried, there was Rafferty, with a bag of coin of his own and the mysterious iron cross she still hadn't found a way to ask him about, the innkeeper and his belt pouch, and—something else. Something out of place.

She made a show of lifting the bed cushion, which was heavy and awkward even missing half its stuffing, and the innkeeper's voice went shrill. "Not to touch! It not yours is!"

"I can't make it worse," Willow said, turning her attention to the broken table. How much searching should she pretend to do, with Rafferty and the irate old man standing right next to her?

"What are we looking for?" Rafferty said.

"Probably nothing. But if Martin had something important in his possession—this looks more like a focused search than just tossing the place for valuables." *Now* she wandered over to the window and casually stuck her head outside. "And it looks like heaven's smiling on us today."

The window looked out on a narrow, stinking alley far below, splotched with dark wet spots where people had dumped their chamber pots out the windows. A thin, weary-looking dog scratched dispiritedly at a pile of refuse, hunting for food. Below Martin's window, someone had hammered a nail into the plaster, and hanging from the nail was a small cloth sack. Willow waited for the old man to turn away, then retrieved it and dropped it into her shirt without opening it. She already knew it held far more gold than anyone living in this neighborhood was likely to have legitimately.

She glanced back into the room. The old man was muttering under his breath, trying to fit one of the table legs back on. "If this is how you protect your guests, I think we won't be staying after all," she said.

"Out!" The man turned on her, waving his arms at them. "Your friend should not return, he unwelcome is!"

Willow shrugged and hurried down the stairs, Rafferty just behind her. "What did you say about heaven?" Rafferty murmured.

"Nothing. Let's get back to your place and I'll explain."

The street was more crowded when they emerged. "The gainfully employed, returning from their gainful employment," Rafferty said, "but we should still be cautious."

The gold was a burning lump against Willow's belly. "You have no idea how right you are."

No one followed them this time, but she moved quickly anyway, fast enough that Rafferty had to stretch to keep up with her. She kept up the pace all the way back to Rafferty's door, where she waited for him to open it for her, noticing that he hadn't locked it. Such a strange contrast.

"We have our own ways of controlling crime," Rafferty said when he saw her interest. "Now, what did you find?"

Willow removed the sack from her shirt and sat, pouring its

golden contents on the floor. Rafferty hissed in shock and dropped to kneel next to her. "There's got to be five hundred guilders here," he said. "Tremontanan coin."

"That doesn't mean anything, necessarily. It's not impossible to get hold of Tremontanan coin here, and someone might want to throw us off the trail, start us thinking Terence Valant was behind the assassination attempt." Willow pushed the coin into a not-so-little heap. "What did you say the people were wearing? The high and mighty types?"

"Purple and silver. With a snake on the chest."

"That's not a sign and shield. Sounds Eskandelic." Willow sighed and pushed her hair back from her face. She really needed a haircut. "Or it could be Terence trying to make us believe it's a principality."

"That's strange," Rafferty said, and plucked a coin from the pile. Willow looked at it with her eyes instead of her magic and saw it wasn't a coin. It was a disk-shaped gold pendant, engraved with curly Eskandelic writing around its edge. In the center, its edges worn down, was the outline of a bird of prey, its wings outstretched. "Does it mean anything to you?"

"No. I wonder what it says." Willow took it from Rafferty's hand and put it into the pouch around her neck. "I'll ask the harem. It might tell us more about our would-be assassin."

"And I suppose you'll give the gold to them too."

"There's no way of proving it was payment for killing Felix, but the harem should see it, too."

"Pity." Rafferty grinned and helped her scoop the money back into the bag. "I could do a lot with five hundred guilders."

"So could I. But I was thinking of saving it for Felix. It seems fitting."

"I agree. It's nearly suppertime, you want to eat with me?"

"I'd better get all this back to the harem. But thanks for the offer."

Rafferty walked her back through the enclave, introducing her to a few men and women as they went. "Are they all here because of the Ascendants?" Willow asked after one of these introductions.

"No, but most of them are, in one way or another." Rafferty nodded at a young man carrying a fat burlap sack over each shoulder.

"The ones who weren't actually insurgents became such after having to flee Ascendant persecution, or losing their livelihoods when an Ascendant decided to take what wasn't his. Maybe it's as well Terence killed Edmund Valant, Willow—Tremontane was already coming apart under his rule, and this has just made the strain more apparent."

"For Felix's sake, I can't wish Edmund dead."

"But you know what I mean."

"I do. I've always wondered how the Counts and Barons feel about the Ascendants. I mean, Countess Cullinan turns a blind eye to Ascendant excesses, but I'd think she might feel their power is a threat to hers."

"We've heard rumors that Countess Huddersfield has raised her standard against Terence Valant. Funny, I always thought she and the Ascendants were in each other's pockets."

"I guess not."

They reached what Willow recognized as the edge of the enclave, and Rafferty slapped her on the back in a friendly way. "Come again, and bring the boy if you think it's safe," he said. "I find I miss him, though I'm sure he doesn't feel the same about me."

Willow nodded. "He knows he can trust you, and that's what matters. I'll let you know if I learn anything."

Chapter Nine

It was late afternoon, and the markets were beginning to close down. Vendors packed up their wares, toted them inside the doors and furled the awnings that had protected them against the sun's glare. Willow threaded her way through the bustle, thought about buying a skewer of meat and vegetables from one of the sellers vocally hawking the last of his food, but decided against it. The Serjian Principality always served an excellent evening meal.

The streets were growing more crowded as men and women headed home for their own suppers, and Willow had to move quickly to avoid bumping into people. If she'd been a pickpocket, this would be her time, all these bodies in close proximity, most of them careless about their possessions. She'd already seen five people whose belt pouches she could have lifted without their even noticing. She twitched her shoulders and felt the pouches around her neck settle more securely, put her hand on her belt pouch, and dodged out of the path of one person—and directly into someone else.

The woman, dressed in dark robes and heavily veiled, gasped and pulled away. Her veil shifted, slid, and she grabbed it, but not before Willow saw her face. "*Imara?*"

Imara turned to run, but Willow grabbed her wrist and pulled her to a halt. "You know, if you'd just stayed put, I wouldn't have suspected you of anything," she said. "But that was too guilty a move for me to ignore. What are you up to? I'm going to guess you're not supposed to be out of the Residence unaccompanied."

"It is not your concern. Let me go."

"Felix was nearly killed twice in the last ten days. Anything suspicious is my concern."

The veil once again concealed Imara's face, but Willow could guess at the mulish look she was probably wearing. She wrenched at Willow's hold, but Willow tightened her grip. Time to push harder. "Were you meeting your young man?"

Imara gasped again. Then she pulled her veil aside. "How *dare* you spy on me!"

"It was accidental. You're terrible at hiding."

Her shoulders slumped. "Do not tell my mother. Please."

"I won't tell anyone anything if you can convince me you're not a threat to Felix."

"I would never harm him!"

"No, but you might leave him open to harm." Willow let Imara go. "Let's just talk, shall we?"

They walked to one of the little parks in the center of Umberan, cool and green in the late afternoon heat. It had a small white fountain whose basin was littered with coins, mostly copper and a few silver. Willow stared at them, marveling. No one in Aurilien would just leave coin lying around like that.

Imara sat on one of the white marble benches flanking the fountain and removed her veil entirely. Her red hair was matted at the temples with sweat, and she was flushed as if she'd been running. That dark fabric couldn't be comfortable in the heat.

"I do not know where to start," Imara said. "Petrosh Pieran is the man I intend to marry. We met at school—he lives here in Umberan, and we correspond on scholarly topics, or at least that is what my mother believes. He is not poor, but he is not wealthy enough to support a wife yet. I tell him I will work as well, but he will not hear me. He wants my parents to respect him, and he thinks that means money."

"I don't understand why you have to sneak around. If you—"

"Mother wants me to join a harem." Imara's voice was low and bitter. "She thinks I will waste my *talent*—" she spat the word like a curse—"if I do not. I cannot convince her otherwise."

"Surely Janida doesn't want you to be unhappy."

"She thinks I will be unhappy anywhere else. And no man is good enough for me, according to my father."

"But—is Pieran such a bad choice? I mean, why do they reject him?"

"They do not. They have never met him."

"Sweet heaven, Imara, how can you say they think he's not good enough for you if they don't know him?"

Imara's lips pressed tight together. "I know what they will say."

"Maybe, but you really ought to give them a chance to prove you wrong."

Imara glared at Willow. "I did not ask you for advice."

"No, you didn't. And it's none of my business. So what's your plan? Are you going to run away with him?"

"I do not know." Imara shrugged. "I am tired of lying."

"Then tell Janida and Salveri the truth. At worst they'll do exactly what you fear and forbid you to meet with him. But I think you should trust them."

Imara stood and settled her veil over her face. "You are hardly one to advise trust, when you do not trust yourself."

The unexpected blow made Willow recoil. "What did you say?"

"I see how you look at my brother, and how he looks at you. You do not speak the words you should because you are afraid."

"It's more complicated than that."

Imara made a dismissive sound. "It is not that complicated."

"Kerish and I have things—problems we can't resolve. No amount of words can change that."

"You will never know unless you speak them." Imara ducked under two of the close-growing trees and set off in the direction of the Residence. Willow watched her go, stunned. Who else had noticed what lay between her and Kerish? Catrela? Janida? Imara was just wrong. It didn't matter what Willow wanted. Kerish had still chosen his magic over her, and he would do it again if he had to make the choice over again. Love wasn't enough to overcome that. *You wouldn't change either*, a little voice told her, but she ignored it.

Imara had vanished into the crowd when she emerged from the little park. Willow found she didn't really care. It was remotely possible that Imara's sneaking out might provide someone access to Felix, but it seemed unlikely, and Willow wasn't interested in solving Imara's problem for her. She trudged through the streets toward the Residence, occasionally rubbing the spot where Martin's golden guilders burned through the cloth. It wasn't a real burn, wouldn't leave a mark, but it hurt as much as if it were.

She arrived back at the Residence just before Salveri and Janida took their places at the supper table. Imara regarded her coolly, daring her to speak, but she felt drained by the sun, by the encounter with Amberesh, and she ate in silence, speaking only to answer Felix's occasional questions. Felix was cheerful and full of commentary about Gianesh's zoological collection, not at all subdued or frightened, and it eased Willow's heart.

"Did you learn anything, Willow?"

Janida's voice brought Willow out of her fugue. "I think so, but we should discuss it after supper," she said, inclining her head toward Felix. Janida nodded in understanding.

"What did you learn, Willow?" Felix leaned forward and accidentally jostled his glass. Willow made a grab for it and kept it from falling over. "Did I tell you I fed the monkeys today? They're messy eaters, and they fling their—"

"Yes, I don't think we need to discuss that at the supper table, Felix," Kerish said. "I'd like to hear what you learned, Willow. If it concerns…" He nodded slightly in Felix's direction.

"Very well," Janida said. "We will discuss later."

Willow met Kerish's eyes briefly before he returned his attention to his food, and thought about what Imara had said. She was wrong, much as Willow wished otherwise. They'd already been honest with each other, and it still hurt—but was it really honesty, when it was cruelty, too? She'd said things, horrible things, and maybe the core of them had been truth, but she'd dressed them up in hurtful words and that had been wrong. Maybe she needed to apologize, not for sticking to her principles, but for doing it in a way that hurt him.

When supper was over, Willow put Felix to bed and then went to the harem's chamber, where the five women and Kerish waited. She stripped the assassin's purse off the cord around her neck and held it out to Janida. "The assassin's name was James Martin. This was concealed in his rooms. Somebody made a huge mess trying to find it."

Janida opened it and poured some of the coin into her hand. "This does not tell us who hired him."

"No, but I have some more evidence. He was hired by someone wearing purple and silver, with a snake design on his chest."

Catrela sucked in a breath. "Hajimhi."

"Unless that's just what someone wants us to think. Paying in Tremontanan guilders is another hint—or possibly another false clue." She dug into her own pouch. "And this was in the purse with the money."

Catrela took the disk from Willow's hand. "I do not recognize this. It is not Principality insignia."

"May I?" Kerish held out his hand. He turned it over, brought it close to his eyes, then ran his fingers over the engraving. "It's the emblem of a men's organization. The kind rich men join to make themselves seem important. Amberesh—" He shut his mouth abruptly.

"Go on," Janida said. Catrela had gone pale at the mention of her son.

"Amberesh belongs to this one, which is how I recognize it." Kerish closed his fist on the pendant. "But so do about five or six hundred other men. It isn't terribly exclusive. The lines here—" He traced the outer edge of the pendant. "According to Amberesh, these are unique to the owner, but I don't know enough of the members to be able to identify whose this is. It's just a famous line of Eskandelic poetry," he said to Willow.

"I bet that's what the person who tossed the room was looking for," Willow said. "It's unlikely he gave it to Martin freely, so Martin probably stole it, maybe as insurance."

"Which means whoever hired Martin was a member of this organization."

"That does not eliminate Terence Valant as behind the assassination attempt," Catrela said. "He might have influenced one of the Principalities."

"But it does mean a Principality was immediately responsible," Willow said. "Hajimhi or not."

"It makes much work for us," Catrela said. "I think it impossible to find the owner of that pendant is."

"But a place to start," said Alondra.

"Indeed." Catrela still looked pale. "And I must investigate Hajimhi, though it pains me. Gessala will devastated be if they the culprits are."

"But we know more than we did. Thank you," Janida said. "In

three days you will join us for…it an evening party is, but not of friends. It is a meeting of the undecided, at which you will attempt the key *parjenisur* to sway. Until then, rest and prepare. Alondra will help you study."

"All right," Willow said. Janida was good at dismissing people without telling them to go.

She left the room and found Kerish following her. "How's Rafferty?" he said, handing back the pendant, which she dropped into her pouch.

"Well. He seems happy here, though I'm sure he'd rather be home."

"Is that how you feel?"

They were walking down one of the long covered walkways between the buildings of the Residence. The sea wind had picked up, and the fronds of the trees blew wildly in the air, lashing the arched window openings. Willow's hair ruffled in the wind, and she smoothed it down. She stopped to look out across the Residence grounds toward where the sun was setting over the ocean. "Umberan is nice, but Aurilien is home. Not that I miss the city in summer."

"I see. That makes sense." Kerish sounded as if the conversation didn't matter to him. Willow remembered her earlier impulse, the feeling that she should apologize, and immediately her palms began to sweat. How could she bring it up without sounding like a fool?

"Willow," Kerish said, "I want to apologize."

It startled her so much she could only manage a strangled, "For what?"

"I…wasn't exactly gracious with you when we set out. You did more than you had to, and I was so caught up in feeling useless I took it out on you. I hope you can forgive me."

"Kerish…" How to explain she'd forgiven him everything a long time ago? "I haven't always been kind to you, either. All those years ago—I think calling you Terence's hound was the least of the things I said to you. I should never have said all that. I'm sorry."

She risked a glance at him and saw he was looking out over the garden, toward the invisible ocean. "We were awfully hard on each other, for two people in love, don't you think?"

"We were." It couldn't have hurt so badly if she hadn't loved him, which made no sense. "I'm sorry for that, too."

"So am I." Kerish took a breath, as if he were going to say something else, then let it out in a long, thin stream. "I should get to bed. I have an early day at the scholia tomorrow."

"Oh." She struggled with herself briefly, then said, "I still haven't seen the ocean. Up close, I mean. Do you think…you did say you could arrange it."

Kerish nodded. "Maybe sometime soon. I'll talk to Felix's guards. They shouldn't have any trouble taking you both."

"I meant—" Willow's chest ached, cold and tight like ice lodged in her heart. "Yes. Of course. That would be nice."

She parted from Kerish at the end of the walkway and trudged the long way through the halls, not seeing much of anything until she reached the top of the stairs and found Felix there, freshly bathed and bouncing on his bed. Ernest trotted back and forth beside him, yipping happily. "Ernest had a bath, too!" Felix shouted. "He likes baths!"

"That's nice. Stop jumping on the bed, you'll ruin it." Willow rescued the wrinkled sheets and tucked Felix in, urging Ernest to cuddle up on his own bed, though she knew he'd end up with Felix once she was gone.

"Are you sad, Willow? You look sad."

"I'm not sad. Just tired."

"Hilarion says it's all right to be sad if something bad happens, but never to let sadness rule your life. Did something bad happen?"

"No, Felix." Willow straightened the blankets one last time, unnecessarily, and stood. "I just wish I had the chance to make different choices, that's all."

"Did you do something wrong?"

Willow sighed. "I don't know. Probably it wouldn't make a difference."

"Hilarion says wishing distracts from the now. But I think wishing is how you get what you want, to start with, anyway."

"And what do you wish for?"

Felix yawned. "I can't tell you or it won't come true. But it's a nice wish, and you're in it."

"Thank you, Felix, I'm happy to be part of your wish. Now, go to sleep." He was already halfway there, his eyes heavy-lidded and his mouth gone slack. She envied him his ability to fall asleep in seconds. She, on the other hand, was going to lie wakeful in her bed for at least an hour, replaying old arguments and wishing beyond reason she had the chance to make them come out differently.

Chapter Ten

Willow followed Alondra through the arched doorway of the Melikjian Hall, not bothering to disguise her awe at the size of the structure. The sandals Caira had insisted Willow wear had soles thin enough that she could feel the rough surface of the tiled floor through them. The grouted gaps between the diamond-shaped tiles were worn down with time, making the floor feel lumpy, uneven and tricky underfoot. She might as well be wearing her own midnighting shoes, though those weren't ornamented with tingling brass studs shaped like flowers and would have looked odd with her silken robes. Even so, she'd have been more comfortable, less off-balance.

The walls were tiled, too, though with tiny squares in deep red and rich gold making abstract patterns that spread from the floor to the domed ceiling high above. It wasn't just a single dome, but many small ones that intersected with each other to create patterns of lines and curves, and Willow couldn't help but stare, trying to trace each one back to a source. Kerish had told her the Melikjian Hall was one of the oldest buildings in Eskandel, but it didn't look old, just intimidating.

Willow drew in a breath and smelled the hot tarry charred odor of torches—no newfangled Devices here—and the perfumes of the harem, all five of which mingled into a single delicate scent. Did the harem coordinate its fragrances the way it had its clothing? The five women wore shades of gold that matched the walls perfectly, with plenty of gold jewelry that burned in Willow's magical sight. The walls burned, too, in places where some of the thumb-sized tiles were actually made of gold.

She couldn't help comparing the hall to Aurilien. They had buildings of roughly the same age and size, but they looked ancient, all old crumbling stone and frigid drafts even in the heart of summer. On the other hand, Old Tower was taller than anything they had in Umberan, taller than the Jauderish, and the thought was obscurely comforting.

She walked forward, trailing Kerish, toward one of the gaudy statues that stood randomly throughout the room. They were odd, completely out of place in this beautiful, elegant chamber. They stood directly on the white tiles, for one, no plinths or anything. For another, they'd been painted solid colors over their stone, forest green and crimson red and cobalt blue like the gaudy doors of Umberan. Each depicted a young man or woman in perfect physical condition. She could see they were in perfect physical condition because each was carved in a form-fitting bodysuit that went from ankles to throat and turned into a hood covering the statue's hair.

Willow stopped in front of a red statue of a young woman. "I don't understand the point of this," she said, then stifled a shriek with her hand as the statue blinked, slowly.

Kerish laughed. "This is one of Eskandel's most famous performing troupes. They're living sculptures. Over the course of the evening they'll gradually change positions, and if you watch closely, you can see them interact with one another."

"That's astounding." Willow walked around the "statue." "I could watch this all night."

"Not that you'll have the chance. You're supposed to talk with the other principalities, aren't you?"

"Now I'm starting to regret the necessity." She realized, now, that the exposed parts of the woman's body, her face and hands and feet, were painted over with thick red cosmetic paste. They must have a hell of a time getting cleaned up after a performance. No wonder her hair was covered. "Felix, come and look at this."

"How do they stand so still, Willow? I couldn't do that." Felix circled the statue the way Willow had done. He was dressed, like Kerish, in black trousers and formal knee-length robes embroidered all over with fanciful creatures. Willow's robes were unadorned dark blue silk that reached the floor and would be impossible to run in. She cast a quick glance around the room for Felix's bodyguards — there they were, standing a discreet distance away, their eyes roving their surroundings without a pause. Willow flexed her wrist slightly. She'd won the battle with Caira about the forearm knife on the grounds that the full sleeve would conceal it completely. She hoped to heaven she didn't need it tonight.

Kerish nodded toward the doorway. "That's the first of them.

Good luck." He walked away toward Catrela, standing at the far side of the chamber. It felt like being abandoned. Willow missed his strong presence briefly before reminding herself that she was Felix's guardian and needed to stand on her own. She looked down at Felix, who stood next to her still admiring the "statue," and sent up a brief prayer to heaven that she wouldn't let him down that night.

She didn't recognize the newcomers, who were dressed far more gaudily than the Serjian Principality and looked like a flight of parrots trying to intimidate swans on their own turf. Was "flight" the right word? Felix would know. "Come on," she said. "We have to meet them."

"I don't know what to say," Felix said.

"Just be polite, answer their questions, and remember you're the King and you outrank them."

Felix nodded. He looked like he wanted to hold her hand. Willow felt the same way.

Janida and Salveri were conversing with the newcomers. The rest of the Serjian harem was spread throughout the room, pretending to be interested in the performers. Janida switched to Tremontanese when she saw Willow and Felix approaching. "Najarhian Yesemia, may I present King Felix Valant of Tremontane to you," she said, "and his guardian and *eskarna*, Willow North."

Najarhian Yesemia looked like sixty pretending to be thirty-five. She wore more cosmetics than Willow had yet seen on an Eskandelic woman, and her black hair had a sheen to it that said it owed its color to artifice rather than nature. She smiled at Willow, a cold expression that didn't reach her eyes, then turned to Felix and said, "You the King of Tremontane are?"

"Yes," Felix said, and Willow cheered inside at how his voice didn't tremble.

"What of Terence Valant?"

"He's my uncle. He's not supposed to be King. Ascendants aren't allowed."

"Please excuse us to our other guests to speak," Janida said, and Willow realized the Torossian Principality, headed by the tall blond Kharalin, had just walked through the door. It was a relief to see someone friendly to them — someone not this dried-up woman with her friendly-seeming comments that hid something nasty, Willow was certain.

"Serjian has spared no expense," Yesemia said to Willow. "But you as strangers will not know this."

"No, we don't, but we're honored to be welcome at this gathering."

Yesemia cast her eyes down. "We a wealthy Principality are not," she said, "but we do not flaunt our wealth. Najarhian is a name that means modesty."

The clothes the five women wore, as well as the robe and trousers of the man who had to be the Najarhian Prince, were woven with real gold threads that made Willow feel as if she were in Aurilien on a sunny day. "That's quite a name to live up to."

Yesemia nodded. "We must protect our own interests." She looked down at Felix again. "You think a boy King can protect what his is?"

This conversation felt uncannily familiar, though Willow was certain she'd never met Yesemia before. "I think with support from strong Eskandelic principalities like yours, he can regain his throne."

"And what does he promise?"

Willow was ready for this. "Better trade relations. Stronger ties between our governments. A reduction in tariffs. There is a lot Tremontane can offer Eskandel that Terence Valant won't give you."

"Hmm." Yesemia smiled her nasty smile again. "I was thinking of something more…informal. A gift, between two respectable parties."

You mean a bribe. Willow was utterly certain at that moment that Yesemia would go on dangling the promise of her support in front of Felix, no matter what he gave or promised. Suddenly she realized what was so familiar about it: this was how Nan had made people dance to her pipes, down to the day she died. "I'm afraid that's not possible. Felix is trying to regain his throne, and all his resources are devoted to that."

"What a shame." Yesemia even managed to look regretful. "I think we convinced are not, this boy King to support."

Willow managed to match Yesemia's regretful look. "You're right, that *is* a shame," she said, and rejoiced to see Yesemia's expression falter. "But you must do what's best for your principality. Don't you agree, your Highness?"

The Najarhian Prince, a thin, long-faced man probably a decade younger than Yesemia, looked startled at being addressed directly. "I…agree," he said.

"But you want our support," Yesemia said quickly.

"Well, yes. But not at the cost of your own needs." Willow thought back over her lessons and pulled a name out of memory. "And Felix does have plenty of support. We have spoken to Torossian, Dekerian…Khalajian."

Yesemia's eyes widened fractionally, though it was hard to tell behind all her cosmetics. "Khalajian?"

"They were very vocal about Felix's cause. Felix, you remember Khalajian Iratia, right? The nice lady with the cats?"

Felix's eyes were round, and he opened his mouth to say something. Willow glared at him, and he just nodded.

"Khalajian is not nearly the *parjenisur* Najarhian is," Yesemia snapped. "You cannot trust them."

"Really?" Willow let a frown wrinkle her brow. "But they were very open with us."

"Najarhian will lend you its support, but only if you reject Khalajian." Yesemia crouched stiffly to be on Felix's level. "You like cats?"

"I do. I like dogs better, but cats are nice."

"You will come to my Residence and meet my cats. They will like you." She stood to face Willow. "What say you?"

"I have your word that you will vote to support the Serjian question? And be *parjenisur* for us?"

"You have my word," Yesemia said, but Willow was looking beyond her, at the Prince, who nodded slightly. It probably didn't matter, it wasn't as if the Prince had any real power, but Willow had a feeling he had more of a say in how things went in the Najarhian Principality than most princes. He was looking at her with a smile that suggested he, too, knew how to make Yesemia bend.

"Well…it's true Najarhian is powerful, and Felix appreciates that. I promise he won't forget you when he reclaims the Crown." Willow made the bow of one just barely subordinate to another, and was relieved to see Yesemia's returning bow didn't claim much greater superiority to her, because showing disrespect to Felix was something Willow would be forced to confront her on, and then all her work would be for nothing.

She graciously excused herself and Felix, who was jigging uncomfortably as if he had to use the facilities. "Come with me, and we'll find a chamber pot," she said.

"I don't need to piss," Felix said.

"Felix! Where did you learn that kind of language?"

"From you. Willow, you *lied* to her!"

"Sort of. I implied facts that were not true."

"...I think that's the same as lying. The Khalajian lady was rude to me and she was mean to her cats. I didn't like her and she said we should never come back."

"That's true. But in politics, sometimes you can let someone believe something's true for the sake of getting that person to do what you want. And that's my job as your *eskarna*. Najarhian Yesemia didn't like the idea of her rival getting any benefits that she couldn't have."

"Oh." Felix stopped wiggling. "So you tricked her."

"Yes."

"And tricks are all right?"

"Sometimes. In this case, definitely. But if Felix plays tricks on Willow he will be in trouble."

Felix laughed. "They could be *funny* tricks."

"Willow?" Alondra appeared beside them. "There is another you should meet."

The next ones were, thank heaven, the Sarhafian Principality, one of those on Willow's list as a powerful neutral party. They were also extremely pleasant, chatting with Willow and Felix in a friendly way, though Sarhafian Jennea, their *vojenta*, never thought to introduce their prince, who looked as if he'd rather be somewhere else. At the end, Willow had no idea whether she'd swayed Jennea to Felix's cause, but at least she hadn't made an enemy.

She turned away from making her bow to Sarhafian and nearly ran over another woman, whose brown hair was piled high on her head and looked in danger of falling down. She looked familiar. "Excuse me," Willow said.

"Of course," the woman said, and at the sound of her deep, somewhat scratchy voice, Willow remembered where she'd seen the woman before. Sahaki Beppinda, formerly *vojenta mahaut* and Mahnouki's puppet. Why was *she* here?

Willow quickly made a respectful bow and saw Felix do the same. "Thank you for accepting Serjian Principality's invitation, Sahaki Beppinda," she said.

"We interested in the Serjian question are," Beppinda said, which made Willow take a quick look around. Beppinda was standing alone, though Willow could see the prince, Sahaki Karalhi, in conversation with Kerish on the far side of the room. "A daring proposal, Eskandel's fortunes to Tremontane to tie."

"Not to disagree, but Eskandel's fortunes are already tied to Tremontane," Willow said. Beppinda was positively dripping with gold necklaces and she was starting to feel scorched. "The ploy of the pretender to steal the Crown of Tremontane just made it more obvious."

"You are correct," Beppinda said, startling Willow. "Tell me, young King, why should Sahaki support you?"

Felix faced her down without a hint of fear. "Because it's right," he said.

"Right is not enough, when it politics is. What does it benefit us?"

Felix glanced up at Willow, who said, "Felix will build up ties between Eskandel and Tremontane. You'll have better trading positions and lower tariffs. And I'm sure you'll find a huge market for, um, *surabhi* in Tremontane."

"You speak for him? He cannot King on his own be?"

"Felix is still a child. I am *eskarna* for him until he's old enough."

"His regent?"

"Probably not. His guardian, though."

"A thief as guardian? That daring is."

"I suppose. I haven't really thought about it," Willow lied.

Beppinda nodded. "Sahaki will *vojenta mahaut* be," she said. "This true is. And I will remember this conversation." She bowed, an abbreviated bob of superior to inferior, and walked away.

"Is that right? You'll still be my guardian once I'm King?" Felix asked.

Willow replayed the conversation in her head and cursed. Then she looked more closely at Felix, at how hopeful he was, and the world rearranged itself so quickly she felt dizzy. "Felix," she said, squatting down to be at his eye level, "I will stay with you for as long as you need me. That's a promise."

Felix's face lit up with a smile. "I'm glad," he said, and threw his arms around Willow's neck. Willow hugged him back, not caring who might be watching. She felt no fears about making that promise, no uncertainties. The Willow she'd been a month ago wouldn't have been so cavalier about tying her fortunes to one small boy. Of course, the Willow she'd been a month ago had been lonely, suspicious, and obsessed with her work. She saw Kerish watching them from across the room, smiling, and discovered she didn't miss that Willow at all.

"Willow North," said a familiar voice, and Willow stood up to find herself facing Hajimhi Fariola and a short man who stood close beside her. Probably Prince Giaveni. "And this is Felix Valant."

Felix bowed to her. "I'm sorry, I don't know your name," he said.

"This is Hajimhi Fariola, Felix," Willow said, "and the Hajimhi Prince, Giaveni?"

Both Hajimhis nodded politely. Fariola said, "We thank Serjian for the invitation. It pleases us with you to speak, young man. You claim to be King?"

"My father is dead, and that means I'm King of Tremontane," Felix said.

In a quiet voice, Giaveni said, "Why do you not rule, then?"

"Because my uncle killed my father and tried to kill me. He wants to be King."

"We have no proof that you Felix Valant are," Fariola said.

"Well, I am." Felix's voice trembled.

"What proof would you accept?" Willow said, putting her hand on Felix's shoulder to calm him.

"Terence Valant would say if it his nephew is," said Fariola. "Return the boy to him, and we shall see."

"Terence will kill him if he gets his hands on him. As to his identity, you have my word and that of Serjian Kerish."

Fariola ignored her. "What did they promise you, child, this lie to tell? Riches? What would please a boy your age enough the King to pretend to be?"

"I'm not pretending. I am the King." Felix's voice was quavering noticeably.

"Stop it," Willow said.

"Or do you have a family in Tremontane that will benefit? Eskandel does not like a fool to be made. Speak truth now and we will understand."

"It's true," Felix said. "I mean, that I'm the King. I don't tell lies."

"I do not believe you, boy."

"*Stop it,*" Willow shouted. Peripherally, she was aware of people turning to look in their direction, but she was so furious she didn't care. "Is that your idea of repaying hospitality? Tormenting a little boy? If you want to attack someone, Fariola, maybe you should try attacking me and we'll see what you get."

Fariola's smile was disdainful. "You cannot bear questioning? I think the truth should withstand my inquiries. It seems it does not."

"Those aren't inquiries, that's just you being nasty. You want to know the truth? It's what we've been saying all along. This is Felix Valant, he is the true King of Tremontane, and Terence Valant is a usurper who would love for you not to support Felix because that will keep him on the throne. You even know Terence has asked for Eskandel to return him, which more or less proves Felix's identity. But I suppose if you're stupid and arrogant enough to cling to your ridiculous theory about how this is all a hoax, you're stupid enough to believe Terence is the rightful king."

Fariola's smile vanished. "You *dare*," she said hoarsely.

"I dare," said Willow. "Hurt Felix again, and we'll see what else I dare."

Prince Giaveni put a hand on Fariola's shoulder and said something to her in Eskandelic. She shrugged him off and without another word strode off in the direction of the door. Willow watched her go, realized her hand was still gripping Felix's shoulder tightly, and released him. Gradually, a few other women, one of them Gessala's curly-haired lover, detached themselves from the crowd and followed Fariola, with Giaveni bringing up the rear. The room was as silent as if it were empty.

"Willow?" Felix whispered.

"What?"

"Is she going to vote against us?"

"Probably." Willow patted his shoulder. "I'm sorry. I lost my temper."

"Can I use the facilities now?"

Willow took his hand. Every eye in the room was fixed on her. She held her head high and led Felix away in the direction of the chamber pots. So she'd just thrown away the support of one of the most important *parjenisur* on her list. So what?

She stood in the hall outside the tiny chamber, waiting for Felix, and kicked herself mentally. That had been monumentally stupid. Fariola's words couldn't hurt Felix—well, that wasn't true, words could be weapons, but it wasn't the kind of hurt that mattered. And yet the memory of facing her down was so satisfying…no, she shouldn't have done it, she should have found a way to deflect Fariola's attention from Felix and gotten them both out of there as quickly as possible. Why had Fariola done it? Was she looking for an excuse not to support Felix? Willow kicked the wall. Hajimhi was still on her list of possible assassins, and this pushed them all the way to the top.

They returned to the grand chamber to find conversations had started up again, and Willow grabbed herself a glass of dark red wine and drank deeply. She didn't want to get drunk, but a little wine might loosen the tension in her muscles.

"May I have some wine, Willow?" Felix asked.

"Not tonight. Maybe some other time."

"That was a rather spectacular show," Kerish said, startling her into fumbling her glass. "Sorry. I can't believe you let me sneak up on you."

"Apparently I'm failing at a lot of things tonight."

"Don't be too hard on yourself. I was too far away to hear most of it, but Giaveni looked like that explosion was planned."

"I still should have been more self-controlled. I don't know what I'm going to say to Janida."

"Probably that—"

"Excuse me," said a deep voice, and Willow turned to find an elderly gentleman at her left elbow. His white hair was thick and bushy, like his eyebrows, and his eyes were a startling blue in a deeply tanned face. "I wish the young King to meet. Jamighian Vijenci, and may I introduce our *vojenta*, Issobela."

Another name from her list. Willow stood frozen momentarily, but Kerish bowed, managing to nudge her discreetly with his elbow, and that broke her out of her daze so she could bow as well. "You speak with great ferocity," Vijenci said.

"That's a really polite way to put it," Willow said without thinking, and both Vijenci and Issobela laughed, surprising her.

"You are like *najabedhi*, fierce in defense of her young," Issobela said. She was younger than the Prince, with blond-streaked brown hair and warm brown eyes. "Hajimhi Fariola should have known that."

"Please don't judge Felix by my bad behavior," Willow said. "I lost my temper, and I shouldn't have."

"That true is," said Issobela. "When it a question is, one must controlled and cautious be. You are young and I think you have not learned this lesson."

Willow's face burned as if the *vojenta's* bracelets were pressed against it. "I'm sorry."

Vijenci and Issobela exchanged looks. They were the kind of looks only long-married couples could produce. "We impressed are at your loyalty to your King," Vijenci said. "You care for him more than for politics. That unusual is, here in Eskandel."

"I'm only involved in politics out of necessity. I hope to leave them behind as soon as possible."

"Abandoning your King?"

"Never." Willow felt Felix's hand creep into hers and she clasped it tightly. "I look forward to the time when the Crown is restored to Felix and he can go back to learning how to be a good King, and I can just be his guardian."

Again the knowing looks passed between *vojenta* and Prince. Then

Issobela said, "Will you be as fierce in your defense of his Crown as you are of his person?"

"They're sort of the same thing right now, so yes, I will."

"Then Jamighian will support Serjian in its question," Issobela said, loudly enough to draw attention from nearby guests. "And we will bring our allies to your cause."

A murmur went up that spread outward from them to the farthest reaches of the chamber. "Thank you," Willow said, giving Issobela and then Vijenci a low, respectful bow.

"It may not be enough," Vijenci said in a low voice, pitched to carry no farther than the five of them. "Mahnouki's question has captured the imaginations of many princes, and some of those have great sway over their harems. But we will add our voice to yours, and pray heaven it will suffice."

"Thank you," Willow repeated. "We're both very grateful."

Vijenci gave Willow an amused look. "Our youngest son is but a few years older than the King," he said. "We hope, if we were gone, that he would find as fierce a protector as Felix has in you."

"I hope it never comes to that," Willow said.

Vijenci and Issobela bowed to Felix, then to Willow and Kerish. "Good fortune to you," Issobela said, and then they were gone.

"Sweet heaven," Kerish said in a low voice. "That was unexpected."

"I remember they weren't going to vote for Mahnouki, but I had the feeling that didn't mean they would vote for us." Willow drained her almost-forgotten wine glass and handed it off to a passing servitor. "How much longer do we have to be here?"

"I haven't even looked at the people," Felix complained, nodding at the nearest human statue, a muscular young man painted a deep violet.

"Let's look around, and hope no one else wants to talk," Kerish said, taking Felix's other hand. They probably looked like a little family, the three of them, and the thought made Willow uncomfortable. She almost let go of Felix's hand before realizing she was being stupid. So what if it looked like she and Kerish—that they were—she gripped Felix's hand a little more tightly and held her head high, daring someone to make an issue of it.

Either Willow's explosion, or the surprise declaration of support from Jamighian, deflected anyone else from approaching them. Willow managed to steer Kerish and Felix away from Janida, who had the look of someone biding her time and would no doubt have much to say to Willow that Willow wasn't interested in hearing. They stood by one of the statues and watched it move, so slowly, and argued in a friendly way over what it depicted. None of them could agree on anything except that the man was running in extreme slow motion.

Eventually, the crowds began to thin, and Willow's tension returned. But Janida only said, when she finally approached them, "It time to return is."

Felix fell asleep on Willow almost before the carriage began moving. It was close to midnight, so that made sense. Willow stroked his hair and yawned. "I hope Janida waits until tomorrow to yell at me."

"If she hasn't yelled at you yet, you're probably safe until morning," Kerish said.

"Maybe she won't yell at me at all. Maybe it's not as bad as I remember."

"Oh, it was bad. I hope you never rip up at me like that."

"I won't. I would never do that." *I could never bear to hurt you*, she cried out silently. But she already had, hadn't she?

"I'll hold you to that." Kerish was looking off into the distance, his face in profile to her, the moonlight casting strange shadows across his cheeks. She wished she could curl up in his arms as she had so many times before, and closed her eyes against the desire.

She drifted into a half-awake state, waking only when they neared the black gateway and she had to be alert. But no one attacked. Back at the Residence, Kerish carried Felix up to their suite, laid him on his bed, and bade Willow good night. Willow undressed in the darkness, then stood at the window, looking out over the Residence grounds, which were mostly layers of dense shadow striped by moonlight. This wasn't passion, it wasn't mere desire. She loved Kerish, and she wanted desperately for him to love her too.

But they'd been here once before, hadn't they? And he'd chosen

Terence Valant and she'd chosen midnighting, and neither of them had been willing to compromise. She could be honest with herself about it now: she'd been afraid to give up the thing that made her who she was, afraid to take a chance on finding something else. Something better. And since she was being honest, she could admit that she still wasn't ready to give up midnighting to allay Kerish's fears. Which meant she didn't love him as much as all that, didn't it?

The hollow, icy feeling in her chest returned. How could she want something so badly and still be unwilling to do what it took to have it? She left the window and crawled into bed, lay hugging her knees, and eventually drifted into a fitful sleep.

Chapter Eleven

The carriage neared the gate to the private neighborhood where the Serjian Residence lay, and Willow sat up a little straighter in the carriage, flexing her left wrist out of habit. No one had tried to kill Felix here since the first time, but she couldn't stop seeing the bottleneck where the street funneled into the black pointed archway, the tall hedges lining the wall where someone might stand concealed even at midafternoon. Felix drooped in the curve of Kerish's arm, exhausted from a morning spent playing in the waves and sun. He looked so innocent—but then he didn't look much different when he was awake, did he?

Kerish had nodded off too, and Willow spent a moment admiring his sleeping profile. She'd been surprised when he attached himself to their party that morning, and had to conceal just how happy it made her. It was tempting to go over and cuddle under his other arm, let him hold her. But even if she could, watching out for Felix's safety was more important.

One of Felix's massive bodyguards leaned forward and said something in Eskandelic to the driver. Willow followed the exchange uncomprehendingly. If Felix's enemies bribed the driver, or the guards, she might not have any idea of the treachery until it was too late. She flexed her wrist again. Maybe Kerish needed to start going armed, while they were in public with Felix. Maybe she needed to ask Janida for a second pair of guards, and alternate them so an enemy would have more trouble getting them alone long enough to bribe them. Or maybe she needed to control her paranoia so it didn't get Felix killed.

The carriage swept up the private street and came to a stop at the end of the Serjian drive. Willow shook Felix and Kerish awake, then helped Ernest down from the carriage as Kerish did the same for Felix. "I like the ocean," Felix said with a yawn. "So does Ernest. We should go every day."

"I don't know about that, but we can certainly do it again," Willow said. "Now you need to bathe so you're not covered in sand and salt, and then it will be time for supper."

"All right. Ernest, come!"

Felix raced ahead of them to the front door, followed by a guard who swore under his breath as he trotted after the young King. Willow controlled a smile. Felix was always considerate of his guards, but he had trouble remembering that most people didn't enjoy running everywhere.

Kerish held the front door for Willow, and the two of them moved at a more sedate pace down the long front hall, cool and shady after the heat of midday. They reached the top of the stairs and began crossing one of the arched walkways between the buildings of the Residence. The breeze felt good against Willow's cheeks, telling her she'd probably burned her face again. She really needed to be more careful or her skin would be permanently peeling and she'd look ridiculous. "Do you think—"

Light footsteps, running footsteps, echoed in the corridor ahead, and Gessala appeared, running with her hands over her face. She bumped into Kerish, who caught her before she could fall. "Gessala, what is it?" he said.

Gessala let out a string of Eskandelic words. She lowered her hands to reveal a tearstained face, gabbled something else to Kerish, then looked at Willow. Her face crumpled, and she burst out sobbing, then tore herself from Kerish's hands and ran away past the two of them. Willow watched her go. "What's wrong?"

"She said her life is over. Let's find Mother."

They found Janida in the hallway outside her suite, the hall that led to Willow and Felix's rooms. She was just shutting the door to Catrela's apartment, carefully, as if it might break if she handled it poorly. She saw Willow, and her lips tightened in anger. "Willow North," she said. "You see what your rashness and violence have done?"

Willow shook her head. "Is it something to do with Gessala?"

Janida grabbed Willow by the upper arm and dragged her along the corridor toward the stairs. "Do not act so innocent," she said, her voice low and grating. "You think Hajimhi will permit you disrespectful to be? That there will no repercussions be? Hajimhi Fariola sends word that the Hajimhi Principality's offer to Gessala rescinded is. No more than this, and yet you are not stupid except when you angry are, so you will understand why."

Janida's hand gripped Willow so tightly she felt numb. "Because of me."

"Mother, that's not fair," Kerish said.

"Fairness there none is," Janida said. Her accent was growing thicker. "Gessala tells us, Catrela and me, that it a love match is. Hajimhi hurts itself in not offering for her. But they have no political intent and therefore can afford...spiteful to be. Gessala suffers because of *you*, Willow North." Janida released her with a force that set Willow's arm swinging. "When will you learn yourself to govern?"

"I'm sorry." Willow managed not to rub her sore arm. "I can apologize—I can ask them to reconsider—"

"Fariola was in the wrong, Mother, and we all know it," Kerish said.

"What we all *know*," Janida spat, "is how this game played is. Fariola tested your honor and you *failed*. There no apologizing for that is. Worse, you insulted her in a way that forced her to rescind their offer or appear weak before others. You will be silent, and you will control yourself in future. Have you forgotten what at stake is? Felix can survive his feelings hurt to be, can survive scared being. He cannot survive if this vote fails. Do not forget." Janida headed off in the direction they'd come. "And avoid Catrela for a time," she added, not looking back. "You now the cause of pain to two of her children are. She does not forgive easily."

When the sound of Janida's footsteps had faded completely, Kerish said, "She was too harsh."

"I don't think she was," Willow said. "I let Fariola needle me, and I should have remembered that Felix is strong enough to handle such petty taunts. This is my fault, Kerish."

"It's not your fault they withdrew their offer. That was just spiteful and stupid. If Gessala fell in love with Giaveni—"

"Not him. One of the harem sisters. I don't know her name."

"Really? Oh. Well, either way, it's hard on both of them to deny that love just because Fariola was embarrassed last night."

"I get the feeling love isn't the most important thing when it comes to Eskandelic politics."

"True. But it still matters. We're families as well as political entities." Kerish took Willow's hand briefly, startling her, but he released her after a quick squeeze and said, "Come on, we both need baths as much as Felix does, and then there's supper, and everything will work out eventually."

There were two empty spots at the supper table that evening. Gessala had disappeared, and Alondra said—blushing, and unable to look at Willow—that Catrela was feeling unwell and chose to eat in her rooms. Willow sat with her navel inches from the freezing iron hooks and concentrated on eating, though the food sat in her stomach like a leaden weight, but without the red-rimmed black emptiness real lead would have had in her vision. Janida ignored her except once to ask her to pass a particular dish. It was worse than being yelled at.

Abruptly, Janida said, "Imara, have you completed your assignment for the scholia?"

"Yes, Mother," Imara said, not looking at Janida.

"It too early to think of the Review is not," Janida said. "Next year you will eighteen be, a good age. I married into Serjian Principality when I eighteen was."

"I do not choose, Mother."

Janida slammed her fist down on the table, making the dishes nearby rattle. "You do not choose? This all you say is. Not enough! *Why* do you not choose?"

"I do not want to join a harem!"

Janida's voice softened. "It all right to be nervous is," she said. "You do not yet understand the joys of sisterhood."

"No!" Imara rose to her feet, kicking her section of table loose so it hung canted against its neighbors. Her glass tipped over and poured a flood of pale wine across the tilted square that Alondra, sitting next to her, tried to stem. "I will not, and you cannot force me to!"

"Force? Why force? Who speaks of force?"

"Janida," Salveri began in his deep rumble, but she cut him off with a curt gesture of her hand.

"I do not force you," she said. "I want you to see what is best for you. You will be *vojenta* someday, Imara, you may even be *vojenta mahaut.* How can you not see—"

"*You* do not see, Mother," Imara shouted. "I am in love and I will marry my love."

Janida recoiled as if Imara had slapped her. "Who?"

"Petrosh Pieran. He loves me and—"

"That *scholar*? The poor one? Do you expect your parents to consent to this, to a daughter of Serjian Principality living in poverty, wasting her talents on someone who no one is?"

"He is not no one! He grows better-known every year. And they are *my* talents to waste!"

"Imara, sit down," Salveri rumbled.

Imara remained standing. "I do not need your blessing," she said. "I am of age and I can marry where I wish."

Janida sucked in a breath. "You *dare* threaten us?"

"I am telling you, Mother. Permission or none, I know what I will do. I will go to him tonight if you tell me I must abandon him."

"No one has said you must abandon anything," Salveri said. "Should we not at least meet him?"

"You will just tell me he is not good enough."

"You do not put words in my mouth, child." Salveri's placid expression turned hard.

"Janida," Alondra said.

"When it your child is, then you may speak," Janida said. "Imara, *sit down.*"

"No," Imara said, and left the room. Janida rose to follow her.

"*Stop,*" Salveri said, and to Willow's shock Janida did. "Leave her be. She will sensible later be."

"And if she leaves?" Janida shot back. "If she runs to this man?"

"You'll only make things worse if you try to stop her," Willow said without thinking, then successfully kept from cringing when Janida turned on her, glaring.

"I think your opinion was not asked for, Willow North," she said.

"I know how little you care for my opinion right now," Willow said. "I also know Imara has been afraid to tell you the truth for weeks, maybe months, and now that she's done so, even if it was in the stupidest way possible, she's probably even more afraid than before."

"That makes no sense."

"Doesn't it? Janida, she cares about your opinion. She didn't want to disappoint you, but she's in love and she didn't want to give that up either. Now she thinks you're furious with her choice when what you're really upset about is the way she told you. For all she knows, she's just thrown away her family — and I guarantee you she's not nearly so certain about her future with Pieran as she sounds."

The anger faded from Janida's face, replaced by her familiar neutral expression. "You know him?"

"Um, no. I...the truth is, I discovered their secret a couple of weeks ago, so all — don't give me that look! It wasn't my secret to tell, and it didn't threaten Felix, so I didn't feel obligated to tell you. But I did tell Imara she should be honest with you and Salveri."

"A fine honesty, that disrespects its parents."

"Sometimes, when you're angry, you say the wrong thing," Willow said. "And then you have to figure out how to make it right when you can't take it back."

Janida narrowed her eyes. "True," she said, almost grudgingly. Then she turned and left the room by the same door Imara had used.

Alondra cleared her throat. "We should finish this meal, and then speak more in the morning," she said.

Willow picked at her food, and nibbled the sweet, iced dessert the servants put in front of her, but didn't rise when Salveri and the others did. "Are you all right?" Kerish murmured.

"I'm fine. Look, I'm going to put Felix to bed, and then I think I'm going to turn in. It's been a really long day."

She took Felix's slightly sticky hand and led him back to their chambers, where she supervised his washing and dressing. She sat on the bed next to him as he wiggled around trying to find a comfortable spot, exactly as Ernest did.

"Is Imara in trouble?" he asked.

"Not really. Sort of. It's complicated."

"Doesn't she have to marry a principality?"

"No more than Kerish does. It's just that sometimes parents want things for you that you don't want for yourself. And then it gets...complicated."

"How do you know which to choose?"

"Hmm?"

"Aren't you supposed to do what your parents want? Hilarion says you should always obey your parents, because you owe them your life. But what if they want something that's bad for you?"

Willow smoothed his hair back from his forehead. "Felix, mostly parents care about their children and do things that show that caring. But everyone has to grow up sometime, and when you do, sometimes you find out that what's best for you isn't what your parents want. And that doesn't mean your parents are bad, just that they don't know everything."

"So you have to choose?"

"Eventually, yes. And since I'm your guardian, I'll do my best to think of what *you* need and not just what I think you should do."

Felix yawned. "I know. I love you, Willow."

"I love you too, Felix."

To her surprise, Janida was waiting in the antechamber of their suite when Willow left Felix's bedchamber. Willow shut the door quietly behind her and said, "Can I help you with something?"

"Imara is gone," Janida said. "She took a few things, not enough...she is gone."

"I'm sorry." Willow braced herself for an outpouring of rage, but Janida just looked tired. "I know a place where she and Pieran met. I could check on it if you want."

"That would welcome be, but it can wait until morning. I think...if I follow her tonight, it will drive her farther away. I choose to believe she safe is with her..." She sat uninvited and covered her face with her hands. "I believed I doing the right thing was."

"I understand that." Willow took a seat nearby.

"Yes, I think you do. I harsh with you was, this afternoon." Janida lowered her hands and sighed. "We learned this morning that Khasjabi Principality has been secretly treating with Mahnouki, their question to support. Donia has lied to me and I cannot forgive her for her greed or myself for my blindness."

"Then they could be the assassins!"

Janida shook her head. "They are not behind the attempts. They merely intended to make us believe they would support our question, then take their supporters unexpectedly to Mahnouki. Bad enough."

"It is. But it still leaves us not knowing who wants Felix dead."

"Catrela will learn, once she recovers her good sense. Salveri will spend the night with her and they will give each other comfort."

"Leaving you to sleep alone," Willow said without thinking. "Though I guess you're used to that, with Alondra."

Janida gave her a level, considering look, which made Willow squirm. It was the kind of look that said Janida was weighing her options and scathing ridicule was one of them. "You think I weak am, that I do not defend my rights?" she said.

"I didn't mean that. I—"

"You think your customs better than mine are?"

"No! They're just different. I didn't mean to insult you. I just...I don't think I could share my husband with another woman he loved more than me."

Janida pursed her lips. "You think love all of one thing is," she said, "but there many ways to love are, and many ways a marriage to build."

"You all seem happy. I'm sorry I criticized you."

Janida made a dismissing gesture with one hand. "Not all principalities so fortunate are. Some torn are by jealousies and hatred. You wrong are not that it difficult is. Salveri and I love each other. Salveri and Alondra love each other. These the same are not."

She again turned that level look on Willow, who tried not to squirm. It looked as if Janida were thinking something over, so Willow stayed quiet, though it was like trying not to cry out when your hand was being crushed by some enormous weight.

Finally, Janida said, "My husband before Salveri was Serjian Lukan. He the love of my life was." She smiled, and her expression was filled with such joy that Willow couldn't breathe for a moment. "We three years together were before the accident that killed him. For a while I wished as well to die. But I had his daughter to care for, and my sisters would not let me fall into despair. I resented Salveri when he chosen was. I agreed to him, for no Prince may be chosen except all agree, but I would have resented any man who dared take my Lukan's place."

She paused for a moment, and Willow had the feeling she was offering her the chance to speak, but interrupting her seemed impossible. "It custom is that the new Prince spend a night with each of his wives, in order of seniority. That does not mean sex, always, if a wife does not choose, and I was determined him to reject. The idea of being touched by another sickened me. I junior then was, and it the fourth day was when Salveri entered my chamber. But he did not give me the opportunity to speak. He saw that I grieved and told me it was for me to decide when he might share my bed. Then he left.

"It was…astonishing. More astonishing that in the days that followed he did not court me, merely treated me with friendship and respect. I grew to admire him and eventually to feel love for him, though it the same as what I felt for my beloved Lukan is not. Now Salveri my dear friend is, and I have given him two children and take joy in them, and in him. My love for him, and his for me, a warm and wonderful thing is, but our closeness is not that of two who burn for each other."

She paused again, and this time Willow said, "So that's why you don't mind about Alondra?"

Janida shook her head. "It the whole of the story is not, Willow. Each of us loves Salveri in our own way, except for Giara who feels only indifference to him. Maitea does not have sex with him and sees him as a younger brother. Catrela a passionate woman who loves physical affection is, and she and Salveri have a very free relationship. And then there is Alondra."

"Who adores him."

"You think it disgusting is, that he loves so young a woman?"

"I didn't say that."

"You did not have to." Janida was smiling a little, though. "Alondra an accomplished artist is and well-known throughout Eskandel. Many principalities wanted her, but ours old and venerated is and we have acquired much political power. The way in which women join a harem complicated for you to understand is, but the least of it is joinings between the woman and the principality, for understanding and…compatibility to have. There many such meetings are, some formal and some not, before an offer made is. Alondra much liked from the start was, and not for her artistic talents but for her kindness and beauty of spirit.

"The night after the third joining, Salveri came to me in much distress and asked that we withdraw our offer to Alondra. He would not give a reason except that he believed her a poor match to be."

"I bet you didn't let him stop at that," Willow said.

"You very observant are. He resisted my questioning, but in the end broke down and confessed with many tears that he falling in love with Alondra was in a way he had never before experienced, as if he a youth in the throes of his first passion were. He thirty-four years her senior is and knew that he a suitable lover for a young woman was not, and could not bear the thought of imposing his feelings on her when she could not return those feelings.

"'I am old,' he said to me, 'and were I indifferent to her, we might find a common ground. But it shames me that I should feel this way, as if I taking advantage of her belonging to this principality to force myself on her were. I cannot do this thing to her.'"

The idea of Serjian Salveri, so physically imposing, displaying his weakness to anyone shifted Willow's perception of him. "So what happened?"

"It broke my heart to see my husband so in pain, and to remember that I too had once loved in this way. So I told him he should Alondra court, to show her the kind of man he is. That love need not bound by age be. I told him if he decided she would not come to him willingly, I would withdraw the offer and give my sisters a suitable lie. But it was Salveri I lied to."

Janida's smile became smug. "A woman considering a harem to join looks at its Prince in speculation, considering what union they might make. What kind of bed partner he will be. But when Alondra spoke to Salveri, she looked at him with shyness and with hope. It the look of a woman considering where she will trust her heart was. Salveri fell in love with Alondra because she first fell in love with him. It took not long for him to realize she did not see him as a…a lecherous old man who looks only at young women to recapture his lost youth, but as the man she loves, body and soul. And then there no question was that Alondra would our sister be, and Salveri's wife."

Janida put her hand over Willow's and squeezed, gently. "Every time I look at Salveri and Alondra, I remember my joy in Lukan. I love my husband. How can I not wish him the same joy?"

"I understand now," Willow said. "I'm sorry I thought so poorly of you. Of all of you."

"It is not an easy thing to understand, when one must share her heart," Janida said, and withdrew her hand. "I had in mind to offer to negotiate on your behalf with a harem. You would strong be and make a principality stronger. But I think such a sharing in your nature is not."

"It's not, but I'm honored by your offer. Besides, I'm not sure Eskandelic royalty is ready to welcome a midnighter into their ranks."

"You are more than your profession, Willow North," Janida said. "You hide by training, but you were born to lead, to stand out and draw all eyes to you."

"By heaven, I hope not!"

"It is not a joke, Willow. When you spoke to the *vojentas* they heard what I did—confidence and power and the will to show others where truth lies. If you choose not to take up that role, it will not be because you incapable of it are."

Willow gaped at her. "I think you're wrong."

"No, you *wish* me wrong to be, because you fear my words. And you should. Becoming who you are meant to be means leaving behind who you were, and that never painless is. But I think the bird never regrets learning its wings to use."

"But there's no point! Even if you're right, and I'm not agreeing that you are, who would I lead? It's not like you wake up one morning, decide you're going to be in charge, and go out and find something to be in charge of."

Janida shrugged. "If you do not take the opportunity something greater to become, you will certainly never discover the answer to that." She stood, then offered Willow her hand. "We will yet win, Willow North. Control your passions, and I think there little you cannot achieve is."

Willow clasped Janida's hand. "Thank you for having faith in me.

127

In our cause. Felix appreciates it."

"It is not Felix I concerned for am," Janida said cryptically, and then she was gone.

Willow stared at the door for a few moments, mulling over those words, then walked to her own bedchamber to undress and settle in for the night. What greater thing could she be than she already was?

Chapter Twelve

A chill wind blew the morning's overcast ahead of it as if herding dark gray sheep, and Willow wrapped her light shawl more closely around her head to keep her hair from blowing wildly with it. Almost everyone she passed on the narrow residential streets had their heads down and moved quickly, racing the storm. The dirty yellow light turned the bright doors strange colors, green becoming blue and red turning dusky orange. High above, a man opened a window and took a pot of red trumpet-flowers inside. Willow quickened her pace. If Imara wasn't at the place she'd met Pieran before, she'd have to hurry to Rafferty's and hope to find shelter there against the storm.

She casually ran her finger along the leather cord around her neck, not touching the gold pendant that hung from it. Wearing the assassin's bird of prey pendant—or, rather, the pendant of the man who'd hired him—in the hope of drawing him out was probably pointless. There had to be at least a million people in Umberan, most of whom were innocent of malice toward Felix. Still, the idea of someone lunging at her screaming about being found out amused her enough to try the experiment. And it was pretty, even if it did make her neck feel hot with burning gold.

She turned onto the street where Imara had gone to meet Pieran, sparing a thought of gratitude that Amberesh wasn't around. She hadn't sensed him at all on her journey through the city, and figured he must be at least smart enough to stay out of the weather.

Willow knocked at the blue door. No one answered. She knocked again, harder, though she had a moment's thought about how pointless it was to think a louder knock would somehow fill an empty house. The wind picked up again, blowing dust into her eyes. As she rubbed them, muttering curses under her breath, she heard the door open. She blinked away tears and saw the blond man looking at her in puzzlement. "Yes?"

"Is Imara here?"

His puzzlement deepened. "Who?"

So he was going to play that game. "Serjian Imara. Your lover?

Look, I'm not here to drag her back to the Residence. Her parents just want to know that she's safe."

"It is all right, Pieran," Imara said, emerging from behind Pieran. "Willow. Come in."

Willow entered and wiped the dust off her sandals on a mat by the door. The room was divided into two unequal sections, one of which had a couple of cupboards and a sink with a water pitcher beside it. The other was covered with floor pillows in unattractive shades of pink and green. Stairs led up to the next floor where Willow knew the bedroom was. She removed her scarf and wrapped it around one hand. "Very cozy," she said.

"We will not live here long," Imara said, rather defensively, Willow thought. "Once we are married, we will return to Gibrelt, where Pieran's family lives."

"Or I will find work at a scholia," Pieran said quickly. "It is not yet settled."

Imara hooked her arm through Pieran's and smiled at him. "So long as we are together, I do not care where we live." She looked at Willow, and her smile disappeared. "You can tell my mother that."

"I didn't tell Janida or Salveri where this place is," Willow said. "And when I go back, the only thing I'll say is that you're safe. Unless you want me to tell them something else."

"They will only make me leave, and I swore not to leave Pieran." Imara's grip on Pieran's arm grew tighter.

"They care about you. They won't—" Willow cursed. "I can't believe I'm saying this, but could you try to see it from their perspective? All they know is you've suddenly declared you're in love with someone they don't know, you haven't given them any opportunity to learn what you've been feeling and thinking, and then you ran away to heaven knows where. That's a lot to take in all at once."

"Mother knows of Pieran. We have communicated since many years ago."

"That's not the same as knowing him as your potential husband. It was clearly a surprise to her."

"They will try to talk me out of this, as if I were a child. I know what I want and I mean to have it."

"If it's truly what you want, they shouldn't be able to talk you out of it."

"I have said to Imara, we must speak to your parents," Pieran said. "I do not like this subterfuge."

"Imara, do you really want to cut off all ties to your family? To your *majdrani* and siblings? Because if you can't make this right with your parents, that's how it's going to be."

Imara's face was still set in a stubborn frown. "They will not listen."

"Then that's their problem. But I think they will, especially if you're as eloquent as everyone keeps telling me you are. I'm not saying they'll be happy about it. But they really do want *you* to be happy."

"Imara," Pieran said, "it is right." He held out his free hand to Willow. "You did not say your name."

"Oh. Willow North. I'm…" She mentally examined a dozen responses, and went with, "a friend of the Serjian family."

Imara snorted an indelicate laugh. "She and my brother are one, or should be."

"That's not important," Willow said, managing not to blush. "Can I tell Janida you will be coming back to talk? You and Pieran?"

Imara sighed. "I will consider it."

"We will come," Pieran said. "And thank you."

"Will you—I am sorry, I should have offered you refreshment," Imara said.

"That's all right. If I hurry, I can get back to the Residence before the rain comes." Willow shook Pieran's hand, nodded to Imara, and let herself out.

The streets were packed with hurrying people, silvery streaks of belt knives jostling with the brass studs of dog collars and fizzing silver and itching copper bouncing along in pouches at nearly every waist. Willow bumped into someone and apologized. The person shrugged and hurried away. She discreetly checked her purses, both the obvious one and the hidden one, accidentally touched the pendant and swore as her fingers burned. The pendant was becoming uncomfortable. Maybe she shouldn't have been so cavalier about wearing it.

She cut across to a side street that wasn't nearly so busy. Arched doorways led to quiet courtyards, most of them empty of anything except the occasional bench or fountain. The sound of running water was drowned out by the rising wind, which gusted and then died away briefly before rising once more. Willow wrapped her scarf across her face to keep out the dust carried by the wind. When the rains came, they'd be falling nearly horizontally if the winds stayed this strong.

Something struck her hard across the back of her head, sending black and yellow lights flashing before her eyes. A hand covered her mouth, pressing the scarf firmly against her lips. Dizzy, she staggered, and an arm snaked around her waist and half dragged, half carried her through one of the arches into a courtyard and flung her to the ground. She caught herself with both hands, scraping her palms on the rough stone of the courtyard, and struggled not to throw up from the pain in her head.

"Now we see you, you are not strong," Amberesh said in a voice barely loud enough to hear over the rising storm. Willow cried out as he kicked her hard in the stomach. She rolled away from him, fetching up against a marble fountain. "I strong am."

Willow managed to stagger to her feet just as Amberesh aimed another kick at her stomach, and he caught her shin instead. She groped for the fountain and put it between them. Why hadn't she sensed him? Her addled brain fought for control. *Use your eyes, damn it.* He wore no sword, and his shirt fit him closely—no room for a mail shirt underneath. "Lose your sword, Amberesh?" she said.

Amberesh's face became furious. "I to eat must sell," he shouted. "You do this to I. You I make suffer." Then his eyes widened. "*You* to steal it?" he said.

"Steal your sword? You're out of your mind."

Amberesh pointed at her throat. "He say, lost is." He burst out laughing. "He not to say, is steal is. He...*embarrassed* is, a woman to steal is."

So the ploy actually worked. Too bad I might not be around to appreciate it. Willow risked a quick look around. The courtyard was mostly concealed from the street, which wasn't very busy. Screaming would be pointless. And Amberesh was drawing a wicked-looking long knife

132

from his belt. Willow let her forearm blade fall into her hand. "A friend of yours?" she said, taking a few steps to the right. "Son of a principality, is he?"

Amberesh mirrored her, a cruel smile on his face. "I take it him to give, when you dead are."

"You're awfully cocky about that."

"I fight good. You woman are, fight bad."

"You are going to get a nasty surprise, Amberesh."

He was between her and the street. She just had to get past him…he outweighed her, his knife was longer by a few inches, and he'd no doubt had the same martial training Kerish had, which meant Willow and her street fighting skills were probably outclassed. She had to get away, and quickly. She might be able to hold him off for a few exchanges of blows, but too long a fight would mean her death.

She took another step, away from the shelter of the fountain, and Amberesh lunged at her. She brought her knife up to deflect the blow and snatched her belt knife out of its sheath, brought it around and had it deflected in turn. It was shorter than her other blade, but she was grateful for any advantage, two blades to his one. She struck at Amberesh's chest, then had to leap backward to avoid his hand, groping for her shoulder to bring her in close for the kill.

"Women dance," Amberesh said with a nasty grin, and thrust for her stomach. She brought both her knives down to catch the blade and was forced back again. She had no idea what was behind her and prayed she wouldn't trip.

Amberesh lunged again, and she tried to block his strike. She felt a sharp, burning pain as he feinted left and scored a deep line across her left arm. She cried out, and his grin broadened. "Hurt you first," he said, "hurt you much."

"Big talk," Willow gasped, and swung at his face, too wildly, because he dodged easily out of the way without giving up any ground. Willow darted to the left, putting the fountain between them again. It was about four and a half feet tall, scant cover, but her heart was racing and she would take whatever shelter it offered.

"Taking your revenge on a woman?" she continued. "Very noble of you. Very brave. Do you think if you drag my body back to your family, they'll be grateful? Or will they just spurn you again for a coward?"

Amberesh roared and ran at her, leaving himself open, but Willow wasn't interested in continuing the fight. She darted around the fountain and made for the street, then screamed as pain lanced up her left leg and it buckled under her. She fell, rolled again, and landed in a one-legged crouch with both her knives held before her. Amberesh's knife was dark with blood. Her blood. He came toward her slowly, no longer grinning.

"I not you care for family," he said, "I not you be Serjian."

"That makes no sense," Willow said. "You should work on your language skills."

Amberesh roared and thrust for her throat. Desperate, Willow brought both knives in front of her, blades crossed, and caught Amberesh's knife between them. It kept driving toward her, and in desperation she twisted, forcing the knife to the right so it plunged deep into her shoulder instead of her neck and threw him off balance.

As his weight bore down toward her, she disengaged with her left hand and brought her forearm blade around in a sweeping arc aimed at his throat.

The knife sang through the air and kept going, tearing through Amberesh's throat and sending a gout of blood spraying across Willow's face and chest.

She just had time to register the look of stunned horror on Amberesh's face before his falling body knocked her over, crushing her bad leg under her. She cried out again, and then thunder crashed, and rain began falling as if heaven itself wept over the fallen man. *Why would it bother with a waste of air like Amberesh?* Willow thought crazily.

Then the full meaning of what she'd done struck her, and panic set in. She shoved Amberesh's body until she was free, then pushed herself up. Amberesh stared up at her with wide, uncomprehending eyes. She was covered in his blood. She had to get help—but for whom? Amberesh was beyond helping, and she...

She limped to the edge of the courtyard and had to grab onto a skinny pillar for support. Her leg was a long streak of agony, as bloody as the rest of her, and her shoulder throbbed with alternating fire and ice. "Help," she said, cleared her throat, and yelled, "Help!"

No one answered. Rain pounded the pavement, soaking her and making Amberesh's blood, and her own blood, stream off her in pinkish trails. She staggered a few more steps, then collapsed. What was she going to tell Catrela? How could she possibly explain herself to the Serjian Principality?

Harder, louder rainfall nearby turned into running footsteps. Someone gabbled at her in Eskandelic. She raised her head and saw a man holding a thick scarf over his head. It wasn't doing him much good, because it was saturated with rain and dripping onto his enormous nose. He said something else. *"I don't speak Eskandelic,"* Willow said. The man touched her bloody shirt, then looked past her at the courtyard. He cursed, loudly, then released Willow and ran away, shouting.

Willow knelt on the pavement and tried to control her rapid breathing. Someone would come. Someone would figure all of this out. She knew she wasn't thinking clearly, that she should at least get out of the rain, but moving seemed beyond her.

More footsteps. Then someone grabbed her and dragged her to her feet, shouting in Eskandelic. Willow looked at him, feeling too dull to respond even if she knew the language. This man was taller than the first, broad in the shoulders, with longish black hair under a white headwrap gone dark with rain. He wore a sleeveless green tunic whose cheap dye ran in the rain and, strangely, boots instead of sandals.

"You? Who do this?" he shouted in Tremontanese. "You?"

"I killed him," Willow said. "He was trying to kill me, and it was all I could think to do."

The man wasn't listening. With one hand he forced open her left hand, which was still clutching her knife, making it clatter to the pavement. With the other he spun her around and kicked the back of her knee, making her collapse again with a cry of pain as she landed hard on the leg Amberesh had knifed. Then he wrenched her hands behind her back, securing them with ice so cold she let out another short scream. Iron manacles. She ground her teeth against the freezing pain.

The man started speaking in Eskandelic, something long and fluid that harmonized with the falling rain. Then he said, "To stand now," and hauled upward on her bound arms, sending agony lancing through her wounded shoulder. She stumbled, managed to catch herself, then stood, leaning heavily on her good leg.

More people dressed in the same cheap green tunics arrived, and a few of them worked together to carry Amberesh out of the courtyard. Someone else collected the three knives. The man prodded Willow in the small of her back. "To walk," he said, and Willow limped away, her mind numb with so many kinds of pain.

The rain let up as abruptly as it had begun, and the wind picked up again, chilling Willow in her wet, blood-drenched clothes. She limped in the direction the man kept prodding her, though she could just as easily have followed the others with their gruesome burden. Probably he just enjoyed prodding prisoners.

Prisoner. She was a prisoner.

Panic swept away the fog she'd been moving in since Amberesh— She stopped, turned around, and said, "You have to send word to the Serjian Principality."

"To walk," the man said. He had a knife in his hand, about twelve inches long, and he poked her lightly with it.

"No, this is a mistake," Willow said. "Serjian Principality. They'll tell you I'm—" She stopped. What *would* they tell the guards? No one knew Amberesh had been following her. No one knew he'd threatened her life, or that she'd killed him in self-defense. No, what this looked like was the killing of a son of one of the most powerful principalities in Eskandel by a foreign woman, and Willow was in serious trouble.

The man brought his blade up to point at Willow's chest. "To walk," he said, in a more menacing tone. Willow turned around and walked.

They passed through the center of Umberan, drawing all sorts of attention. Willow didn't meet anyone's eyes. There wasn't any point. None of them could help her. Or could they? "Someone tell the Serjian Principality to come to the—where are you taking me?" she said over her shoulder. The man was silent. "Are you taking me to prison?"

"To walk," the man said. "Is to talk not." Willow felt the cold silvery streak of his knife press against the side of her throat. Willow shut up.

The street they ended up on was broad enough for three ox carts to pass side by side without brushing one another, paved with those same large round-edged bricks that were outside the Serjian Residence's neighborhood. It was lined with buildings like piles of cubical blocks, faced with marble and decorated with enough gold to make Willow's skin burn. In Aurilien that gold would have been picked clean by scavengers ten minutes after construction was completed. The men carrying Amberesh's body went around the side of one of these buildings, but Willow's captor prodded her in a different direction.

They walked down a short flight of stairs and into a low-ceilinged corridor of rough granite lit by smelly lanterns behind green-tinted glass. The corridor continued for more paces than Willow could keep count of. Her head hurt, her shoulder throbbed, and her injured leg had gone numb half a mile back. Just as she realized the corridor sloped gently downward, her guard grabbed her bound wrists and brought her to an abrupt halt. Willow blinked, and saw there was a door in the wall beside her, almost invisible, its lock plate rusted iron.

The guard sheathed his knife, then yanked the pendant off over Willow's head, followed by her neck pouch. When she protested, he slapped her hard across the face. He next took her belt pouch, then patted her all over, briskly, with no sign that he enjoyed it. "You have to tell the Serjian Principality," she said. "Tell them what happened. They'll make you let me go. Serjian Principality!"

The guard shrugged and spun her around. A lock clicked, and the freezing manacles were gone. Willow rubbed her wrists vigorously. "Tell them—"

"To inside go," the guard said. He brought out a giant iron key and inserted it into the lock, and the barely visible door swung open, revealing darkness. The guard shoved Willow, who stumbled through the doorway and fell to her knees. She scrambled around, but it was too late. The door shut, and she was alone in the dark.

Part Five

Chapter Thirteen

She lay in the darkness, breathing in the smell of stale piss and wet stone. Her injured leg throbbed a counterpoint to her shoulder, which burned alternately hot and cold. She shifted her weight, hissed involuntarily at the pain that shot through her body, and lay still again. With her cheek pressed against the rough stone floor, she should have been at eye level with the crack under the door, but there was no light, no breath of cooler air. The cell was hot enough she felt she was being broiled alive. Drops of sweat rolled off her forehead and prickled under her arms. She closed her eyes. It wasn't as if she needed them.

Grunting with pain, she got her good arm under her and pushed herself to a sitting position, then had to lean against the invisible wall until the dizziness passed. It was no cooler sitting up, though she thought she felt a draft of warm air from above. Possibly they didn't want prisoners dying in here before they could be properly executed.

The stone walls absorbed the sound of her labored breathing. She heard nothing else, no passing footsteps or screams of agony. The silence was more frightening than either of those things would have been. She rubbed her fingers against the damp stone of the wall. Its grittiness reminded her of a room she'd once rented, though that had had plaster walls rather than stone, but both had a texture that rubbed off on her fingers and smelled sour, like boiled cabbage. Her stomach tried to growl at the idea of food, but she hurt too badly to feel hunger.

She tried to stand, but her leg wouldn't support her. It felt slick with blood when she gingerly touched it, and the long cut burned when she moved. She reached across with her good arm and tugged at the seam of her sleeve, tears of pain trickling down her face as she jogged the painful wound in her shoulder. The stitching was finely done, and she cursed whoever had made the shirt so well. Her Tremontanan clothes would have come apart with practically no effort. She tugged harder, ignoring the pain.

138

Finally, she heard a couple of threads tear, and wormed one finger into the hole to widen it. More threads parted, then, with a ripping sound, the sleeve came loose from the shirt. Carefully she worked it off her arm, then used it to bind her leg. It felt marginally better when she was done, and she wished she had some way to bandage her shoulder, but it was throbbing now thanks to her exertions and she didn't want to make it worse.

She got on her hands and knees and made a crawling circuit of the room, one hand occasionally brushing the wall to orient herself. She felt no metal other than the hinges and lock plates of this and the neighboring cells, and it made her feel blinder than the darkness did. Feeling out the dimensions of the cell wouldn't help, but she felt desperation whimpering at her like an injured dog, growing more insistent with every moment. Movement let her tell herself she was doing *something*.

After a few halting steps, her hand came down in a puddle, splashing up a nose-clenching whiff of ammonia. She shook her hand to rid herself of the piss, then wiped it on her trousers and clenched her back teeth together to keep from vomiting. That probably wouldn't make the cell smell worse, but it felt like defiance, like proving to her captors that Willow North couldn't be defeated so easily.

She kept going, not sure what she was trying to achieve—it wasn't as if she could get out of this place—and realized she'd circled the little room twice just as her shaking arms threatened to give out. She sat back against the wall again and tried to calm her breathing. Her shirt clung to the wound in her shoulder. She thought the bleeding might have stopped, but she was afraid to touch it in case she made it start bleeding again. Her ears rang with a faint, high whistle she could hear even over her breathing, the sound that comes just before unconsciousness. She lay down on the stinking floor, feeling around first for more puddles, and closed her eyes again. This wasn't defeat. It was a temporary setback, nothing she couldn't handle.

She fell into a waking stupor, unable to sleep for the pain of her wounds, but too exhausted from the fight and the heat to stay fully conscious. Someone would come for her eventually, and she would make that person send to the Serjian Principality. *If they even care. You killed Amberesh, you ruined Gessala's life, you were complicit in Imara's flight...they might just let you rot here.*

"You stupid chit," Nan said. "Get up and stop lazing!"

"Yes, Nan," Willow said.

Nan was hazy in her vision, bending over Willow and shaking a fist in her face. "You think that's clean enough? I said scrub it, not give it a swipe and a promise!"

Willow felt a twinge in her shoulder as Nan struck her with her cane. "Just like your father, you are. Never saw a bottle he didn't like the bottom of. You're going to be just like him."

"Shut up, Nan, you're dead," Willow whispered. Nan struck her again, but it was a phantom blow, and Willow closed her eyes against the vision.

Others came to her, one at a time, Rufus and Albie and Marion and dozens of other friends from Lower Town, most of them saying things that in her brief moments of lucidity made no sense. Gnawing aches in her belly told her she was hungry, that time really was passing somewhere outside the cell, but soon they vanished along with the nagging pain in her leg and shoulder. Far away in her mind, a tiny voice shrieked that she was becoming dangerously dehydrated, that blood loss, heat, and hunger were weakening her, but it was an easy voice to ignore, stupid and ineffective and completely unable to do anything to help her situation.

She waited for Kerish to come, if only because he was going to say 'I told you so.' Everything he'd ever warned her about, all his fears she'd scoffed at, and now they'd come true. "They don't lock you up, they cut off your hand," she protested, but Kerish was gone and he was never coming back, because he was a Serjian and all the Serjians hated her for killing Amberesh.

The thought made her heart ache worse than her shoulder, and she sobbed, wishing Kerish were there so she could apologize for caring more about midnighting than she had about him. And now it didn't matter anymore. She ran out of tears before she was done crying, and sat with her forehead against the wall, heaving great dry-eyed sobs until she drifted back into befuddled hallucinations.

She was talking to her childhood friend Amaris about some game they'd both loved when Amaris cut off mid-word and vanished. Half a breath later, the door ground open, stone on stone, and Willow covered her eyes against the horrible glare of the lantern-lit hallway. A man in a green tunic shouted at her in Eskandelic. *"Do you speak Tremontanese?"* she choked out, then fell into a coughing fit because her throat and tongue were too dry to make her words heard.

"Out," the man shouted. Willow tried to stand. Her arms and legs shook so badly she could barely get to her knees. The man cursed and came into the cell, grabbed her bad arm and hauled her up. Willow screamed, a weak, thready sound that went nowhere. The man slung her up against the wall and took a close look at her shoulder. He muttered something in Eskandelic, then said, "Come," and put his hand under her other arm, not as harshly. Willow blinked away tears of pain and hobbled along with him.

The green-glass lanterns of the corridor, still stinking of the sour-fish odor of whatever fueled them, made the guard look corpselike. Willow didn't want to know what they turned her into. The walls looked dull, as if they'd been painted over by something that absorbed the light rather than reflecting it with the myriad glints of specks within the granite. The cell doors all fitted the walls so closely she wouldn't have known they were there if she hadn't sensed their hinges and locks. No wonder she hadn't heard any screams. She shuddered despite the heat.

At the end of the corridor was a heavy door, black with age, banded with dark iron. Beyond she sensed more doors, set closer together and more numerous, with brass knobs and locks rather than freezing iron. Not cells, then. Willow was so grateful she hardly minded when the guard slapped another pair of iron manacles on her, though this time her arms were bound in front. The freezing chill was almost welcome after the stifling heat of the cell.

The guard unlocked the door and shoved Willow through. She stumbled, caught herself on the wall, and staggered forward into another corridor. This one was lit by clear white Devices, but was as narrow as the first. Willow counted hinges: ten doors along this corridor, plus another one at the far end. "Where are you taking me?" she said, enunciating clearly.

The guard just prodded her again. She walked down the hall, assessing each room: silvery steel knives, some silver or bronze or gold jewelry, assorted metal objects she didn't have names for. Occasional fragments of conversations came to her ears, muffled enough that she couldn't tell what language they were in. She was lightheaded enough that the sounds filled her with elation, this simple evidence that she wasn't alone in the prison.

She was so preoccupied with counting someone's belt purse—fifteen *ryad*, seven *obat*, two *galt*—that she hardly noticed when the guard unlocked the door at the end of the corridor and marched her inside.

The windowless room, dimly lit by Devices instead of smelly lanterns, was cool by comparison to the hallways and downright chilly after the heat of her cell. The low ceiling, and the lack of light, made it feel like a cave someone had set up home in—a rough, unpleasant home. Benches lined the walls adjacent to a pair of iron-bound doors that looked capable of stopping a riot. A few men and one woman sat there, their hands manacled as Willow's were. A couple of men in green tunics stood near each prisoner, their hands placed loosely on their knife hilts. They eyed Willow as if thinking about how they'd stop her if she tried to escape.

A tall desk roughly knocked together out of unfinished wood, the least elegant thing Willow had ever seen in Eskandel, stood opposite the doors. It was chest-high to Willow and was paired with an equally tall stool on which another guard sat. He was fatter than the others and his face shone with sweat. He alone didn't look at Willow when she entered. His attention was all on the man standing in front of him.

Kerish.

Kerish turned toward her when the door opened, and a look of such terrible fury crossed his face that Willow felt lightheaded again. She'd never seen him look that angry and she'd never dreamed he'd turn such a look on her. Tears prickled her eyes again, but she blinked them away. Crying wouldn't change anything. Though his being here made no sense. If the Serjians wanted her punished for killing Amberesh, they'd just leave her there—unless they wanted to carry out that punishment personally, which Willow could see Janida doing—

Kerish began speaking in Eskandelic in a low, level tone that promised violence was an option. The man at the desk tried to reply and Kerish cut him off without raising his voice. Then he gestured and spat out a few more words. The man looked at Willow's guard and motioned with his hands. Willow sighed as the manacles were removed. The relief from freezing pain was almost enough to ease her battered heart.

Kerish began speaking again, still in that level tone. Willow caught only "Serjian". The man's face turned dark red, and he began nodding. Then he got off his stool and bowed low, one of the most servile gestures Willow had ever seen, and she'd seen people grovel before Ascendants. Kerish ignored him. "Come with me," he said to Willow.

"Wait," Willow said. Her voice was hoarse and she had to clear her throat to continue. "They took my things—my—" She stopped before mentioning her knives. She didn't want to remind him about Amberesh at all.

Kerish turned to the man and said something that ended in a question. The man glanced at Willow, shrugged, and said a few words. To Willow's shock, Kerish grabbed the front of the man's ugly tunic and shoved him against the wall, shouting. Terrified, the man gabbled something, and Willow's guard left the room at a run, disappearing through the door they'd entered by.

Kerish released the man with an oath and turned away from Willow, clenching and opening his fist the way he did when he was under extreme stress. Willow felt her leg beginning to shake. Another few minutes, and she was going to collapse. She limped over to one of the benches and sat, not caring how it looked.

"Are you badly wounded?" Kerish said.

Willow shrugged. Speaking was just too difficult.

Kerish turned away again. Willow tried not to care. She focused on planning her next move. Janida wouldn't kick Felix out just because she wanted Willow punished, but she surely wasn't going to give him her support anymore. Willow would have to contact Rafferty and see if he could take Felix. It wasn't as good a disappearing act as she'd intended to pull, but Rafferty could protect him—no, this was all wrong. Damn it, she'd been *defending* herself! Janida had to see that.

She'd show Janida the truth, and then she and Felix would leave the Residence and—

The guard burst into the room, carrying her things. *All* her things, including her knives, minus a few Eskandelic coins. She accepted them from the guard and stood holding them, dully incapable of figuring out what to do next. Kerish said, "Is that everything?"

She chose not to make a fuss over the missing coin. "Yes."

Kerish said something that by the tone of it was scathing, then said, "Let's go," and held one of the double doors for her. It opened on a stairwell that ascended into a bright Umberan morning, the sun a few inches over the horizon and the sky a cloudless blue that would be sweltering in a few hours.

They were still on the street with all the buildings that looked like piles of cubical blocks, as if anyone might swoop down and rearrange them into nicer shapes. Willow felt she'd never appreciated the sky before now. She stood and stared up at it, watching a couple of seabirds wheel and dance, white against blue, until Kerish said, "Willow." Then she drew in a deep breath of untainted air and followed him.

One of the Serjian carriages stood waiting at the side of the street. To her fuddled brain, it looked taller than she remembered, the short steps too high off the ground. She half-lifted one foot, wobbled, and put it down again. Her hands were full. She needed her hands to balance. She looked from the things in her hands to the carriage and back again. She couldn't think what to do next.

"Give me that," Kerish said, and removed the little pile from her hands. He made no other move to help her, which stabbed at her heart—he was too angry to bear to touch her?—so she took hold of the side of the carriage and managed to crawl into it, collapsing on the pearl-studded satin without caring that she'd probably ruin it. It was soft, and warm from the sun's rays, and she closed her eyes, pretending everything was all right. She heard a couple of thumps as Kerish dropped her things on the floor of the carriage. He spoke to the driver briefly and the carriage jolted into motion, jostling her shoulder and making her wince.

She opened her eyes, daring to look at him. His lips were set in a tight line, and his eyes looked everywhere but at her. "Are we going to the Residence?" she croaked.

"We're going to the scholia for healing," Kerish said.

They both fell silent. Willow struggled to find something to say, but she didn't want to talk about Amberesh and she *really* didn't want Kerish to yell at her. "Is…Felix all right?"

"He's fine. I didn't tell him where you were. No sense frightening him."

More silence. "I guess that makes sense."

Kerish finally looked at her. "Nothing about this makes sense," he said.

The carriage turned in at the scholia drive, but instead of following the familiar path to the Devisers' building, it turned right when they emerged from the hedges onto the lawn and followed the flowering wall around to a smaller, domed round building. Pillars supported a wide verandah that looked as if it would be shady at all hours. Men and women in brightly colored robes sat on benches beneath it, talking quietly or playing some kind of game with blue and white boxes. They looked curiously at the Serjian carriage and openly stared at Willow. She had no idea if they were astonished at her nationality or her battered condition. She must look terrible and probably smelled worse.

Kerish stepped down from the carriage, then to Willow's surprise offered her his hand to help her descend. His touch was so gentle it brought tears to her eyes, which she blinked fiercely away. She had no desire to let him know how miserable she was. As soon as both her feet were on the ground, he released her, abruptly, and walked toward the building, fast enough that she had trouble following him on her bad leg. The ache in her shoulder had swelled to fill all of her. Why had Janida sent him, of all people? She'd almost rather have been left to rot than endure his anger and scorn.

The door was a single sheet of glass set in an iron frame. Willow had never seen anything like it. Weren't they afraid of someone breaking it? It was so impractical, and so beautiful. How very Eskandelic.

The door opened not on a hallway or entry chamber, but on a large room, curved in a way that suggested the entire building was one room, bisected by a single straight wall. Light filled the room from large windows near the base of the domed ceiling, making the white walls glow as if lit from within. Light Devices hung from the ceiling on long chains and trembled in the movement of air imperceptible to Willow. Multicolored low sofas scattered throughout the room gave the impression that it was ready to host a party, but it was so still, so silent, it was hard to imagine anyone being willing to speak at more than a whisper. Willow felt suddenly exhausted and eager to lie down on one of those beautiful sofas and just sleep for a thousand years.

An elegant rosewood desk, its front panel carved into an asymmetrical lattice, took up most of the straight wall, and a man and a woman sat behind it. Both wore sleeveless shirts with deep V-necks, as white as the walls, and they both looked so incredibly clean Willow felt embarrassed to be there.

Kerish spoke. The woman replied, looking at Willow, then said something else that sounded apologetic. Kerish glanced at Willow, then shook his head and pointed at her shoulder. The man came around from behind the desk and plucked at the bloodstained shirt, pulling it away from the wound. Willow hissed in pain. The man said something to his companion, then patted Willow on her unwounded shoulder and gestured to her to follow him. Willow looked at Kerish for guidance, but he'd taken a seat on one of the sofas and didn't even look up. She swallowed, trying to moisten her painfully dry throat, and followed the man through a white-painted door into the next room.

Cascades of gauzy curtains filled the space, reminding Willow of the Review and its little cubicles of fabric. Sunlight from more windows near the ceiling filtered through the curtains, filling the room with a diffuse, comforting light. The man led Willow through a corridor formed by the curtains, past cloth-bounded spaces occupied by sleeping men and women. More people dressed in the same clothing her guide wore stood near their patients, apparently doing nothing. Willow had never been healed by magic before, never seen it done, and had no idea what it looked like. For all she knew the healers were performing miracles under her ignorant eye.

The man stopped and parted a curtain, indicating that Willow should enter ahead of him. The little room shrouded in white contained nothing but a low cabinet with two doors and a narrow bench. It was curved in a stretched-out S-shape, like a frozen wave, so anyone lying on it would have their head higher than their feet. It was padded lightly, the cushions the same white as the curtains, and Willow thought about her filthy, bloody clothes and hesitated when the man indicated she should lie down. The man gave her a little push and pointed at it, so she sat on the lower end, trying to keep as much of herself from touching it as possible. The man shrugged. Then he took hold of the hem of her shirt and began to pull it up over her head.

Willow squeaked and batted at his hand, then crossed her arms tightly over her breasts and shook her head vigorously. The man said something she guessed translated as "don't be so stubborn." She just shook her head harder. The last thing she needed, after her ordeal, was some strange man seeing her naked. The man shrugged again, then pushed aside the curtain and left.

Willow sat there feeling stupid. He probably did this all the time. How did she expect him to care for her injuries if she wouldn't even let him look at them? Eskandelics were casual about nudity, if the Review was anything to go by. But she was Tremontanan and she had limits.

Eventually the woman from the desk came through the curtain. She said something that sounded like a question, pointing to herself. Willow hesitated only a moment, then tried to pull her ruined shirt off over her head. Sharp agony stabbed through her shoulder, and lights danced before her eyes. She lowered her right arm, breathing heavily and trying not to faint.

The woman laid a gentle hand on her uninjured shoulder and shook her head. She brought the largest pair of scissors Willow had ever seen out of the cupboard. Willow held very still as she cut through the shoulder seam of Willow's ruined shirt, then cut the other shoulder and down the sleeve so the shirt fell apart around her waist, the front sticking to the gory wound. The woman gently peeled it away while Willow clenched her teeth against the pain, though it wasn't as bad as before.

The woman then indicated she should take off her trousers, and Willow did so, praying she wouldn't ask for her to take off her undershorts as well. The little room felt private, the curtains were heavy and thick, but there were no doors with sturdy locks and Willow was conscious of all the other people wandering around the building. Then she felt ashamed. Here these people were helping her and all she could think about was being naked in front of strangers. What mattered more, her modesty or her health?

The woman seemed satisfied with Willow's state of undress. She indicated with gestures that Willow should lie down on the bench, so Willow lay back with her arms to her sides and tried to relax. It was surprisingly comfortable, and she didn't feel cold despite her nakedness. Such a difference from seeing Kerish stitched up by that physicker outside Perelton, all those weeks ago.

The woman examined her shoulder with her eyes and her fingers, and it hurt, but not as much as it probably could have. She lifted Willow's leg and unwrapped the makeshift bandage to examine the wound on her calf. It hurt more than the shoulder. Willow stared at the ceiling, which seemed to shift thanks to the soft movement of the curtains. Eskandelics were fond of domes. Here, the Jauderish, that building where she'd met with the *vojentas*, all domed. Even the harem's meeting room in the Residence had a dome. They made all those places seem more spacious. Why didn't they have more domes in Aurilien? She was halfway to thinking about whether Felix might construct a new building in Aurilien with a domed roof when she drifted peacefully off to sleep.

She woke as slowly as she'd fallen asleep, happily rising up from a deep rest back into a body that felt no pain anywhere. Even the slight tenderness of her sunburned face was gone. She was still mostly naked, but she was alone on her bench and heard no speech anywhere nearby. The silence of the room was unnerving.

She sat up, crossing her arms across her breasts, and looked around. The little cubicle was empty of anyone but herself. Soft light filtered through the curtains, not enough to make them transparent, not enough to cast more than the faintest of shadows. A faint floral scent drifted through the air, almost too faint to be noticeable. She could sense bits of metal nearby, odd shapes of silvery steel she couldn't identify, plus a few straight, thin objects she thought were skinny knives. Surgical implements? Would healers even have a need for those? More distantly, she sensed a larger knife, someone's belt knife, possibly Kerish's, and a curved sword. She hadn't realized he was armed until now.

The curtains shifted, and the woman appeared. She smiled at Willow and said something in a friendly voice, held up a finger in a "wait there" motion, and left. Willow waited. It wasn't as if she had any other options. The room was comfortably warm, but there was a draft from somewhere that made her feel a little chilly. And now that she wasn't in pain anymore, she was conscious of how filthy she was, her hair matted with dried sweat, traces of blood—not as much as she'd expected—on her chest.

She looked down at her shoulder and saw, not a bloody mess, but a coin-sized scar, white and raised against her pale skin. She prodded it; no pain. It was almost miraculous. She twisted her leg around and saw her calf was uninjured—looked as if it had never been injured. Why had it healed cleanly when her shoulder hadn't? Something to ask the healer, if she'd been capable of speaking Eskandelic. She was too grateful to make an issue of it. Maybe Kerish would know, since he'd received healing here too.

Thinking of Kerish brought the heartache back. Well, the Serjian Principality couldn't want her dead if it was willing to have someone heal her, right? Which meant they had something else in mind. Like rejecting her and Felix. She breathed in deeply, let out the breath slowly. Clothes, and then she could face Janida. She hoped the healer woman was bringing her clothes.

On that thought, the curtains parted again, and the woman returned with a pile of fabric. It turned out to be a sleeveless tunic like the one the woman wore, only dark yellow instead of white, and a pair of black cotton trousers. Willow dressed quickly while the woman waited, tactfully turning her back. Strange, considering she'd already seen almost all of Willow during the healing, but Willow took it as a kindness, deference to the foreigner's strange customs.

When Willow was fully dressed, the woman held the curtain for her and led the way back to the front room, where Kerish waited. He was sitting in his accustomed pose, his elbows on his knees and his head bowed, and Willow was struck so hard by longing she had to remind herself to breathe.

He raised his head when they entered, then stood and said something questioning to the woman, who replied with a nod. "*Thank you*," he said in Eskandelic, then to Willow, "Let's go."

Chapter Fourteen

In the carriage, seated across from her, Kerish said, "I had to use your money to pay. I didn't bring enough."

"It's my healing. I think that's fair," Willow said.

Kerish nodded. His mouth was set in that straight, hard line again, and it made Willow's heart hurt more. "I'm sorry," she blurted out.

"Sorry for what?"

"For everything. For killing Amberesh. I swear I didn't mean to, Kerish, but he was trying—I know you're angry with me—"

Kerish's eyes widened. "I'm not angry with you."

"You certainly look like you are." To her horror, her voice trembled.

In one swift movement, Kerish was beside her. "Willow," he said. His arms encircled her, and it was so comforting, so familiar, that her eyes burned again. She clutched the front of his shirt and buried her face against his chest, and felt him stroke her hair.

"You looked so angry," she murmured.

"Of course I was angry. I was furious. It took them the whole damn day to bother sending word to us that you'd been arrested. Amberesh dead, you gone missing, and when we found out you'd actually told them to tell someone—" His arms tightened around her. "The guard didn't come until just after breakfast, when we were preparing to send out search parties. He's lucky Mother was there, because I'm sure he was just a poor grunt who didn't deserve what I intended to do to him. His boss wasn't so lucky."

"Thank you for coming for me."

"As if anything on earth could have stopped me. Oh, Willow, *khaladesi*, forgive my slowness."

Khaladesi. Beloved.

"It's not your fault," she murmured. "I killed Amberesh. You should hate me."

"Never." He brushed a kiss across her forehead that made her tingle all over. "I know whatever you did was in self-defense. It's true, he was my *fuoreno*, but if I had to choose between you, I would pick you every time. If he'd killed you…"

"He nearly did. I was lucky."

Kerish's arms tightened on her again, almost painfully, but being held by him was so blissful she didn't care. She put her arms around his waist and closed her eyes, breathing in the cinnamon and cloves smell of him and trying not to remember the awful cell.

He stroked her hair again, so gently. "After last night—after this morning—I realized you still hold my heart in your hands. I love you. I have never stopped loving you. Just…let me hold you, please, if only for a little while."

His quiet voice, his gentle hands, brought back everything she'd felt in that long, dark night. "I love you," she whispered, and felt his hand still against her hair, heard him take in a quick breath. "Kerish, I love you."

She felt him kiss the top of her head, and it sent another tingle through her. "I hoped," he said. "Sometimes, the way you looked at me…it was as if all those years had never happened."

"All those years. I never stopped loving you, either. I tried to forget—did forget, for a long time—but there was always a part of me that knew the truth."

"There hasn't been a single day since we parted that I haven't thought of you. I was angry with you for so long, and then I was angry with myself, but I couldn't have felt that way if I didn't love you more than my own life." His hand trailed down to caress her neck, sending shivers up and down her spine.

"I'm sorry I wasn't willing to change. I was afraid—I didn't know what I wanted—"

"I don't care about any of that now. I just don't want to be without you any longer. Even if it's only until the end of Conclave or until the end of this drive, I'm yours."

Willow's heart was pounding so hard she was sure he could feel it. "Even if nothing's changed?"

"Don't you think it has? We chose our own paths once, and I've been miserable without you for five years. I think it's time for a different choice." He drew back to look at her. "I know I can't go back to being a dowser, so maybe it means nothing when I say I'd give it up for you, but the truth is I would give up *Devisery* to have you. And I wouldn't regret it for one moment."

She couldn't look away from his eyes. "Kerish," she said, and then she threw her arms around his neck and kissed him, felt him return her kiss.

She barely noticed when the carriage stopped. It felt wonderful, kissing him, touching his back and his shoulders and his face, feeling his strong arms embracing her. The scent of him filled her, wonderful and spicy, taking her back to the night they'd first met, that first kiss that had changed her life forever. Then it made her realize how awful she must smell. She pulled back, reluctantly, and Kerish kissed her forehead and wiped away a tear she didn't remember shedding.

"I'm giving it up," she said. "No more midnighting, I swear it. I couldn't stop thinking of you while I was in there, that it was your worst nightmare—"

"My worst nightmare was last night, when you didn't come home," Kerish said grimly. "It was what I always feared, that you'd disappear and I'd never find out what happened to you. Seeing you come out of the jail looking like that was maybe third or fourth on the list."

"It doesn't matter. You were right. I don't have to be a thief to survive. I should never have put what mattered to you second. And I wish to heaven I'd realized that five years ago."

Kerish drew her close once more. "I think, five years ago, you weren't the sort of person who could realize it, any more than I could see beyond the needs of my magic. You're sure you're not going to end up resenting me for it?"

"No. Never. I love you too much."

"I love hearing you say those words," Kerish said, and kissed her again.

The courtyard door opened, and Willow broke away from Kerish quickly. She felt shy, as if she'd been caught doing something wrong. Then anger filled her. She'd longed for him all these years, throughout this whole journey, and she was going to let embarrassment interfere with that? She looked at him, a little afraid of what she might see—had she offended him, pulling away so abruptly? But no, he was smiling at her, that wonderful smile that said he loved her more than anything, and she smiled back and took his hand. *I can endure whatever the Serjians throw at me.*

"Inside," Janida said. "We have much to discuss."

***

Janida walked rapidly, her bare feet slapping the stone of the corridor, and Willow and Kerish had to hurry to keep up with her. Willow put together a dozen openings and discarded all of them. Better to let Janida speak first, probably. If she was going to tear Willow apart, there wasn't much Willow could say in her own defense.

Janida led them through the house to a room filled with low-slung sofas upholstered in bright tapestry shot through with silver threads. Windows as tall as Willow lined two adjacent walls, giving a view of the central courtyard that was the twin of the one at the Serjian Principality. The sound of cool water in the fountain made Willow itch everywhere with dried sweat and blood. Distantly, she smelled lamb being roasted for the noon meal. She was suddenly starving. How long had it been since she last ate? Nearly twenty-four hours, probably.

The whole of the harem, and Serjian Salveri, were gathered in the little room. No, not the whole: Catrela was missing. That was one burden lifted. She'd have to face Catrela eventually, but not having to do it in front of the entire principality was a relief. Maitea looked grim, her dark eyes focused uncomfortably on Willow. Giara looked neutral, as if this were all just one more meeting. Alondra's hands were clenched tightly in her lap, but her expression was placid — well, there was one member of the Serjian Principality who wouldn't mourn Amberesh long or loud. Salveri was standing at the window with his hands clasped behind his back, looking out at the courtyard, and didn't turn around when the three of them entered.

"She is uninjured," Giara murmured.

"We went to the scholia for healing," Kerish said. "Willow was badly hurt and suffering from dehydration and loss of blood."

"You should have come here to prove it," Giara said.

"I think Willow's health is more important than proving she was nearly killed," Kerish retorted.

"Enough," Janida said. "Alondra, send a runner to the Domian scholia to summon the healer who treated Willow. His or her testimony will have to be enough." Alondra nodded and rose from her sofa. Salveri turned slightly to watch her go, then returned to staring out the window.

"We must decide how this catastrophe to lessen," Janida continued when Alondra was gone. "By now the story will have spread, that a guest of the Serjian Principality has killed one of its own."

"Amberesh a Serjian was not," Maitea said. "He banished was."

"A technicality that will be lost on many," Giara said. "And he was still our *zuareto*."

"First I wish to hear from Willow North," Janida said. "What led to this disaster?"

Willow swallowed. It dawned on her that no one had offered her a seat. She felt as if she were on trial, facing not one judge, but five, all of whom had good reason to want her punished. "Amberesh has—had been following me since we arrived in Umberan," she said. "I didn't mention it because I didn't think he was dangerous, and I was afraid of having my freedom of movement impeded if you all thought I needed a bodyguard, like Felix."

Janida spat out a blistering curse. "You fool," she said. "You thought nothing of your own safety?"

"He was bad at hiding. I—thought I could stay out of his way."

Janida dismissed this with a wave. "Go on."

Willow took a deep breath, then told the story of her fight with Amberesh, keeping her voice steady and not leaving any details out. She saw Salveri's hands clench so tightly the knuckles turned white, but he said nothing. No one spoke until she finished telling about her time in jail and Kerish's arrival, at which time Alondra returned and took her seat wordlessly. Then, after a few moments, Maitea said, "That could have been avoided."

"Hardly," Giara said. "Amberesh would not have stopped until Willow dead was. He dogged in pursuit of a goal was."

"A bodyguard would have dissuaded him."

"Possibly. But a bodyguard a short-term solution is."

"This a short-term problem was."

"What might have been does not matter," Janida said. "We must deal with what is. We have expended great political capital to buy private justice for Willow. This leaves us weakened with regard to our enemies. We must make a new plan."

"What do you mean, private justice?" Willow asked.

"A foreigner has killed an Eskandelic citizen," Janida said. "This a simple thing is not. Any other foreigner, any other victim, and you would executed be, with no trial other than the evidence. We are Serjian, and not without influence. And it our *zuareto* is, and you our guest are. We demanded the right to punish you as we choose."

Willow stiffened her shoulders against the blow. "And what punishment is that?"

Janida looked at Salveri. "We believe it self-defense was."

"And...?"

"And what? Amberesh attacked you, you fought back. Should you punished be, for fighting to stay alive?"

"*No!*" Salveri roared, turning around fast and taking a few steps that brought him inches from Willow's face. "She is not to pay for his death? My *son*, Janida! He should be avenged!"

"Willow did not seek his death, husband," Janida said in a level voice. "He violated hospitality by attacking her."

"We do not know that! We have only the word of this *foreigner*." He spat the word, and traces of spittle flecked Willow's face. She managed not to flinch. Kerish gripped her hand harder, but said nothing. "She has brought nothing but pain upon this house," Salveri continued, "demands much and gives little. I want her gone."

"This her fault is not, Salveri," Alondra said in her soft voice. "You grieve. It has disordered your thinking. Would you punish Felix too?"

"We should never have agreed the boy to sponsor." Salveri gazed down at Willow, hatred in his eyes. "It too late to refuse is not."

"We committed are," Giara said. "If we retract our question now, we will lose power for many years. I will not see this happen."

"We may lose power anyway," Maitea said. "If we cannot show a united front, we will lose not only the undecided, but allies as well. We must stand together."

"I will not support this woman," Salveri growled.

"You will, and you will show no sign of discord," Janida said. "This we have decided."

"Catrela has not, and will not," Salveri said.

"Catrela will see sense. Sit *down*, Serjian Salveri."

Salveri glared at Janida. "You cannot force me," he said, and shoved past Willow and Kerish to leave the room.

There was silence for half a minute after Salveri's exit. Willow's cheeks burned. Her hand in Kerish's was the only thing that kept her from fleeing, finding Felix and gathering their things and going to the Tremontanan enclave for safety. Finally, unable to stand the silence any longer, she blurted out, "I'll go. You shouldn't have to suffer discord on top of grieving for your *zuareto*."

"You will stay, Willow North," Janida said, her voice silver steel. "Serjian has chosen a path and we will stay the course. This is but a moment's pain. Or do you think grief a good reason to ruin a country?"

"That's a bit dramatic. Not supporting Felix won't ruin Eskandel."

"We convinced are that Serjian best to rule Eskandel as *vojenta mahaut* is," Janida said. "If our question rejected is, that will not happen. We mourn Amberesh, but we do not blame you for his death."

"Salveri does. Catrela does."

"They know in their hearts it irrational is. The heart knows what it wants and sensible is not." Janida eyed their clasped hands. "As I think you know."

Willow flushed again. "I think I've done a damn poor job of repaying your hospitality. I don't know if I can face Catrela."

"You will not." Janida took a seat near Giara. "Easier for all if you do not until after Amberesh buried is. You will remain in the Residence until then, three days from now. Then we will attempt to make up for the loss of those three days."

"Felix safer is, to stay inside," Alondra said. "We still have an assassin to find."

Willow gasped. "I left it in the carriage."

"Left what?" asked Kerish.

"The pendant. Amberesh—he told me, before…he said it belonged to someone he knew. A son of a principality."

Janida and Maitea exchanged glances. "He said no name?" Maitea said.

"No. But, Kerish, you said the characters around the rim are unique to the owner. Wouldn't Amberesh be likely to recognize his fellow's mark? He said...he said the man claimed it was lost, but Amberesh thought it had been stolen and the owner was just ashamed to admit to it."

"That makes the list of suspects smaller," Maitea said, "but does not solve the mystery."

"It has to make a difference! Can you...do something with that?"

"Catrela can," Maitea said with a scowl. "If we can rouse her to her duty."

"She a fool is not," Janida said.

"She dramatic is," Giara said dismissively.

"Give her time to grieve," said Alondra. "He her son was. Dramatic, yes, but she sincere in her grieving is."

"You very generous of spirit are," said Janida, exchanging glances with Giara that told Willow the harem knew exactly what Amberesh had done to Alondra. "And sensible. Catrela will have her mourning time, and we will tell the story our way these next three days. Willow, go to your King and reassure him of your safety. And do not again disregard a danger to yourself. Did you not think of what would happen to Felix without you?"

Willow ducked her head. "I'm sorry. For everything."

"You should be. Go," said Janida.

Kerish stayed with her, his fingers intertwined with hers, as they crossed the open walkway to the long hall and stairs leading to her chambers. "They'll forgive you eventually," he said.

"I almost wish they wouldn't. I can barely stand to look at them, knowing—"

"Stop," Kerish said, bringing her to a halt in the middle of the corridor, opposite Catrela's apartment. Willow looked at the door nervously, wondering what the possibility of Catrela flinging open the door and launching herself at Willow's face was. "Amberesh tried to kill you, Willow. I saw what you looked like when they brought you out of the jail. You were perfectly justified in defending yourself and it was just bad luck it was against a member of the principality. It's going to be painful and awkward, but you need to stop feeling guilty that you're alive and he's not."

"I feel guilty at not feeling sorry he's dead, when all of you cared about him."

"I feel guilty about that too. He was always a selfish bastard, and when we returned I found I had even less in common with him than I did when we were children. I don't miss him at all. Mostly I feel sorry for my *majdran* and Gessala and Posea. And for my father."

Willow thought of how Salveri had looked, looming over her, how much pain there was behind the anger. Did he know how Amberesh had treated Alondra? How much difference would it make if he did?

Willow heard voices before she was halfway up the stairs, children's voices and the high yapping of Ernest. She pushed the door open and found Felix and Posea chasing each other around the room under Caira's eye, climbing over the furniture like scaling the city walls and flinging themselves onto the sofa cushions they'd piled on the floor.

Felix saw her and changed direction so rapidly he stumbled into Posea and they both landed on the floor. "*Willow!*" he screamed, and hurtled toward her, grabbing her around the waist and hugging her tightly. "Where were you? Why didn't you come home last night?" His face scrunched up in a nose-wrinkling scowl. "You smell really bad."

"I know, and I'm going to take a bath," Willow said. "I was..." *Never lie to him.* "I was in jail, Felix."

Felix's eyes and mouth went wide. He shouted, "You said you wouldn't get caught! You *promised* me! They could have cut off your hand!" He looked at Willow's hand, joined with Kerish's, and said, in a calmer tone of voice, "Why are you holding hands?"

Willow had to quell an impulse to snatch her hand from Kerish's, again as if they'd been doing something wrong. "Because, well, Kerish and I..." What to say? What were they now to each other?

"Because I love Willow, and she loves me," Kerish said, squatting down to look Felix in the eye. "And we like holding hands."

"Oh." Felix looked concerned. "Are you going to get married?"

"Um..." Willow said.

"Not right now," Kerish said.

"Hilarion says marriage is a natural state for two people in love. He says no one should live in sin. I don't know what that means."

"Um…"

"Don't worry about it," Kerish said.

"I won't." Felix started running around them in a big circle, Ernest yipping along behind him. "If you get married, you can adopt me!"

"Oh, Felix, we—we can't do that." Willow was starting to feel dizzy from more than Felix's rapid motion. "Besides, you couldn't be King if you were adopted by someone else."

Felix came to a stop in front of her, his cheerfulness gone. "I forgot," he said. "Can I go back to the scholia now?"

Willow glanced at Posea, who was watching this exchange in mute incomprehension, then at Caira, whose face told her she had known where Willow had been. "I have to stay in the Residence for the next several days. I…killed someone. That's why I was in jail. I didn't get caught stealing."

"Did that person attack you? Because it's all right to fight back if that happens." Felix looked uncertain. Willow released Kerish and put her arms around the boy.

"Yes, I had to fight for my life," she said. "But the person I killed was Amberesh, so things are…complicated."

"Amberesh?" Posea said. Felix turned and said a few words in Eskandelic. Posea looked confused and said something in reply. Felix shook his head. He appeared to be searching for words, though Willow was impressed at his growing fluency. Finally, he said something that included Amberesh's name. Posea began to cry, noiseless tears that streaked her face and made Willow wish to be anywhere but there.

Kerish put his arms around his *suorena* and hugged her tight, murmuring to her in Eskandelic. Posea nodded violently. "I'm going to take her to Catrela," he said. "I don't think anyone explained to her that Amberesh is dead before now. I'll be back later, with food."

When the door closed behind them, Caira began picking up the sofa cushions and restoring them to their places. "You alive, he not. Is good is."

"I'm trying to keep that in mind," Willow said.

Felix said, "Posea didn't really like Amberesh. He used to tease her, and not in a funny way. But he was still her brother."

Willow sat down on one of the cushions on the floor and buried her face in her hands. "I wish I could leave this place. I'm a constant reminder of what happened."

"We could go to Mister Rafferty."

"We could. But if we did, we'd be giving up any chance of regaining the Crown."

"Oh." Ernest came over to Willow and licked her hands, inviting her to pet him. "Is that still going to happen?"

"I don't know. I found out more about who hired the second assassin, so that should help." She almost said *Unless there's more than one* and decided against scaring Felix any more that day. "Were you worried when I didn't come back?"

Felix sat down on Willow's lap and put his arms around her. "I was, but Hilarion says worry is a waste of imagination, so I tried not to."

"I've heard that one before. I'm not sure I believe it."

"I think you should take a bath now. You smell like the horse stalls."

"Thank you, Felix, for that lovely compliment."

"I'm supposed to be truthful. Besides, I think you already know."

"I do. I'm just not sure I need a reminder."

Chapter Fifteen

Willow shut the door to her rooms behind her, took a deep breath, and descended the stairs. They'd never felt so much like a gallows march as they did just then. She hadn't been down them in three days, the whole time the Serjian Principality mourned Amberesh. It hadn't taken Janida's command to keep her there; she didn't want to encounter anyone for whom she'd be a living reminder of why they mourned. So she'd stayed inside, and eaten off trays Kerish brought for her and Felix, and went slowly mad with captivity.

Now it was time to face her victim.

The funeral had been held at dawn, the family had returned well before noon, but Willow had delayed, pretending she was giving Catrela time to recover from the funeral. It was a lie. She'd just been too cowardly to approach her. But it was drawing close to suppertime, and Willow had run out of time and excuses.

The hallway below her rooms was empty and silent as usual. Janida and Catrela's apartments both opened off this hall, and neither woman spent much time there during the day. But Willow knew Catrela had confined herself to her rooms during the days of mourning, and hoped the woman wasn't quite fully recovered, because she wanted privacy for what she had in mind. Then she felt guilty, all over again, at intruding on Catrela's grief, for imposing herself on her, for making demands...

She stopped in front of the apartment door and knocked. Felix's safety was at stake. She could endure embarrassment and guilt for his sake.

The door opened. A young woman dressed in the shift of a *zetesha* stood there. Her inquiring expression became flat and cold when she saw Willow. "*Yes?*" she said in Eskandelic.

"I need to speak to Catrela."

The woman's lips were tight with anger. She said something in Eskandelic Willow couldn't understand, but her tone of voice clearly said Willow wasn't welcome.

"This isn't about me, it's about Felix. Please tell her I'm here."

"I know you are here, Willow North," Catrela said from farther inside the apartment. "I have no interest in speaking with you."

"It's about Felix," Willow repeated. "Please. Just five minutes. I don't want to intrude."

"Too late for that, it is," Catrela said, then spoke in Eskandelic. The unfriendly *zetesha* stepped aside and held the door open for Willow. She didn't bow even a little bit.

The room resembled the harem chamber, though it was square instead of round. It had the same low sofas cushioned in green and blue and violet, the same floor pillows scattered throughout the room, and a small multi-sectioned table beneath a stained glass lantern. The smell of sandalwood came from somewhere, and Willow had to stifle the urge to sneeze, it was so strong. She held her breath until the urge passed, then walked forward onto a carpet so plush she was sure she was leaving footprints in it.

Catrela sat on a floor cushion next to the table. She held something in her hand that sparkled with dizzying bronze, from which dangled a gold chain. She played with the chain, running it through her fingers, tangling it into a web. Willow kept walking until she stood about five feet from the woman. "Catrela," she said, then couldn't think how to continue.

Catrela just looked at her. Her lips thinned into a taut line.

"I'm sorry," Willow said. She felt as if the words were boiling out of her. "I never wanted to cause you pain, and I didn't want to…and I don't want to make excuses, as if that will make it all right that your son is dead, but he would—"

"You correct are, that it not all right is," Catrela said. Her voice sounded distant. "I would have seen you dead in his place. But that a mother's right is."

"I can see how you'd feel that way. I'm not sorry I'm alive. He attacked *me*."

Catrela tangled the chain around her fingers again. "You think he deserved death for that?"

"No. I'm sorry he's dead." A tiny lie. "But I won't apologize for being alive."

Catrela sighed. She put the chain around her neck, and Willow could see the sparkling bronze was a pendant, fat enough that it was probably a locket. "I cannot forgive you his death," she said, "but I am not a fool. Amberesh made many bad choices, and I blame myself for his behavior. I indulged him far too greatly, my oldest child, my only son. How he treated Alondra..." She shook her head, then stood up, leaning heavily on the table as if she were an ancient crone. "I can forgive you for having survived when he did not."

"Thank you," Willow said. "I wish I'd told someone he was following me. Maybe this would have turned out differently."

"Secrets necessary are but not safe, to ones such as we are." Catrela took a seat on one of the sofas and waved in the direction of the other. Willow sat. "But there another secret is, and I think it your purpose in coming is."

"I need to know who's trying to kill Felix. And I need your help to do it."

"It a difficult prospect still is. Your information good is, but not enough."

"I don't know. Kerish said it was a large organization—the one Amberesh belonged to—but he couldn't have been close to many of the members." Willow watched Catrela carefully for some reaction to her using Amberesh's name, but Catrela just had her thin eyebrows narrowed in thought.

"I know the names of his friends, and can discover which of them belong to that organization," she said, "but determining which of them has lost his pendant, more difficult is."

"If you can tell me who to investigate, I can find that out."

Catrela raised an eyebrow. "You confident are."

"I have a plan. It might not be a good plan, but I think it will work. Do they have a...a house or a building or somewhere they all meet?"

Catrela shook her head. "But there are other events, other locations. What do you intend?"

Willow smiled. "I intend to be bait."

***

The morning light struck the pool surrounding the Varisi Palace and turned it into a brass mirror, reflecting not the palace but the sky, high above. A brisk, warm wind blew, surprisingly, from inland, bringing with it the scents of exotic trees and flowers Willow couldn't begin to picture. The carriage was approaching the palace along a causeway whose surface was about a foot above the water. Willow looked over the edge and saw her own reflection, yellow and wobbly. Probably not a good idea to take its imperfect image seriously, because the *giorjanesh* she wore was outlandish even by Eskandelic standards, but it was also beautiful, and its night-blue satin suited her coloring. The fitted bodice and narrow skirt slit to the knee were actually comfortable, even if the cropped bodice did expose several inches of her midsection to view.

It was the drape, three feet wide and six or more feet long and embroidered with silver stars, that made the whole thing awkward. It wrapped around her in a complicated fashion, and Caira had cautioned her about standing from a sitting position. Willow hitched it up and flexed her feet again. She definitely missed her own shoes.

The palace looked more like a collection of warehouses than a palace, and she only called it that because Kerish had. It didn't even have a domed roof, or a series of domed roofs. The stone was dark yellow, stained green at the bottom where the water level had changed over the years. At present, the water in the pool was low enough to reveal that the palace stood on enormous pillars like the causeway, the gaps between them coming to pointed arches through which little boats floated, propelled by men wielding long poles. Willow watched one of them glide through and disappear into the darkness beneath the arches. The boat had passengers. Was that something anyone might do?

She turned to ask Kerish about it and was interrupted by Felix, saying, "Do you think Nanitan will win?"

"She's been best in her class twice now, though not last year. I think she has a good chance." Kerish pointed. "That's where the dog owners enter, there at the top. We'll go in below, straight to the competition floor."

A round courtyard large enough to fit a dozen carriages stood in front of the main palace entrance, a ten-foot-tall pair of doors made of beaten brass that had Willow's skin vibrating when she were within twenty feet of them. It would be a pleasant buzz so long as she got away from it soon. One nice thing Aurilien had over Umberan — no solid metal doors to make her tingle or itch.

They waited in line for a few minutes — Kerish was apparently less willing than his mother to trade on the family name — until their carriage arrived at the door. Willow stood, gingerly, certain the *giorjanesh* drape was going to collapse in a pile of fabric around her, and with Kerish's help managed to wobble out of the carriage. She kept a grateful grip on his hand when she was on solid ground and adjusted the gold pendant that burned a little patch of skin just above her breastbone. "Now what?"

"Now we walk around and let people get a good look at us," Kerish said. He was worth looking at in his trousers that bloused at the ankle, a fine linen shirt with full sleeves, and a vest heavily embroidered with an abstract pattern. "And see if we can find our suspects."

"I don't like being looked at," Felix said. He was dressed in the same kind of clothes Kerish wore, but he'd managed to rumple himself in the ten-minute drive from the Residence. His bodyguards hovered nearby, sweating in their armor.

"They'll probably be looking at Willow, because she's so beautiful," Kerish said.

"Kerish," Willow said, blushing at the look he gave her, intimate and knowing.

"That's all right, then," Felix said. "Can we go see the dogs now?"

Willow held her breath as they passed through the doors, which at that proximity gave her a full-body tingle too intense to be pleasant. Gooseflesh rose up on her arms, and she clutched Kerish's hand more tightly. "I forgot about the doors," Kerish murmured in her ear. "They must be a misery."

"I can endure." Willow rubbed one arm and ran her tongue over her teeth, stilling the vibration the brass had sent up inside her mouth. "Not that it's enjoyable. Besides, it's passing. And this place is beautiful."

The interior of the palace was comfortably cool, and looked cooler thanks to the blue mosaics covering the walls and ceiling, laced with yellow tiles that picked out a lovely floral pattern. Willow's shoes were thin enough that she could feel the ripple of the stone tiles underfoot. They might be more like her own shoes than she realized.

The hallway was full, but not crowded, and no one seemed inclined to speak to them. Willow kept a tight grip on Kerish's hand and clutched Felix's with her other hand. Crowded or not, the last thing she needed was to lose the boy in these halls.

Ahead, she heard the murmur of many voices in a large space, and sharp echoing sounds that she realized were dogs barking. Then they came out of the hall, and Willow stopped, momentarily overwhelmed by all the metal. It wasn't so much that there was a lot of it as that it was everywhere, in dog collars and lead chains and knives and cages. The room was as large as the Conclave chamber in the Jauderish, but where that was a vast open bowl, this was a flat plain, studded with pillars holding up the ceiling. A draft from somewhere carried the faint smell of hundreds of dogs. That it wasn't stronger, Willow put down to a miracle of engineering.

Felix grabbed her hand and tugged her along. "Come *on*, Willow, let's get closer."

"Slow down, Felix. The dogs aren't going anywhere." Though they did seem to be in motion, dogs going from marked areas on the floor to an oval near the center, where boxes and hoops and tiny fences were set up. A black dog that looked like Maresh was trotting around the oval, leaping over the fences and through the hoops with no apparent instruction from its owner. Other dogs milled about nearby, ignoring each other, which to Willow seemed like a greater feat of training.

A low rope fence separated the dogs from the passersby, most of them dressed the way Willow and Kerish were. Beyond the fence were a series of bays defined by cages and more rope, some empty, but most containing dogs and their owners. Willow hitched up her *giorjanesh* again and held out her hand for a nearby dog to sniff. It did so without interest, and its owner whistled it away. Probably that was inappropriate behavior, interacting with the competitors.

"Kerish," someone said, and Willow turned to see a pair of young women dressed in *giorjaneshes*, one cream and rose, the other shades of green. The one in green said something in Eskandelic, then added in

Tremontanese, "Please introduce us to the young King."

"Of course," Kerish said. "Felix, this is Tarjian Emelda and Jamighian Ruelle. Ladies, his Majesty King Felix of Tremontane, and his guardian Willow North."

"I cannot believe anyone would wish his Majesty to assassinate!" Emelda said. "He sweet is."

"I'm not sweet," Felix said indignantly. The two women giggled.

"We'll find the ones behind the assassin and stop them," Willow said. "I won't let it happen again."

The two women eyed her. "I suppose you would stop him," Emelda said. "Permanently."

"Excuse me?"

Now the two women eyed each other. "Some call you murderer," said Ruelle, "but we think you had reason. Amberesh a...I do not know your word. A *rial-shaad* was."

"He was my *fuoreno*," Kerish said tightly.

"Then you know it true is," Ruelle said. She touched Willow's arm in a confiding way. "You have done us all a great favor."

"I was just defending myself," Willow said.

"Willow killed someone to protect me," Felix said. "But that doesn't make her a bad person."

"Of course not, your Majesty," said Emelda, crouching to put herself at his eye level. "You fortunate are, to have so loyal a guardian."

"We have to look at the dogs now," Kerish said, taking Willow's arm and tugging her away.

They walked a few paces down the row of dogs waiting their turn at the oval, followed discreetly by the bodyguards. Willow said, "I'm sorry."

"Don't be. Is it too strange that I don't regret Amberesh's death, but it still makes me furious to hear others speak ill of him?"

"I think it makes sense. What's a *rial-shaad*?"

"A word I'd rather not repeat where Felix can hear."

"I know all sorts of bad words," Felix said. "Some of them I learned from Willow."

"Let's not talk about that," Willow said. "Look, there's another dog starting the course. Do all of them have to perform?"

"This is just one group. The *khetashi*," Kerish said. "The *stevaashi* are judged on their appearance and gait, and the *lehndashi* did their trials last week—they're the hunters. Those have a solo category and a pack category."

"Nanitan is *stevaashi*," Felix said. "Jauman bred and trained her, but he's not allowed to show her himself until he's an adult."

"He must be very excited about today, then," Willow said. She looked around, wondering if any of the young men were the one she was looking for, and instead caught the curious gazes of a dozen bystanders, all staring at her openly. "Kerish," she said quietly.

"What—oh," Kerish said. "I guess you're famous."

"They all look like they're trying to decide if they want to attack."

"Or they could just think you're beautiful, and can't stop looking at you."

"That seems highly unlikely."

"It's why I'm staring at you." Kerish took her hand and kissed it, his lips lingering on her knuckles.

"Kerish! We're in public!"

"Mother would want it to be clear that you're under Serjian protection. And *I*—" he took her other hand and held it—"want it to be clear that your heart has already been given."

Willow gave up. "Can you help me find our suspects?"

"Of course. Let's walk, then."

Even with the bodyguards flanking them, she still felt uncomfortably exposed, and vulnerable, with Kerish holding one of her hands and Felix the other. The short sleeves of the *giorjanesh* made wearing the forearm knife impossible. If someone else decided assassination was a good idea, she'd be powerless to defend Felix. She listened to his chatter with half an ear and glared at anyone who met her gaze. *That's right, I'm dangerous, so don't try anything.*

She shrugged to shift the annoying pendant to a different spot. She hated carrying gold, and if she cared about such things she'd be annoyed at having to wear something that clashed with the rest of her clothing, but her plan depended on the right person recognizing the pendant.

"There four men are," Catrela had said, "friends of Amberesh and members of his organization. They the most likely culprits are."

"Gharibi Cammean, Hajimhi Jherjesh, Abakian Terjalesh, and Khazanjian Ojman," Willow had said, referring to her sheet of notes. "I still think it's Hajimhi."

"We must not jump to conclusions. All four will be at the *sheteshi* and Kerish will be sure you meet them. I do not like it."

"What don't you like?"

"This, much guessing is. We have no proof that it one of these men is, and if it one of them is, we do not know how he will react to being confronted. This may not bring us closer to proof."

"Amberesh recognized who the pendant belonged to. One or all of these men must know it, too. And if I'm wrong, and none of them respond to it, we try something else. But all of these principalities except Khazanjian are in opposition to Serjian, which suggests they *could* be behind the assassinations. And Khazanjian isn't exactly friendly. It's worth trying, Catrela."

Catrela had sighed, but said nothing more, and now Willow rubbed the spot where the pendant lay against her chest, with only the fabric of the *giorjanesh* between it and her skin. Catrela was right, this was fumbling in the dark, but it was all they could do for now.

She wasn't happy that Felix was with them. This was a kind of midnighting, and having a child along while she was working made her feel anxious, worrying about his safety as well as getting the job done. But Felix had pleaded with her—it was the last day of the *sheteshi*, the famous Eskandelic dog show, and there would be so many animals there—and in the end she'd given in. So long as Willow and Kerish and the bodyguards were there, he was protected. Even so, she felt more on edge than usual. She really shouldn't have given in to his pleading.

"Hajimhi," Kerish said in a low voice, pointing. To her dismay, Willow saw Hajimhi Giaveni standing in one of the bays where the cages sat. Giaveni was deep in conversation with a much older man, lean and sinewy. A younger man crouched in front of the cage, brushing a brindled gray sighthound.

"Is that Jherjesh?" she asked.

"With the dog, yes."

"What do you think the odds are that Giaveni is going to start shouting at me when I approach?"

"Leave that to me. Wait here, and once I've got him talking, come around the long way." Kerish strolled off in the direction of the two men. Willow waited, her attention divided between Jherjesh and Giaveni. What was Kerish thinking? Giaveni had to be as angry at Serjian as he was at Willow. Though…Kerish had said it had looked like Hajimhi Principality had set Willow up to fall into that trap, so maybe his animosity was feigned.

"I want to go look at the dogs, Willow," Felix said.

"In a minute, Felix." Kerish had reached Giaveni and was making his bow. Giaveni paused a long moment before returning it—that couldn't be good. There, Kerish was telling the man something. Giaveni responded. Kerish said something else, and suddenly Giaveni was paying very close attention to Kerish. His older companion took a few steps in Kerish's direction, also very intent on him. Willow shook herself out of her stupor. "Come on," she told Felix and the bodyguards.

The long way around was very long, since Willow was sure walking on the oval when you didn't have a dog was frowned on. She skirted a few more competitors, keeping her eyes on Jherjesh and resisting the urge to see if Giaveni was watching. If he was, there wasn't much she could do about it.

Jherjesh had set the brush aside and was trimming the dog's claws when they arrived. He glanced up at them. "Tremontanans," he said. "Stay away."

"I like your dog," Felix said. "What's her name?"

Jherjesh laid down the little knife and regarded Felix. "You must the would-be King be," he said. "And you his keeper."

"I'm Willow North," Willow said. She'd expected antagonism and wasn't surprised to be the recipient of it. "And this is King Felix Valant."

The dog whined and put a paw on Jherjesh's knee. The young man scratched her head absently. "You murdered Serjian Amberesh," he said.

"Killed him in self-defense." That one still struck a nerve, no matter how prepared she was for it.

"You too small to fight well are. You must have tricked him."

Willow casually reached up to fiddle with the pendant. "I was lucky. So, Amberesh was a friend of yours?"

Jherjesh made a dismissive sound, something between a grunt and a whistle. "I grew up. Amberesh did not."

"I don't understand what that means." *Fiddle, fiddle.*

"Amberesh liked drinking and women and nothing else. I have other concerns. We had little in common these last two years."

"Well, I'm still sorry for your loss. I didn't want to kill him." Was the man completely unobservant?

"You should have executed been. No son of a principality should be cut down like a dog by a foreigner and not avenged be." Jherjesh's eyes narrowed. "His pendant. You *dare* wear that, like a trophy?"

His last words were a shout. Willow took a step back and put herself between Jherjesh and Felix. "This isn't Amberesh's," she said in a level voice. "You don't recognize it?"

"Give it back," Jherjesh said, reaching for her throat. Willow took a few more steps backward, nearly tripping over Felix. Jherjesh's dog started barking, not at anyone in particular, but there was an edge to its voice that made Willow nervous. She glanced around quickly. They were drawing a *lot* of attention, but none of it was the kind she could depend on to come to her aid. The bodyguards hovered, one placing himself near Felix, the other looking as if he wanted to intervene in her conflict with Jherjesh but didn't want to lay hands on the son of a principality if he wasn't a direct threat to Felix.

Then Kerish was there, stepping between her and Jherjesh. He said something that sounded harsh. Jherjesh responded, his voice husky and furious. He shoved Kerish, who stood firm and gripped the young man's wrist, twisting it up and spinning him around. Jherjesh made a pained sound. Kerish leaned forward and spoke at some length into Jherjesh's ear.

A new voice cut across Kerish's. Hajimhi Giaveni grabbed Willow's shoulder in a painful grip. She twisted away. "Get your hands off me."

"You think this family more to insult? Get away now before I have you thrown out," the Prince said. Kerish looked back at Willow, then released Jherjesh with a little shove. He took Willow's hand and towed her and Felix away from the oval and away from the Hajimhis.

"Slow down," she protested.

"Not until we're at a safe distance," Kerish said, but he slowed his steps. Eventually they came to a halt near the mouth of the corridor, where a dozen people watched Willow curiously. She ignored them. "Did you learn anything?"

"Jherjesh thought the pendant belonged to Amberesh and that I'd taken it off his body. He said he and Amberesh hadn't been close for a couple of years. I don't think he's the one."

"That's good. I don't want to encounter Giaveni again. All the Hajimhis are proud of their family honor, and we seem to keep insulting that."

"I don't care anymore. If they want to be stupid, let them."

"You're speaking rather loudly, Willow."

"I don't—all right, I care a little. The more I antagonize them, the more likely they are to actively campaign against Serjian. Anyway, that's one name down. Who's next?"

"I saw Khazanjian Ojman in the crowd as we rushed past. Let's go talk to him."

Kerish aimed for a spot where the crowd was thickest. Laughter issued from the center of it, but it was strange laughter, echoing and discordant, with a lone voice letting out a mirthless laugh and then a dozen people joining in a moment later. Willow gripped Felix's hand tighter. Now was not the time to lose hold of him.

With some shoving, Kerish managed to get them to the center of the knot of people just in time for another one of those horrible laughs to go off. The man doing the laughing had a cheerful, handsome face, with an aquiline nose and high, prominent cheekbones. He saw Willow, and the cheerfulness disappeared, replaced by a sly, appraising expression. He said something to Willow that made the crowd laugh. "*I don't speak Eskandelic,*" Willow said.

"This is Willow North, guardian to King Felix of Tremontane," Kerish said, "and you can apologize to the lady right now."

"Of course," Khazanjian Ojman said, his smile widening. "I welcome a beautiful lady to Eskandel. You beautiful are, for one so fierce."

"Thank you," Willow said, feeling Kerish bristle. "I like your country."

"It the best is," Ojman said. "You live here now?"

"Until Eskandel decides to support Felix's claim to the Crown of Tremontane."

Ojman looked down at Felix. "So young, King to be." Felix said nothing. "I must show you Umberan, beautiful lady," he said to Willow.

"Willow already has a guide," Kerish said.

"I think she wants a better one." Ojman gave Willow another sly glance.

"That's very nice of you," Willow said, cutting off Kerish's retort, "but I don't think I need a guide."

"Then I think I show you…something else," Ojman said, with a gesture that left no doubt as to what he meant.

Kerish dropped Willow's hand and shoved Ojman, who couldn't go very far thanks to the press of the crowds. He laughed and shoved Kerish in turn. "Stop it, both of you!" Willow shouted. "Ojman, I'm not interested."

Ojman glanced at her where he was still wrestling with Kerish. His eyes widened slightly. Then he began laughing, an amused sound that was so different from his earlier mirthless laugh Willow couldn't believe it had come from the same person. "You and I both out of luck are," he said to Kerish. "Another man has got there first."

Kerish shoved him once more and broke free of his grasp. He said something furious in Eskandelic that made Ojman laugh harder and respond at length.

Willow gasped. "Did he just say Terjalesh?"

"You play him false," Ojman said, jerking a thumb at Kerish. "Abakian Terjalesh has claimed you for his own."

"He has *not*," Willow replied hotly.

Ojman reached out and fingered the pendant. He managed to turn it into a caress, and Willow slapped his hand. That just made him laugh more. "He gave you this as love-token, and you wear it openly. Kerish is too stupid to know this. You bold are, Willow North."

"Thank you," Willow said. "Kerish, let's go."

The bodyguards had to shove hard to make a path out of the crowd surrounding Ojman, and Willow ultimately picked Felix up to carry him rather than risk him being crushed. "He's disgusting," she said.

"I didn't think he'd be so overt about it," Kerish said.

"It doesn't matter. He told us who the pendant belongs to. We have to talk to Abakian Terjalesh."

"Willow, can't we please just look at the dogs?" Felix said.

Willow looked out across the great oval. So many people, so many animals…finding Terjalesh in this place might take some time. "All right," she said. "Dogs first. But then we have an assassin to find."

Chapter Sixteen

They came to the far end of the room, where Felix pulled free of her grasp and ran to the edge of the rope barrier, crying out, "Oh, *look* at the puppies!"

Several small areas had been roped off and filled with cages that were open on top. Inside each, four to eight puppies romped or slept, watched over by men and women dressed all in silvery gray tunics and trousers. "These are purebred Kazhari sighthound pups," Kerish told Willow. "They're all the offspring of champions and very valuable. Most of them have probably already been purchased and are just being held here until the end of the competition."

"They're adorable. Felix—"

"I know not to touch them." He was leaning as far forward as he could without overbalancing.

The woman at the cage Felix was next to said something inquiring to Kerish, who shook his head. "She just wanted to know if we were in the market for a dog," he told Willow. "They start at three hundred *galt*."

Willow whistled. That was the equivalent of almost four hundred Tremontanan guilders. "Is Ernest worth that much?"

"Probably."

"I wish I'd known that. I wouldn't have allowed Felix to accept that kind of gift."

"They wouldn't have offered him to me if they minded," Felix said, not turning around. "Besides, it's too late now."

"I won't take Ernest away, Felix."

"I know." Felix squatted beside the cage and watched a tiny black head poke its nose through the bars.

"So, do you have any idea where to find Terjalesh?" Willow asked.

"None. He's not exhibiting this year, and if he attends, it might be at any time. Do you have a backup plan?"

"Another event? Go to the Abakian Residence and knock on the door? I'm just hoping he's here and we can find him."

Felix laughed. One of the puppies was washing his face with its wet pink tongue. Willow glanced at the dogs' keeper, but she didn't seem to mind, so Willow just watched them play. Four hundred guilders. It was astonishing what people would pay for the most ordinary things. She'd never been hired to retrieve anything living, and her mind started churning over the possibilities — some kind of drug to keep the dog still, probably, because she wasn't good with animals. Getting it out of the cage with all those keepers watching so closely would be even more difficult, but still possible —

"I can't wait for next year!" Felix said. "Do you think the keeper of the kennels would help me find someone to enter Ernest? Or maybe Gianesh will do it!"

"Felix…" His small face was so alive with excitement it felt wrong to crush his dream. "Time enough to plan for that next year," she said, and immediately felt awful, because if it wasn't a lie, it was its next-door neighbor. "You'll be in Tremontane then, remember?"

The eagerness left his face. "I forgot," he said. "But I'll be King, so I could visit, right?"

"Sure. Now say goodbye to the puppies, and we need to move on."

It was probably her imagination that Felix took her hand with less enthusiasm than he had earlier.

They walked slowly around the oval, Willow scanning the crowds though she had no idea what Abakian Terjalesh looked like. Almost everyone they passed stared at her, whispering, women in their bright *giorjaneshes* and men in bloused trousers and embroidered vests. What were they thinking? That Serjian was a fool for buying private justice and then not exercising it? That Willow was arrogant in walking around in public, just as if nothing had happened? She returned their stares coolly, keeping her head high even though she wanted to hide. This was far worse than just being known as Felix's guardian.

Kerish came to an abrupt stop, jerking on Willow's hand. "Did you see him?" she asked.

"No." His lips were barely moving. "But Mahnouki Adorinda is coming this way."

Willow looked around fast. There Adorinda was, with two of her harem sisters, her eyes fixed on Willow. Running and hiding was not an option. "Kerish, what do I do?"

"Don't let her rattle you. And remember who you are." Kerish squeezed her hand, which comforted Willow a little. But only a little.

Adorinda moved gracefully in the center of an empty space that surrounded her, a space that grew naturally as people nearby seemed to realize they had elsewhere to be. Her *giorjanesh* was pure black, embroidered with real gold that burned a tracery of fine lines beneath Willow's skin. She smiled at Felix, a thin expression that didn't reach her eyes.

"You like our dogs, young King?" she said.

"I have a sighthound. I want to enter him in the *sheteshi* next year."

"Felix is good with animals," Willow said, feeling defensive. The gold didn't help.

"I would not think a King would have time for such things," Adorinda said.

"True. This time next year, Felix will be busy in Aurilien. But that doesn't stop him thinking of what might be."

"Better he spend his time thinking of what is, do you think?" Adorinda transferred her thin, humorless smile to Willow.

"If you never imagine things beyond your grasp, you'll never achieve them, will you?" Adorinda had something in mind, but Willow had no idea what. She felt herself skidding along an icy lake once again, terrifyingly aware of the frozen depths beneath her and of just how thin that surface was.

"You care for the boy, yes?"

"I do."

"Then why are you cruel to him?"

Here it came. "I beg your pardon?"

Adorinda returned her attention to Felix. "Your Majesty will have no support from Eskandel," she said. "We will not vote to support your question on the *adjeni*. Better you know this now and prepare to accept defeat."

"You're very confident, Mahnouki Adorinda," Willow said, overriding whatever Felix might have said in reply. "But I don't think you can see the future."

"I need not see the future when I can read the present. A vote for

Mahnouki, a vote for riches and prestige for Eskandel is." Adorinda spoke more loudly now, pitching her voice to carry past the conversations going on quietly around them—not that there were many, since everyone close enough was watching their interaction. "The principalities of Eskandel sensible are."

The gold was a fine thread of burning pain just inches from her body. Willow breathed in deeply, willing herself to ignore it. "You're right, Adorinda," she said in the same loud voice, ignoring too the gasps coming from all around. Damn. She'd forgotten the polite way of addressing a harem member. Too late now. "Eskandel is sensible. Your principalities have governed this country well and sensibly for generations. Which is why the Mahnouki question is bound to fail."

Adorinda frowned. "You are bold."

"Just following your example. What *sense* is there in sending ships on a voyage into mostly unknown waters, to a new country you know nothing about? What *sense* is there in assuming that country is unpopulated and open to your pillaging it? Eskandel won't waste its resources like that."

"Instead to waste its resources supporting a child-King's bid to take the Crown of a foreign nation?"

"It's not a waste of resources to ensure good relations with a neighboring country and economic growth."

"A King who cannot himself gain his Crown, too weak to make good relations is. But let us say for discussion's sake that Eskandel fool enough is to follow where the boy leads. What of the repercussions if he loses? Eskandel will have now an enemy on its northern border and not an ally."

"He won't lose."

Adorinda's cruel smile widened. "I think you cannot see the future."

Willow didn't flinch as Adorinda threw her own words back at her. "Which leaves us both where we started. You backing your question and me defending Serjian's. And you're right, neither of us can see the future."

The smile faltered, just the tiniest bit. "I know where my support lies. Do you?"

"I don't, actually. To be honest, I'm not worried about it."

"You are arrogant." Adorinda spoke even more loudly.

"I can see how you'd think that way. People always see their own worst traits in others."

Adorinda flinched. Before she could speak, Willow said, "No, I'm not arrogant. The reason I'm not worried is that I have faith the rulers of Eskandel will see what's best for their country and will vote accordingly. Supporting Felix is best for Eskandel, Adorinda. Supporting Mahnouki only benefits you."

"You do not use my name, girl," Adorinda said in a low, cutting voice.

"I apologize. I don't know your customs well and I mean no disrespect."

"Do you accuse me of profiting by my question?"

"No, but I'm guessing you'd come up covered in glory if that voyage is successful." Willow lowered her voice and made a logical leap. "And I bet if someone dug into the ownership of those vessels, they'd find the Mahnouki name written all over them. Is that legal, Adorinda?"

"*Lies,*" Adorinda said.

"No lie is needed when the truth will bind you better. Someone very wise told me that once." Willow raised her voice again. "I'm not Eskandelic. I can't tell the principalities how to vote. All I know is that Felix is the rightful King of Tremontane, and I'm sworn to protect him and help him regain the Crown. I hope Eskandel chooses to side with him. Good day, Mahnouki Adorinda." She hitched the drape of her *giorjanesh* higher, bowed to Adorinda — the perfunctory bow of equal to equal, because she didn't think she could get away with implying Adorinda was actually her inferior — and swept away down the hall, towing Felix behind her. *Leave a meeting on your terms.*

"Slow *down,* Willow," Kerish said in a low voice.

"Not if there's any chance she's chasing me. She isn't, is she?"

"I think you might have paralyzed her with rage." Kerish put his hand on Willow's arm. "That was incredible."

"Was it? I can barely remember what I said."

"It was effective. I wish Mother had been here to see it. Of course, if she had been, the fight would have been between her and Adorinda, and you wouldn't have been involved at all. Do you really think Mahnouki is illegally profiting off the proposed voyage?"

"I don't know what's illegal or not, but she sure acted like someone with something to hide. I'll have to tell the harem and let them ferret it out. It might make a difference."

"She's wrong, isn't she? About the voting?" Felix's voice had a tremor in it. Willow squatted, carefully, and put her arms around the boy.

"We don't know how the vote will go. Adorinda just wanted to scare us. You're not scared of her, are you?"

"Of course not. Hilarion says fear is the unwanted visitor we choose to entertain, and a King should rule his fear and not let it rule him."

"I might have known Hilarion would have something to say about that."

"But what are we going to do if they vote against helping us?"

"Don't worry about that. I have a plan."

"Does it mean running away?"

"Sort of." Felix didn't sound frightened anymore, just curious. "Would it make you feel better if I told you what it was?" He nodded. "Then tonight before you go to bed, we'll talk about it."

"All right." Felix took her hand again. "Can we watch the dogs now? I want to see the *stevaashi* parade, because they're the prettiest."

"We're going to take one more walk around this place, and then we can watch the dogs," Kerish said. "If we don't see him by then, we'll have to think of something else," he told Willow, who nodded.

The exhibition hall had grown more crowded and stuffy with the smell of warm bodies and warm dogs all in one place. The draft Willow had felt earlier was gone. She hitched the drape of the *giorjanesh* higher for what seemed like the hundredth time and surreptitiously scratched her armpit. Her clothing was beautiful, but the fabric was heavy and *hot* and she wished for a cool linen tunic, or better yet, a cool bath.

They walked, pushing against the current of attendees, toward the entrance, where the air was marginally cooler. Willow found a spot where an occasional breeze whistled past her face. It smelled of sweat, but she didn't care. "Maybe we should forget about this," she said. "There have to be other places where we can encounter him."

"Don't tell me you're giving up already."

"I'm not. Well, maybe a little."

"May we see the dogs now?"

Willow sighed. "All right, Felix, we'll go watch the dogs." His constant requests, however polite, were starting to grate on her, but she controlled her impatience. He was only eight, after all, and this…quest of Willow's didn't mean anything to him. Even though, technically, it meant life or death to him.

She shifted her grip on his hand. If the Abakians were behind the assassination attempts, she would make them pay. There had to be something she could do to make them suffer.

The noise was becoming intolerable, all those people trying to be heard above everyone else, a thunderstorm someone had let indoors. Willow tugged on Felix's hand, leading him away from the entrance. Better the stuffy heat than the unbearable noise.

Behind them, a boisterous mob of men came through the entrance, laughing and shouting at each other as if they were separated by the length of the exhibition hall instead of shoulder to shoulder. They bore down on the crowds without stepping out of anyone's way, moving like the lords of creation they no doubt believed themselves to be.

Willow took a few quick steps to the left, then darted right, trying to anticipate their movement, but they swept over her and Felix like an inexorable tide, not even bothering to try to avoid them. One of the bodyguards moved in front of her, breaking the tide with his body; the other, Willow couldn't see. Willow drew Felix closer, shielding him with her body, and looked around for an escape. Should she try to get out of the crowd, or wait for them to pass?

She felt a tug on her hand, then a harder tug, and suddenly Felix was gone, swallowed up in the mass of alarmingly large and energetic men.

"*Felix!*" she shouted, diving after him, but he was gone as if he'd never been there.

"Willow! There he is!" Kerish shouted. Willow looked around wildly. He was pointing in the wrong direction. Felix had gone missing to her left. Where had the bodyguards gone? She ignored Kerish and shoved her way past a couple of older women who gabbled at her in Eskandelic. It didn't sound friendly, but Willow didn't care. The men continued to swarm around and past her. One jostled her elbow and muttered something in Eskandelic that could have been a curse or an apology, but spared her no more than a glance.

"Felix!" she cried out again. She was almost free of the mob, but still saw no sign of Felix. He had to be *somewhere*. He couldn't have simply vanished, unless… Willow shoved past a few more people, trying to control her panic. No one would try to kidnap him, would they? *They absolutely would.*

Then she saw him, standing by himself in an open space, and her leaden heart lightened. She ran to his side and hugged him, felt him throw his arms around her and cling to her. "I'm sorry," she said, "I should have held on more tightly."

"I was trying to go to the dogs and I let go," Felix said. "I won't do it again."

"Let's find Kerish, and this time we'll both hold on tighter."

Felix's grip on her hand was almost painfully tight. She could hardly blame him. One of the bodyguards came staggering up, then the other. "Where the *hell* did you go?" Willow shouted. "Anything could have happened to Felix!"

The first bodyguard said, "I see him, but he—" He made a little motion with his hands that Willow couldn't interpret. His companion said something rapidly in Eskandelic. Willow wanted to take both of them by the hair and crack their heads together. The bloodthirsty image stopped her cold. She was frightened, and tense, and that weakened her when she needed to be strong.

"Never mind," she told them, cutting across the first guard's attempt to translate for his comrade. "Never mind. I don't want to hear it. Stay close, and you can explain yourselves to Janida when we get back to the Residence. Now we're going to find Kerish."

She looked around, but Kerish had disappeared as thoroughly as Felix had. She swore under her breath. This was a really bad idea. She should never have taken Felix into such a crowded, public place.

"I see him!" Felix said, pointing. "Talking to that man."

With relief, Willow looked where Felix pointed and saw Kerish in conversation with someone else. The man was enormous, taller even than Kerish and broad in the shoulders and belly. His arms were twice the size of her own, and his fingers looked like knobby sausages. He wore the same vest and trousers almost all the men did, but on him they looked undersized, the vest straining across his stomach and the trousers tight instead of billowing. Whatever Kerish was saying had both of them on edge. Willow moved toward them, dodging more people — why was she the only one getting out of anyone's way?

" —*jeh dua din*," Kerish was saying as Willow neared. He hooked his arm around her elbow and drew her closer. "Abakian Terjalesh, this is Willow North. Willow, Abakian Terjalesh."

"So what?" Terjalesh said. His voice came from somewhere very deep, possibly well beneath the bottom of the pool the building was built over. "Abakian wants nothing to do with Serjian."

"Are you sure about that?" He hadn't noticed the pendant. Willow reached up and found it had slipped beneath the neck of the *giorjanesh*. She hadn't even felt the burning, she'd been so caught up in finding Felix. She pulled it out and settled it where it was visible. "From what I hear, Abakian has been very involved in Serjian affairs."

The big man looked puzzled, as if he didn't quite understand her. Then he said, "You hear lies. I leave now."

"Wait! I want you to meet someone," Willow said, not quite daring to put a restraining hand on his arm. "This is King Felix Valant."

Terjalesh took a few steps and loomed over Felix, who miraculously didn't flinch. "This the King is?" he said. "He puny is."

"I'm eight," Felix said. "I'm still growing."

A nasty smile spread across Terjalesh's face. "True. For now." Felix took half a step backward. Terjalesh followed him. The bodyguards moved forward to intercept him.

"Terjalesh!" Willow said. "Missing something?" It was brash, but the amount of metal in the room just kept growing and the drunk feeling was growing with it. She ran her finger under the leather thong holding the pendant, making it shift and gleam in the low light.

She'd managed to confuse him. He turned back toward her, mouth open to frame a question. Then he saw the pendant, and his mouth dropped open farther, making him look like the monkeys' older, uglier, fatter cousin. "How do you have that?" he said. "That yours is not."

"I know. Whose is it, Terjalesh? Someone you know?"

Terjalesh's meaty hand whipped out, far too fast for a man of his size, grabbed the pendant, and yanked it hard enough to break the cord. Willow cried out at the pain of the leather cutting into her neck. Kerish grabbed Willow and put himself between her and the giant. "Don't touch her again, Terjalesh, or we'll see how far Serjian privilege will take me," he said, laying a hand on the hilt of his sword.

"You steal this. I tell everyone so." Terjalesh's fingers closed around the pendant, hiding it entirely.

"Then *I'll* tell everyone where I found it—in the property of a dead assassin," Willow said. "An assassin hired by you in Hajimhi colors. Who do you think they'll believe?"

"Not you." Terjalesh smiled again, an unpleasant expression. "Abakian wields great power. Will *vojenta mahaut* this year be. The boy king nothing is."

"You might as well stop hiring assassins. He's protected."

"For now." Terjalesh turned back to Felix, unconcerned by the bodyguards' looming presence. "Do not sleep easy, boy King."

"Don't you *dare* threaten Felix!"

Terjalesh laughed. "We know who the true King of Tremontane is and we respect him. Abakian prepared to treat with him is. Serjian building on false hopes is. The more fools you."

"Willow," Felix said in a small voice.

"How does it feel, that your own uncle wants you dead?" Terjalesh said to Felix. "And if we his right hand are, you can prove nothing."

Kerish drew his sword and shouted something in Eskandelic, gesturing the bodyguards back. *He keeps picking fights,* Willow thought wildly, but Terjalesh only laughed and replied with what sounded like a challenge. Felix stepped closer to Willow. "He scares me," he whispered.

"Don't be scared. He's not going to hurt us," Willow said, hoping it was true.

The shouting had drawn quite an audience, men and women forming a lopsided circle around them and whispering to each other. Kerish replied at length, his voice cool and commanding, and gestured with his sword. Terjalesh went rigid, and for a moment Willow saw uncertainty in his slab of a face. Then he laughed again, a forced sound, and turned away, saying something over his shoulder. Kerish stood there, his hand balled into a fist, his jaw rigid. "Kerish?" Willow said.

"It's all right," Kerish said. "He was afraid."

"He didn't look afraid. He looked like a beast barely under control."

"He wouldn't have walked away if he weren't afraid of what might come out if we dueled." He sheathed his sword and turned his back on the retreating giant.

"Dueled? Would you have fought a duel?"

"Over you? Of course. We can't afford to have people thinking you're weak. And I object to seeing the woman I love treated so disrespectfully."

"But wouldn't they think I'm weak if I don't fight my own battles?"

"It doesn't work that way. You'd be…it shows your status, that you have powerful people willing to fight for you. But it doesn't matter, because he refused my challenge. He's big, but he's not stupid. I may not have fought often in the past eight years, but I still have a reputation as a skilled swordsman—more skilled than he ever was. He might even have been grateful for the excuse to turn me down."

"That's because the Abakians are doing Terence Valant's bidding. They're not doing it of their own volition, they're doing it because he wants them to and they want stronger ties with Tremontane."

"That's quite a leap, Willow."

"It's what he said—about being Terence's right hand in his wanting Felix dead. And all that stuff about Abakian becoming *vojenta mahaut*, and planning to treat with him—I'm convinced they're behind the assassins."

"It won't be enough proof for the other principalities."

"No. But it's a start."

She realized Felix's grip on her hand was painfully tight. Felix's face was ashen and drawn with fear, and he stared at nothing, unblinking. She crouched, not caring what it did to the *giorjanesh*, and gathered Felix into her arms. "You're very brave, you know that?"

"I don't feel brave."

"Hilarion says bravery is doing the right thing even when you're scared."

A weak smile broke over Felix's face. "Hilarion never said that."

"Well, he would have if he'd known me. And it's true."

"Is that the man who hired the assassins?"

"Yes. And we're going to stop him. Now, let's go watch the…what did you call it? *Stevaashi*? We'll watch that, and then we'll go have dinner and a nice cool bath, and you can show us Ernest's new trick."

"All right." He still looked pensive.

"Is something wrong?" *I should say 'is something else wrong?'*

"Did we miss Nanitan's trial?"

Willow burst out laughing. If he could still worry about the dogs, he would be all right. "Let's go over there, and find out," she said.

Chapter Seventeen

"I realize it's not proof enough to condemn them in public," Willow said, "but it's enough to justify searching for more evidence."

"Agreed," Janida said. "Catrela?"

Catrela stood and began pacing the harem chamber, weaving a path between sofas and floor pillows. "Definitive would be to catch them in the act of arranging for another assassination," she said, "but that complicated is. We would have to have our own 'assassin' in place to accept the commission, and find someone acceptable to all a witness to be."

"And I'd rather not risk Felix's life again," Willow said.

Catrela nodded acknowledgement. "Less complex but more difficult, documentation to find. A letter from Terence Valant requesting their services would convince all but Abakian's staunchest supporters."

"I do not understand how it can both less complex and more difficult be," Alondra said. She held Caderina over one shoulder and rubbed the baby's back gently.

"It's less complex because it's as straightforward as finding the letter, but difficult because we'd have to get into the Abakian Residence," Willow said. "Which I can do."

"The Abakian Residence a fortress is," Giara said. "I think you overconfident are."

"I've spent the last ten years of my life breaking into places people thought were impregnable," Willow said. "And I'm not overconfident. It will take some doing, and I'm not saying it won't be hard, I'm just saying that with enough time, I'm sure I can find a way into anywhere."

"But you cannot read Eskandelic," Alondra said. "How will you know what evidence to take?"

"Kerish told me Terence doesn't speak Eskandelic. Anything he sent to Abakian will be in Tremontanese." Willow watched Catrela pace. "You know I can do it."

"Catrela should," Giara said.

"Moving about secretly in a home I have been given access to, that I can do with ease," Catrela said. "But entering a home uninvited, unlocking doors and bypassing sentries—this I cannot do without much preparation. And preparation something we have time for is not."

"What do you mean?" Willow asked.

"Conclave nearly over is," Janida said. "Nine days from now the vote on the *adjeni* is. For this information effective to be, we must have proof five days from now."

"That's not enough time," Willow said. "It usually takes me that long just to work out a plan of approach for something as well-defended as you say the Abakian Residence is."

"Then we must think of something else," Giara said. "Can we trick Raena into revealing the truth?"

"Raena a crafty old woman is," Maitea said, with the air of someone who was herself a crafty old woman. "She will not speak to us even to gloat."

"We might trick Terjalesh," Alondra said. "I know him. He cunning is, but not intelligent."

"No," Willow said. "It will have to be the break-in."

"That impossible is," said Catrela.

Willow shook her head. She could see the future laid out before her, all those possibilities, but only one led to the success of their cause. "I'll just have to work more quickly. And take advantage of your knowledge. Surely some of you have been inside the Abakian Residence?"

"I have," said Alondra. "Before I married was. Abakian courted me as *harima* and I visited the Residence twice. But I do not see how that helpful will be."

"The more I know about its interior, the more successful this will be. Alondra, can you draw a map of the parts of the Residence you remember? Catrela, where would they keep an incriminating letter like the one we need?"

"Every Residence has a room like this one. All business is carried out here. If it is not kept in the harem chamber, it might be in Raena's apartment."

"Unless it has been destroyed," Janida said. "This is foolishness."

"Raena would not destroy anything so valuable," Catrela said. "If she needed to turn against Terence Valant someday, she has only to produce the letter and claim he attempted to suborn Abakian. With no evidence that she hired assassins, it would make her look noble and him look weak in the eyes of others."

"But Janida's right, there's a possibility it might have been destroyed," Willow said. "Or that it doesn't exist. Abakian still might have done this on their own."

"And yet you will try anyway," Janida said.

"It's a risk, but it's one worth taking."

"If you are caught, it over is." Janida looked more stern than Willow had ever seen her. "Do not caught be."

"I've never been caught and I don't intend to be caught." Willow regretted her brash words immediately. Feeling cocky was a sure path to failure. "But I'm going to be careful. You said we need proof in five days? I'll make my theft in four. Which means I need to start…not immediately, I dislike making an initial approach in the dark. Tomorrow morning. And I need that map as soon as possible."

"I will draw it tonight," Alondra said.

Willow nodded. "I'm going to put Felix to bed now, and…thank you. All of you. You've done far more for him than I could have hoped."

"Thank us when he King is," Janida said. "You did not say you had spoken to Mahnouki Adorinda."

Startled, Willow said, "Who told you that?"

"Kerish. You should not have confronted her."

"*She* confronted *me*. Besides, there wasn't any way to avoid her. I didn't exactly want to talk to her." Belatedly, she remembered how that conversation had ended—something that had been driven out of her mind by the conflict with Terjalesh. "But I did learn something. Is it legal for a principality to invest heavily in the proposed southern voyage?"

"It illegal is not," Catrela said, "but…bad manners is, to promote out of altruism something that a personal benefit is. Did Adorinda say this?"

"She failed to credibly deny it."

Janida's lips curled in an unpleasant smile. "This a thing we can use is."

"So it wasn't so bad that I talked to her, was it?"

The smile vanished. "Willow North, you brash and impetuous are at times. Think of Hajimhi Fariola, and your insults to Abakian Raena at the Review. You *eskarna* for a King are, and should not speak so unguardedly. Adorinda is cunning and eloquent and can turn your words against you. But..." Her eyes narrowed in thought. "Kerish very clear was, that you clever and confident were. Perhaps you will yet learn to think before you speak."

"Thank you. I think," Willow said, and made her escape.

Willow's usual path from the harem chamber to her rooms felt darker than usual, though the Device lamps gleamed as brightly as ever. She crossed the open corridor without looking out over the grounds toward the invisible ocean. Part of her wanted to leap to the ground and go running off toward the Abakian Residence, start investigating the place, counting guards and timing their paths. But that would be stupid. Lurking around the building with no idea what she should look for would only get her caught. Not to mention that she didn't know where the Abakian Residence was. No, waiting for daylight was safest, even if it did set her nerves jangling with tension.

The sitting room was empty when she pushed the door open, so she went to Felix's bedroom and knocked softly. On a muffled reply, she entered. Felix was sitting on his bed, already in his nightshirt. Ernest was, for a miracle, asleep in his own bed, his doggy head resting on his front paws and his left ear twitching in his sleep. "I didn't think Ernest knew what that was for," Willow said.

"I wanted there to be room for you, and besides, it's good for him to obey," Felix said. He lay down, scooted well over so there was a place for Willow to sit.

"Are you tired? It's been a long day."

"I wanted you to tell me your plan."

"My plan?" She wondered how he'd known they'd made a plan to break into the Abakian Residence. Then she remembered what she'd said that morning. "Oh, you mean for if the Serjian question loses.

191

Which it won't. And I don't want you thinking fatalistically."

"I don't know that word."

"It means expecting the worst. If you do that, you can weaken yourself by not having confidence in whatever you're doing. You have to have confidence that we'll win."

"I do. But I'll feel better if I know what will happen if we don't win."

"All right. Here, sit up with me. You have the most extraordinary ability to fall asleep in the space of two breaths." Willow scooted over and put her arm around Felix. "Comfortable?"

"Yes."

"Then here it is." Willow squeezed his shoulders briefly. "If Eskandel won't support you, there's no way we can regain the Crown on our own. So we'll disappear into the city. There are plenty of Tremontanans living here in Umberan, and with a change of hair color and clothing, we'll look just like an ordinary mama and her little boy. Then we'll go to one of the other Eskandelic cities, change our names, and find work there. We'll move around like that for about a year, then come back to Umberan and settle in under yet another set of assumed names."

"That sounds easy."

"It's not, because there are all sorts of ways we can give ourselves away if we're not careful. But we'll both be careful, right?" There was another possibility, that of going to one of the Tremontanan provincial lords and asking for his or her help, but the idea made Willow's skin crawl. Not the need to ask for help; she wasn't that proud. No, it was the fact that it would be far harder to get Felix away from a Baron or Count who wanted to use him as a figurehead — and who would likely kill Willow as his first step in that process.

"Can I be Adam again?"

"Sure. But remember, that's not likely to happen."

"I remember." Felix snuggled closer, a little motion that made Willow's heart ache. "Will Kerish come with us?"

"I...don't know." In all her plans, she'd never thought to include Kerish, mainly because she'd made most of them before they were reconciled. Now it didn't seem so simple. Kerish had said he would give up Devisery for her, but she'd asked him to give up his magic once before and she wasn't going to make that mistake again. And a Deviser would draw far too much attention to them. But if they loved each other, shouldn't they make that decision together? The thought of leaving him behind made the ache grow harder and colder.

"Was that man today the one who wanted to kill me?"

"He hired the assassins, the one who killed Fedrani and the one your guard killed."

"He didn't know who I was. Why would he want to kill me?"

"Because your uncle asked him to. Felix, I'm sorry."

"Why are you sorry?"

"That you have to endure all this. If Terence wasn't such an arrogant, self-centered git, you'd still be in the palace and not fearing for your life."

"But I wouldn't have met you."

"That's true. And I would still be midnighting in Aurilien." Would Kerish understand that this plan, stealing from Abakian, wasn't the same? Or would he think she was breaking her promise to him? "I guess neither of our lives went the way we'd planned."

Felix was silent. Willow looked down at him and saw he'd fallen asleep. Carefully, she laid him down on his pillow and tucked him in. No, her life definitely hadn't gone as she'd planned.

When she emerged from Felix's room, she found Kerish sitting on one of the sofas, leaning back with his eyes closed and his arms stretched out across the sofa back. "You're not asleep, are you?" she said. "Because I'd have to wonder what it is about me that the men in my life fall asleep in my presence."

Kerish smiled. Without opening his eyes, he said, "I was just enjoying the quiet. Posea was having a shrieking fit just down the hall from my room and I wanted to get as far from her as possible."

"And 'as far as possible' turned out to be my room?"

"I might or might not have had ulterior motives. Come, sit with me." He opened his eyes and smiled at her, that wonderful expression that never failed to make her heart beat faster.

She sat down, and Kerish immediately put his arms around her. "There, that's better," he said. "I was hoping to spend some time alone with you."

"So was I." Willow rested her head against his shoulder and breathed in the wonderful smell of him. "It's been a long day."

"Culminating in a long meeting with Mother and my *majdrani*. Were you talking about the Abakians?"

"Yes." Willow fought a brief but urgent battle with herself, torn between honesty and cowardice, and won — or possibly lost. "I'm going to break into the Abakian Residence to find evidence linking them to Terence."

"*What?*" Kerish disentangled himself from her and grabbed both her hands. "Are you out of your mind?"

"Kerish, I know I said no more midnighting, but this is different!"

"You're damn right it's different. If you get caught, you'll not only be executed, you'll ruin Felix's chances entirely. You can't possibly think this is a good idea."

"It's not a great idea, true, but it's not — no, *listen* to me, Kerish! If I can find this evidence, Janida and the others can use it to erode Abakian's support and build ours. Not to mention preventing them from hiring any more assassins. This is crucial to Felix's survival."

Kerish swore a blistering oath. "Abakian was never going to vote for us anyway. This changes nothing."

"Then it protects Felix. Either way, this is a good thing."

"I thought I was done having to worry about you."

It hit her like a brick to the face. "I wouldn't do this except for Felix's sake. I made you a promise, and I intend to keep it. Please, Kerish, can you understand this?"

Kerish looked away. She could see the taut line of his jaw, his clenched fists, and a tiny thread of fear wound itself through her heart. Had she just ruined everything? She reached out to touch him, but withdrew her hand before it could rest on his, fearing what he might do.

Finally, he sighed. "I don't like it," he said, "but it makes sense. I just…Willow, *please* be careful."

"I will. I always am."

Kerish chuckled and put his arms around her again. "Remember when you broke into the Bank of Aurilien vault?"

She flushed. "That was different. I didn't know there were two sets of guards. And they'd put the second pair on duty the afternoon before my theft, so that wasn't carelessness, that was just bad luck."

"You came back so shaken I had to hold you for an hour to get you to calm down. I don't think you've ever come so close to being caught."

She smiled at him. "Only once before. When I found myself in a strange man's bedroom."

"I see. And I suppose that man turned you in for the reward."

"There wasn't a reward. And he didn't turn me in. He gave me my first kiss."

Kerish brushed his lips across her forehead, making her shiver with pleasure. "Did he? Was it a good kiss?"

"The best."

"Let's see if we can improve on that," Kerish said.

***

Early the next morning, Willow borrowed some clothes from Caira, a *zetesha's* short-sleeved robe and wide sash, and asked her to bundle up some clothes for her to carry. Caira rolled her eyes, but said nothing, and just after dawn Willow set out for the Abakian Residence, hoping she looked enough like a *zetesha* on an errand for her mistress to pass casual scrutiny. She'd donned the gray headwrap herself, and with that covering her hair and her skin tanned by weeks under the hot Eskandelic sun, she wasn't obviously Tremontanan. She hoped.

Umberan at dawn was cool and fresh, smelling of dew and the salt brine of the ocean. The usual overcast was thin and high, promising a blistering hot day as soon as the sun got around to burning it off. Willow walked slowly along the street in the kid leather shoes she'd made herself and felt as if she were home again, though Aurilien didn't smell of the sea and its houses weren't plastered white. Her special shoes were thin enough to let her feel the stones of the street, and if she really were a native of Umberan she'd be able to walk the length of the city blindfolded, just relying on the shoes. But she wasn't a native, and her eyes had to be her guide.

She'd passed the Abakian Residence twice in her earlier wanderings through Umberan without knowing it, and hadn't paid it much attention other than to observe how big it was, easily a third again the size of the Serjian Residence. Its walls, forty feet high and squared off at the top, were built of the same pinkish-tan stone, but in blocks the size of a carriage that must have taken dozens of laborers dozens of hours to haul from wherever they were quarried. All she'd seen of the building were a couple of domed roofs beyond the massive walls, but at the time she hadn't been interested in its construction. Today was different.

The Abakian Residence wasn't located in its own private neighborhood the way the Serjian Residence was, fortunately for Willow's plans. A private neighborhood meant twice as many guards to elude. A completely unnecessary iron fence surrounded the stone walls, with crushed stone and the same spiky desert plants Willow had seen back at the Serjian Principality filling the space between the two. Two guards stood sentinel at the gate. They looked far more alert and ready for violence than their Serjian counterparts. Too bad she couldn't just suborn them, get them to protect Felix instead of the Abakians. But that was a different kind of job, and not one she had any gift for.

She kept walking, observing the place covertly while appearing intent on her shoes. So. She'd need to find a way through or over the wall and then tackle getting inside the house. The wall was too sheer a face to climb without assistance, and she couldn't tell if there were guards at the top, but she'd bet on it.

She stopped, removed a shoe and pretended to search it for a small, annoying stone. The guards hadn't noticed her, on the far side of the street, though they gave close attention to anyone passing near the gate.

Past the Abakian Residence, a row of tall, narrow houses extended to the end of the street, similar in shape to Rafferty's place, but built of granite rather than wood and stucco. They looked expensive, and much easier to get into than the Residence, and Willow had a moment's regret that they weren't her target. On the other hand, they might be able to help her with the real job.

Willow put her shoe back on and crossed the street at the corner, then kept going, looking for access to the rear of the houses. She found it immediately, a narrow alley barely wide enough for a small wagon to pass, cluttered here and there with barrels and crates. It smelled faintly of human waste, but the paved surface was clean, with no noxious puddles or unpleasant clumps that could be mistaken for dirt. There were doors but no windows on the side facing the alley—on either side, because the other "wall" of the alley was a row of identical houses. Aside from the narrowness, it was nothing like an Aurilien alley, but it still felt comforting, familiar, and Willow felt a tingle of excitement she hadn't felt since leaving home.

The alley ended at a blank stone wall about seven feet high, too smooth for her to climb. Willow found a convenient crate, empty, but solidly built, and dragged it over to the wall. With its help, she was able to stand tall enough to peer over the wall's top, if she pulled herself up a bit. Wishing she had her special gloves, she gripped the stones and hoisted herself up.

She could just barely see the guards at the Residence front gate, but they weren't looking her way in any case. The space between the iron fence and the stone wall of the Residence was narrower on this side, but still filled with crushed stone and desert plants. A hard-packed dirt path ran from a wide double door in the wall around to the back of the Residence, with little stones scattered across it where the gardeners—could you call them that, if there was no garden?—hadn't been thorough in sweeping its surface. The double door, its wood dark with age, was iron-banded and had a massive lock visible from where she was as a black smudge on the iron faceplate. This was probably where deliveries came, which meant there was likely another gate at the back of the house.

Willow dropped lightly to the ground, put the crate back after a moment's thought, then ran back down the alley and turned left. Unless there were streets she hadn't guessed at, this one should take her around to the rear of the Abakian Residence.

This time, she strolled with her hands swinging freely by her sides, dangling her bundle and enjoying the fresh breeze off the ocean and the comforting sounds of the city. Carriages passed her, their wheels rumbling along the cobblestones like approaching thunder. She felt like waving at the occupants, but that was out of character for the *zetesha* she appeared to be, so she contented herself with watching them drive past and wondering what their stories were.

What would they think if they knew what she was planning? Aside from immediately turning her over to the authorities. Just over a month ago, she wouldn't even have considered stealing from the Abakian Residence—too much danger for too little payoff. And now she was planning what might well be the most dangerous heist of her career. The only thing more dangerous she could think of was sneaking into the palace grounds to climb Old Tower, and she wasn't likely to do that any time soon.

She turned another corner. The new street was parallel to the one the Abakian Residence faced, and was its mirror image: a row of narrow stone houses, then the back of the Residence and the continuation of its iron fence. There was another entrance here, but no stone arch, just a metal gate set into the fence. It was rusted in places and, more interestingly, unguarded. A corroded brass bell hung from its top, no doubt a way for drovers to signal the arrival of deliveries. Children must pull this bell all the time, annoying the guards. She thought about yanking the cord and then running away, but that was too juvenile a prank to pull even on the Abakians.

Willow stopped, set down her bundle, and stretched, pretending to need a rest from carrying that heavy parcel while really examining the back wall of the Residence. No doors on this side, and no windows—well, there wouldn't be any, would there?—but—

Willow let her gaze continue traveling casually across the top of the wall, but her heart thumped once, painfully, when a guard wielding a crossbow appeared out of nowhere and looked directly at her. There was no way he could know what she had in mind, but she felt as if her guilt was written on her forehead in large letters. *No fear.*

She pretended she hadn't seen him, stretched again, and picked up her bundle and strolled off. Well. That was one question answered. It was going to be hard, plotting the guards' movements when they were barely visible, but the truth was, if she couldn't see them, they likely had as much trouble seeing anyone near the base of the wall. So it was all a matter of timing.

Once she was out of sight of the Residence, Willow picked up the pace. Back to the Serjian Residence to change into her own clothes, and then the real work began.

Chapter Eighteen

Thunder rumbled in the distance, a big-bellied chortle from one of the lost gods. Willow eyed the oncoming storm. It would reach Umberan just after sunset, darkening the sky and pouring rain into the streets. She was counting on it spending itself and moving out over the ocean well before she had to be at the Abakian Residence, because otherwise she was going to get very wet. Tracking water all over the inside of the enemy Residence would go a long way toward getting herself caught.

There was a click, and the lock sprang open. Willow set it aside and picked up the next. She hadn't been able to get close enough to the side door to test her skills on its lock, so she'd done the next best thing: bought a bunch of assorted locks to practice with. There was little difference between Eskandelic and Tremontanan locks, but she didn't want to take chances. She was getting really sick of lock picking, but her speed had improved and she'd honed her skills to the point that she could open each of these locks in under a minute. She *needed* to open the door in half that time, but this was the best she could do.

Click. One more lock. She let her fingers do the work and scanned the horizon. Streaks of lightning illuminated the clouds like threads of light. The wind had picked up, blowing the leaves of the trellis vine so they rustled around her. She'd taken to practicing in the rooftop garden, which was a riot of color, bushes with dark green leaves and trumpet-shaped flowers of purple and pink, squash plants in the vegetable garden shedding the last of their yellow flowers, green tomatoes beginning to blush red. It smelled deliciously sweet and spicy, even more so with the coming storm, and Willow enjoyed the peaceful quiet and the coolness at midday. The sounds of the city were muffled, distant, and she could pretend she was a lady with a country manor and leisure time to…well, pick locks, which no lady would ever do. It was a nice, irrelevant fantasy she didn't actually wish for.

Click. She set the last lock aside and stretched, then put away her picks. Four days wasn't nearly enough time to prepare herself for this, but she'd had to make do. She'd stitched up a pair of gloves with roughened palms, wishing she'd known to take all her midnighting gear with her when they left Aurilien. She didn't actually plan on climbing anything but the iron fence, but having some protection from the freezing bars was worth a little extra effort. Rafferty had taken her to a used clothing shop in the Tremontanan enclave where she bought dark, fitted trousers, a charcoal-gray shirt with loose sleeves—not too loose—and a knit cap that concealed her hair entirely. Nothing black, which stood out at night. How many aspiring thieves had learned that lesson the very hard way?

"I thought I'd find you up here," Kerish said. He emerged from the dark hole of the stairwell and crossed the garden to sit on the bench opposite her at her table. "It's almost suppertime."

"Thanks."

"I brought you something. I'm not sure if it will help, but…"

He held out his hand. Willow took the squat cylinder, no longer than her middle finger and half that around, and braced against its tingling brass. "What is it?"

"A prototype light Device. You twist the two halves, and it makes a light. Not a very bright light, I'm afraid."

"Bright light is generally a bad thing, for a thief." She gingerly took the thing in her other hand and twisted. One end of the cylinder began glowing with a warm pinkish light that flickered slightly, not as much as a candle would, but more than the Devices lighting the Residence did. "That's amazing. Please tell me you stole this."

"I didn't steal it. I may have borrowed it without permission. So don't lose it."

"I won't. Now I'm glad I have the gloves. This is much better than matches or a lantern."

"I'm glad I can help. Are you nervous?"

"Not nervous. Just—ready to go." She'd tried to explain the feeling to him several times, but maybe there were no words for that sense of urgency, the knife-edged clarity to everything around her, the way her skin fizzed like silver and all her senses were tuned to the highest pitch. Saying she was on edge gave entirely the wrong impression.

Kerish reached across the table and took her hand. "I'll be waiting for you, however late it is."

"I know. I'm sorry. I know how this must feel for you."

"Do you?" There was an edge to his voice that made Willow want to pull away from him. But he gripped her hand more tightly and said, "Sorry. It's just—I'm a strong, skilled swordsman, I'm trained to fight, and yet you're constantly facing things I'm powerless to protect you from. Why can't you be menaced by pirates for once?"

Willow laughed. "After all this, we'll go to sea and sail around waiting for pirates to attack, and then you can defend me."

"I'd appreciate it. And then you can appreciate *me* in an appropriately grateful way."

Willow moved around to sit next to him. "I do appreciate you," she said, "all the time."

He kissed her, his lips gentle in a way that made her long for more. "True. But there's always time for more."

"Not if it's almost suppertime."

Kerish kissed her again, more deeply. "They can wait."

"Mmm. If you kiss me like that again, they can wait all night."

"That sounds like a request."

He put his arms around her waist and drew her closer, kissing her until she was breathless and dizzy. His hand stroked the soft skin at the base of her neck, making her tingle from more than just the Device she held. It was like a miracle, his love for her, and she pressed herself against him until she could feel the beat of his heart in rhythm with hers.

A quiet cough brought her back to herself, startling her into pulling away from Kerish more abruptly than she intended. Gessala stood there, expressionless, with her arms crossed over her chest. "It is time for supper," she said, and turned and left the roof.

"She still hates me," Willow said.

"She doesn't hate you."

"I ruined her life. What would you call it?"

Kerish put his arms around her and pulled her close, resting his forehead against hers. "All right, she's angry, and maybe that makes sense, but Gessala isn't the sort of person who holds grudges."

"She's your *suorena*, so I guess you'd know." That hadn't been a friendly look. Willow resolved to stay out of Gessala's way in future.

Supper was even more quiet than usual. Willow ate lightly and reviewed her plan in her head. It was detailed to begin with, then became more of a sketch, because she knew from experience that plans tended to diverge from the ideal almost immediately. She tried to be grateful for the lack of conversation, so distracting, but the silence felt oppressive, as if she were going off to her death. She took a large bite of her *cabra*, savoring the rich herbs of the curried lamb stew. It was her favorite — was that on purpose? Had the cook, not privy to the plan, somehow divined what she intended that night and prepared her a last meal? Suddenly the food wasn't so appetizing anymore.

She walked with Felix back to their rooms. Felix hadn't spoken at all during the meal, which concerned Willow. "Something wrong?" she said. Felix shrugged. "Is this because of what I'm doing tonight?"

"Don't you ever get scared of things that might happen?" he said. "Like getting caught?"

"No, because if you're scared, you make mistakes, and making mistakes is what gets you caught. Are you scared for me?"

Felix nodded.

"Well, don't be, because that will only make you feel worse and it won't help me at all. Be brave for me instead." Everyone was treating this like some kind of suicide quest. That was not the mindset she needed to be in right now.

She tucked Felix in and returned to the sitting room. The frond tree, caught in the wildness of the approaching storm, lashed the window with dry, scratching sounds. She looked out over the city, which was tinted strange colors, orange and red for the sunset, pale yellow for the light that reflected off the storm clouds. Five hours before she had to leave. She wished she could go immediately, wanted to be moving, acting, but that was a fool's errand, and she couldn't afford to be a fool.

Kerish had offered to wait with her, but she'd turned him down gently. She needed this time alone for final preparations. She took out a blank sheet of paper from the stack on the writing desk, sat at the table and began sketching. Alondra's map had been not only detailed, but beautiful. Willow had forgotten she was an artist. Willow's version was rougher, but the important thing was that she was able to draw it from memory. She certainly couldn't afford to take any map with her to the Abakian Residence.

She compared the two maps. Perfect. Well, not *perfect*, but she hadn't left out any details and she knew where everything was. It would be a more useful map if she were able to go in the front door, but it would have to do.

She traced the lines with her forefinger. Past the iron fence, the giant stone wall surrounded a courtyard, which in turn surrounded the Residence. Wide marble stairs led up to the main doors, which according to Alondra opened on an entrance hall with several doors and stairs leading off it. Alondra knew two of those exits went to reception rooms, places she'd gone as *harima*. Unfortunately, she'd never been to the harem's meeting chamber, but she'd been able to eliminate two more exits as leading down and to each side, probably to offices and servants' quarters on the first floor. "There a dome is," she'd said while going over the map with Willow, "and that the harem chamber will be. It in the center of the Residence is."

"And at the top," Willow had said. "So I just need to keep going up."

Now she wondered if she'd been too cavalier. The Abakian Residence was four stories tall, and there was a lot of unknown space between the entry hall and the harem chamber, wherever it was. And Willow wouldn't be going in by the front door. After passing through the wall, she intended to use the Residence door closest to that side, a little door that led to the kitchens. Probably. Some sort of servants' rooms, anyway. Willow was fairly certain one of the stairs Alondra had identified ended up near that door.

She pushed the sketch map away and lay down on the sofa for a quick nap. It would leave her rested and keep her edge sharp. *I wish Kerish were here*, she thought as she drifted off, but that was a bad idea, a distracting one. They weren't sleeping together, but not for lack of desire. Willow didn't have any remaining family bonds to interfere with having sex with someone she wasn't married to, but she still had enough respect for her religion not to break that taboo. Being alone together in her rooms, or his...the other night she'd had the hardest time telling him goodbye, saying no to his devastating kisses. He didn't seem disappointed, but suppose he was just good at hiding it?

She shook away those distracting memories. She'd go to him first thing upon returning. It was something she owed him.

When she woke, the clock on the wall above the door read just after one o'clock. Excellent timing. She changed into her midnighting gear, checked the fit of her knives and the wire stashed up her sleeve, tightened her belt pouch and put on her gloves. Then she drew in a long, comforting breath and let it out slowly. This was her time.

She left the Serjian Residence by the kitchen door and made her way from shadow to bush until she reached the wall. Call it a warm-up for the night's activities, eluding the guards at the gate, even if the raindrops lingering on the bushes did dampen her shirt and trousers. She pulled herself up and over and landed lightly on the other side. Janida needed to know that security was still lax, though if Willow succeeded tonight, it might not matter so much.

Dodging the guards at the black arch took more effort, which cheered her. Success came down to her magical edge, perceiving the guard outside before she ran into him. She waited for her opening, then ducked past him and ran along the outer wall, listening for sound of pursuit. She heard nothing but the sound of her breathing, light and easy, and the fainter sound of her soft shoes striking the stones of the road. One hurdle down.

The storm had passed, leaving a clean scent in the air and sweeping away the odors of human and animal waste. She avoided the puddles, but her shoes were still soaked from the grass of the Residence. Nothing she could do about that now. Tiny white birds cooed and whistled overhead, swooping across the still-cloudy sky in pairs. Willow squinted up at them once or twice, their bodies light-colored blobs against the darkness of the sky. She'd never seen them before. It always astonished her, the things that came out at night. It was like a different world.

She turned the corner, heading toward the center of town. It was a fifteen-minute walk to the Abakian Residence at night, when the streets were empty of all but a few patrolling guards. She'd tried to map out as much of their routes as she could, but with only four days to prepare and a million other things to do, she'd fallen back on sticking to the side streets and hoping for the best. Umberan didn't have a curfew, but she guessed they would be suspicious of anyone out late and she couldn't afford to be caught.

She saw movement, and a flash of silvery steel, half a breath before the guard stepped into sight, barely enough time to duck into the dubious shelter of a doorway. Heart pounding, she listened to the tread of his boots crossing the street only feet away. She was *not* going back to that cell, he was *not* going to catch her… Her breathing was too loud, surely he'd hear it and come storming over — no, his footsteps were receding, and she made herself breathe slowly, closing her eyes against her memories. No cell. Not ever again.

She walked more carefully after that near-miss, sticking to the alleys and listening hard for signs that anyone else was abroad that night. *Wouldn't it be funny if I met another thief? We could exchange notes.* Not that thieves tended to be friendly with each other — too much competition, and she wouldn't speak an Eskandelic thief's language anyway. But the idea amused her all the way to the Residence, where she stopped across the street, concealed in the shadow of a tall building, and examined the Residence one final time.

Light Devices glowed at the iron street gate, which was unguarded, and at the wall where the heavy front doors were a dark blotch against the lighter pinkish-tan stones. No one stood at those doors, either. She'd concluded Abakian counted on the sheer impregnability of the wall to discourage casual attempts at breaking in. She loved that kind of arrogance in a mark.

High above, lights like moving stars floated past as the guards walked back and forth along their paths atop the wall. She'd watched them for two nights and seen the same thing both times: they kept irregular patterns, sometimes pausing for minutes at a time, presumably to chat about women or gambling or whatever it was guards found interesting. Nothing she could take advantage of. The first night, it had been discouraging. The second night, she'd stopped wishing for what couldn't be and made a plan.

She circled wide around the Residence, wishing the wall at the end of the alley weren't there. The alley would have been perfect for her plan. Instead, she crept along the front of the row of tall houses, sneaking from doorway to doorway until she crouched as near as she could get to the iron fence running along the side of the Residence. It was fifteen feet from where she lurked and radiated cold even at that distance. She tugged her cap more firmly over her head, snugged her gloves close to her fingers, and waited. This was the second most dangerous part of this job, getting to the wall without being seen. Which was why she'd arranged for a little help.

Time passed. Willow watched the guards pass, two of them on this side, and wondered what the Abakians were so afraid of that they needed so much security. Their paths had them meeting in the middle, pausing for the inevitable conversation, then separating to walk back to opposite corners. That left her an opening, but not enough of one. She liked lax guards, but sometimes they just made trouble.

She flexed one foot, which had started to cramp. More of the tiny birds swept overhead and disappeared past the roof of her shelter. This had to work. She didn't know what time it was, but her distraction certainly did. If Rafferty arrived late, or worse, had been early…

She heard singing, far in the distance. It was a powerful, melodious voice, and the notes echoed off the houses on the next street over, making the words unintelligible. Willow knew the tune, though. It was a popular Tremontanan folk song about a young man and his walking staff, heavy with innuendo and a hundred verses. It was so unexpected she almost laughed. Rafferty had assured her he'd keep the guards' attention on him, but hadn't said how.

The singer was coming closer, and Willow tensed, ready to run, watching the guards. There. One guard reached his corner at the rear of the wall and stayed there, looking down. Willow couldn't see Rafferty, but she could hear him clearly and knew he'd stopped outside the fence. Another racket arose, this one of a metal stick banging against the bars of the fence. Willow grinned. The second guard left his path to join his fellow at the back corner, and Willow sprinted for the fence.

Chapter Nineteen

Gravel crunched underfoot as she ran, feeling every sharp-edged pebble through her soft soles. Time for pain later. She grabbed hold of the icy crossbar at the top of the fence, barely able to reach it in a leap, and used her momentum to pull herself up and over. Her shirt snagged and tore, and she cursed under her breath. Landing lightly, she rose from a crouch and ran again, wincing at how loud her footsteps were. Was the gravel another security measure on the Abakians' part? Probably not, but it was serving them well tonight, or would be if anyone were paying attention.

She didn't bother avoiding the desert plants dotting the ground, and they sent up spicy fragrances wherever she trod. The ruckus was wild music to her ears, her feet crunched the gravel underneath, her breath came in quick pants, drawing in the damp, cool air, and then she was in the shelter of the doorway arch. It wasn't much more than a few inches of stone protruding from the wall, but it would have to be enough. She rattled the latch gently, just to be sure—she'd once managed to lock an unlocked door she'd thought was locked—then whipped out her picks and went to work. The lock was older and bigger than her practice locks, big enough she could almost fit her pinky inside, and the slim picks gave alarmingly as she worked the tumblers. Already her plan was going south. She closed her eyes and watched the icy tumblers shift, too slowly.

The banging sound had become rhythmic as Rafferty started using the fence as a percussion instrument. Shouts joined the melody, drifting down from above. The guards sounded as frustrated as she'd hoped, and she grinned despite the tension gripping her neck and shoulders. She owed Rafferty again. Not that she was in a position to grant favors other than perhaps the use of the Serjian Residence bathhouse. He'd only be there a few more minutes, and this lock was taking *forever* to pick, she was wasting her distraction—

With a squeal that set Willow's teeth on edge, the tumblers ground into a new position. Willow jammed her picks into her waistband and eased the door open.

Barrels and crates surrounded the door, piled neatly to head-height. Willow put a hand on one of them, and it shifted: empty. These were waiting to be collected by merchants and wine vendors in exchange for full ones. Willow slid through the narrow gap between door and frame and crouched behind a stack of crates. The smell of old wine and rotten food almost overwhelmed her, and she breathed shallowly through her mouth to avoid the worst of the stink.

She moved a few inches to the right, hoping for a better view of the Residence and the door she knew would be there. The ells and blocky wings of the Residence looked tacked on to the main building, exactly as if some giant child had constructed it out of whatever blocks were handy. In the center, rising high above the rest, was a golden dome that gleamed in the lamplight. By day it would be blindingly brilliant and probably unspeakably gaudy, but it had an immense dignity by night. That dome was her goal.

She could see the guards on the opposite wall more clearly. The wall-walk was open on the inside, and steps led down the wall. They weren't more than stones protruding from the sheer face, but the guard descending them trotted down them as if they were the broadest of ballroom stairs. Willow watched him for a few moments before she realized he was coming her way.

She cursed, and wormed her way deeper into the pile of barrels and crates, praying it was enough concealment, praying the guard would be too focused on his annoyance with Rafferty to pay much attention to his surroundings. She hadn't considered that the guards might take a more direct approach to her diversion if it continued too long. If the guard realized the door was unlocked…and he would certainly lock it on his way back in…she'd counted on that door being open if she had to leave in a hurry, and this meant recalculating everything. She made herself breathe more quietly. No panic. First, avoid being seen. Worry about the rest later.

She crouched in her stinking hole and listened to heavy booted footsteps approach. The man was grumbling in Eskandelic, and she heard keys clink over the sound of the footsteps. She caught a glimpse of dark hair, then the key was in the lock—she clenched her fists so tightly they ached. More muttering, and the key turned again. The door opened, then shut again with a loud, frustrated bang. Willow stood and ran for the Residence.

Picks in hand, she made a straight dash, counting on all the guards' attention to still be on Rafferty. The stone of the courtyard sent little jolts through her soles to her knees as she ran, praying to remain unseen. The guard at the door hadn't done anything to indicate he realized it had been open, so maybe her luck was holding.

The side door was nearly black against the light stone of the Residence. Willow grabbed the latch, grateful for the gloves that shielded her against its icy numbness, then breathed out in relief when she discovered the door was unlocked. She was inside in moments, panting with exertion and excitement.

The hallway beyond was black, not illuminated by candle or Device. Willow leaned against the door to catch her breath and let her senses build up a picture for her. Three doors to the right, five to the left. Iron lacework cages for the lanterns that were currently unlit. A *lot* of copper and iron somewhere to the right; that had to be the kitchen. Above, silver blobs of candlesticks at the very limit of her range. The hall smelled faintly of roasted pork and spicy chickpea paste. Willow blinked, and saw dim light at the end of the hall. Using the door latches and hinges to keep herself oriented, she moved toward it.

The light grew brighter and more yellow the farther she went, until she came to a T-junction where a hall branched off from hers to the left. Golden lamplight burned just a few steps away, illuminating the stone-paved hall and a couple of doors beyond. Willow looked back down the continuation of the dark hall. You didn't leave lights burning in places that weren't used. She quietly made her way down the new hall.

The first door she came to, its iron hinges black with long use, was locked. She didn't bother opening it. The mess of metal beyond told her it was a storeroom. She shook off the pleasantly drunk sensation it gave her and moved on. Her shadow came and went beside her as she passed the lamps, a partner in crime, though a silent and useless one. Rufus had often suggested she partner with someone, but she'd always hated the thought. Her shadow was the closest she'd ever come to a companion.

The next storeroom was also locked. She regretted, as she usually did at this point in a theft, that there wasn't some way to make a clock you could carry with you. Maybe that was a Device Kerish could invent. Or maybe some clever Deviser already had, and no one knew about it because it lacked artistic unity. Willow pushed those thoughts aside. *Stay focused. Move quickly but efficiently. Stop daydreaming.*

Ahead, she saw another door, identical to the others, and next to it, a staircase leading up. Willow ran to its base and up a few stone steps, listening. She heard nothing but her own breathing and the slight scratching noise, so faint, of her shoes on the steps. More light came from above, silvery rather than golden, and steady, not flickering. Probably Devices. She crept up the stairs, one hand trailing along the cold stone of the wall.

A silver-white Device light in a cage of polished steel that to Willow's senses intensified the light illuminated the landing, where the stairs doubled back on themselves. At the top was another landing, this one tiny, next to a blank wall, and a double door sheathed in brass that made her feel like sneezing from the tingling. She pushed the door open an inch or two, then stopped as it made a high-pitched *skree*, loud enough to shatter the stillness, though probably not as loud as it seemed to Willow's keyed-up nerves. She left it for the moment and moved to explore the hall leading away from it.

More doors, very little metal — there were the candlesticks to the right, a big empty nothing space studded with icy nails to the left. She checked that room despite what Alondra had said about the harem chamber being at the top of the house. It really was empty, some kind of reception room or ballroom. For the first time she wondered if Eskandelics had dances the way Tremontanan nobles did. Something to ask Janida when she returned to the Serjian Residence.

The hall ended in a stairway leading up, this one of wood. Willow tiptoed up a few steps, which didn't creak, then paused. This didn't feel right. She was almost directly over the kitchen, so the dining room had to be nearby, but what else would be above the kitchen? Apartments, that's what, with easy access for servants bringing breakfast or midnight snacks.

She retreated down the hall to the brass doors and stood, bracing herself against the tingling. She should have thought to bring oil, and she cursed herself for her carelessness. There was no help for it. She leaned against one door and slowly, so slowly, pushed it open. The doors went *skree* again, but a thinner, higher sound Willow could barely hear. She slipped through the narrow crack, her teeth buzzing with proximity to the doors, and took a few quick steps away.

Two silver-white Device lanterns faintly illuminated the room, which smelled of roses from narrow vases flanking a pair of wide, ornately carved doors. This had to be the entry Alondra had described. The tall, narrow room rose two stories to a mosaic ceiling depicting something Willow couldn't make out in the dimness. Tiles covered the walls in an abstract design, shades of gray in the lamplight, and benches of white marble here and there stood in contrast to them. Willow moved forward to stand at the center of the room and looked up. A pair of spiraling staircases, wrought iron painted white, ascended to the next floor, and several doors led to rooms with little metal in them.

Willow cast about to orient herself by her memorized map. She'd come up the servants' stairs — no wonder they came out at such a tiny landing, the Abakians wouldn't think servants needed much space — and there was a second stairway leading down to the first floor a few yards away. Then there were the iron staircases, which had her shivering already, and the front doors, and the smaller doors leading to the salons Alondra had seen, plus the doors she'd noted but not entered. Willow tried one of them. It led to a long, narrow room with floor cushions stacked high in piles near the door and one of those fat-bellied musical instruments propped on a stand at the far end. Music room. She shut the door.

It was possible one of those smaller doors led to stairs going up, but what was the point when you had two beautiful staircases available right in the open? Willow swallowed hard and tried to calm the beating of her heart. Why hadn't Alondra said they were made of iron? *Because to her it didn't matter*, she thought, and before she could dither any longer, she made herself take the first step.

Sweet heaven, it was *cold*. She wanted to run, but even her soft, slow steps caused the treads to let out a quiet, musical tone, hollow as if she were striking them with a mallet. *It's all in your head, it's not real, you're not freezing.* Her hands were shaking, her feet were practically numb, and despite herself she moved faster, desperate to escape. She flung herself off the last step and crouched, shivering, as far from the staircase as she could get.

When the shivering subsided, she examined her surroundings. This was little more than a landing that overlooked the entry hall. The light from the Devices burning below didn't reach this high, and there was only one light, a steel lantern cage hanging from a stand that didn't do much more than brighten the dimness. Windows cut into the dome of the ceiling would illuminate the room far better during the daytime, but now they only showed the black, cloud-covered sky that was a thief's best friend.

She turned her attention to the three doors on the opposite wall. Each was mahogany, with brass hinges and wooden doorknobs, and as far as Willow could tell, they were identical. There were no other openings off this room, or gallery, or whatever it was.

Willow crossed the tiled wooden floor, grateful for its silence, and examined each door. She couldn't sense any metal beyond the hinges, could perceive nothing that might tell her what was beyond each door. The air was still and warm, warmer than it had been on the first floor, and surrounded her like a gentle caress, relaxing her. She shook the feeling off. Relaxed was deadly.

This floor was where the apartments were, and at least one of these doors, possibly more, opened on the Abakian living quarters. If she was lucky, one of them would lead to stairs. If she was unlucky, and those stairs were in the heart of the living quarters…

She tiptoed to the door farthest to the left and took out Kerish's Device, twisted it, and held it up to the door. People used it all day long, in and out, so how would that show itself on the door? Time was sliding away from her. She moved to the next door. Identical.

In the distance, she heard footsteps.

She twisted the light off and dropped it into her shirt. The doors were identical as far as her eyes and her magic were concerned. She stripped off her left glove and felt the knob of the leftmost door. It was smooth from hundreds of hands, slightly grainy where the lacquer had worn off.

The footsteps grew louder. Closer. She ran to the next door. Smooth, but less grainy — or was that her imagination? She tried the third door, then ran back to the first. Both of them felt more worn than the middle. The footsteps were nearly to the entry hall. Breathing out a desperate prayer, she turned the middle doorknob and pushed the door open.

Chapter Twenty

Once again she was in darkness, but this time there was no metal to guide her, only the tingling sensation of the brass hinges at her back. The warm, damp air clung to her like a shroud. She reached out with her bare hand and felt around her, but found nothing. For a moment, she was transported back to her cell and had to force herself not to panic. She reached into her shirt and pulled out the light Device, twisted it, and wanted to laugh at how much the dim pink glow reassured her.

The walls of this little room were tiled with tesserae the size and shape of her thumbnail, tracing out blooming flowers and angular lines. It was too bad she couldn't see it in full light, because what she was able to make out was beautiful. Ahead, stairs ascended beyond the range of her light. Their treads were tiled as well, with extraordinary blossoms and vines that Willow was almost afraid to step on. They were slippery underfoot, and Willow had to move slowly despite the inner voice that was shrieking at her to hurry.

The stairs ended at a wooden door, plain by comparison to the walls. This one was locked. Willow set to work opening it. Moments slid past as the tumblers shifted, not fast enough. The scratching sound of the picks was driving her mad, and if she weren't so damned *slow* she'd be done already. She concentrated on her fingers, on her sense of the lock's inner workings, and made herself breathe slowly, regularly. She wasn't slow, and rushing this would only get her caught.

Click.

She pushed the door open and turned on the light Device again. Sofas, floor pillows, richly colored carpets and a modular table — this had to be the harem's meeting chamber. It smelled of cedar and sandalwood, but sourly, as if the woods were old and used up. She pinched her nose briefly against the smell. Silver cages spaced evenly along the walls of the hemispherical room contained light Devices Willow didn't dare turn on. She closed the door behind her and scanned the room again. What she needed was a desk, or a cabinet, something that might contain paperwork.

She found it almost immediately — or, rather, found them, because there were two desks and an ebony cabinet that resembled ones she'd seen in the Serjian Residence. Holding the light in her mouth, she set to work searching the cabinet. Its three drawers held stacks of paperwork, not very tidy ones. Willow shuffled through the papers as quickly as she dared, trying not to be distracted by how her lips and tongue tingled. Everything was in Eskandelic except for two papers in Veriboldan script, which Willow could recognize but not read.

She lost track of time entirely. Her whole self was narrowed down to her two hands, moving papers around, and her lips, beginning to go numb. She tried gripping the light Device with her teeth, but that just set her skull buzzing and made it impossible for her to see. She finished one drawer and started on another. This was going to take forever, and she didn't have forever. If that person she'd heard had seen something and was looking for anything out of the ordinary —

She stopped and took the Device out of her mouth. She wasn't thinking like a thief. Raena Abakian absolutely knew what she was doing was not only wrong, but would be frowned on by the rest of the Conclave. She wouldn't keep incriminating documentation with the rest of her papers; she'd have a secret place to hide it.

Willow pulled the drawer out entirely and felt along the back and bottom. Nothing. She repeated the trick with the other two drawers and came up similarly empty. With the drawers lying on the floor, she dragged the cabinet away from the wall and found nothing. She put everything away the way it had been and surveyed the rest of the room. It would be someplace accessible, so not inside the sofa cushions or floor pillows. It would be someplace non-obvious, so probably not the desks.

Her eye fell on the table, with its many little linked squares. Why not? She dropped to her knees and ran the light underneath the table. Each square section had four legs, with hooks to connect it to its neighbors, and a frame into which fitted the piece of tile that was its top. Iron rods crossing the frame gave support to the tile. And there, near the head of the table — or what Willow guessed would be the head — were some folded pieces of paper wedged between the iron rods and the tile.

Willow held the Device in her mouth once more and lifted the square tile, which was unexpectedly heavy. She set it to one side and gathered up the papers. Two were in Eskandelic. The third was in Tremontanese and bore a chipped wax seal with the sign and shield of the Valant family. Willow skimmed the page, just to be sure. Terence had been cagy, but there was no doubt what he'd asked of Abakian. She tried to summon up fury at Terence's foul demand, but felt only relief at having found it. This could save Felix's life.

After a brief hesitation, she took the other two papers and folded all three away into her shirt. Let Raena wonder what the thief had really been after. And maybe Janida could make something of the other documents. She put the tile back, went around the room straightening everything up, then slipped out the door and locked it. Then she took a moment to calm herself. This was the time when she was in the most danger, not just because she had no idea how the situation outside might have changed, but because she was fizzing with success. Time enough to celebrate when she was back at the Serjian Residence.

She moved carefully down the stairs and listened at the door, and heard nothing. If anyone was waiting outside, they bore no metal. She'd just have to take the risk. Willow eased the door open just wide enough to slip through the crack, then shut it behind her. She crept to the edge of the landing and peered over. Whoever had nearly caught her was gone.

Willow let out a soundless breath of relief and descended the iron stairs, clenching her teeth against the cold. Back the way she'd come, then a quick dash to the side door—it would be locked, but there were all those crates to hide behind, making it only a small bump in her path to freedom. She reminded herself again not to be cocky. Anything could happen between there and the gate.

Still shaking with cold, she eased the brass door open, unable to tell if the tingling in her fingers was from cold or from the metal. The hinges protested again, but she slid through the gap and decided to leave them ajar—once she was free of the Abakian Residence she didn't much care if they found out they'd been burgled.

Down the corridor, one of the doors opened.

Willow darted into the stairwell and down to the landing. Behind her, the brass door swung shut with a terrible screech. A woman called out something in Eskandelic, but Willow rounded the landing, pattering down the stairs as fast as she dared. Just as she saw the light at the bottom of the stairs grow brighter, felt ice where there hadn't been any before, a man's voice responded, and Willow reached the bottom of the stairs in time to run headlong into the speaker. He was slender and elderly, but he grabbed her wrist and held her tightly. He held a lantern in his other hand and brought it close to Willow's face, gabbling something in tones of surprise.

Willow twisted, wrenched her arm away from his grip, a trick she'd learned from Kerish years before, and shoved the old man, making him stumble and catch himself on the wall. Then she ran down the corridor, not stopping to look behind her. Her shoes skidded on the worn stone of the hallway as she rounded the corner into darkness. Ten more paces, five more paces, and she was at the outer door, which was thankfully still unlocked. She heard someone coming after her, felt the lantern's approach as the glow behind her brightened, but then she was through the door and slamming it behind her.

Swiftly she jammed one of her picks into the lock mechanism and leaned on it hard, snapping it off in the lock. Someone rattled the latch, but she ignored it and scanned the walls. The guards were still making their rounds, high above. No one had yet raised the alarm. She waited, counting the guards' paces, then ran for the gate in the wall.

Immediately she knew she'd made a mistake. The hammering of her heart had propelled her forward too soon, and she felt in her bones they'd seen her. Then the shouting began. She sprinted for the door. Concealment was now impossible. Speed was all that would save her.

The shining steel head of a crossbow bolt flew at her, landing several yards short. That wouldn't last long. More bolts, these from the side and above. Could crossbows fire straight down? She was about to find out.

She skidded the last few feet to the gate and went to her knees before the lock. She hadn't paid attention to which pick she'd broken, and if it turned out to be the one she needed… She flung herself to one side, avoiding another missile. The shining steel swords were closing in on her. She forced herself to breathe slowly, focusing all her attention on her lock picks. There was no way to avoid capture but through the gate, and no way through the gate but this one. She heard footsteps now, running boots pounding the hard-packed earth of the courtyard. More missiles, slowing her down—

Click.

She dropped the picks and hurled the door open, then bolted for the fence. Men piled through after her, came running from the front of the Residence—they'd tried to cut her off in both directions! She slipped on the gravel, caught herself, and kept running. The first of them was just steps behind her, but she was almost at the fence—

She leaped for the top bar and hauled herself up and over just as a hand gripped her ankle and jerked her off-balance. She lashed out with her other foot and sharp pain stabbed through her leg as she connected hard with his face. His grip loosened as he cried out, and she shook frantically free of him and fell, landing on her side and knocking the air from her lungs. Gasping, she got to her feet and staggered away, forcing herself to keep moving. Behind her, a couple of men were trying to climb the fence, and others were breaking away to run to the front of the house, to use the gate there.

Her leg hurt when she put weight on it, but Willow kept running, not caring where she was going, just putting as much distance between herself and the guards as possible. Most of them were free of the gate now and running after her, and she pushed herself harder. If she could still sense them, they were far too close.

She turned right into a warren of tiny streets, familiar to her now after a few weeks' exploration of Umberan. She'd planned an escape route, but in her need to get away quickly, she'd panicked and gone the wrong way. Now she reviewed her mental map of the city and began plotting a new route. The guards were still far too close, and there were a lot of them. Her best bet was to get up high and wait for them to decide she'd eluded them.

Nothing presented itself. Willow turned a corner, then flung herself backward as she felt two silvery swords running toward her street. They'd seen her come in here and they knew enough about the city to trap her, tightening the noose of their search until it was solidly around her neck. The only thing protecting her now was the overcast night and her magical senses, and those wouldn't be enough.

Willow backtracked into an alley that was barely wide enough for her to fit. No windows—you'd just be looking into your neighbor's home if there were any—and no room for a night wagon to collect waste, though it certainly smelled as if people used it for that purpose. She might hide there. It was darker even than the street, and stank badly enough that the guards might not want to investigate. But Willow had a feeling they would rather get themselves covered in muck than have to tell Abakian Raena they'd failed to catch the thief. Particularly once Raena figured out what had been stolen.

She reached the middle of the alley, about equally distant from each end, and looked up. The buildings were three stories tall, she judged, and had the typical flat roofs of most of Umberan. They'd be a perfect hiding place, if she could reach them. But the surfaces were too smooth for free climbing…unless there was another way.

Willow stretched out both arms. She could easily reach both sides of the alley without extending her arms fully. That meant it was narrower than she was tall, which meant…

She pressed her back flat against one wall and brought up one of her feet to press against the other. Swiftly she raised the other foot until she was wedged between the two walls. This was probably the most dangerous thing she'd ever done, but if the Abakians got hold of her, her life would be forfeit, so it was definitely the lesser of two evils. She raised one foot, shoved hard with the other, and slid upward a few inches, thanking heaven for the roughened soles of her shoes.

She pressed her palms flat against the wall behind her for balance and took another "step." The wall caught at her shirt, pulling it down and choking her, but she didn't have spare hands to loosen it. Push, shove, step. It wasn't as hard as she'd feared, but she felt tension in her legs and back and guessed the hard part would come when she was two-thirds of the way up—high enough that a fall might break bones, if not kill her outright.

Slowly, she inched her way upward. The swords had come to a decision and were searching the warren methodically, closing in on her location. The stench of human waste made her stomach clench even as it reassured her that they might choose to search this place last. High above, she heard the fluttering of wings and prayed the little white birds wouldn't be so curious as to investigate this strange creature who dared invade their territory. She took another step. Sweat slid down her neck and pooled where her shoulders met the rough stucco of the wall. Just a few more feet.

Willow was so focused on her movements, step, slide, step, that she reached the top without knowing it. Panting, she paused for a moment, feeling her limbs shake with exhaustion. She hadn't thought about how she'd get out of the narrow space. She saw a rooftop garden over the edge of the wall and smelled night-blooming flowers, which were a delicate contrast to the stink of the muck below. If she could reach that, she could rest.

She shifted her hands around and pushed herself up another step. That was impossible. If she tried to lean forward, she'd fall to her death. But if she went backward—as far as her magical senses were concerned, backward was a blank void, empty of metal and just as dangerous as falling forward. Backward could be anything. But she didn't have much choice.

She felt around, twisting her arms into painfully awkward positions, until she felt the edge of the roof. She got both hands on it, palms splayed flat across the surface, then with a fervent, short prayer, kicked off with her feet, shoved hard with her hands, and rocked backward to roll over the edge of the wall into whatever waited there.

Her back slid sickeningly down the wall as gravity wrapped its fingers around her. She arched backward, clawing at the top of the wall in desperation. She cracked her head hard on the flat roof and kept going, rolling backward and making her neck pop painfully. Then she collapsed into an awkward tangle of limbs, breathing heavily and trying not to cry tears of pain.

She had no idea how much time had passed before her legs and arms stopped shaking and she could sit up. She was lying in a patch of tomato plants she'd crushed under herself, sending up waves of sweet-tangy smells that stirred her stomach to hunger. She crouched and brushed as much tomato pulp off herself as possible, then crawled to a bare place on the roof and lay down, reaching out to track the Abakian guards. Nothing. She was too far up.

She crept to the far side of the roof, staying low, and looked down on the street side of the building. A guard walked past, not looking up. They almost never looked up. Willow slid down to lean against the short wall protecting the roof. She'd just have to wait them out the conventional way.

Minutes passed, turned into an hour, maybe two. The Abakians might be evil, murderous opportunists, but they hired good help. Or maybe these were members of the family, which would explain their diligence. Willow ate one of the uncrushed tomatoes, not quite ripe, and wiped her mouth on her sleeve. Kerish must be going mad by now. The thought tore at her heart. She'd made him a promise and been forced to break it for Felix's sake, and as justified as her actions were, they didn't hurt him any the less. She'd go straight to him when she got back, let him hold her even though she was covered in tomato juice, and maybe it would be all right.

Another hour. She hadn't seen any passing figures in half that time. Willow crawled to the hatch next to the garden and hauled up on the loop of rope, revealing a black hole that smelled of warm incense. She used Kerish's Device to illuminate the space and saw rakes, hoes, shovels, and wooden boxes. Well, that made sense.

She dropped lightly into the gardener's room and took a moment to orient herself. She hadn't been able to close the hatch behind her without making noise, and the fresh air followed her down into the murky space. Where the incense smell came from, she had no idea, but she only cared that all the metal she could sense on this floor was stationary. She found the door and let herself out.

The Device light led her down a hallway to stairs, which she descended quickly, all the way to the ground floor. No one moved, which was fortunate. Willow was tired and her reflexes were dulled, and what she didn't need was someone getting up for a late night—or, more accurately, early morning—snack and stumbling across her.

She found the front door, which was locked. Cursing silently, she dug around for her remaining picks. She was running out of good fortune, but she still had one wrench and a couple of picks, and this ought to be the last lock she picked that day. Wearily, she set to work. Her gloves were torn from her passage up the wall, and her fingertips hurt, but she could easily sense the positions of the tumblers, and in only a few seconds the lock clicked open. She sighed and put everything away.

If there were swords lurking outside, they weren't anywhere nearby. She slipped through the doorway, offering up a silent prayer that heaven would protect the house from actual theft, because she didn't have time to lock the door behind her. The streets were quiet save for the cooing of the white birds. Where did they go during the day? Breathing in the cool early morning air, Willow headed off down the street.

Almost immediately, she perceived them — two curved swords positioned at the end of a nearby street. Willow detoured around them and kept going, more carefully. The new street ended in guards, too. Willow hid in the shadows of a doorway and reviewed her options. She could wait until morning, when the streets would be teeming with people, but hurting Kerish like that was unthinkable. But getting caught would be worse.

Willow did some calculating. There had been eight guards, not enough to cover all these streets, especially if they were doubled up. Based on what she'd seen, they were watching the streets that led most directly to the center of Umberan, which made no sense. Better they should guard the streets a thief would find it easiest to conceal herself in. But their foolishness didn't matter to her. Turning around, she returned the way she'd come.

She found her way out in a tiny, well-kept alley where all the doors were painted in what by daylight would be bright colors and flowers bloomed in pots by the windows. No guards lurked nearby. Willow took her time, moving from doorway to doorway, just in case. The Abakian guards weren't the only ones she needed to worry about.

It took her nearly an hour, she guessed, to make her roundabout way through the silent streets of Umberan and back to the black arch, where she was too tired to hide from the guards. It was almost cheering to see how quickly they accosted her. "I'm a guest of Serjian Principality," she said to the man who drew his sword on her, demanding something in Eskandelic.

The man didn't lower his sword. Another man said, "Serjian

Principality?"

"You can send for someone to vouch for me. They even know I'm out here."

The second man ducked back inside the arch. Exhaustion had crept over Willow, and she wished she could lie down and sleep right there in the road. Instead, she smiled brightly at the man with the sword, who didn't waver. She thought about complimenting his diligence, but decided that was too condescending, and he wouldn't understand her anyway. Finally, the second man came out through the arch with a companion, a man Willow recognized. "Serjian Principality," he said. "You go now."

"Thank you," Willow said, and trudged away up the street toward the Serjian Residence. The sky in the east was beginning to glow pink, turning the clouds fluffy and soft instead of ominous, and Willow moved a little faster. If she could return before dawn…it was a little thing, but it might make a difference.

The guards at the Residence were alert despite the hour, and challenged Willow the way the ones at the black arch had. Willow waved at them, and they let her past without comment. She was too tired to make trouble for them. Her eyesight was blurry, her legs and back had cramped up painfully, and her fingertips were sore.

She was most of the way to her bedroom before she remembered Kerish and had to reverse her path. The sun was just peeking over the horizon, making the stones of the Residence glow, when she knocked on his door.

It opened almost immediately. "Willow," Kerish said. She put her arms around him and let him hold her up.

"I found it," she said.

Chapter Twenty-One

After reporting in to the harem and handing over the letter, Willow slept all morning, waking briefly to relieve herself, then returning to her bed for more sleep. She dreamed fragments of her theft, saw herself wandering halls that multiplied the more doors she opened, or climbing an endless chimney whose end was always more distant the higher she went. She never felt metal in her dreams, even when her dreaming self picked up a weapon or a fork, which drove her deeper into dream, chasing memories. When she finally woke, sometime after noon, she felt rested physically, but mentally exhausted. She lay on her bed, blinking up at the canopy, mustering the will to stand and hunt for food.

Outside her room, she heard someone moving around. "Hello?" she called out.

"Willow!" Felix shouted, and her door banged open. Felix ran into the room and jumped onto her bed, narrowly missing landing on her stomach. "You're all right! You slept a long time."

"I was tired. Why aren't you at the scholia?"

"Kerish went to the gymnasium to spar, and I don't like going to the scholia without him."

"You have guards."

"I think Kerish is a better fighter than they are, don't you?"

Willow remembered how gracefully he'd taken down his opponent in the courtyard. "Probably. But if they weren't good, Janida wouldn't have given them to you."

"I know. I wanted to wait for you to wake up, too." Felix flung his arms around her so tightly it hurt. "I was scared. Hilarion says it's okay to be scared if you don't let it make you do something stupid."

"It's all right. I'm back, and I found what we needed, so it was worth being scared, right?"

"I guess. Will *you* take me to the scholia?"

"After I eat. Did you have dinner yet? Let's go see if Derona will feed me. She thinks I don't appreciate her hard work, so maybe you will have to convince her." The Serjians' chief cook took her job very seriously and didn't like people eating between meals, something Willow was prone to do.

Felix convinced Derona, in his halting Eskandelic, to give Willow some bread and cheese. Willow did her best to express gratitude, though her stomach growled at the smell of the leftover midday meal. Heaven forbid she get any of *that*, even though most of it would go to the dogs. She folded the bread and cheese together and took a large bite. "We'll get more when we go into the city," she told Felix when they were out of earshot of the kitchen. "Or some sugared nuts. You like those, right?"

"I like candied fruit better. May I have some of that?"

"Sure. Now, why don't you tell your guards we're going to the scholia?"

The clouds that had given Willow so much protection the previous night were gone, and Willow was grateful for the canopy shielding them from the sun's rays. Most people were indoors, napping away the midday heat, and the air hung heavy and still like a down comforter over the carriage. Felix licked his fingers, sucking up the last of the sweet stickiness of his candy. "I'm glad they didn't catch you," he said.

"So am I." She decided not to let him know how close a thing it had been. "I had to hide for a bit, but they weren't as smart as I am, so I got away…maybe not easily, but it wasn't hard either."

"You're not going to do it again, are you? Kerish said you said you gave up being a midnighter."

"Did he?" Irritation swept over her briefly, and she had no idea why. "It's true. I don't need to be a thief to survive. But if I had to do it to protect you, I would. So it's only mostly true."

"Oh."

"What did that mean, 'oh'?"

Felix said nothing.

"You're unhappy about something," Willow said. He shrugged. "Tell me what's wrong, or I'll make up something Hilarion would say about little boys who keep secrets."

That made him smile. "I was just thinking about Fedrani. He died because he was protecting me. I don't want you to die because you're doing something you could be punished for, for me. Just because I'm

King."

"Felix—" Words failed her. "Felix, I protect you—and Kerish protects you—because we love you, and that's what you do for people you love. Not because you're King, though it's true a lot of the things we protect you from only happen because of that. And someday you'll be a grown man, and you'll have people in your life you'd die to protect. That's just how things work."

Felix nodded, then gave her a sticky hug. Willow put her arms around him and cursed Terence Valant for what seemed like the thousandth time. Felix smelled of sweat and candied orange peel and the indefinable smell of little boy, and she closed her eyes and for a moment indulged a fantasy in which they were just an ordinary mama and her son. Then she gently detached him and squeezed his hand. "You're going to need to wash when we reach the zoological collection."

"I could let *najabedhi* lick my hands," Felix said with a grin. "I wish Gianesh would find one with babies. Don't you think her babies would be pretty?"

"They would be," Willow said, "like big kittens. But I doubt she'd let you play with them. She's probably a fierce mama."

"Like you," Felix said.

***

Willow sat cross-legged on the soft grass and regarded *najabedhi*, who stared back at her with total unconcern. The bars were far enough apart that Willow could reach between them and stroke the big cat, if she felt like losing a hand. *Najabedhi* was never anything but totally relaxed, but Willow wasn't stupid enough to think that made her tame.

Behind her, Felix laughed and said something in Eskandelic. She half-turned to see him watching the monkeys, who were throwing...oh, lovely, they'd started throwing turds at each other again. Felix thought it was the funniest thing ever, and Gianesh had said it was a sign of intelligence. Willow just thought it was disgusting. "Don't stand too close, Felix."

"They're not throwing at me this time. Don't you think it's funny? I think it's a game, because if they wanted to hurt each other, they'd throw rocks."

"Then they must be intelligent, if they can make that distinction." *Najabedhi* yawned, and Willow found herself responding in kind. "It's time for us to go."

"Can't we stay just five minutes longer?"

Willow sighed. "All right, but if any of that stuff gets on me, you'll have to visit the monkeys without me in future." She wasn't terribly worried. The monkeys had good aim, but their…missiles…didn't fly far from the cage. She propped her chin on her hand and regarded *najabedhi*. "I bet your children don't play with their messes. You wouldn't stand for it."

She felt relaxed for the first time in days. True, the vote on the *adjeni* was approaching fast, with no certainty that Serjian would win, and Hajimhi Fariola probably still hated her, and Imara hadn't come home yet, and she had no idea if Janida could neuter Abakian's ability to hire assassins, but after last night's successful theft, Willow felt she'd won a victory. The enclosure of the zoological collection contributed to that, with the occasional noises of the animals soothing her spirits. She'd even gotten used to the smell.

"I see you have made a friend," Gianesh said, coming to squat beside her.

"I know she'd probably tear me to pieces if not for that cage, but it doesn't stop me wanting to pet her." Willow stood up and stretched.

"*Najabedhi* is fierce in the defense of her children, but she can be playful and friendly. Though I would not risk her teeth and claws, myself." Gianesh patted his leg, and Maresh the sighthound came trotting to his side. "Thank you for bringing Felix. I have grown fond of him."

In the next cage, a monkey scored a direct hit with a noxious clump on one of his friends. Felix cheered and laughed. "He loves this place. I should thank you for welcoming him."

Gianesh nodded, and opened his mouth, then closed it without saying anything. "What is it?" Willow asked.

"Nothing. That is — Felix is well suited to this life."

His carefully casual tone set off an alarm inside Willow's head. "Meaning he's less well suited to the life he has?"

"It is not my place to judge. Forgive my speaking out of turn."

"No. That is—I understand. But Felix is King, and it's the life he'll have to live. Maybe he'll start a zoological collection of his own in Tremontane, when this is all over."

"Perhaps." Gianesh nodded to her and walked away to stand by Felix. Willow watched them, feeling disturbed. So Felix was suited to being a scholar. He could do that when he was King, couldn't he? He'd have all the freedom, all the resources—there was no reason he couldn't do both.

Flanked by Felix's guards, they walked back to the carriage. It was later than Willow had realized, nearly sunset, and hunger gnawed at her stomach. She hurried Felix along. She had no intention of missing another of Derona's meals.

They were rounding the side of the Devisers' building when, to her surprise, Willow saw Kerish approaching from the other direction. He veered away from the entrance to meet them. "I didn't know you were here," he said.

"I thought you were at the gymnasium," Willow said.

"I was, until an hour ago. I had some things to finish here and I was just about to put away my new project."

"Could we see it?"

Kerish shrugged and gestured to them to follow him. Willow regarded him closely. He'd sounded remote, as if she were just another acquaintance, and it chilled her. She made herself smile and nod.

They waited for the bodyguard to check the Devisers' hall, then entered the room where the source resided and found another Deviser standing within the source circle with her hand held out. She didn't look up when they entered.

"Imbuing motive forces is a meditative activity," Kerish said, as if apologizing for her bad manners. "Fiolina's a new student at the scholia, but she's learning fast, at least as far as imbuing motive forces goes. She doesn't have any interest in building Devices, but she seems happy doing what she's doing. And we can always use people imbuing source. It's left me free to work on my new project, for one."

"What is it?"

"You'll think it's boring."

"I'm never bored by what you come up with. Just knowing it

interests you fascinates me."

"So you care about my opinion. That's good to know."

His voice was harsh, cutting, and she felt as if he'd slapped her. "What is that supposed to mean?"

He glanced in Felix's direction, but the boy was standing next to the Deviser, rapt in his contemplation of the glowing disk on her palm, and wasn't listening to them. "It's nothing. Forget I said anything."

"This is about last night. Kerish, I thought you understood."

"So did I." He turned away from her and picked up something thin and gold from the nearest table. "Willow, tell me the truth. How close did you come to being caught last night?"

She wouldn't lie to him. Ever. "Reasonably close. I think one in a hundred thieves could have made the escape I did."

He swore under his breath. "Mother could have dealt with Abakian another way. You risked your life—"

"For Felix. And I'd do it again if I had to."

"Meaning you don't care what I have to say about it."

"Kerish, you love him too. Are you really saying his safety doesn't matter?"

"Of course it matters. But—damn it, I should have just fought Terjalesh. An honor duel would have forced the issue."

"As if anyone who'd conspire to murder a little boy has anything resembling honor. Kerish, I'm *sorry* I hurt you." She felt her voice shake, and swallowed. "You're a swordsman. You're willing to fight to defend Felix, and that could mean your death, the way you Eskandelics handle these things. Why is that all right when it's not all right for me to defend Felix my way?"

Kerish shook his head. "It's different," he said, "because I love you, and you make it impossible for me to protect you."

"I thought there was a plan involving pirates."

"This is serious, Willow."

"I know. I'm sorry. I just don't see how it helps any of us if your…your motive force is your ego."

Kerish raised his head. "Did you just suggest I'm some sort of Device?"

"I don't know. All the metal in this room is starting to make me drunk. All I know is that I love you, and I depend on you for so much more than your strong right arm." She touched his hand. "Can that be enough for you?"

"Enough?" Kerish smiled and put his arm around her. "More than enough." He drew her close enough that she was pressed against him, feeling his steady heartbeat.

"Kerish, we're not alone."

"They're not paying us any attention, and I feel I haven't seen you in days."

"You saw me just this morning. You were the first one I went to, you know."

"I know. Thank you." He kissed her, slowly, his fingers brushing the side of her face. Willow put her arms around his neck and kissed him back. His mouth tasted deliciously of honey and cinnamon. She kissed him again, feeling warmth spread across her back where his hand touched her…warmth that quickly became a burning sensation…

She twisted away, gasping. "What are you holding?"

His eyes widened. "I'm so sorry, I picked it up a moment ago and I forgot—are you all right?"

"Yes, but—what is that thing? It felt like a brand."

Kerish brought his right hand around and displayed a rod of pure gold, about twelve inches in length. A thin disc of silver was impaled on the narrow end, and a cuff of inch-wide copper encircled the fatter end. "My new project. Gold works, but it's impractical. Far too expensive, and I want this to be readily available. So I'm planning to make the next one out of iron or brass. Maybe wood, if I'm skilled enough."

"What does it do?"

"It's to speed up imbuing a motive force. This thing takes about an eighth of the time a Deviser does to imbue the average motive force. It only seems to work for *ezdalha* that are made of silver so far, so it's not practical—"

"I thought practical was something Eskandelics were allergic to."

Kerish grinned. "They'll probably want this to be etched with floral patterns or something, but practical is all right if it's also productive. And right now we're experiencing something of a bottleneck with regard to producing fully imbued motive forces. Hence everyone's pleasure at Fiolina being willing to do it for hours on end and not demand to be allowed to use the motive forces she imbues. Also, this Device can be used by a non-Deviser, so if I can get it to work properly, we can bring in others to use them."

"A non-Deviser? Can I try it?"

"Sure. Point it at the source circle, and twist the copper ring."

Willow took the rod and pointed it as directed. The copper made her fingertips itch, so she gripped it more tightly. Kerish reached toward her. "Actually, you're pointing it—"

She twisted the ring. There was a soft sound, the disk went from matte silver to palely glowing blue, and she felt as if her bones were sucked out of her body. It wasn't painful, strangely, just a steady pressure that lasted for a few moments and left her ears ringing and her skin tingling.

"—the wrong way," Kerish said. His voice was coming from very far away. Slowly, she touched her face. It was still there, but it took her some effort to move her arms. She felt as if she were swathed in warm cotton wool, sounds and sensations all dimmed. She blinked a few times.

"That was strange," she said, and could barely hear her own voice. She felt deaf, and the lights were all wrong, like the sun was setting within the Devisers' hall and her eyes were trying to cope with the gradual dimness. Blind, and deaf, and—

The rod was gone. Had she handed it back to Kerish? No, it wasn't gone, it was still in her hands, but it felt inert, no warmth, no itching. She brought it close to her eyes, peering at it in the dimness, and felt no heat scorching her face. She couldn't sense it at all.

She couldn't sense any metal in the entire room.

Willow turned and ran to one of the many filigree boxes in the room and plunged her hand into it. Nothing. She might as well be touching glass marbles for all her senses reacted to the little discs. She closed her eyes and tried to orient herself, but it was as if all the metal in the room, in the nearby rooms, had vanished. She opened her eyes. The bodyguards' steel swords shone with nothing more than reflected light. "What did you do?" she whispered.

"Willow, what's wrong? You look as if you're about to faint. Sit down." Kerish guided her to sit on the floor—there were no chairs in the room—and put his arm around her.

"What exactly does this thing do?" she asked.

"It's too complicated for a non-Deviser—"

"But it takes magic out of a source, right?"

"That's the basics, yes."

"Kerish," Willow said, "I think it took source out of me."

Kerish blinked. "That's not possible."

"Why not? The disc is glowing. And you said I was holding it the wrong way around."

Kerish touched the disc lightly, as if he expected it to feel different. "Because you're not an Ascendant. Nobody dowses for you."

Willow lowered her voice and glanced at Fiolina and Felix, both of whom continued oblivious. "But my magic comes from *somewhere*. All magic comes from source."

Kerish chewed his lower lip in thought. "You absorb magic passively from the lines of power, so yes, you contain source. But you aren't filled with it the way an Ascendant would be. And that tool is meant to draw magic from the intersection of lines of power, not from a person."

"It looks like you ended up with a side effect."

They both looked at the rod in Willow's hand. "Put it back," she said.

"Put it back, how?"

"I don't know." The strange silence, the dimness of her eyesight, was starting to unnerve her. *This is what it's like to be normal,* she thought, and it terrified her.

"Well, it's not like that thing has a reverse setting."

"Then dowse for me. Do something."

"Willow—"

"In about half a minute, I'm going to start screaming. It's that bad, Kerish."

Kerish helped her stand, then took her hand and led her to the circle. "Felix, could you show Fiolina the prototype hall? I want to do one last thing with this Device."

232

At least one of them was thinking clearly. Willow couldn't see beyond her need to have her magical senses restored, but it occurred to her that Kerish couldn't dowse for her without Fiolina realizing Willow had inherent magic. She waited, tense and miserable, for the bodyguards to perform their ritual dance and Fiolina and Felix to leave the room.

"Just stand here," Kerish said, and put one hand on her lower back and held the other in midair over the circle, presumably in the center of the source. Willow nodded and tried not to move, or breathe, or do anything that might distract him. Kerish closed his eyes and lowered his head.

Music, delicate and flowery, sprang from nowhere, bypassing the cotton wool her ears were stuffed with and going straight to her brain. She smelled flowers, honeysuckle and lilacs, tasted the burnt-sugar deliciousness of *khaveh*, and closed her eyes against the rainbow veils that swept across them. She became faintly aware of the golden rod she still held in one hand, its warmth trickling through its length into her palm, gradually warming to a blessed scorching heat. The tingling, itching, fizzing sensation of assorted metals emerged from the fog, making her want to weep for the sheer joy of no longer being blind and deaf and numb.

All the sensations were reaching a painful peak, and she stepped away from Kerish, breathing as heavily as if she'd run a mile. "Enough," she gasped. "Please."

"Sorry. I forgot you wouldn't know how to signal…sweet heaven, are you all right?"

"I am now." Everything was clear-edged and bright, painfully sharp, but she welcomed the pain, evidence that she was herself again. "Thank you." She handed him the rod and rubbed her palm against her leg. It was going to hurt for a while.

"Willow…I had no idea."

"I know. It's not your fault."

"No, but I should have thought—"

They looked at each other. "It takes source out of people," Willow said.

"Completely negates their magic," Kerish said.

"It's a weapon. Against Ascendants."

"This isn't a war, Willow."

"Isn't it?" Willow's heart sped up again. "Terence isn't going to just let Felix have the Crown. He's going to fight. And he's got all those Ascendants who are as good as an army—"

"Which he also happens to have. This isn't a solution. There's only one Device!"

"For now. And it's part of the solution. If we had an army of our own, that Device could turn the tide of battle in our favor."

Kerish shook his head. "We don't even know if the Serjian question is going to succeed. This is all completely premature."

"Nevertheless...Kerish, I think you should focus on making more of these."

"I think you're insane."

"I'm not insane. I'm thinking of Felix. Just...I just want to be prepared, that's all."

Kerish sighed. "I'll see what I can do. Let's just go home, all right? We'll have supper, and put Felix to bed, and then I want to show you the rooftop gardens at night."

"Kerish, I know you just said 'rooftop gardens' but what I heard was 'kissing until we can't breathe.'"

He brushed her hair off her forehead with his gentle fingers. "You," he said, "have *excellent* hearing."

Chapter Twenty-Two

Willow lay wakeful in her bed, watching the moonlight trace shadows over her wall. She drew shapes in her imagination: a bridge, a dragon, a pig with only one ear. If only she could make sense of life so easily. Catrela was speaking to her again, but tersely, only about things that mattered to *eskarnas*. Willow could hardly blame her for that. And Kerish…she could hardly blame *him* for wanting to protect her. It wasn't as if his fears for her were irrational; she was in a dangerous line of work. Had been in a dangerous line of work. Her promise only to use her midnighting skills in aid of Felix didn't seem to ease his mind at all.

She rolled over and stared at the canopy, dark and lowering like a cloud. At this time of night, she found her deepest fears waiting, all her many failures lined up to parade themselves across the field of memory. It didn't matter that she'd secured evidence Janida could use against Abakian Raena: she'd alienated one of Felix's best supports, had ruined Gessala's happiness, and had failed utterly at convincing Imara to return home. The girl hadn't even returned for her *fuoreno's* funeral. And the vote on the *adjeni* was in four days. Things were not looking good for the Serjian question.

Maybe it was time to start looking for an exit. She regretted giving Janida the assassin's money now. She could have used that to support herself and Felix for a long time. In the morning, she'd go to Janida and explain…what? That she was a quitter? No, she wasn't going to give up yet. Even if she had no idea what to do next.

She rolled out of bed and went to Felix's room, more to give herself comfort than to check on him. He was sleeping as he always did, sprawled across the bed and leaving very little room for poor Ernest, who ought to be in his own bed anyway. Not that Willow cared. She knelt by Felix's head and smoothed the hair back from his forehead. How extraordinary, that she'd gone from being deliberately alone to having this young boy in her life. Was this how mothers felt, this tender desire to protect Felix from everything that might hurt him? She touched his hair again, then stood. "Don't think I approve," she whispered at Ernest, whose ear twitched in sleep.

She settled in a chair in the main room and thought about calling for a servant to bring her hot herbal tea or something that might calm her. No, she wasn't going to disrupt someone else's sleep just because she was restless. She drew up her legs and leaned her head on one arm. The moon was in the wrong position to shed light on this room, but Willow found the darkness comforting. This was still her time, even with all her fears, even if she'd given up midnighting. The time when she felt most in control.

There had to be *something* more she could do. Sitting and doing nothing would drive her mad. The harem was probably doing something with Abakian Raena's letter, but whatever it was didn't involve Willow at all. She didn't understand the rules of this strange society she floundered through, couldn't contribute by writing letters or hosting a party, and there wasn't a single thing she could do to aid Felix politically or make amends for the mistakes she'd made.

Unless…no, that was a terrible idea. The Hajimhis didn't want to hear from her, after that disastrous party, even though Fariola had been at fault too. And what would she say? "I'm sorry you provoked me into rudeness?" That wouldn't achieve anything. And she'd probably just mess everything up, blundering around and proving she was an uncouth foreigner.

Or she might humble herself, hope Fariola was as honorable as everyone had said, and maybe correct one of her mistakes. She was having trouble shaking the idea.

Sleep on it, make a decision in the morning, she thought, but it was at least another hour before she calmed enough to sleep.

***

In the morning, she fortified herself with several cups of *khaveh* before turning to her resident expert on Eskandelic culture—the part relating to dress, anyway. "I need to visit someone this morning," she said. "Someone not friendly who hasn't invited me. What should I wear?"

"Someone not—to say, enemy is?" Caira began going through Willow's wardrobe.

"Not really. Someone I want not to be my enemy."

Caira clicked her tongue. "This," she said, holding out a pale yellow silk dress fine enough to be nearly translucent. "Over this."

Willow struggled into the narrow cotton shift and let Caira slide the silk dress over her head. It had been made for someone curvier than Willow, but it still looked good, and Willow wished Kerish were there to see her. Where was he, anyway? Usually he ate breakfast with them before taking Felix to the scholia for the morning. "You can play with Posea this morning, all right?" she told Felix.

"Can't I come with you?"

"That would be a bad idea. Besides, it's probably going to be…" *Boring* was not the right word. There was every chance her conversation with Fariola would turn into a shouting fight. "Not interesting to a little boy."

"All right. But I want to go to the ocean later."

"We can probably do that." She hugged Felix, tousled his hair, then ran to the courtyard, praying she wouldn't meet anyone she might need to explain herself to. With gestures and a few words of Eskandelic, she convinced a servant to harness a carriage for her, then directed the woman to drive her to the Hajimhi Residence.

The Hajimhi Residence lay near the palace where the Review had been held and was made of the same yellow stone. That was where the resemblance ended. Where the Review had looked delicate and fairy-like thanks to its lattices of carved marble, the Hajimhi Residence was built along the same lines as the Abakian Residence. It looked like a fortress, a single blocky building surrounded closely by trees easily fifty feet tall with dusty green needles.

The stones used in its construction were half the size of the carriage and rough-faced as if no one had bothered to shape them into more than a basic rectangular block. The side facing the private drive was windowless, with only a pair of doors to indicate it was more than a strange yellow wall erected in the middle of Umberan. Willow could climb it, probably, thanks to that rough surface, but it didn't seem to lead anywhere more accessible than the front door. And breaking in would give the wrong impression.

She asked the driver to wait, climbed awkwardly down from the carriage, and walked the long, long path from the street to the door.

The Residence was on a hill about fifteen feet above street level, turning the needle-strewn path into a stiff climb that had Willow's calves aching by the time she reached the front door. This was probably the stupidest idea she'd ever had, but she was there and the worst that could happen...all right, Fariola might take such offense at Willow's effrontery she'd make it her mission in life to eliminate all Serjian's support on this and every other issue. Willow paused with her hand on the bell rope. She really hadn't thought this through.

No fear. Before she could stop herself, she pulled the rope. She heard nothing, but she already knew from the Serjian Residence that the bell rope was attached to a bell deep within the house, so she clasped her hands in front of her and waited.

A breeze brought the smell of flowers to her nose. Bushes of unfamiliar flowers, big fat clusters of blue and white blossoms, grew around the base of the Hajimhi Residence. The contrast to the building was amusing, like seeing one of Felix's stolid bodyguards dressed in a dainty pink skirt. The bushes were large enough that Willow could easily conceal herself beneath or behind them, and she looked closer, imagining some Hajimhi servant crouched there, with instructions to observe callers and pass the information to whomever decided who was allowed to enter.

The door opened. A man wearing purple Hajimhi insignia on a comfortable tunic and black cotton trousers stood there. He looked very surprised to see her. So much for her servant in the bushes theory. "*Yes?*" he said in Eskandelic.

"Willow North to see Hajimhi Fariola," Willow said, enunciating clearly.

That startled him even more. He said something in rapid Eskandelic, then backed away, holding the door open wider. Willow entered.

The room was a tiny version of the entry chamber back at the Serjian Principality, with a floor tiled in gold and silver and a couple of benches against the walls. Willow sighed at how comfortably cool it was. It was still early, but the silk dress was surprisingly warm despite its thinness.

The servant indicated that Willow should take a seat on one of the benches, then left the room by one of its three arched doorways. Willow leaned against the wall and enjoyed the feeling of cool marble against her back. They hadn't kicked her out, which was either good news or meant the servant didn't know who she was. In either case, she was going to enjoy the room while she could.

She heard footsteps down the hall the servant had left by, and sat up straight just as a couple of women and the door servant entered the chamber. One of the women carried a basin, the other held white towels. The man spoke in Eskandelic, then paused, waiting for a response. *"Do you speak Tremontanese?"* Willow said. The three exchanged glances. They were glances that said each was hoping another would take charge.

Finally, the woman with the basin said, "To wash, guest is," and knelt on the floor, extending the basin to be at chest level to Willow. Willow splashed her hands in the cool water, then wiped her face, keeping an eye on the man. He didn't wince or do anything else that might indicate she'd made a misstep, and she accepted a towel to dry her face and hands with, then handed it back. Finally, the basin woman stood, bowing to Willow, and she and the towel woman left the chamber. The man made a little gesture that meant "stay there" and left by a different door.

Willow sat with her hands clasped loosely in her lap and waited. She examined the domed ceiling, which was painted with a mural depicting five women kneeling before a man. Interesting. They were dressed in traditional Eskandelic garb, open jackets and full skirts, but they all wore their hair long and gathered high on their heads in a style Willow was unfamiliar with. There was no telling how old the mural was from where Willow sat, and she was in the process of assessing the room's potential as a climbing surface when the man reappeared and said, "Come."

The hallway he led her down smelled faintly of roses, though Willow saw nothing except the same silver and gold tiled floor as the entry and a high arched ceiling set with round windows. By the shadows, the sun would illuminate the room most directly around two o'clock in the afternoon. At the moment, the windows let in a diffuse morning light that revealed dust motes floating through the air, caught

Melissa McShane

by the same drafts that brought the scent of roses wafting past Willow's face. The servant had a ring of iron keys somewhere inside his tunic, but aside from that Willow sensed no metal nearby.

The hallway ended at an arched doorway with strips of gauzy fabric hanging down over it like a tattered curtain, though since the fabric was embroidered with real gold it was unlikely to be tattered by accident or use. The servant parted the fabric for Willow and bowed. Willow returned the bow of master-to-servant, feeling slightly guilty at doing so, and entered the room.

It was hemispherical, identical in shape to that of the harem in the Serjian Residence, though its walls were painted a cool, pale green and the cushions were deep blue and forest green and a rich burgundy. Hajimhi Fariola sat on one of the sofas, her back straight, her face expressionless. Light Devices filled the room with a silvery glow that made her look carved of marble.

Willow let out a long, slow breath, then sat on the sofa across from Fariola. She perched on the edge of the sofa, afraid of being swallowed by the pillows. Silence stretched out between them. Willow guessed she was supposed to speak first, but in the face of that marble visage all her conversational gambits deserted her.

Finally, she said, "Thank you for agreeing to see me."

"You dare much, in coming here," Fariola said. "Or perhaps you do not know this."

"I don't know what it signifies, in your culture. I'm sorry if it's bad manners. In my culture, my coming to you means I want to make things right, if I can."

"You think to impose your culture on me?" Fariola's voice sounded remote, not at all as if she took offense despite her words.

"No, I thought it better not to pretend I understand more of your rules than I do, as if my short time in Eskandel could make me a master. I intended to show you respect the way I would...anyone back home." Probably better not to tell her that whatever Willow knew of respect, she'd learned from Aurilien's dukes of crime. She already felt as if she were skimming along a crust of ice, forced to keep moving if she wanted to survive.

One corner of Fariola's mouth twitched, not in amusement. "And this respect demands what of me?"

"Nothing. I show respect for my own sake. It's to indicate that I apologize for my rudeness."

"And demand forgiveness."

"I said it's not about demanding anything. My honor requires that I demonstrate… contrition. I behaved badly and I embarrassed both of us in public. I apologize for this."

"You think this is enough?"

"No. If you were a…lord in Aurilien, I would offer amends — something concrete, usually a payment or a public statement. But that would place the burden of response on you, and I told you I don't expect anything from you."

Fariola was silent for a moment. Willow kept her hands from winding tightly into the silk of her dress. Finally, Fariola said, "You abase yourself. No Eskandelic woman would do so unreservedly."

"I'm not Eskandelic. I've done my best to abide by your rules, but there are some things in which I have to be Tremontanan. And by my rules, I can stand proud."

"You would give me such power over you?"

"That's up to you." Willow swallowed to moisten her suddenly dry throat. "But I think you prize honor and plain speaking, so I think you're not going to leave it at that."

Fariola's jaw went rigid briefly. "What do you imply?"

"In your culture, you'd demand something in return for an apology, right? I don't want anything but the answer to a question. Why did you attack Felix that night? Why push the issue of him being an impostor when you know full well he isn't?"

"I testing him was," Fariola said. "A King cannot weak be, even if he a child is. Your King unprepared for the question was. You at fault for that are, Willow North."

"*I* am? Those questions are supposed to be directed at me! That's my job as his *eskarna* and guardian."

"You cannot protect him from everything. He must answer his own questions eventually. You his strength and his weakness are. I say Felix Valant unsuited King of Tremontane to be is."

"That —" Willow had to turn away, bite back a reply that would ruin everything she'd worked so hard to regain. "You're entitled to your opinion."

Fariola smiled. "That cost you much to say, I think."

"I disagree with you. Felix is young, yes, but he'll have good advisers and he'll learn."

"With you as one of them."

"I don't understand politics. I'm his guardian."

To Willow's surprise, Fariola chuckled. "You understand more than you think. Do not..." She said something fluid in Eskandelic. "It a phrase is that means thinking less of your abilities than you should and thereby losing a greater good. False humility. If Felix Valant regains the Crown, you should remain as his adviser, not just his guardian. This the *opinion* of one well versed in politics is. Do not disregard me."

"I...all right."

Fariola smoothed her skirt over her knees. "I will not apologize, because I did nothing wrong," she said. "But...you may tell Serjian Janida that Hajimhi Principality asks for a *khojabi*, at their earliest convenience."

"*Khojabi*," Willow repeated.

"At their earliest convenience. You must say this to them this as well."

"I will."

Fariola stood, so Willow scrambled to her feet and returned the woman's bow, not trying very hard to match her depth for depth. Then she turned and left, feeling Fariola's gaze sharp on the back of her neck. The cool appearance of the room was an illusion; she was sweating as if she'd run the length of Lower Town at noon on Midsummer Day. Had that been a victory, or no? She needed to talk to Janida immediately.

Back at the Residence, she ran through the halls—she couldn't get any sweatier than she already was, right?—to the harem chamber, where she found Maitea and Janida in conversation that broke off when she entered. "Hajimhi Principality wants a...a *khojabi* at your earliest convenience," she panted.

Maitea's eyebrows climbed nearly to her hairline. "How do you know this?" Janida said. She looked as expressionless as Fariola had.

"Because I talked to Hajimhi Fariola this morning, to apologize for what happened at the party." Willow braced herself for an outpouring of fury.

"You did *what?*" Maitea shouted. "A fool, are you? Wish to ruin all Felix's chances, do you?"

"I don't think I made it worse. What's a *khojabi?*"

"There are *rules* about these things. You did not even ask for advice." Maitea looked as if she might explode.

"She succeeded," Janida said.

"Yes, but out of luck, no doubt," said Maitea.

"I will take luck where I cannot have skill," Janida said. "A *khojabi* is a request for a meeting, but not of equals."

"I'm sorry," Willow said. "I gave her more power over us, didn't I?"

"Hajimhi Fariola acknowledges in requesting this meeting that she the supplicant and therefore of lesser status is." Janida stood and gave the bell-pull near the door a good hard yank. "And 'earliest convenience' means, contrariwise, that we to set the time and place are, ceding power to us."

"I don't understand. Why would she do that?"

"Because Fariola acted hastily in rescinding Gessala's offer," Maitea said, "and she essentially prostrates herself and Hajimhi Principality in the hope that we will overlook her bad behavior. What did you say to her?"

"I just apologized for being rude. I told her I didn't expect anything from her in return."

Maitea and Janida looked at each other. Then both women began laughing. Willow looked from one to the other. "I don't see the joke," she said irritably.

"You put Fariola in a terrible position," Janida said. "You humbled yourself without asking a reciprocal favor, which took away her power over you. Renewing their offer to Gessala is her response. It…I cannot explain easily."

"I think I understand," Willow said. "If I were Eskandelic, I'd have, what, asked for her forgiveness? And then she'd have been magnanimous in giving it to me and she'd have power over me. But I didn't ask for anything, which gave *me* power over *her*. So to regain that balance, she had to offer something, and since she never really wanted to rescind the offer to Gessala, she can ask you to accept it again. But that puts her in our power again, so…does that mean Hajimhi will have to vote our way? Because she was pretty clear she doesn't think Felix should be King."

"Hajimhi is pragmatic as well as honorable," Maitea said. "We will say nothing of the vote at the *khojabi*, but they will judge our behavior and make a decision. And a vote for our question is not necessarily a vote for Felix, but for the *vojenta mahaut*."

"You see clearly," Janida said. "Though you wise to go untutored to Hajimhi were not. Maitea is right. You might have ruined things further."

"It's true." Willow sat and took a small pillow in her hands, turned it around. "But I think it's truer that I'm not Eskandelic, I'm Tremontanan, and everyone knows that. I'll do my best to honor your customs, but I'm never going to have the knowledge you do. And I think most of the principalities respect that. And the ones who don't — well, we're not going to win them over, are we?"

"True," Janida said. "And since you have succeeded, I see no reason to chastise you further."

"That's very generous of you."

"Do not try my patience, Willow North," Janida said, but she was smiling.

Chapter Twenty-Three

The Jauderish was no cooler than the last time Willow had been there, the day of the opening of Conclave. The antechamber was at least shielded from the sun, which only meant the day outside was broiling. The dozens of arches and pillars glowed as if their yellow stone was lit from within, though Willow realized this time she couldn't see any light sources in the vast hall other than what came through the entrance. The gilding around the tops of the arches and the bases of the pillars was a low-grade burning that she easily ignored, but she stayed as far from the tingling brass front doors as she could manage.

She hoped Janida wouldn't think anything of how she kept close to the second set of doors, the ones that led to the Conclave bowl and were made of wood instead of metal. It wasn't a comfortable position, with gusts of warm air blowing through the doors at unexpected times, but Willow far preferred it to the sensation of being trapped in a jar full of brass bees.

The sound of rhythmic Eskandelic came to her ears again. She was certain it was unintelligible even to those who spoke the language, because the Prince currently giving his speech stood at the bottom of the bowl, near the Solstice altar. The bowl was awe-inspiring, big enough to hold ten thousand people, but much farther than halfway up it swallowed the words of anyone speaking.

Willow twitched the neck of her sheer blue robe and listened with half an ear to Felix's chatter. It was about the zoological collection, and she'd heard it all before. The boy must be bored out of his mind, just standing there watching people who were staring openly at him. Or maybe she should be grateful he could talk instead of being overwhelmed. She was too warm to be overwhelmed. The heavy white linen of the trousers and loose shirt she wore under the robe made her sweat, and she was grateful it wasn't also shot with real silver.

"Willow, are you listening? I asked when we can eat." Felix tugged on her hand.

"I'm sorry, Felix, I was thinking about something else. Janida said we don't eat until after all the speeches are done. So it will be later."

"I'm hungry now," Felix said, but he didn't sound unhappy. "Why doesn't anyone try to talk to us?"

"I don't know." All right, so she was a little overwhelmed by the attention. She wished she could read their minds, all these Eskandelic royalty passing and whispering things to one another about the Tremontanan strangers intruding on one of their most important political meetings. She smiled and nodded at anyone whose eye she met, but she was starting to wish Janida hadn't insisted on her and Felix being present.

"Enjoying yourself?" Kerish emerged from the crowd, smiling in a way that eased Willow's heart considerably. "I'm sorry about this."

"Hilarion says we have to endure what we can't avoid," Felix said, "but I think he would be bored, too."

"It's more interesting when you can understand the speeches," Kerish said. "Most of them are rhetorical masterpieces. They collect them every year and make copies for the libraries."

"What's this one about?" Willow said.

Kerish rolled his eyes. "An exception to the rule. It's about tariff reform and I don't think I've ever heard anything so dull. It's why things are so crowded up here right now. Most of the principalities have already made up their minds how they're going to vote on the question and don't need to listen to Nersesji Gharan drone on about how it will be disastrous for Eskandel."

"When will Salveri speak?"

"Second to last. We lost the draw on that. Mahnouki Ghanetan is going to speak last." Kerish looked grim. "That's not the best position for us to be in."

"I can imagine."

"At any rate, there are about another half-dozen speakers before my father, so—I wish I could provide entertainment for you." He stepped closer and said, in a lower voice, "What I *wish* is that I could find us a quiet, private corner. You look extraordinary in dark blue."

"Your mother would kill us both. She made it clear we can't let it look like Serjian has a personal interest in this question. But I don't see how we can help it. You and I were conspicuously together at the *sheteshi*."

"That was different. This is…official, I suppose you might say. Much as I might wish otherwise. I don't like how some of my acquaintances are looking at you."

"Are they really? I hadn't noticed. Any of them who might be worth meeting? I'm not attached to anyone right now, according to Janida."

"You have such a sense of humor." Kerish touched her hand briefly. "I would introduce you, but Mother said you were to remain available for conversation. Not that anyone seems interested in doing more than stare. Sorry."

"That's all right."

The babble of Eskandelic from the doors ceased. Moments later, the volume of conversation in the antechamber increased as men and women pressed forward through the wooden doors toward the Conclave bowl. Willow took Felix's hand and drew him nearer. "Should we go in?" she asked Kerish.

"We'll wait for the crowd to pass," he said. "There's a ten-minute recess between speakers so everyone has a chance to get settled, but we're sitting above the principalities, so we shouldn't need that long to reach our seats."

"I'm tired, Willow."

"I know, Felix, but you have to be patient. It's only a few hours longer."

"Can we go to the scholia afterward?"

"Maybe. Let's—"

A strident voice said something in Eskandelic that made Kerish turn around fast, his hand on his sword. Willow flexed her wrist, feeling the comforting pressure of her knife, and put Felix behind her, close to his guards, who hadn't moved forward in response to the threat.

She turned to see Abakian Raena bearing down on them, her small eyes narrowed in anger. She spoke again, vicious, harsh words whose content Willow could guess.

"You aren't a fool, Abakian Raena," Kerish said, "so I know you didn't just threaten the King."

"You spread lies," Raena said, coming to a stop inches from Willow. "I will not allow it to be so."

"I don't know what you're talking about," Willow lied. "What lies are those?"

Raena's face reddened. "Abakian does not do the bidding of a foreign King. You have no proof."

"I think, if I didn't have proof, you wouldn't be so worried. And I think you're *exactly* the sort of person who'd try to kill a defenseless child. Why else would you come to me here, trying to frighten him, instead of taking it up with Serjian Janida?" She gripped Felix's hand tighter and felt him press into her side, and prayed he wouldn't display whatever fear he felt.

Behind Raena, a giant of a man loomed. Abakian Terjalesh was impassive except for his eyes, which gleamed hatred at her. He, too, had his hand on his sword hilt, and Willow chased away a moment's fear at his size and menace. "*Majdran,*" he rumbled, "does this touch your honor?"

"It does, my *zuareto,*" she replied.

In an instant Kerish had his sword drawn and stood between Raena and Willow, who took a step backward in surprise. "Then let's settle this as honorable men," he said.

Terjalesh's eyes widened, and his mouth fell open slightly. "I fight the woman," he said. "She a thief is."

"You have no proof," Kerish said, "and her honor is mine. Go ahead, Terjalesh. Draw your sword."

"She must fight," Raena said.

"Much as I'd like to see her humiliate your *zuareto,*" Kerish said, "the laws of the honor duel permit the challenged to choose a champion. Which I assure you she has."

Willow became aware that all conversation around them had stopped. They were surrounded by a ring of onlookers, men and women as intent on the confrontation as they'd been on Willow and Felix earlier. "Kerish," she began.

"Don't worry, Willow," Kerish said. "Well, Terjalesh?"

For a moment, Willow was sure the big man was going to back down. His eyes darted from Kerish to his *majdran* to the crowd without pause. Then his eyes narrowed, and he drew his sword, a massive thing that looked more like a bludgeoning weapon than Kerish's elegant slim blade. He said something in Eskandelic that Kerish answered. Willow couldn't see Kerish's face, but his tone of voice was tense, challenging. Willow grabbed Felix and retreated just as the rest of the crowd did the same, backing away through the many pillars that surely weren't the best ground for a duel.

Terjalesh growled and swung at Kerish's head. Kerish dodged and struck, faster than Willow could follow, a blow Terjalesh only barely deflected. He swung again, and Kerish again dodged the ungainly blow, this time taking a step backward.

Terjalesh grinned. He pressed the attack, forcing Kerish back. Kerish dodged each stroke easily, but kept backing away, and Willow discovered she had her fists clenched. Why didn't he attack? He was going to be trapped against a pillar eventually, and it would all be over.

She heard murmuring nearby, and saw a couple of Eskandelic men exchanging words that even she could tell meant they were betting on the outcome. "Stop it," she said. "Stop!"

They looked at her as if she were crazy. One of them said, "Is good, not to worry."

"This isn't—"

She heard a clang, and turned her attention back to the fight. Sweet heaven, it had happened, Kerish had his back to a pillar and Terjalesh's sword had just connected with it beside his head. She could see Kerish's face, and he was...smiling?

Kerish brought his sword up to catch Terjalesh's next wild swing, forcing him back and around so Kerish was away from the pillar. He slashed, parried, slashed again, and now Terjalesh was the one backing away, stumbling over his own feet. Kerish bore down on him relentlessly, his sword flicking in and out so fast Willow could barely follow. Terjalesh looked terrified, and his swings grew wilder, not connecting with anything but air.

Then he grunted, and folded up over Kerish's sword emerging from his stomach. Raena screamed. It happened so quickly Willow missed the blow, just saw the sword stuck through the big man's body like a pin impaling the world's ugliest butterfly. Kerish stood with his hand on the hilt, breathing heavily, speaking something to Terjalesh Willow couldn't hear. Terjalesh nodded.

Raena screamed again. Kerish withdrew his sword and wiped it on Terjalesh's shirt. "If you take him to the healers quickly, he'll live," he said, then called out something in Eskandelic. The watching crowd roared an assent. Kerish turned his back on the Abakians and returned to Willow's side, sheathing his sword. "You weren't worried, were you?" he asked.

Willow unclenched her fist. "Of course not," she said.

Kerish smiled. "An honor duel is...it's not just about who wins, but how you fight it. I had to make it clear that I controlled that fight down to the last stroke. And in giving ground like that, I made Terjalesh look like a fool for daring to challenge me. I was never in any danger except maybe from falling over laughing."

The two men Willow had seen wagering approached Kerish. One of them said something in a rueful tone of voice that Kerish laughed at. The other grinned and punched Kerish lightly on the arm. Kerish pretended to be hurt, which made the other two laugh as they walked away. "Those two have been my sparring partners for years," Kerish told Willow. "They wagered on how long it would take me to win that duel. I think Arjan has never once won that bet no matter how often they make it."

"Is that man going to die?" Felix asked.

"No, Abakian Raena is too smart for that. Though not smart enough to realize what would happen if she challenged Willow to an honor duel. I don't know what she was thinking. Possibly that a foreigner wouldn't know our customs enough to ask for a champion. Even so," Kerish added, "if Terjalesh had lost to you, it would have looked even worse for Abakian than me defeating him."

"You just fought a duel for me," Willow said. "I had no idea how incredibly romantic that would be."

Kerish laughed. "I'd ask for a kiss as my reward, my lady, but we're still being discreet."

"I can wait. Felix, are you all right?"

"I'm fine. Just hungry."

Willow tousled his hair. "Patience."

The crowd was dispersing, though with plenty of glances at the three of them. Willow again nodded and smiled just as if a man's life hadn't been at stake. The dry rainfall of spoken Eskandelic washed over her as they maneuvered through the crowds and took seats on an upper bench, flanked by Felix's guards. The Prince standing near the altar had stopped speaking. Apparently the duel had delayed people's entry enough to disrupt the meeting. Willow didn't care. Surreptitiously she took Kerish's hand and squeezed it gently, felt him run his finger down the back of her hand in response.

They sat through two speeches, then Kerish rose and beckoned to Willow. "Another uninteresting one," he said, "though Mother and my *majdrani* will stay to listen, hoping to woo that principality to our cause. We can stretch our legs a bit."

Willow followed him, Felix in tow, back to what she'd begun to think of as her spot. At least she didn't have to explain to Kerish why she didn't want to stand near the cooler exit with its brass doors. More people passed, brightly robed or clad in white, none of whom stopped to talk. Willow's face hurt from all the meaningless smiling. "How many more speakers?" she asked.

"This one, then two more, then Father and Mahnouki Ghanetan." Kerish shifted his weight. "I should go—I'll be back before the next speech."

"All right," Willow said, trying not to feel abandoned. Then she grabbed his hand, not thinking how it would look. "Who is that?"

Ahead in the crowd, a woman dressed in the white clothing of a harem sister, wearing the gold bracelets of a *vojenta*, approached them at speed. She was flanked by three other women, all of them as intent on Willow as the first. People made way for them, glancing from the women to Willow and back. A susurrus of whispers went up, growing in volume to rival the sound of the tide coming in.

"Um," Kerish said. "That's the Takjashi harem. They look angry."

"If they're Abakian's allies, they probably want my blood. I don't think we can avoid them." Willow sucked in a deep, calming breath and let it out slowly. "Let's get this over with." At least none of the women were armed. She wasn't sure she could handle another honor duel, even one Kerish fought for her.

Takjashi Lucea came to a halt in front of Willow. She was a short woman with fine brown hair that blew in wisps across her round face. Her lips were set in a tight line, and her brow was furrowed over expressive brown eyes. Willow cast about desperately for something to say that wasn't an apology — she felt no shame over exposing Abakian for trying to have Felix killed, and no guilt over Terjalesh's injury — and came up empty.

"Willow North," Lucea said. Her voice was deep and warm like her eyes and completely void of expression. Then she bowed, dipping a low curtsey that Willow could never have managed even in her own clothes. To her sides, the other three women did the same. Willow felt Kerish grip her arm tightly. She'd never seen that bow before. How was she supposed to respond?

Lucea and the others stood upright again. Willow, praying she was doing the right thing, returned the bow of equal-to-equal. Without a change in her expression, Lucea nodded, then walked on past Willow toward the Conclave bowl, followed by her sisters. The whispering stilled as they passed, then resumed at a louder volume once the four women were through the door. Now everyone was looking at Willow, but she was too stunned to care.

"Kerish, what just happened?" she said.

"Takjashi Principality made itself *parjenisur* to you," Kerish said. "To you directly, not to Serjian Principality, though I guess it's the same thing — "

"To *me?*"

"I don't understand it either — unless this is Takjashi's way of showing they won't follow a child-killer like Abakian. I can't imagine any other reason for Lucea to do that so publicly. And it's not as if Mother isn't here. She could as easily have pledged herself to her. No, Lucea did that on purpose, pledging to you."

"That was unsettling. Like being savaged by a butterfly."

Kerish blew out a long, heavy breath. "I think," he said, "the tide has just turned in our favor."

"But Ghanetan is still speaking last. And the Mahnouki question is popular."

"Neither of which we can do anything about. I'm taking a moment to feel optimistic."

Willow smiled, but the knot of tension she carried around with her permanently these days didn't unravel. Time enough for optimism when they'd won.

Though...once they'd won—she refused to think in terms of "if"—what next? She'd focused so much on how to get Felix safely out of Umberan that she hadn't given any thought to plans for the opposite contingency. Terence wasn't just going to give up the Crown because Eskandel backed Felix, and it was definitely going to come to war. Could Eskandel send Felix back to Tremontane with troops? Wouldn't that be more like an invasion? They'd need support from at least some of the Counts or Barons, but how could they manage that? Willow didn't even know which of the provincial lords had laid claim to the Crown in their own name. She sighed. This was a conversation to have with Janida later. Three days later, to be precise. The vote on the *adjeni* was day after tomorrow.

Kerish left. A handful of people stopped to speak to her and Felix, most of them assuring her of their principality's support of the Serjian question. Willow felt too overwhelmed to remember all of their names, though she was sure Janida would want to know the details later. Felix tried to sit on the floor and she had to haul him up and remind him about his dignity. He scowled. Willow didn't have the heart to reprimand him when she felt the same desire to sit and daydream about the coming meal.

Finally, Kerish returned and ushered them back in to listen to Salveri's speech. Willow wished she understood his words. Salveri's deep voice, always pleasant to listen to except when he was yelling at you, turned into molten honey that captivated Willow. The Conclave bowl was almost full during his speech, and Willow watched the listeners, all of whom were intent on his words. Kerish leaned forward with his knees on his elbows, rapt in concentration. When Salveri finished, a sigh went up throughout the bowl. Willow had wondered at the lack of applause, which in Tremontane would have followed any artistic performance, and these were clearly performances. Kerish just shook his head and didn't try to explain.

Salveri took his seat with the Serjian harem. No one else moved, not even to switch seats for a better view. Willow realized her fists were clenched again and made herself relax, then wiped her sweaty palms on her knees. "Why doesn't Mahnouki Ghanetan just start speaking now?"

"Tradition. Everyone gets that ten-minute recess. And he's not here."

"What do you mean, not here?"

Kerish grimaced. "It's a ploy to indicate disrespect for Serjian and suggest others ought to share in that disrespect by voting against us. But it can backfire. We're—Serjian, I mean—we're staying to listen to his speech, which could give us the moral high ground...or it could be interpreted to mean we feel weak enough that we're compelled to listen to our opponent. There's no way to tell how others will read each interaction."

"And his speech is going to be compelling."

"I assume so. I've never heard him speak before. He can't be as good as Father. Maitea and Giara are excellent writers, and Mahnouki may not have anyone of their caliber. Too bad Imara isn't allowed..." He trailed off, looking down at his knees. Willow nodded. Imara still hadn't returned, and Willow was having trouble not feeling guilty over that. If she'd been more persuasive...

Motion nearby drew Willow's attention. The Mahnouki Principality emerged from the doorway at the top of the bowl and made its way down through the benches to their traditional seats. Mahnouki Ghanetan, his long brown hair spilling straight and gleaming down his back, descended the steps to stand near the altar. He paused for a few moments, waiting for silence. Then he spoke, raising his hand to salute the crowd, and Willow's heart sank, because she knew a performer when she heard one even if she couldn't speak his language.

Ghanetan was a master, his voice dipping down low enough that Willow had to strain to hear it, then filling the bowl with a few powerful words. It was like listening to the ocean in all its moods, calm, or stormy, or furious with the oncoming tide, or quiet enough to soothe a restless heart. Willow watched the audience and her empty stomach burned from more than hunger, because so many of those faces were avid in their attention to Ghanetan and the story he told. She glanced at Kerish. His eyes were closed, and he looked as intent as he had when his father spoke, but his lips were thinned tight with anger and his breathing came a little too rapidly.

Ghanetan spoke a few final ringing words, and another sigh went up from the audience. This one sounded excited, and Willow, to her horror, heard a couple of claps that were quickly stilled. "Let's go," she said.

Kerish was already on his feet, holding out a hand to Felix. "I'm hungry," Felix said. "That's not complaining if it's true."

"I think I've lost my appetite," Kerish said.

"Was it as bad as I think?" said Willow.

"Probably worse. Even I wanted to vote for their question, and I know it's a fool's errand."

"You can't be serious."

"Not really. But I'm sure a lot of people felt that way. I'm regretting my earlier optimism."

Kerish led them down the small, dark corridor that led to the carriage yard, a back way that kept them away from prying eyes. Willow didn't feel like conversation, let alone the kind anyone who'd heard Ghanetan speak might feel inclined to start. The passage was dimly lit, and comfortingly small, not like the enormous antechamber with its twenty-foot-high ceiling and all those arches standing at attention like stone soldiers.

They had to stop at the end of the passage to allow one of Felix's bodyguards to exit first. Kerish was armed, but neither of the burly men relaxed in his presence, not even after the duel with Terjalesh. Willow was grateful for their paranoia. Janida must have reamed them out after the incident at the dog show.

Finally the man gestured to them to proceed, and they crossed the vast expanse of the carriage yard, looking for the blue and copper of the Serjian carriages. The late afternoon sun hammered down on their heads, and Willow in her blue head scarf and heavy linen felt like wilting beneath it. A bath was definitely in order.

Someone shouted. Instantly the bodyguards took up protective positions around Felix, pushing Willow to one side. Felix cried out. Willow let her knife fall into her hand and scanned the crowd, looking for assailants. Kerish shouted in return and began pushing his way through the crowd, sword drawn. Willow hesitated, torn between her need to protect Felix and her desire to find out what the hell was going on. She couldn't see or sense anyone coming at them with a weapon. Everyone nearby was craning their necks, looking for the speaker.

Then Kerish was back, sheathing his sword and crouching to speak to Felix. "It's all right," he said, "let's just get back home as quickly as possible, all right?" He said a few words to the bodyguards, and one of them scooped Felix up and carried him behind his companion. Kerish took up the bodyguard's place behind Felix. "Don't sheathe that knife," he said in a low voice. "I need both hands free, just in case, but I want to remind people we're not afraid of committing violence on Felix's behalf."

"What—who was that?"

"I don't know." He hesitated, then finally said, "Whoever it was shouted 'Death to the foreign King.' I think it's just words, but…"

"But nobody stopped whoever it was," Willow said, "which means at least a few people here agree with that sentiment."

"Right. I'm not going to be comfortable until we're home."

Willow nodded. In her heart, she'd already implemented her escape plan.

Chapter Twenty-Four

The wooden handle of the hairbrush felt smooth against Willow's palm. She'd bought it herself in the marketplace, provoking an outburst from Caira, who liked the silver-backed set they'd found waiting in the dressing room when they arrived at the Residence. Willow usually compromised by letting Caira use that one to brush her hair, enjoying the fizz against her scalp. But today she needed all the tranquility she could muster, so she brushed her short hair herself and practiced breathing, in through the nose, out through the mouth. It was a calming ritual she'd invented for herself. It wasn't working.

She set the brush down and moved to the window. A big storm was coming in, gray clouds massing on the horizon and wind blowing them so rapidly she could see them tumbling over each other in their haste to reach land. Did heaven care anything for what would happen today, that it sent this storm as portent of things to come? That seemed unlikely.

The fronds of the trees lashed the window, scratching the glass with a high-pitched *skree* almost too faint to hear. The wind was strong enough to shake the sturdy trunks, and the trees bobbed their heads in a bow of servant-to-master. Not that they would make good servants, rooted to the ground and incapable of doing more than offer scant shade at noon. Though in Umberan, perhaps that was enough.

A soft knock sounded at her dressing room door. "Willow?" Felix said. "Are you ready?"

Willow crossed to the door and opened it. "It's almost time," she said. "Do you wish you were going?"

"Not really. I'm going to teach Ernest a new trick." He sounded cheerful, and Willow's heart ached for him, so successfully concealing his fear over the upcoming vote. "Besides, you said it wasn't safe."

"I don't want to take any chances. But you don't have anything to worry about. I'm sure we'll win."

"Kerish isn't sure. I can tell. And Janida watches me with her eyebrows squinched up when she thinks I'm not looking."

"Well, I have confidence." She hadn't lied to him, ever, and it wasn't entirely a lie, but she still felt guilty. She knelt beside him, feeling her robe pool around her feet, and hugged him close.

"I know you'll take care of me," Felix said, his voice muffled where his face was pressed into her shoulder. "That's why I'm not worried."

"You're very smart. Now, have fun with Ernest, and I'll see you in a few hours."

She fastened her complicated sandals, inwardly groaning at how hard they would be to climb in, and left her rooms for the courtyard and the Serjian carriages. The wind was strong enough that she had to wait inside, listening to its howling voice and watching what little she could of the men and women preparing the carriages for the short journey to the Jauderish. She adjusted the dark blue headwrap so it covered most of her face. The wind carried too much dust to be comfortable.

"It's going to be an unpleasant ride," Kerish said, putting his arm around her. He was dressed in dark gold tunic and trousers, and wore a headwrap with its ends hanging loose, ready to cover his mouth and nose.

"Is it strange that the storm feels comforting?" Willow said. "It's like a reminder that there are things bigger even than this vote."

"Nothing feels bigger than this vote, right now. Is Felix all right?"

"I think he's just good at hiding his fears, which is sickening that a boy that young should be capable of doing that. This *will* be all right, won't it?"

"I won't lie to you, Willow."

Willow leaned into his embrace. "I know. But I thought, just this once let's pretend everything will go our way."

"You idealistic are not, Willow North," Janida said. She was invisible in her white veil and robes, trailed by the rest of the harem and Serjian Salveri, who brought up the rear.

"No, I'm not." Willow straightened, and Kerish's arm fell away from her. She wished she knew what Janida thought of their relationship. Did she think they were sleeping together? Willow tried to be discreet, but Kerish never cared who was watching when he kissed her—not that this bothered Willow. Much. She hadn't realized how private a person she was until she was in the heart of the Serjian Principality, surrounded by dozens of people who all watched her like a beggar watches a rich man's coin. Or, worse, did Janida *expect* them to sleep together, and was she disappointed that they weren't?

"We have done our work, and now we can only pray for success," Catrela said.

"Then let us go, and may heaven bless our efforts," Janida said.

She took a few steps into the courtyard, then halted, causing Willow to bump into her. Willow moved to one side, her mouth open to apologize, then she saw what had brought Janida to a stop. Another woman, this one fully veiled in black robes, approached across the courtyard. Willow didn't need to see her face to recognize the robes.

Imara.

Janida stood still with her robes fluttering around her. Despite the wind, she put back her veil. Her face bore no expression, not even annoyance with the storm. Imara raised her own veil. Willow thought the two had never looked more alike, red hair peeking out from beneath the veils, blue eyes blinking away dust, faces dispassionate as if this were any other meeting.

Imara shifted her weight, a nervous movement that transformed her into an uncertain girl not sure of her reception. "Mother," she said. The wind captured her word and blew it away so rapidly only Willow and Janida could hear.

Janida took two steps forward and put her arms around her daughter, drawing her close. She said something in Eskandelic that the wind carried away, but Imara laughed, a choked sound that was almost a sob, and returned Janida's embrace. Then Salveri was there, gathering up both women in his arms, and Willow took a step back, feeling like an intruder. She felt Kerish's hand on the small of her back and looked back at him, but despite his touch his attention was all on his parents and sister.

Maitea, clearly recognizable despite the veil, came forward to shout something over the howl of the wind. Janida nodded, and gestured at the lead carriage. Imara shook her head, plucking at her dark robe, and pointed back at the Residence. Janida shook her head. "They're arguing over whether Imara is dressed properly for the voting," Kerish said, his face pressed close to Willow's ear. "Mother says it's irrelevant. She's probably going to win the argument. But we'd better hurry. Being late could be fatal to our cause."

Kerish was right. After only a minute of arguing, Imara climbed into the carriage, followed by her mother and father. Willow ended up in a carriage with Kerish, Giara, and Alondra. The four of them rode in silence. Willow couldn't think of anything to say, so she held Kerish's hand and blinked away the specks of dust the wind blew into her face. If not for the wind, she could appreciate the coolness that came before the storm. The rain would come in the middle of the vote. How would it sound, all that water drumming away on the roof of the Jauderish and its elaborate glass lens?

Only a few people walked the streets that morning, most of them with their heads bent against the wind. The impromptu markets that sprang up wherever the roads met and widened were gone. A donkey brayed and planted its feet near a fountain, determined to get a drink no matter how its owner cursed it. Willow watched the little drama until the carriage turned a corner. Whatever had happened to Rosamund, the ill-named mule that had carried them from Tremontane to Eskandel? She hoped the creature had found a good home in Belenda.

More carriages swung into line behind them, painted all sorts of bright colors, some with real gilding. Willow didn't recognize any of the emblems that flew wildly above each carriage, and the occupants were mostly anonymous in their white robes and veils. It should have felt like a celebration, all that white, but Willow felt instead as if she were going to a funeral, possibly her own. She shook her head to dispel the image. "Something wrong?" Kerish said.

"Just trying not to entertain disturbing thoughts."

"Do not fear, Willow," Alondra said. "Catrela correct is. We have done all we can."

Willow said nothing. They were right, there was nothing she could do, and that drove her mad with frustration. She returned to going over her contingency plan: pack the bags she'd bought a few days before in the Tremontanan enclave, leave a note for Janida, give the bodyguards the slip and disappear into the city. She glanced at Kerish, who sat in profile to her. She still hadn't discussed the plan with him, and now she wasn't sure why not. Possibly she just didn't want to face the possibility that he'd tell her goodbye—or the possibility that he wouldn't. *He might want to marry me*, she thought, but he hadn't said word one to her on the subject and she felt shy about bringing it up. What did he want, really?

The carriage drew up to the base of the wide stairs of the Jauderish, and Kerish helped Willow down, then offered her his arm. As the carriage rattled away to take Giara and Alondra to the principalities' entrance, Imara alit from the other carriage, her veil once again secured over her face. She took Kerish's other arm. "It is good to see you again, brother," she said, "and better to see the two of you as one."

"I'm glad you came home," Kerish said. "What about Petrosh Pieran?"

"He will attend upon Father tomorrow, to ask his blessing upon our union. But I will go with him no matter what Father says." She sounded mulish. Willow suppressed a sigh. Imara coming home was a step in the right direction, but she and her parents had a long way still to go.

They joined the others ascending toward the beaten brass doors set in their keyhole arch. There were far fewer than there had been on the solstice, and all of them were veiled against the wind. Willow had to use her free hand to keep her headscarf from flying away and saw several other women doing the same. She and Kerish weren't the only ones hurrying through the doors, though they were undoubtedly the only ones hurrying to get away from the buzzing, tingling sensation of the brass.

This time, Kerish led Willow and Imara to a spot near the middle of the bowl, just above the wide aisle that divided the spectators' benches from the padded seats belonging to the principalities. "We want to hear everything clearly," he said, "and there's no reason to get up and leave in the middle, so we don't need to sit near the doors."

"Our question is last on the *adjeni*, isn't it?"

"Yes. That's good for us. If Mahnouki's question fails, some of those who voted in favor of it might decide, as long as we're spending resources, to support ours."

"That doesn't seem likely."

"It's not. I was trying to be optimistic again."

Willow squeezed his hand. "Kerish, I wanted to talk—"

At the base of the bowl, near the altar, a woman dressed in black who did look as if she were officiating at a funeral began speaking. Kerish hushed Willow. "It's starting," he said. "That's the *voleni* responsible for overseeing the voting. She and her assistants are all scholia masters—that's supposed to make them beyond manipulation. Really, they're no less corruptible than the average person, just because they're masters, but in practice they take their roles very seriously."

Someone behind them said something irritable. Kerish turned his head and replied, shrugging, then gave Willow an apologetic look. She nodded in understanding. Time to listen, not that she understood any of it.

She knew how the system worked because Janida had explained it to her the night before. "This," she'd said, extending a brass coin toward Willow, "a voting token is. Each token stamped with the name of a principality is, and enameled black or white. Black for no, white for yes, you see? For each question, a principality puts one of these into the voting box. They counted are, and the names of each principality recorded are. So all can see who has voted in what way."

"You don't keep that secret?"

"With so many *parjeni* and *parjenisur*, it important is to know if one's proxy is honest. If not, a principality may choose to withhold support from its *parjeni* the following year, or may extort greater promises in exchange for overlooking a bad vote."

"That's a lot of votes to cast."

"Many principalities will have already delivered their voting tokens to their *parjeni*, for them to prepare their votes. Only a few will cast their votes directly. Once the votes counted are, the answer to the question recorded is, and preparation for the next vote begins."

"Serjian is *parjeni* to a lot, though, right?"

Janida had shaken her head. "Not as many as makes me comfortable. But we have powerful allies, and it will have to be enough."

Now Willow looked around the Conclave bowl at those allies. She recognized the Dekerian Prince, and could identify tall Torossian Kharalin despite the veil. Jamighian Vijenci's white hair made him stand out, though Willow couldn't tell which of the sisters was Issobela. The *vojentas* didn't seem to have designated seats the way the princes did. But there were enemies, too—Sahaki Karalhi to Vijenci's left, and the Gharibi Principality, and of course Mahnouki Ghanetan, just taking his seat. Felix's future depended on these men and women.

Brief fury gripped Willow, that a child's life could be so controlled by the whims and desires of others. Of course, you could say that about all children, as Willow knew from experience, but it just seemed so much more *wrong* in Felix's case, so unfair. Nan had made Willow's life hell, but at least she was related. These were effectively strangers to Felix.

The *voleni* finished speaking and took two steps to the right, which put her directly behind a wooden lectern carved with tropical flowers. "Abakian," she said.

"*Yes*," Abakian Benjedan said.

"Altiri."

"*Yes*," said an old man, his voice so faint Willow had to strain to hear it.

The *voleni* called out more names, all in alphabetical order. A roll call. At one point, the *voleni* spoke a name and got no response. She waited a few moments, then repeated the name. After a third repetition with no answer, she moved on, and one of the assistants drew a line on a sheet of paper, presumably crossing out the name. Willow wished she dared ask Kerish or Imara what it meant—would a principality just not show up if they wanted to protest the whole *adjeni*?—but she was conscious of the irritable man on the bench behind them and stayed silent.

Eventually, the *voleni* reached the end of her list with only two other principalities not responding. She nodded to her assistants. Eight of them picked up wooden boxes and carried them to the ends of the rows of seats. The *voleni* raised her head and spoke a long sentence in a clear, ringing voice that surely carried to the top of the bowl. Immediately, several Princes stood, some of them holding cloth bags.

The assistants moved along the rows, offering the boxes to the Princes, who dropped brass tokens or bags into them and resumed their seats.

As soon as all the Princes were seated, the assistants brought their boxes to a long wooden table containing several deep trays. Willow had to resist the urge to fidget; even the soft sound of fabric rustling would have echoed in the silence. The assistants gathered around the table, dumping out the contents of the little sacks and sorting rapidly. The ringing clatter of brass against brass chimed through the silent room. Another black-robed assistant stood nearby, rapidly scribbling on a sheet of paper. Willow discovered she was leaning forward and made herself sit back, wishing the bench had a back to it.

Finally, the assistant handed the sheet of paper to the *voleni*, who scanned it and handed it back. She returned to her lectern and spoke again. The assembled crowd, including the ones near Willow and Kerish on the benches, murmured quietly. "They voted against lowering tariffs on certain Veriboldan goods," Kerish said. "Nothing earthshattering. The next question is about *raising* tariffs on those goods."

"Are there any other exciting questions? Other than the obvious?"

"A few."

The man behind Willow again said something in an irritable voice. Kerish responded at length, something that included his name, and the man jerked backward, then scooted down the bench away from them. Imara chuckled. "I hate trading on the name, but it's sometimes effective," Kerish said with a grin. "The next one's starting."

Willow surreptitiously stretched her back. How many questions were on the *adjeni*? This was going to be a very long day.

The next vote, and the next, went the same as the first—Princes dropping their tokens into the boxes, the clinking of brass on brass, the announcement of the outcome. The result of the fourth vote caused an uproar stilled only by the *voleni* banging on her lectern with a stone-headed hammer. "They voted to recall the ambassador to Tremontane," Kerish whispered. "That's a huge mark in our favor."

"Because it indicates they question the legitimacy of Terence's rule?"

"Exactly." Kerish gripped Willow's hand. "It's not enough, but it's something."

The voting continued. Kerish whispered the results into Willow's ear. Funding for various government projects, including one to open a new scholia dedicated to inventing and researching Devices. That one was voted down. "Next year," Kerish said. A few more relating to Devices. One or two proposing laws related to taxation, both of which were approved. Willow's back ached and her jaw hurt from suppressing yawns.

Rain began pattering on the roof after the seventh vote, a gentle sound that turned torrential and forced the *voleni* to shout over it. Willow eyed the lens. Hard raindrops smacked against it, throwing up tiny splashes. Umberan would smell wonderful when the storm passed, fresh and vibrant, the colors of the trees and the flowers magnified by a million tiny lenses clinging to them. She had a sudden memory of Aurilien in spring, when rain fell almost every day and the city was gray and bleak, and wished with all her heart she was home. If the vote didn't go their way, she'd almost certainly never see it again. She closed her eyes. *Dear heaven,* she thought, but couldn't find words for a prayer.

A murmuring rose up from the seats below them, and Kerish gripped her hand again. "This is it," he said. "The Mahnouki question."

It was only her imagination that the Princes rose to their feet with more eagerness than before, dropped their tokens into the boxes with more force. Willow realized she was clutching Kerish's hand so tightly her nails were digging into his skin, though he didn't complain. He sat leaning forward slightly, his eyes fixed on the table where the counting was in progress. Willow made herself breathe, slowly. The clinking continued for an eternity. The scribbler seemed to be taking much longer than before, carefully noting each name and its vote.

Finally, the assistant brought the paper to the *voleni*, who nodded. She returned to the lectern, gripped it with both hands, then paused just long enough to make Willow want to leap from her seat, run to the base of the bowl, and throttle the answer out of her.

The *voleni* spoke, a long, musical sentence that seemed a counterpoint to the rain still thrumming on the roof. The Conclave erupted in exclamations. Kerish's grip grew momentarily tighter, then fell away entirely. "It's over," he said. "They voted in favor of Mahnouki's question. Just barely, but it's a majority."

His words echoed hollowly in Willow's ears. She reached up to touch her face, which had gone numb. "They can't," she said, even though she'd been expecting it. "I thought—"

"There's still a chance, if Serjian becomes *vojenta mahaut*."

"We needed to win the question for that to happen," Imara said.

"I know."

He took Willow's hand again, this time gently. "I'm sorry," he said. "What will you do next?"

"I—"

The *voleni* banged her hammer on the lectern for quiet. She spoke at length, gesturing with the hammer toward the lens. "She said there's one more question on the *adjeni* and everyone can shut up until it's answered," Kerish said. "She was more polite about it."

"What's the point? Mahnouki already won."

"It's tradition." Kerish made a sour face. "We might as well stay to the end. It's not as if we have anywhere else to go."

The boxes were already proceeding along the rows. Willow could see Salveri's face clearly. He was impassive, just as if the question meant nothing to him. Mahnouki Ghanetan was openly gloating. Strangely, he was the only one. Even Abakian Benjedan looked dispassionate. But Willow remembered that Abakian wasn't going to vote in favor of Mahnouki's question, so he'd lost as well, hadn't he?

She sat back, surreptitiously straightening her spine. She had a few days before she'd have to implement her plan, plenty of time to gather supplies and prepare Felix for a life on the run. Ernest might be a problem, but she wasn't going to separate the boy from his dog, not after he'd already lost everything else. Maybe she didn't need to elude the bodyguards, if she could convince Janida that she knew what she was doing. And Kerish—

The clinking of brass stopped. The scribbling assistant brought the paper to the *voleni*. The *voleni* nodded and took her place behind the lectern, then spoke a long sentence that included the words "Felix Valant." She paused, and added a few words.

The room erupted in a clamor that drowned out the rain. Princes and veiled harem members leaped to their feet and began shouting. Salveri remained seated, expressionless as ever. Imara gasped. "What happened?" Willow said.

"A miracle," Kerish said. "They voted to support Felix in his claim to the Crown."

Chapter Twenty-Five

"They did *what?*" Willow exclaimed, leaping to her feet. Everyone around her stared, but she had eyes only for Kerish, who looked as stunned as she felt. "But—"

"I don't know. Mother was very clear that Eskandel couldn't do both." Kerish grabbed Willow's hand and pulled her down to sit with him. "It's going to be down to the *vojenta mahaut* to figure it out. Sweet heaven. This is going to mean political turmoil for the next year."

"Or longer," Willow said. "If that voyage doesn't pay off, your economy is going to hell."

Kerish hushed her, nodding toward the lectern. The *voleni* was addressing the audience, and when she finished speaking, everyone rose and made their way to the exits. Kerish stood and drew Willow up next to him. "Fifteen minutes for using the facilities," he said, "and last-minute maneuvering, if I know Mother."

Willow followed him and Imara out of the bowl, but found she didn't need to relieve herself and instead took a walk around the antechamber, stretching her legs. She stayed well away from the brass doors; she didn't need any more agitation. Both the Mahnouki and Serjian questions answered in the affirmative? She wished she knew by how great a margin the Serjian question had passed. Kerish had said it was close for Mahnouki. Not that she understood how that translated into deciding on the *vojenta mahaut.*

She stopped near the doors leading to the Conclave bowl and looked down at the altar with its blackened top. Suppose Mahnouki became *vojenta mahaut.* They'd be bound by law to support Felix, but that support could be as weak as withholding recognition of Terence as King of Tremontane. It was a qualified victory, because what they needed was troops, something to protect Felix while he rallied the Counts and Barons behind him. But could Eskandel even do that, send their own military into a foreign country? That struck Willow as being aggressive and potentially a declaration of war.

She sighed, and began making her way back to her seat. This was all still premature. But she resolved, if Mahnouki became *vojenta mahaut*, she wouldn't wait around to see what kind of lukewarm support they'd give Felix. Disappearing was still an option.

"What are you thinking?" Imara said, startling Willow, who hadn't heard her approach.

"Wondering what I'm going to tell Felix. It almost would have been easier if they'd rejected the question."

"Hope is not lost," Imara said, but she didn't sound very certain.

Kerish joined them, and the three returned to their seats. "Did Mother explain about the voting for the *vojenta mahaut*?"

"She said it wasn't like voting on the *adjeni*, where each question just needs a simple majority of votes to win. The new *vojenta mahaut* has to win more than two-thirds of the vote in order to be elected. Which by tradition is three hundred and thirty-five votes."

"That's right. And only a few principalities are eligible. Some years, it takes only one round of voting. This isn't one of those years."

"Who's eligible?"

"Serjian and Mahnouki, obviously. Abakian, Sahaki, Jamighian, Takjashi, Hajimhi, Najarhian. Maybe a few others. I have no idea where their support lies."

"Jamighian doesn't want it."

"How do you know?" Imara said.

"I…just do." Willow remembered Jamighian Vijenci's bright eyes, Issobela's smile when she spoke of their son. "They've pledged their support to Serjian for this as well as the question. They won't accept others' votes for them."

"I'm not sure it works that way," said Kerish.

"I don't know how it works. I just know what I know."

"All right. What about Takjashi?"

"If their ties to Tremontane are as strong as Catrela said, they're weakened with regard to the *vojenta mahaut* because of having to support Felix's claim over Terence. I think it's unlikely they'll get many votes."

"When did you become such an expert on Eskandelic politics?"

"I'm not. I didn't. This is all just me thinking out loud." Anything she knew about politics, she'd learned from watching Rufus Black and his fellow dukes of crime. It simply made sense to her. "And I think

Sahaki might not have distanced itself sufficiently from Mahnouki."

Kerish closed his hand over Willow's knee. "I guess we're about to find out."

Streams of white-clad men and women filed back into the bowl, taking their seats in near-silence. The *voleni* waited for everyone to return, then spoke at length, gesturing with her hammer. "She's instructing them on how to vote," Kerish whispered, "following their consciences and not being moved by fear, things like that. They all have slips of paper the Princes will write the name of their choice on. Then they're collected and counted twice, and then, if there's no winner, the *voleni* will read the names who received votes and how many votes each got. Then they repeat the process until someone gets the magic number."

"That could take forever."

"It does, sometimes. If there's no *vojenta mahaut* by sunset, they continue in the morning."

"I don't think I'll survive that long."

"That hasn't happened in over forty years. Of course, this is the kind of year where I could see it happening again."

The boxes were passing along the rows again. This time, every Prince took part. "No *parjeni* for this," Kerish said. Willow caught herself leaning forward, as if she could read the papers from where she sat. She straightened and watched Salveri, whose expression was perfectly composed. Were they allowed to vote for themselves? Probably, or they'd take steps to prevent it.

The rain on the roof still pattered away, but quietly, like mice on a bare stone floor. It was still enough to drown out the sound of shuffling papers as the *voleni's* assistants sorted the names into piles. Willow craned her neck. Four—no, five little piles, some of them substantially bigger than the others. More assistants were counting the piles, once, twice. They spoke to the *voleni*, who held a wooden tablet on which lay a sheet of paper. She wrote down whatever they told her—*or maybe she makes it up, she's got tremendous power, no wonder they want her to be unshakably honest.*

Finally, the *voleni* returned to the lectern and began speaking. Names spilled out into the Conclave bowl, and a sigh passed through the room. "No winner," Kerish said. "Mahnouki two hundred and one, Serjian one hundred seventy-eight, Jamighian eighty-two, Sahaki thirty, Abakian six."

"Mahnouki's ahead."

"For now."

Willow watched Jamighian Vijenci, who sat perfectly erect in his chair and glared at his peers. She could practically hear him warning them off—no more votes for Jamighian. Salveri still looked impassive, but he had his pen in hand and was tapping it on the desk in front of him. She wished she could see Janida's face, but at that distance she couldn't even sense her golden bracelets to know which of the white-veiled figures was the Serjian *vojenta*.

The assistants distributed fresh paper. The Princes wrote. The boxes traveled along the rows. Willow fidgeted. Now she was grateful there wasn't any Device you could carry with you to tell time, because she'd wear it out from looking at it all the time. The rain stopped, and watery sunlight trickled down through the lens, not bright enough to mark a spot on the floor.

The *voleni* stepped forward. "No winner," Kerish said. "Mahnouki two hundred and five, Serjian two hundred and two, Sahaki fifty, Jamighian forty."

That put Abakian out of the running. Willow doubted they'd ever had a chance, given their assassination attempts. And Serjian had gained on Mahnouki. Vijenci now looked nearly apoplectic in his silent fury. *Take a hint,* Willow thought. The room was so quiet she could hear clearly the rustling of fabric when Imara shifted her position, could hear the dry shuffling of paper at the table below. The *voleni* took her place again.

"No winner. Serjian two hundred thirty-three—"

Willow gasped and clutched Kerish's hand.

"It's not over yet. Mahnouki one hundred ninety-eight, Sahaki sixty-six."

A murmur passed over the assembled crowd, and the *voleni* didn't bother stopping it, just motioned to her assistants to proceed. The sky was darkening, this time from the approaching sunset rather than the storm. If sunset came before this was finished…Willow had no doubt

Janida would spend the night gathering support, but so would Adorinda, and she had a sudden terrible feeling that if the vote didn't go their way in the next few minutes, they would lose in the morning.

The *voleni* struck the lectern with her hammer. "No winner. Serjian three hundred and six, Mahnouki one hundred seventy-one, Sahaki twenty."

The murmur was louder this time, and now the *voleni* did silence the crowd, speaking to them at length. "This is the final one tonight, she says," Kerish whispered. "Last chance."

Willow gazed out over the assembled Conclave. How much did this matter to them? Another year, and they'd have a chance to change whatever decision they made that night. How powerful a government could they have with such instability, really? She thought of Felix, waiting back at the Residence for her to return. He was just a little boy, when you stripped away all the nonsense about Kings and ruling and inheritance, and he didn't deserve to have his fate held by strangers, even if they were well-meaning ones like the Serjians. She felt stretched taut, like a fiddle string, with someone turning the knob to tighten her further until she must surely snap under the pressure.

There were only two piles of papers on the table now. One was significantly larger than the other, but all that mattered was that Mahnouki keep Serjian from reaching that magic number, and with enough support, this battle could go on forever. Willow watched the hands sorting through the piles and tried to count with them, but gave up when the number got too high. Any moment now...

The *voleni* once again took her place at the lectern, paper in hand. She swept her gaze across the crowd, not just the principalities but the observers above. Willow thought she hesitated when she came to Willow, but the pause was so tiny she decided she'd imagined it.

The *voleni* spoke. A cheer rattled the lens and shook the walls. Kerish threw his arms around Willow and kissed her. "It's over. We won," he said.

***

They waited, hands clasped, for the furor to die down and most of the other observers to leave the Jauderish. "The swearing-in ceremony happens tomorrow," Kerish said. "This is just for our supporters to congratulate Father. It can take a while."

"I don't mind," Willow said, though in truth, now that Serjian was *vojenta mahaut* and the tremendous pressure was gone, she'd started to feel hungry, and her eyes ached from staring at the voting table for so long.

She watched the Serjian Principality, the harem seated and quiet in their anonymous robes, Salveri accepting congratulations from his peers. Salveri still looked impassive, as if this weren't a victory they'd all been working toward for nearly a month. It made him look more gracious than Mahnouki Ghanetan, who'd left his seat practically before the *voleni* had finished speaking. Mahnouki would probably never stop being a problem for Serjian, but for today, at least, they were no longer a threat.

"Felix will be so happy," Willow said. "I still can't quite believe it. I...probably shouldn't admit this, but I didn't have a plan for this outcome."

"That's all right. I'm familiar with your endless optimism." Kerish kissed her again.

"I thought we weren't supposed to let anyone know Serjian had a personal interest in this fight."

"We've won. We can do anything we like." He put his arm around her and drew her close. "Tell me something. Did your plan for losing involve leaving me behind?"

"Kerish..."

"Because I'd just have followed you."

"I meant to talk to you about it, but...everything was so unsettled."

"I believe you." He didn't sound angry, or upset, just amused. "And now it doesn't matter, but I find myself curious about what you meant to say."

She turned in the curve of his arm to look at him. "I don't—Kerish, I—"

"We should leave now," Salveri said. The big man moved too silently for someone of his size. "Supper waiting is."

Willow rose, trying not to feel relieved at his interruption. She still didn't know what she'd have asked of Kerish. What she'd had in mind required stealth, concealment, disguising herself, and a Deviser couldn't do those things and still find work. And she'd asked him to give up his magic once before, with disastrous results—she wasn't going to make the same mistake twice. But leaving him behind...even now that it wasn't necessary, the idea made her stomach hurt from more than hunger.

Alondra talked cheerfully the whole way back to the Residence. Giara was more subdued, but what little she said sounded more hopeful than Willow had ever heard from her. Willow clasped Kerish's hand in hers and tried to make new plans, but her mind felt fuzzy, incapable of planning past food and a warm, soft bed. But first, she had to see Felix.

The bodyguards standing sentinel at the door to her rooms gave her the once-over before allowing her into her own suite. Good. The sitting room was unoccupied, though the chairs and sofas had been pushed back against the walls to leave a big empty space in the center of the room. Felix and Ernest must have been playing again. "Felix?"

His bedroom door banged open, and Felix, dressed in his nightshirt—*thank you, Caira*—came running out. "Willow, it's so late! What happened?"

Willow picked him up and spun around with him. "We won, Felix! They're going to help you regain the Crown!"

Felix stiffened. "No!" he screamed, and burst into tears.

Willow was so startled she nearly dropped him. She managed to set him down gently and tried to put her arms around him. "Felix—"

He shoved her away. "You're *lying* because you think it will make me feel better. It's not true!"

"Felix! I *never* lie to you. Serjian Principality is *vojenta mahaut* and they're going to help us defeat Terence."

"I don't want to! I want us to run away!"

She could barely understand his words through his tears. She reached out to him again, but he wrenched away from her and ran into his bedroom, slamming the door behind him and shutting Ernest out. The puppy whined and scratched at the door, looking at Willow with his big pleading eyes. Willow bent to rub Ernest's head. "That's not what I expected," she told the dog, who whimpered.

The apartment door opened. "Willow, are you coming? Supper's ready," Kerish said.

"Ah...I need to spend some time with Felix. Would you make my apologies, and I'll get something later if I'm not there in time."

"Is everything all right?"

"I'm not sure. I'll tell you all about it later."

Kerish looked skeptical, but nodded and shut the door. He always knew when to leave her alone. She loved him so much. She let out a deep breath and opened the door to Felix's bedroom, letting Ernest scamper in ahead of her and leap onto the bed beside Felix.

Felix was curled up, sobbing, with his face buried in the pillow. Willow sat next to him and laid a hand on his head. "Do you want to talk about it?" she asked. Felix shook his head vigorously. "Then we'll just sit here together and you can cry it out, whatever it is, until you're ready."

She stroked his hair while he cried and Ernest snuffled at his face, licking whatever parts he could reach. Eventually Felix calmed enough to put his arms around the dog and hug him. Willow folded her hands in her lap and waited for the tears to stop. She felt as if she were under tension again, a fiddle string drawn tight, but this time she felt emptiness at her core, cold and hollow and waiting to be filled.

"Can you talk now?" she finally said when the sniffling had stopped.

"I don't want to," Felix said, his voice muffled by the pillow.

"Then why don't I talk, and you can tell me if I'm right." Felix nodded. "You thought we were going to lose, didn't you?" Another nod. "And you've been mentally preparing yourself for what would happen when we did. You let yourself believe you weren't going to be King and...I think you liked the idea."

Felix nodded again. "Well, you don't have to be afraid," Willow said.

"I'm not afraid. I don't want to be King."

"I know right now, all you can see is—"

"*I don't want to be King!*" Felix shouted. "I want to take care of animals and be your little boy and never go back to Tremontane! That was my *wish*, Willow, and I want it to come true!"

Willow sat with her hand halfway to Felix's shoulder, unable to move. She blinked away unexpected tears. "Felix, that can't happen."

"I don't care about Tremontane. Uncle Terence can be King. Please, Willow, let's just go like you said! Kerish can come with us and we can be a family. A real family. *Please*."

"Felix—" She took hold of his shoulder and pulled him close, put her arms around him and hugged him. "I don't blame you for wanting those things. If I could, I'd give you that. But you have—" She couldn't say it. She couldn't tell this gentle, wonderful boy he had a duty that would probably tear him apart no matter what she did to protect him. "What did Hilarion teach you about the responsibilities of a King?"

"I don't care a damn about Hilarion. He said a lot of stupid things."

"It's 'give a damn,' sweetheart. If you're going to swear, do it properly. And Hilarion was very wise about the important things. He taught you to be a good King, and you're going to…you're going to rule, and I'm going to help you. You don't have to be afraid."

"But I don't want to."

"We all have to do things we don't want to. And sometimes, when we do them, they make us happy. I didn't want to go with you and Kerish to Eskandel, not at first, but now I'm so glad I did, because I love you and I want to take care of you."

Felix wiped his eyes. "Do we have to leave tomorrow?"

"I don't think so. There are a lot of plans to make, and I'll talk to Janida about it. It's probably going to be a few weeks, maybe a lot of weeks. So you can go to the scholia as much as you want, and we'll go to the ocean, and everything will be all right."

"And you're not going to leave?"

"I'll be with you for as long as you need me."

"Which is always."

"Then I'll be with you always."

She helped him lie down, then tucked him in, kissed his forehead, and turned out the light, not even bothering to shoo Ernest off the bed. In the sitting room, she stood with her eyes closed and practiced breathing, in through the nose, out through the mouth, until her tears stopped flowing. Then she washed her face and left the room, counting each step as she walked down the stairs.

The meal was almost over by the time she reached the dining room, and she ate rapidly, without noticing what she put on her plate. Kerish put his hand on her knee when she took her place beside him, but said nothing, and she wondered what her face might look like that it dissuaded him from conversation.

Despite the excitement of the day, supper was as quiet a meal as it ever was, with most of the talk centered on requests for a particular dish, which suited Willow. She felt drained, as if she'd turned Kerish's Device on herself again and sucked every ounce of source out of her. She turned down the offer of dessert, but remained seated until Janida rose. Then she said, "I need to speak to you alone, please."

Janida raised an inquiring eyebrow, but gestured to Willow to follow her to the harem chamber. Once inside, she took a seat and indicated that Willow should do the same. "I imagine you have many questions," she said.

"I do, but probably not the ones you're anticipating." Willow sat forward until she was on the edge of her seat. "Why exactly does Eskandel care about making Felix King of Tremontane?"

The eyebrow rose again. "You know the answer to that question," Janida said. "Stability. Economic security. And it the right thing is."

"That just explains why you want someone who isn't Terence Valant," Willow said. "It doesn't explain why *Felix* should be king."

"That Tremontanan inheritance law is. We do not make the decision."

"Maybe you should."

Janida's eyes narrowed. "I do not understand."

"What I'm saying," Willow said, "is I don't think Felix is suited to be King."

The *vojenta's* face turned completely neutral. "You think you suited to make that judgment are?"

"I know him better than anyone. He's a good, gentle, kind person, and he loves animals, and he's incredibly smart, but he lacks the qualities a King needs. Ruthlessness. Decisiveness. Strength of will. And I know he's still got years of a regency to learn all of that, but I don't think it's in his character. I don't think he's ever going to become the kind of man who can rule a country, let alone one who can bring it out of the catastrophe it's fallen into now."

Janida nodded once, slowly. "I did wonder when you would realize that," she said.

"You mean—you knew?" Janida nodded again. "Then why didn't you say anything?"

"It not my place is, to judge another country's ruler." Janida stood and paced the length of the room. "And we had enough difficulties in achieving what we did today without adding uncertainty to that burden."

"All right, but now I really don't know what to do! I can't bear to do this to him, Janida, I can't keep pushing him into a role he's completely unsuited for. And yet I can't watch Tremontane go up in flames. It needs a King who isn't an Ascendant and a murderer, and…" She took a deep breath. "I don't know when I turned into the sort of person who cares about that. Two months ago I didn't care who ruled Tremontane so long as I could go on giving him the finger. But now…maybe it took leaving my country to show me how much it mattered to me. I need help. Tell me what to do."

Janida returned to stand near Willow, settling her gold bracelets more snugly on her wrists the way she did when she was thinking hard about something. "You will have to choose," she said.

"Choose? Choose what?"

"The new King of Tremontane."

Willow burst out laughing. "As if anyone would listen to my opinion on the matter!"

"This is no joke, Willow North. It must either Felix or another be. You have decided it will not Felix be. Who better to choose the other but the guardian of the Crown?"

Willow stopped laughing. "You're serious."

"Very serious. You understand what it means to rule a country. You have the ability to identify those traits in others. And you *eskarna* are, able to bring your will to pass and make others believe it their idea is."

"But they won't listen to me. I'm nobody."

"Eskandel will recognize you as Felix's guardian and chief

political advisor. We will not say regent because that a bargaining token is, but in all other ways we will grant you power. You will do the rest. You are not nobody, not any longer."

"But how am I supposed to find a new King?"

"We will send you to Tremontane with…we will say it an honor guard for the King is, protection while you send word to Tremontane's provincial rulers. They will be his true support, and among them you may find one capable of ruling. Then it will your cause be to give the Crown to that person."

"You make it sound easy."

Janida smiled, a calculating expression that made Willow want to shiver. "It fiendishly hard is. But I think Willow North has never walked away from a challenge no matter how hard."

"Until now, anyway." But Willow knew she couldn't walk away from this. "I can't tell Felix. Everything depends on everyone believing we intend to make him King, and he's young enough he'll let the secret slip. I wish I didn't have to hurt him like that."

"A little pain now better than a lifetime of pain later is." Janida began pacing again. "The fewer people know, the better."

"Agreed. How long before Eskandel will be ready to send troops?"

"Weeks, perhaps months. But it will be long before the snows fall."

Willow thought of Terence's Ascendants clashing with the forces of the provincial rulers, thought of villages and towns on fire. "The sooner the better."

"You will need time to prepare as well. And, Willow?"

"Yes?"

Janida once again regarded her with that calculating expression. "Remember that greatness may come from where you least expect it. Do not confine your search to those who already noble are. Keep an open mind."

"I will," Willow said.

Chapter Twenty-Six

Broken twigs and scattered leaves filled the streets of Umberan, legacy of the previous day's storm. Willow tried not to see symbolism in it—remnants of the past littering the present. How much of the previous regime would Janida have to clear away before addressing new concerns? Thank heaven Willow didn't have those worries. No, she had her own entirely different set of problems.

The swearing-in of the new *vojenta mahaut* had been anticlimactic after the previous day's drama. Even Mahnouki Ghanetan had made his oath with no hint of disapproval or disdain. They'd no doubt try to take over in a year's time, but until then, Serjian held all the power. Not that Willow believed Janida would be so complacent as to let that slide. She'd probably already started campaigning for next year's Conclave.

The Tremontanan enclave was as debris-strewn as the rest of the city, but people were doing something about it. Men and women with brooms swept up leaves and twigs into small piles by the side of the road, while small children gathered up what the brooms missed. They laughed as they tossed their scraps into the piles, then ran off for more. Willow nodded at the workers, who smiled and nodded back. It wouldn't be such a bad place to live, once the Crown was securely bestowed on someone who'd wear it wisely. Maybe she and Felix would end up there.

A knee-high pile of twigs and leaves teetered next to the entrance to the *khaveh*-house, poorly balanced and close to falling over. Willow avoided it and bought herself a cup, then sat under the trellises, sipping the burnt-sugar deliciousness of the drink. Maybe she should learn to make *khaveh*, take it with her to Tremontane. It was something she'd miss.

"I hear Eskandel has a new *vojenta mahaut*," Rafferty said, sliding along the bench toward her. "Congratulations."

"It's just the beginning. But it's a good start."

"So what happens next?"

"Felix returns to Tremontane in the company of Eskandelic troops and begins to gather the support of the Counts and Barons."

"It can't be as simple as that."

"It's not. Deciding how many troops is a subtlety I'm not privy to. Choosing who to approach first is also hard. And Felix's safety is still a priority."

"I imagine Eskandelic soldiers entering Tremontane, even in the company of its King, might be grounds for war."

"That's another subtlety I don't understand fully."

Rafferty drained his cup and set it on the table with a resounding *tock*. "It would be better," he said, almost too casually, "if Felix were backed by Tremontanan fighters."

"True, but we don't have those. Once we command the loyalty of the provincial rulers…but that will take time."

"You don't have an army. That doesn't mean you don't have fighters." He rested his hands on the table and studied his fingernails.

"We don't—" Willow became aware of how many people were listening to their conversation. "Giles, what are you saying?"

"I'm saying maybe it's time for me to head north again. My people strike against Ascendants where they can, but it's gotten us nowhere. We're not in a position to fight the Eminence on our own, but we're clever and strong and know how to attack from the shadows. Do you think a King might find a use for a band of rebels?"

Willow let out the breath she'd been holding. "I think he might," she said. "Can you really bring your rebels to our cause?"

"Promise them immunity from their so-called crimes against Ascendants, promise fair treatment under the new King, and yes, they'll fight for Felix."

"I think Felix can do that, so long as we're not excusing murder. And you already know he's fair and honest."

"I'm more interested in *your* promises. You'll be part of his government, yes?"

"Apparently. I still don't think I'm qualified, but I don't want Felix to be overridden by advisors who have only their own interests at heart. But I won't be regent. Janida thinks that will be a powerful incentive to get the provincial lords to fall in line, the promise of that power."

"It could be dangerous. You'll be giving up control."

"Yes, but I'm *definitely* not qualified to be regent, so it's a chance I'll have to take." Willow set her cup down and sighed. "I don't mind telling you I'm worried. Tremontane is in turmoil and getting the attention of even one of the provincial lords is going to be tricky."

Rafferty clapped her heartily on the back. "I think, if anyone is capable of getting the attention of an arrogant noble, it's Willow North."

***

Kerish and Felix were still at the scholia when Willow returned to the Residence, flushed with excitement over her talk with Rafferty. True, they weren't soldiers, but the rebels — the insurgents — had been fighting for their freedom for years, and what better way to start a new reign than with the help of those who'd fought so desperately against the old one?

She begged food from the kitchen and took it up to the rooftop garden, where she sat at the table and enjoyed the fresh sea air. This was something else she'd miss — well, who said they couldn't eventually return to Umberan? It was a big city, easy for a mama and her little boy to disappear into.

She made herself stop that line of thought before it went too far. Daydreaming about a distant future was an indulgence that could get them killed. Time enough for thinking about the future when she was sure they would have one.

Footsteps echoed in the stairwell, and Kerish appeared, smiling when he saw her. He carried a canvas sack embroidered with purple flowers around the mouth that clanked with fizzing silver and tingling brass when he moved. "I guessed you'd be up here," he said. "I thought you'd like to see what I've been working on."

Willow moved her meal to one side so he could put the sack on the table. "New Devices?"

"As per your request." He opened the sack and withdrew a silver wand, smoothly rounded and narrowing toward the tip. "Five of these, three of brass, and two dozen more in production."

"That was fast work!"

"I made this one specially for you." He handed her a slim baton some fifteen inches long, polished ash with a hidden core of gold. An ivory cuff about an inch wide circled the wand a third of the way from its fatter end. "I don't think I need to tell you which way to point it."

"No, I learned my lesson already." With the buffer of the wood between her and the core, it felt warm but not burning to the touch. "And those discs in the box are all silver."

"It works on copper now, too, but I figured you'd prefer fizzing to itching." He set a matching ash box about six inches on a side on the table. "Your own personal Ascendant-fighting weapon."

"I know I said this was a war, but I have trouble picturing myself going face to face against an Ascendant with so slim a weapon as this." She took a silver disc from the box and fitted it to the tip of the wand, then gestured with it. The disc fell off and struck the table with a dull chime. Kerish retrieved it and put it back more securely.

"If you can strip an Ascendant of her magic, this is all the weapon you'll need," he said.

"I know. I hope I didn't sound ungrateful. Your talent is going to help Felix more than mine will."

"I think that's untrue." He gently removed the wand from her hand and set it aside, then took her hands in his. "You still haven't told me what you intended to say, back when you thought you'd be disappearing with Felix."

"I can't remember now," Willow said, "and I have something more important to discuss with you."

Kerish raised his eyebrows. "You look disturbed. This isn't about how you're leaving me for the kebab seller on the corner, is it? I've seen how he looks at you."

"This is serious, Kerish."

"I can tell. You have me worried. Is something wrong?"

"I—come with me." She drew him up from the table and led him away from the stairwell, away from any listening ears. The sweet smell of roses surrounded them, warm and wet in the afternoon heat. Willow breathed it in and was transported back to Aurilien, to an estate she'd burgled years ago whose copper-bright roses had sheltered her as she hid from the guards. What a memory to have right then.

"Tell me something," she said, cutting off Kerish, who'd opened his mouth to speak. "Do you think Felix will be a good King?"

"I…well, of course, someday." Kerish still looked puzzled. "He's got a long way to go."

"Be honest, Kerish. The truth is, Felix doesn't have it in him to be King. And no amount of time is going to change that."

"It doesn't matter. He's the King. He can't be worse than Terence, and he's got a more legitimate claim. Willow, what's the point of this?"

"The point is I'm not going to let Felix become King. I'm going to find someone else."

Kerish stared at her. Then he laughed. "You can't be serious."

"I am serious. And Janida agrees with me. I'm going to take Felix north and gather support for him, but I'll really evaluate the nobles who come to his side and choose one of them to become King. Then I'll make Felix disappear for good."

"Willow, you can't do that."

"Why not? It means Felix gets a chance at a normal life and Tremontane gets a ruler superior to Terence."

"I mean it's not possible. You don't have authority. You don't even have an army. And the only way Felix can get out of this is if he dies. Do you have a plan for that, too?"

"Not yet. But I will."

Kerish took a few steps toward the nearest rosebush, turning his back on Willow, and she felt cold. "This sounds like my mother's idea."

"That doesn't make it a bad one."

"No, but you're not a noble or a politician, Willow! This isn't your responsibility."

"Felix is my responsibility. His happiness and safety are my responsibility. I love him and I don't want him to have a miserable life. And, much as it surprises me, I want Tremontane to have a good, wise, competent King."

"And you think you can decide who that will be?"

Willow recoiled. "That's harsh."

"I didn't mean it that way." Kerish came back to take her hands. "Why you, of all people?"

"Because if I'm the one saying Felix can't be King, I owe it to my country not to just abandon it." She laughed. "I can't believe I'm even thinking this way."

"Neither can I. Didn't you once tell me you had more loyalty to a rabid street dog than to Tremontane?"

"That was before someone showed up in my bedroom and entrusted me with an eight-year-old King."

"Oh, so this is my fault," Kerish teased.

"In a way." Willow sighed. "This is the path I've chosen, Kerish. And I don't think I can bear to do it alone. I can't even tell Felix. Will you...come north with me?"

The teasing light left his eyes. "That's not really what you're asking," he said.

"It's all I feel I have a right to ask."

"What is that supposed to mean?"

His dark eyes were fiercely intent on her in a way she hadn't seen in years. She said, "I can't—Kerish, Felix and I are going into hiding when this is over. I asked you to give up your magic once before. I'm not going to do it again. I don't want you to resent—"

He stopped her words with a kiss, warm and passionate. "Don't," he said, while she tried to get the world to stop spinning. "Don't say anything about how you plan to sacrifice yourself for my sake, or how you're going to make my decisions for me. Let's just start from the beginning, all right? I love you. I want to spend the rest of my life with you, whether it's here in Eskandel or somewhere in Tremontane or wandering the known world. Maybe that means I can't be a Deviser. I don't think either of us knows exactly what the future holds. I'm willing to take that chance if it means being with you. Marry me, Willow. Tonight."

Her mouth fell open. "Marry you?"

"You sound shocked. Don't tell me—you've already married the kebab seller."

"*Kerish!*"

"That's what I thought." He brushed a kiss across her knuckles. "You wanted to marry me once. I'm taking a chance on you still feeling that way. Because I can't think of anything that would make me happier."

She had to make herself breathe before the bronze sparkles dancing before her eyes claimed her. "Yes," she said, throwing her arms around his neck. His lips on hers were fierce, promising a future together she could barely imagine. His fingers stroked the soft skin at the base of her spine, making her shiver with pleasure. "I want to be married in Tremontane, too," she murmured. "Will you take my name? Start a new North family?"

"So long as you're willing to marry me here, now," Kerish said. "I don't think I could bear traveling with you again and not sharing your bed."

The idea made her shiver again. "And we'll adopt Felix. But we can't tell him yet. If he knows he doesn't have to be King, he'll let it slip eventually."

"You're probably right. Well, it won't be many months, will it?"

"I hope not. Can we really be married tonight?"

"Any *vojenta* can officiate at a marriage ceremony. And I even came prepared."

"What do you mean?"

Kerish released her and began digging in his belt pouch. "This thing is too cluttered...here, hold this."

He held out something she'd thought was a coin toward her, and she gasped. Gold inlaid with stars of silver gleamed in the sunlight. "You kept it."

"Of course I kept it. I'm never without it."

To her senses, the ring burned, like a star giving off bursts of fizzing light. She folded it into her sleeve, closed her hand around it and watched him search. "This wasn't supposed to be so awkward," he said, and came up with a bright silvery spot. He hesitated, then said, "I thought wood might be too plain, and stone couldn't alter if it was the wrong size, so I hope I guessed correctly."

Willow reached out to take the ring in wonder. Solid steel, the only metal she could easily handle, but slimmer than his, and set with a dark blue faceted stone. Sleek, unadorned, something that might fit easily under a glove.

"Sapphire," Kerish said. "I hoped...I know it will take a lot of caring for, but you do like it, yes?"

"I love it." She slid it onto the middle finger of her right hand. "It's only a little loose."`

"Well, it's not as if you have any other rings I could borrow to make a better fit." He took both her hands in his and kissed them, one at a time, his lips lingering on her knuckles. "I love you."

She put her arms around his neck once more. "Show me," she said.

Willow's story concludes in
Champion of the Crown

An Eskandelic Glossary

PRONUNCIATION: j is always zh, -u after an initial letter is -w, kh- is hard k and only comes at the beginning of a word

adjeni--the voting roster for the Conclave

amhiri--tea (black tea)

cabra--flatbread

eskarna (es-KAR-nuh)--harem spy

ezdalha--motive force

fuolero (fwo-LEH-roe) --half-brother in an Eskandelic principality

galt--unit of money almost equivalent to a Tremontanan guilder. Gold coin

giorjanesh--like a sari, brocade and satin

harima--potential member of a harem, pl. harimi

Jauderish--the building where the Conclave meets

khaladesi--term of endearment roughly equivalent to "beloved"

khaveh—coffee, Turkish-style

khedesh (keh-DESH)--how the children of an earlier princeling address the current prince (their "stepfather")

khetashi--dog trained to perform tricks

khojabi--a meeting of supplicant to one of higher status

lehndashi--hunting dog

majdran (mazh-DRAHN), pl. majdrani--how the children of a principality address wives who are not their birth mothers

najabedhi--jungle panther

nastaheh--breakfast

nesh--jam

nouhut--sort of breakfast pancake of flat bread, soft goat cheese, and jam

obat--unit of money equivalent to two Tremontanan coppers. Bronze coin

parjeni--controlling voters in Conclave; those who command the votes of others parjenisur--someone who commands votes, but gives those votes to another

ryad--unit of money equivalent to half a Tremontanan stave. Silver coin

scholia--like a university, but smaller, and often focused on one field of study

sheteshi--big dog show, the most famous in Eskandel

sovi--with personal name, how to address a harem sister

stevaashi--dog that competes on looks and obedience

suorena (swo-RAY-nuh) --half-sister in an Eskandelic principality

surabhi--Device

vojenta (voh-ZHEN-ta)--leader of the harem, the "voice"

vojenta mahaut (voh-ZHEN-ta ma-HOWT)--ruler of Eskandel for a year's term, Conclave to Conclave

voleni--person who keeps order and handles Conclave business; almost always an academic from a scholia

zetesha--personal maid/valet

zuareta, zuareto (zwah-RAY-tah/toh)--how a member of the harem addresses children not born to her

About the Author

Melissa McShane is the author of the Crown of Tremontane series, beginning with SERVANT OF THE CROWN, and The Extraordinaries series, beginning with BURNING BRIGHT, as well as several other books. After a childhood spent roaming the United States, she settled in Utah with her husband, four children and a niece, two very needy cats, and a library that continues to grow out of control. She wrote reviews and critical essays for many years before turning to fiction, which is much more fun than anyone ought to be allowed to have. You can visit her at her website www.melissamcshanewrites.com for more information on other books.

For information on new releases, fun extras, and more, sign up for Melissa's newsletter: http://eepurl.com/brannP

www.ingramcontent.com/pod-product-compliance
Lightning Source LLC
Chambersburg PA
CBHW070309260626
47160CB00003B/779